"Why did you leave the dance?" LeBeau asked without preamble.

"I…I just came out for a bit of air." Norah stepped back and tried to regain her composure. "I didn't mean to wander so far from the tent." Her heart was hammering against the silk bodice of her dress and in the pulse point at the base of her throat.

"You should not be out alone," warned LeBeau. "This is an army post, Miss O'Shea, and you are a beautiful and desirable woman. I advise you not to walk around at night unescorted. It might not be safe."

"Well, I'm perfectly safe with you," Norah answered, attempting a bantering tone out of sheer nervousness. "For you've certainly kept your distance."

Instantly she was in his arms, her breasts crushed against the hard expanse of his chest. His face came down to hers, and his breath misted her skin. The heat of his body warmed hers, but it was the dark desire in his face that ignited her own blood, that sent it singing through her veins and roaring in her ears.

"How safe do you feel now?" LeBeau whispered hoarsely.

MARIANNE WILLMAN

PIECES OF SKY

MIRA

ISBN 1-55166-564-6

PIECES OF SKY

Copyright © 1986 by Marianne Willman.

Visit us at www.mirabooks.com

Printed in U.S.A.

To Jan Greenberg and Loren B. Estleman
with deep appreciation
for their encouragement
and loan of research material.
And of course, to Ky, the Seneca chief.

1

Arizona Territory, 1873

The coach clattered to a bone-wrenching stop, and the lone passenger grasped at the hanging leather strap to keep her balance. Norah O'Shea peered out the streaked side window, her forehead and palms clammy as she fought to retain the greasy breakfast forced down twelve hours earlier in Santa Fe. She was eager for a first glimpse of her new home, but the long plume of dust from the stage's arrival hung like a yellow fog in the heavy air, obscuring the view. As it slowly settled to the ground she was able to make out the general scene, and it did nothing to calm her anxiety.

In all her twenty-eight years she had never looked upon such a desolate scene. Except for a few horses tied to a rail and switching their tails lethargically, the town looked deserted. Straightening her outmoded straw hat, she tried to smooth the wrinkles from her second-best gown of pale blue muslin, then gave up the futile attempt. Her hands were trembling.

Quickly she scanned the street again. There was not a soul to be seen. No idlers in the open door frames, no pedestrians along the crooked wooden sidewalk outside the splintered hotel front. And most vexatious of all, no Abner Slade, eager for his first meeting with his bride-to-be. A small indignant frown formed between Norah's straight dark brows.

She had left Boston for the wilds of Arizona Territory in the merciless June heat, experiencing dirt and discomfort all the way, in order to marry a man she had never seen. Surely it was not too much to expect that Abner would be there to meet the stage, as he had promised in his most recent letter! Since Santa Fe she had visualized him alternately as a dashing hero or a boorish ogre. In her mind he was rapidly assuming the latter identity again. A flare of undiluted Irish ire momentarily vanquished her fears. The slender fingers clenched, then relaxed. *A lady never shows extremes of emotion: Maxim Number Ten from Miss Emerson's Academy for Young Gentlewomen.*

The driver threw open the door. "Greenwood Junction, ma'am."

"Thank you, Mr. Murdock."

He didn't wait to help her alight, and she hesitated, then jumped down gracefully despite her weariness. She was delicately made, with a firm little chin, softly curving mouth and dark-fringed eyes that could darken from a deep sky blue to violet in an instant's time. And beneath her shy and ladylike exterior, there lurked an adventurous woman of fiery spirit and the Devil's own temper, which she constantly fought to master.

So this is Greenwood Junction, she reflected. *How very inappropriate!* No matter where she looked there was neither green nor wood to be seen, except for the bone-colored planks of the sidewalk and the storefronts, cracked and bleached from the relentless sun. The rest of the buildings were formed from adobe and sprung like pale mushrooms from the earth itself—not a comforting sight for someone more used to the neat brick and clapboard structures of the East.

A strange bird cried once, twice, then dipped at a piece of refuse. No one was about, yet Norah had the definite feeling she was being watched. The back of her neck prickled unpleasantly, sending a cold razor of apprehension scraping down her spine. A dull rapping sound came to her ears, but the wind shifted, and she couldn't locate its source. Keeping her head high, her back stiff, Norah waited uneasily.

In the deep shadows of the lean-to at the far end of the dirt street, two men assessed her, one in frank admiration, the other with an intensity unlike his usual controlled manner. "There's a real lady, now, Sergeant LeBeau," the blacksmith said to the man whose horse he was shoeing.

He nodded toward the woman waiting on the boardwalk in a crumpled gown of fine blue muslin and a simple hat of chip-straw trimmed with matching ribbon. "Must be Abner Slade's mail-order bride. Looks like a china doll, don't she?" He drove another nail in place.

A bitter smile twisted the other man's mouth. He was lean and tall, and wore his clothes with indifferent grace: light blue cavalry pants with a yellow seam stripe were stuffed into knee-high cuffed moccasins of soft leather, and a battered gray hat hung by the strap from one callused but well-shaped hand. Like the hat and footwear, his blue fireman's shirt was nonreg-ulation, in the casual style adopted by the Indian Scouts attached to Camp Greenwood. Beneath his red bandana a roughly shaped bit of turquoise dangled from a leather cord.

He wore his shoulder-length black hair pulled back and restrained with a knotted thong at the nape, and beneath the thin and finely molded patrician nose, his mouth was a determined slash. The hair and the high cheekbones hinted strongly of Indian ancestry, but his eyes were the cool dark gray of a lake on a rainy morning.

Abner Slade's bride! To his own distraction, LeBeau discovered he envied the former and pitied the latter. What in holy hell was a woman like that doing with a man like Slade? Didn't she know what he was really like? The damp muslin clung to her shoulder blades and breasts, and her black hair escaped its smooth coils, curling into rebellious ringlets around her face and neck. She appeared demure and elegant and untouched by life. That look of untried innocence would change forever, once Slade got his blood-stained hands all over that slender white body. The thought disgusted LeBeau. His eyes glittered like ice, and his lean features settled in stern lines.

"Mercy Michaels and her girls are going to lose a lot of business." LeBeau's voice was harsh and abrupt.

The blacksmith was startled by the grim tone. He looked at LeBeau to see if he was joking, but there was nothing in the Scout's face to give that impression. Even in profile LeBeau's face had a dangerous and arresting quality that was more than the sum of sculpted bone and taut muscle beneath the darkly burnished skin. It was a face that made women glance his way from under coyly lowered lashes, and made men tread more warily in his presence. There was a rumor that he was part Comanche, but no one knew if it was true or not.

And I ain't about to ask 'im, neither, the smith decided with a sidelong appraisal of the other man. *Likely he don't use his real name. If he even knows it.*

LeBeau did answer to many names and knew them all. In the white man's world he was Sergeant Roger LeBeau of the Camp Greenwood Indian Scouts. In the world of the Comanche he was Storm Caller, Rider-of-Storms: in his heart this was his true name. His father had been a Frenchman, who abandoned his Comanche wife and son to marry a white woman. His mother had died after receiving one of the blankets distributed by the government which had been purposely contaminated with smallpox; yet he had left his ancestral homelands on the Staked Plains to become an Indian Scout for the U.S. Cavalry. Everything about him was a paradox: he was a complicated man leading a simple life, a man constantly at war with Fate and his own self, torn between the two opposing cultures that had formed him, body and soul. Nothing of this endless struggle was apparent as he leaned back and watched the woman.

Norah, standing in the dusty street, felt her temper unraveling from the heat and uncertainty. What a God-forsaken place! Sweat trickled down her nose. Beyond the miniscule town, the parched land lay flat to the horizon in three directions, but to the north the humped spine of a mountain range shimmered blue and purple with distance. The hot wind fanning her cheeks brought no relief, but oh, how good it felt just to stand erect after hours of rattling around in the confined space, like the few coins left in her worn change purse.

With difficulty she refrained from stretching to ease her aching muscles. But a lady didn't do such things. Of course, a lady didn't sweat, either, but she had no control over her body's reaction to the sweltering day, compounded by the many layers of clothes that modesty required.

The driver vanished into the stage office, and it seemed to Norah that there was no one else alive in the vast dun-colored landscape but the yawning guard and herself, slowly wilting under the yellow sun. Where was everybody? And most importantly, where was Abner? Something moved in the street, and she whirled around, eagerly. It was only a yellow dog with scabrous sores on its ribs and a huge, lolling tongue. She dabbed at her forehead with a wadded-up handkerchief, unable to rid herself of the feeling she was being watched.

A welcome idea sprang into her mind. There had been a silly mistake. Somewhere close by there was *another* Greenwood Junction, a bustling town of laughing people, of smartly painted buildings with a green park on the outskirts. Her fingers twisted a knot of ribbon on the muslin skirt. *Oh, surely there has been a mistake...or perhaps some unfortunate accident...*

"Look lively, there!"

She jumped aside as an object hurtled down beside her, followed by two others in quick succession. Boxes of goods, shipped from the East. Two scarred valises made the same short trip from the top of the vehicle. When the guard put his beefy hands on the humpbacked trunk that had come from Ireland with her grandmother, her blue eyes sparkled warningly.

"Sir! If you please, be gentle with my trunk! My grandmother's china set is in there." *No matter what provocation, a graduate of Miss Emerson's Academy for Young Gentlewomen never forgets she is a lady.* Somehow it was becoming more and more difficult to remember that.

The man grinned amiably. A request for careful handling usually caused a sharp increase in the descending velocity of the next piece of luggage, but he felt benign today. She was a pretty little filly, that black-haired lady they'd taken on at Santa Fe. Nice breasts for her size. She'd look damn good naked.

"Sure thing, ma'am." Looping a piece of rope twice around the trunk, he lowered it down the side, wondering what a pretty lady and her grandmother's dishes were doing in a hell-hole like Greenwood Junction. Climbing down wearily, he spit a stream of amber juice around the plug of tobacco that bulged his narrow cheek. "She sure don't belong here," he muttered.

He crossed the street to Mercy's place, eager for whiskey, women, grub and a hot bath; that was the order in which he wanted to have his needs filled, but he knew Mercy would dictate otherwise. "Yer gals is too particklar," he'd complained on more than one occasion, but Mercy Michaels never bent her rules for anyone. He spat again and opened the carved oak door, forgetting Norah as the familiar smells of the bordello welcomed him.

In the lean-to, the smith drove home the last nail with a sure touch. "Nice roan you got here." He scratched his head. "I disremember you having a horse that was shod before."

LeBeau needed a good mount, and the roan was perfect for his needs. He'd be leaving Camp Greenwood as soon as his stint was up. Although it was against regulation, the stable-master would find a place for the horse until then. "I bought him from Abner Slade last week. He is a good horse, nevertheless."

The smith cocked a curious eye at the Scout, and that dangerous trait won out over caution. "Abner Slade is purty successful, what with his trading company and his ranching. He's looked up to by most folks, but I reckon there's bad blood between you and him. He done somethin' to offend you?"

LeBeau shot him so long and chill a look that the man fancied his blood might clot in his veins. "Your respected merchant sells shoddy goods to the Army and rotting meat covered with maggots to starving Indians. And those are among his lesser sins." His mouth thinned to a taut line. "Abner Slade offends me merely by being alive."

The smith wiped his hands on his grimy leather apron. "All set, Sergeant."

LeBeau patted the neck of his impatient roan. The horse was ready, and he should have been on his way. Instead he watched and waited with more than a casual interest. The woman's pose of quiet dignity didn't fool him. He saw the blanching of the fine-boned fingers clasped so tightly and half hidden in the folds of her gown. There was too much white showing around her eyes. He'd seen that same wild-eyed look on horses, just before they bolted. Keeping an intrigued eye on the woman, LeBeau rested his weight against a post of the lean-to. No need to leave just yet.

Another interested pair of eyes observed Norah from the second floor across the street, peering through red velvet draperies in Mercy Michaels's own boudoir. Inside, the room was dark and close, filled with the scented ghosts of whiskey, strong perfume, and stale sex. Mercy gave a little snort of disdain as she watched the newcomer waiting alone on the uneven boards of the walk, the oval face becoming paler by the moment. Beneath elaborately fringed and curled orange hair, the whore-house madam's painted lips curved in a feral smile.

The girl would be no rival, that much was for sure. Why there was nothing to her! Mercy was relieved. Wouldn't she tease Abner about his lah-dee-dah little wife the next time he visited her? Wouldn't she just! And, while she was at it, she'd give him a piece of her mind. She'd expected him last night, and he hadn't shown up at all. He'd pay for that, one way or another.

Mercy's name was no reflection of her spirit. There was no kindness in her, no tender heart beneath the too-tight bodice of gold satin decked out with black silk braiding. Years of drink and dissolution showed in her face despite the careful layers of rice powder and rouge, but Greenwood Junction danced to her piping. She was a woman of power in her restricted sphere, and few people cared to remember that she had been plain Edna Freuhoffer from Buffalo when she'd first arrived. Shrewd and tough, with a heavy-boned, rather mannish build, she was im-placably aggressive and quick to take offense. A small slight was returned tenfold. What a larger insult might result in was unknown: no one had ever tried it.

She set her half-emptied glass of whiskey down on the edge of the dresser. "Well, I won't have much to worry about with that one! Skinny and too dowdy by half..." With a satisfied smile she let the curtain drop and went out into the corridor until she reached the end room. She gave two sharp raps on the door with the back of her hand.

"Get a hustle on, Sal! Stage just pulled in." She hurried back to her vantage point. She waited until she heard the long sigh and rustles of movement within. "And get that new Mex-ican kid ready. Murdock likes the young ones."

Back down in the street, Norah's nervousness had given way to frank anger. Any of the pupils of Miss Emerson's Academy would have recognized the signs: her eyes, clouded with emo-tion, deepened to violet, and the soft lips compressed into a firm line. Wheeling about sharply, she marched along the wooden walkway toward the stage office, the heels of her half-boots echoing in the emptiness.

Eyes fixed on her destination did not see the man stagger out of the saloon. He caromed into her, and Norah was shoved off balance by the impact. She landed on her back in a most unladylike position, slim legs in pale stockings half uncovered and tangled in the hem of her traveling dress. The wind was knocked out of her, and she lay there, staring up at the drink-raddled face of a sodden drifter. His cheeks were covered with uneven stubble, his bull-denim pants caked with dirt, and months of grease stains decorated the front of his leather vest. His gun belt, hung below a protuberant belly, was twisted sideways.

"Wahl, wahl, wha' have we here?" The drunk shook his head as if to clear his vision. "You the new whore for Mercy's crib? Mighty pretty, mighty pretty!" He reached out for her, weaving slightly. A string of spittle hung from the corner of his mouth.

Norah had no breath to speak or even move, but lay there in helpless horror with a generous expanse of white thigh exposed. Before she could even move, a shadow fell over her. She saw a blur of action, had a swift impression of strength and power, and then the drifter was arcing through the air toward the street, like the Human Cannonball she had once seen in Sullivan's Traveling Circus. Her rescuer knelt beside her. His face was not classically handsome, but had a stark beauty all its own, all hollows and angles and frowning gray eyes. As he bent over her, Norah gazed up at him wonderingly. *He is the stuff that girlish dreams are made of!* Her heart skipped in double time. Could this be Abner?

"Are you hurt, ma'am?" The words, the calm impersonal manner, shattered her brief fantasy: she remembered that Abner was fair, his eyes brown. She could do nothing to quell the guilty stab of disappointment.

The man slipped an arm beneath her shoulders, supporting her weight on it. "I am quite unharmed, except for the blow to my pride! Thank you, sir, for your most timely assistance." His arm tightened momentarily, and she had an overwhelming urge to lean her head against his broad chest, but it was gone in an instant, and she held out her hand, completely flustered. "If you will just help me to my feet..."

He pulled her up, and they stood almost touching for a fleeting moment. Norah stepped away and looked down, hurriedly brushing at her dusty skirt. When she turned around, the drunk was still lying in the street. "Is he...is he hurt?"

"I doubt it," the tall stranger said, as if it were of no importance.

As if to corroborate his statement, the drunk began to snore lustily. Norah bit her lower lip to keep from laughing. "Are you going to just leave him lying there in the street, Mr.... ah...?"

"Sergeant LeBeau of the Camp Greenwood Indian Scouts, at your service, ma'am." He bowed, mockingly. "Is there anywhere else you'd rather have me leave him?"

Norah scanned his face. Was that a twinkle in his eye? She couldn't tell. "Well, he might be run over by a carriage," she said, ignoring the lack of traffic. "Or...or trampled by a horse!"

"Would that distress you? In that case I'll remove him to safer quarters." LeBeau stepped off the sidewalk and into the street, picked the man up and slung him over his shoulder with an ease that spoke of the hidden strength in his lean frame. With deliberation he walked over to the barrel set at the end of a dirt-clogged gutterspout in the forlorn hope of catching rainwater. Like a magician, he folded the unconscious drifter in half, then stuffed him into the receptacle, a soiled pimento in an oak-staved olive. All that could be seen were the soles of a pair of scuffed boots, much run-down at the heels, and the battered brown hat that LeBeau set neatly on the man's head.

Norah watched, mouth half open. She didn't know whether to laugh or protest, but was much inclined toward the former. Her sides were shaking with suppressed mirth. LeBeau advanced down the boardwalk with an easy stride that denied the effects of the broiling heat. "Anything further I can do for you, ma'am?"

"Thank you, that is quite enough," she said in her best schoolteacher voice, trying to subdue the unladylike bubble of laughter that fought for release inside her throat. By the smile that quirked LeBeau's mouth up at one corner, she knew he had seen past her pose. She should have been embarrassed: a lady never condoned violence, but she was beyond caring at the moment. Norah ruminated on what further changes these strange Western lands might wreak in her behavior.

LeBeau took pity on her silence. "Isn't someone meeting you?"

"My fiancé was supposed to be here when the stage got in. Mr. Abner Slade. I can't think what has detained him! I'm sure he'll be along at any moment."

"I think you'd better wait inside, or you'll be dead of heat-stroke before he arrives. A sorry end to your romance." Without waiting for assent, he took Norah's elbow and propelled her toward the hotel. Automatically, her feet fell into step with his. Then she stopped in her tracks. Or rather tried to. LeBeau continued on, drawing her along willy-nilly.

"But my things! Everything I own in all the world is in my luggage."

"I don't think anyone here will have much use for your trunks or your grandmother's china set, ma'am," LeBeau replied, without slackening their pace. "Too hard to fit in a saddle bag."

Norah drew herself up and glared at him. His face was still serious, but the way one dark eyebrow tilted at the corner and the way his gray eyes sparkled told her he was laughing at her expense.

"Perhaps such things seem out of place to you here in this…this…*place*. However, my personal possessions have great value to me."

LeBeau didn't answer, merely tucked her arm more firmly under his. He smelled of leather and horses combined with a tinge of juniper, and she was reassured by the scent's faint familiarity: it tugged the strings of her memory, reminding her of happier times when her father had been alive.

Glancing at the Scout out of the side of her eyes, Norah made no further demur. She judged him to be between thirty and thirty-five, although it was difficult to tell age in men bronzed by constant exposure to wind and weather. The rhythm of her heart accelerated, and she was immediately conscious that her reactions to him were, most definitely, not those of a daughter. Hastily, she looked down again, noting the new scuff on the toe of her right boot.

Sunlight glinted off the garnet ring on her left finger, and Norah blushed guiltily: she was a woman legally betrothed, and tomorrow, after a few short vows, she would be a wife. A stranger's wife. Her flush deepened, and her stomach gave an uncomfortable lurch. More than ever Boston seemed like a dream, and Greenwood Junction a nightmare. For an instant she wished she were back in Boston, safe in the confines of her spartan room with the narrow white enameled bed. But Miss Emerson's Academy was no more, and neither was the Norah O'Shea who had taught there for most of her twenty-eight years and only dreamed of adventure. No, now she was living the exciting life she had always longed for, and if this new life was startlingly different, it was still more than a fair trade.

Shrill feminine laughter floated from the window of the building across the street as Norah went through the open hotel door. It felt cooler inside, but only in comparison to the sizzling air outdoors. The lobby was small and sparsely furnished, with two tables, a writing desk, and several wooden chairs set around haphazardly. Behind the dark mahogany counter a thin man of middling age sat in his shirtsleeves and examined Norah with frank curiosity. He donned a rusty black suitcoat that matched his rusty black trousers, and removed the pencil from behind his ear.

LeBeau waved his hand in the direction of the chairs. "If you'd care to admire the artwork, I'll check at the desk."

A set of garish prints hung above them on the fly-blown wallpaper. Limp mallards with death-glazed eyes reposed in feathered splendor among pyramids of autumn fruits and vegetables. Norah wrinkled her nose with amused distaste. "I'm afraid dead game birds are not my favorite still-life subject." She leaned closer. "And I'm reasonably sure this artist has never even seen a duck." A dimple appeared at the corner of her mouth and disappeared just as quickly. "Chickens...*just possibly*. But not ducks!"

LeBeau broke into an open, genuine smile, and it transformed his face. Their eyes met and held in the sudden intimacy of shared humor. They both looked away simultaneously. "I'll make the inquiries," he said abruptly, and she took a seat on the hard wooden chair, perplexed at what had come over her just then. He approached the desk clerk with an economy of movement combined with a lithe grace. Realizing she was staring rudely, Norah busied herself with smoothing out one of the wrinkles in her rumpled skirts.

"Slade, you say?" The clerk cleared his throat. "Checkin' up on him again, eh? Heard tell there was a spot of trouble down in Tucson a while back, but…"

"Has he been here, or not?" LeBeau interrupted sharply.

"Naw, he ain't showed up yet. Paid ahead for the front bedroom for tonight, though. Right here. Mr. 'n' Mrs. Abner Slade, one night only."

Norah gasped and rose to her feet, patches of high color staining her cheeks. Crossing the plain board floor with embarrassed determination, she addressed the clerk. "I believe you have made an error, sir! I am Miss O'Shea. A room was to be reserved in my name. A *single* room."

The clerk opened his mouth to protest, evaluated her martial attitude, and looked again. Silence stretched out as he ran a finger over the smeared page of the registration book again. There was grime beneath the chipped edge of his nail.

"Sorry, ma'am. Mr. 'n' Mrs. Abner Slade, and Reverend Melloway is all I got listed here, 'cept for a patent-medicine salesman and the fellows from the stage. That's it."

"But…but there must be some explanation."

"An eager bridegroom, no doubt," LeBeau murmured dryly. His gaze flickered over her small but womanly figure. "And who can blame him?"

She flushed deeply, the result of anger as well as mortification, and ignored his comment. "Why, I cannot possibly stay alone in a hotel full of men!"

Neither of the men answered, and she recalled with nostalgia the wheezy widow who had been her companion as far as Santa Fe yesterday. How reassuring it would be to see that enormous bulk toddle through the doorway now! "Perhaps you could recommend some lady who would bear with my company, or even put me up for the night if necessary."

Devils danced in the clear gray of LeBeau's eyes, and he grinned unabashedly. The clerk followed suit, and she glared at them both. "I see nothing humorous in my request! Surely it is not unreasonable under the circumstances."

Open laughter greeted her words. Her Irish temper was fully roused now. "Well, if you refuse to help me, I shall have to make arrangements myself. I heard a woman's voice across the street as we came in." She swung around, heading for the door but was stopped before she went two steps. A hand clamped down on her shoulder, effectively fastening her to the floor. She could not budge an inch.

LeBeau was serious now, no touch of amusement in his features. "I am afraid that would be unwise, Miss O'Shea. This is not Boston or Philadelphia or some civilized little hamlet back East with ice-cream socials and a Ladies' Aid Society. This is Greenwood Junction: there are no ladies here."

"But I heard..."

"What you heard, my dear Miss O'Shea, was not a lady. There are several *women* in Greenwood Junction—but as I've already said, there are no *ladies.*" He held her arm in his hard grasp and watched understanding dawn.

"Oh!" Norah's eyes widened.

"Yes. 'Oh!'" He released her abruptly. "You will have to put up here. There's no alternative. Just stay in the hotel and keep the door bolted when you're in your room. I'll see that no one bothers you. Slade will show up soon." He contemplated the bride-to-be. "Whatever else the man is, he is certainly no fool."

Although displeased by the circumstances, she perceived that she had no choice. Ignoring LeBeau, who slouched against the counter as if anticipating further amusement at her expense, Norah addressed the clerk in her most devastatingly proper schoolteacher's tones.

"When Mr. Slade arrives, you will show him to another room for the night. I will take the room that was reserved." And paid for. She signed the register with a flourish. "And now I believe I would like to freshen up from my travels."

"Yes, ma'am. Just follow me, ma'am." She nodded distantly to LeBeau, who was still grinning. "Thank you, Sergeant. You have been most helpful."

The Scout rose to his considerable height and bowed, a tight little smile on his lips. *Dismissed like a servant, by God!* Wondering why he had ever gotten involved, he stalked out, damning Abner Slade and everything and everyone connected to him.

Norah witnessed his departure, then followed the clerk up

the stairway that rose on the left. The treads were covered with a runner of dark brown carpeting, badly worn from the grit and sand tracked in from the street. Small particles glittered like gold dust where the sunbeams struck. The upper landing was darkened by heavy chocolate draperies framing the lone window at the far end of the corridor. The walls were painted a deep ivory, almost yellow, and were punctuated at regular intervals by narrow four-panel doors with tarnished brass numerals. It looked like a shabbier version of every other hotel she had stayed at on her journey, and Norah derived some solace from its nondescript sameness.

The clerk inserted a key in the fourth door on the left. He held the door open, and she crossed the threshold. Hot air met her, tempered slightly by the breeze blowing through the half-opened windows fronting the street. Clean but well-mended curtains of blue and red chintz danced fitfully on either side, and a matching counterpane was spread across the bed. A machine-loomed imitation Oriental rug covered the center of the floor with washed-out tones of red and blue. The wallpaper, which had once been white with red roses, was now gray with faint splotches of dull brown. It was the bed that impressed itself most strongly upon her notice. A double bed of tarnished brass.

"This here's the best room," the clerk said doubtfully, looking from Norah to the faded walls and back. "I'll send Henry up with yer luggage right away. Uh, if yer feeling peckish, there's a mess of stewed prunes and some cold meat pie left from lunch. Otherwise, supper's downstairs in an hour."

"Thank you, but I am not really hungry. I shall only require some warm water for bathing." How could she eat when her stomach was threatening to crawl up into her throat?

"Suit yerself. The bath's behind that there screen in the corner. Tub was brought up earlier."

She hung her hat on an iron hook and smoothed her hair. Her face looked ghostly in the mottled mirror. Lost in contemplation, she jumped and whirled around as the door swung open. It was only a white-thatched porter, whose strength belied his age. He plunked her trunk down in the center of the turkey rug, then left without glancing her way once. A few minutes later he brought up the rest of her belongings, and Norah was alone for the first time in days.

She went to the leather chest and opened the lid. The scents of rose geranium and lemon verbena filled the room, bringing with them the memory of lush summer days, and a sudden pang of homesickness. Atop the other items sprinkled with fragrant bits of dried petals and leaves lay a packet wrapped in silver tissue. She removed it, but left the trunk open, hoping the sweet bouquet would dispel the musty odor of the bedchamber.

Placing the tissue on the shabby coverlet, Norah unwrapped it carefully. Inside, neatly folded, was a gown and peignoir of fine lawn, hand-tucked and trimmed with narrow bands of white satin ribbon. Myriad tiny mother-of-pearl buttons winked in the light as she hung it over the door of the wardrobe to shake out the wrinkles. She was pleased to have a few beautiful items in her trousseau. It helped to salve her pride, coming dowerless as she was to Abner. The door opened again, and a middle-aged woman with a creased red face bustled in, bearing steaming copper cans of hot water. As she spotted the gown and negligee her gooseberry eyes lit up with pleasure.

"Oh, ain't that something like!" she exclaimed, setting the cans down by the folding screen. She beamed at Norah, and her horny hand reached out to reverently stroke the fabric. "As soft 'n' white as snow on the mountains! My Ma said you can allus tell a lady by her underthings, and I never seen anything so fine in all my days!"

Norah hid a smile, glad the awed chambermaid couldn't see the well-worn and carefully mended lingerie that lay deeper in the trunk. "Thank you. It was a gift from my colleagues at the young ladies' academy where I taught."

"We don't get many ladies here. Mostly just salesmen and the fellows from the stage. It's so romantical, you being a bride, and all."

The words brought Norah up short. Everything had seemed like a dream up to this point, but now reality was closing in fast. She was really *here*. And tomorrow, if all went as planned, she would be Mrs. Abner Slade. For some reason the prospect seemed less exciting than it had earlier. Moving aside some other articles, she retrieved Abner's picture in its brown leather frame, and set it out on the dresser.

"That your intended?" the maid asked. "I've never seen Mr. Slade, myself. When he's in town he allus stays across the way at Mercy's...." Her speech broke off abruptly, and her lined face and neck suffused with crimson color.

Norah didn't comment, but her mind was busy with speculation as the other woman peered at Abner's likeness. "My, he's got a hard face, don't he? Lookit that mouth and chin! Now there's a man what's used to having his own way." The maid shook her head and conscientiously straightened the torn doily on the side table. "But then a man needs to be hard out here. 'This land will either make you rich, or kill you,' my Pa said, and it kilt him, sure enough!" She poured most of the water into the bath, reserving some for the china pitcher that stood on its own washstand. Satisfied with her ministrations, she left reluctantly. "I'm Ella Beasley. Just ring the bell if you need anything else, miss."

"Thank you."

The door closed behind the woman, and Norah bolted it, then went back and picked up Abner's picture. She turned to the light and scrutinized his face, as if seeing it for the first time. Yes, there was indeed a look of forcefulness to his features, especially in the sharp lines of nose and chin and jaw. Had his wide, slightly full mouth always had that rather ruthless expression to it? Had his heavy-lidded dark eyes always seemed so determinedly aggressive? How strange that she had never noticed before! Perhaps it was merely a normal prenuptial reaction of her ever-active imagination. Hadn't she jumped at strange shadows and loud noises every night of her journey?

Stripping to her petticoats, Norah poured water into the plain china basin, added a few drops of cologne from her reticule, and began to rinse the dust and grime from her face. She stepped out of her underclothes and into the water, avoiding her reflection in the waist-high mirror. Ripples circled her knees and neck, lapping against the curves of her breasts. The water's warm caress reminded her that tomorrow, for the first time since infancy, another person would see her unclothed. Not just another person. A man. Her husband. A husband who was the next thing to a total stranger, but who would be granted, by the exchanging of a few simple vows, the right to see and touch and invade the intimate places of her womanhood.

She glanced down at her body, then away. Her limbs were well formed, her waist narrow and breasts full. Would Abner be pleased with her? Unbidden, a vision of LeBeau's face intruded. "The heat is unhinging my mind!" she muttered, pushing him out of her mind. Her nipples tingled and contracted, and gooseflesh rose along the back of her arms. Attributing it to the cooling water, Norah finished her ablutions quickly.

After brushing out the tangles from her ebony cloud of hair, she slipped into a thin summer night rail and lay down on the bed, intending only to rest a few minutes. Heat and anxiety over a missing fiancé were no match for exhaustion: she fell almost immediately into a disturbed sleep, awakening hours later to a room softened by the purple shades of evening, with the echo of raucous laughter ringing in her ears. Her gown was twisted up around her slim legs, and her heart bounded inside her rib cage as footsteps sounded along the corridor outside her door. Suddenly every sense was alert. She sat up, listening, but the footsteps continued to the end of the hall. A door opened and closed, and a long sigh of relief escaped her. She hadn't realized she'd been holding her breath.

She lit the lamp, and a gentle radiance banished the shadows. Evidently Abner had not arrived yet. Relief warred with annoyance. What was she supposed to do if he didn't show up at all? Norah was too awake and too edgy to fall asleep again. Her stomach growled reproachfully. She found the bag of dried apricots in her cloak bag, and bit hungrily into one. Warm and fragrant, it tasted like an afternoon in a sunny garden, and she felt somewhat cheered after polishing off a few more.

Through the still-open curtains, the velvet night beckoned. Norah strolled to the window and peered out. The change in the view was almost miraculous, the buildings across the way silver-plated with moonbeams. Greenwood Junction was drastically altered, unreal, and no longer threatening.

The night breeze fluttered wisps of hair along her brow. She blinked and stared at the brilliant needles of light that pricked the indigo sky. *How bright the stars are here. How much larger, how much closer they seem!* She leaned out the window, hypnotized by their beauty, and forgot that only a gauzy nightgown covered her bare flesh. Between the starlight and the lamplight behind her, she might as well have been naked.

Two men stood on the boardwalk opposite, and one looked up at Norah's lighted window. "Damn, will you look at that? A woman!" a male voice shouted into the silence.

"Christ, you're drunk, Archie," another voice slurred. "The women are back there at Mercy's place."

"I tell you there's a woman up there," the other protested. "C'mon, I'll prove it to you."

Norah retracted her upper body into the room like a snail into its shell, belatedly remembering that this was a town where a civilized woman was a novelty. She flew across the carpet and checked the door again. Still bolted. There was shouting from down in the lobby, and then a raspy voice bawled out the refrain of a maudlin lovesong. Slowly dragging her hump-backed trunk along the rug, Norah pushed it against the door. Her arms and back ached with the exertion, but she was glad she had taken the precaution. The song grew louder, accompanied by the uneven tramp of heavy boots. The men were coming upstairs in search of her.

"Come on out, purty lady," a gruff male voice cried from the hallway. "Come out 'n' lookit the stars with me." Loud guffaws followed this sally, and someone began knocking on a door at the other end of the corridor. "Come out 'n' let me see those—"

The voice cut off in mid-sentence, to be replaced by a series of dull thuds and then several crashing thumps, as if something—or someone—had been thrown down the stairs. Norah was sure she distinguished the timbre of LeBeau's deep voice down in the lobby, but the words were low and indistinguishable through the thick oak door. She was shaking. More than ever she realized the awkwardness of her position, as a woman alone in a town of men.

There was a brief scuffle out in the street and then silence. Norah was just starting to relax when she discerned stealthy footsteps coming up the stairs. Arming herself with a pair of sewing scissors and an empty water can, she prepared to defend herself if necessary. Over the turbulent pounding of her heart she heard another sound from just beyond her door. Seconds ticked away.

A discreet knock. "Miss O'Shea?"

She recognized the voice. Without hesitating, she set down her weapons, dragged the trunk away, and unbolted the door. LeBeau stood there, his body rigid, and a dark red smear across the knuckles of one hand. His eyes were smoked crystal in the dimly lit hallway, his strong cheekbones accented by the darker hollows beneath. He looked angry. And dangerous.

Stepping across the threshold, he stood just inside the room, towering over her. "You're much too trusting, Miss O'Shea. I hope you are not in the habit of opening your bedroom door to anyone who knocks."

She drew herself up haughtily as anger banished her earlier fears. "Thank you for your concern, Sergeant. However, I am able to take care of myself."

"Yes. I've already seen two examples today of *exactly* how able you are!"

Her hand tightened on the edge of the door, and she prepared to shut it in his face. LeBeau put his palm flat on the carved panels and pushed, lightly but deliberately. The opening widened as she gave ground before his superior strength, and Norah retreated in disorder, clasping her hands nervously to her breasts. He shut the door quietly behind him and advanced upon her menacingly. She backed up until the hard edge of the bureau caught her in the back.

Norah remembered how thin her gown was, how transparent, and folded her arms across her chest. He reached out and captured her wrists, forcing her arms slowly down to her sides. His breathing quickened. For a moment his gaze roved over her, pausing at the pulse that beat wildly at the base of her white throat, and lingering along the upper curves of her breasts until she was afraid to breathe. Without warning he pulled her close, and as their bodies came in contact a jagged bolt of sensation sizzled up her spine and out along her nerve endings. She was so inexperienced she mistook it for fear.

LeBeau cursed silently as she recoiled. She was lovely. She was innocent. He had lost his innocence long ago. Desire grew, and he fought to remember his purpose. He had meant to frighten her into using discretion, to make her realize the precariousness of her situation, and instead he had caught himself in his own trap. A lifetime of steely discipline came to the rescue.

"How able do you feel now, Miss O'Shea?" he said in a husky whisper. "How capable of protecting yourself now? Look!"

He swung her around to face the mottled mirror. Her dusky hair tumbled wantonly about her shoulders, accenting the camelia skin exposed by the half-buttoned bodice. She gasped at her reflection. Heat and dampness had molded the wispy fabric to her body, and the rosy aureoles showed through quite clearly. Surprise and fear had frozen her tongue, but anger thawed it.

"Let me go! Let me go at once, or I will shout the house down!"

He spun her around to face him again and caught her chin firmly in his hand. "And have some of those ruffians downstairs decide to join us? I think even you have better sense than that."

His grip relaxed and she flung herself away. Snatching up her ivory-handled button hook from the dresser, she brandished its wickedly curved end in his direction. "Do not come one step closer," she demanded in a shaking voice. "I would not like to harm you, but I shall not hesitate to do so in the least."

She was hopelessly outmatched, but her proud defiance made her look like a little mouse defending its burrow. An unexpected spurt of laughter shook his chest. "Have no fear, Miss O'Shea. I have no designs on your virtue." A flush spread over his cheeks at the lie, and he hoped she was too distraught to notice. "But I do think you should know the risk you take in opening your chamber door to a man. Any man."

"If that was your intention, Sergeant, there was no need to humiliate me in the bargain. How dare you!" She caught up a shawl from the chair and wrapped it about herself protectively. "A gentleman would not have treated me so!"

The hurt and vulnerability on her face filled him with fury. It was a crime to leave a woman like this alone and unprotected in such a rough-and-tumble town. He chalked up one more score against Abner Slade. "Perhaps I am not a gentleman, then."

He grabbed her arms above the elbow and gave her a teeth-rattling shake. "Listen to me, and do as I say! Do not lean out that window again, do not leave your room until morning, and do *not*, under any circumstances, open your door to anyone but Mrs. Beasley. Do you understand? I may not be around the next time to save you from your own ignorance."

Despite her indignation and something bordering on fear, Norah was mesmerized, unable to look away from his face, his terrible, chiseled beauty. His expression was fierce and impossible to decipher, yet strangely stirring. A door banged somewhere, and she came to her senses. What on earth was she doing, standing like this in her nightdress, staring into the face of a man she didn't even know? Breaking free of his spell, she moved back toward the door.

"Thank you again for your concern, Sergeant. I shall be more careful so that you will not be required to rescue me again." Her voice quavered slightly.

A muscle twitched at the corner of his mouth. "Remember—don't open your door to anyone."

"Be assured that I shall not open it to anyone until morning. Not even you," she added disdainfully.

The brief, self-mocking smile did not reach his eyes. "*Especially* me!"

LeBeau stalked out. Norah slammed the door shut, shooting the bolt home with a satisfying click. She leaned against the jamb a moment. Her whole body trembled with reaction. Never before had she been spoken to in such a way! And never before had she been held roughly against a man's strong frame, been so intensely attuned to the differences between male and female. She could still feel the weight of his body against hers. For several minutes she stood in the center of the rug, trying to sort out her emotions. It was no use. Her head was whirling. She went to shut the casement, wishing she could shut out the memory of her last encounter with LeBeau as easily.

In the dappled moonlight a man leaned back against a hitching post, looking up at her window. Although she couldn't see his face, she knew his identity beyond a doubt: Sergeant LeBeau of the Indian Scouts. She dropped the curtain as if it burned her hand. For some time Norah wandered about restlessly, arranging and rearranging her toilet articles on the worn dresser scarf, checking the door bolt a dozen times more. Aimlessly she prowled the room as unnamed needs and longings awakened from their long slumber. She did not know what it was she wanted, only that she felt a lack, a hollowness of spirit that cried out to be filled.

She paced the room a long while, and when she looked out again LeBeau was still there, keeping his vigil over her like some dark angel. He had angered her, insulted her, and yet Norah felt immeasurably safer for his nearness. Perhaps she had found a friend in this strange and alien world. That was a comforting notion. But where was Abner Slade, the man she was to marry in the morning? Perturbed over what the morrow held in store, she flung herself atop the cotton coverlet and lay awake till dawn.

Down in the street the Scout brooded over his own uncharacteristic behavior. Why had he embroiled himself in the affairs of this woman? It was an awkward situation, at best: tomorrow she would be Slade's wife; and in a few weeks, she'd be his widow.

Because as soon as LeBeau's suspicions of the past months were confirmed, he was going to kill Abner Slade.

2

Norah woke to a golden glory of sunlight pouring through the window. It was so heartening she almost forgot what a fierce white light it would become as the day lengthened. She donned her best dress of rose silk. Today was, after all, her wedding day. If the groom showed up, that is! Her stomach complained in earnest about its lack of dinner, and sent her down the stairway in search of an early breakfast. There was no clerk manning the hotel desk. Her impatience for news of Abner would have to wait a while longer.

"Morning, miss," someone called. "Breakfast is in here."

She followed the voice, which belonged to a cheerful slattern, into a small dining room, currently unoccupied. Breakfast consisted of a flinty biscuit only partially softened by an enormous quantity of gray-brown gravy. Two small sausages lay like lead bullets on the heavy ironstone plate. Norah sighed and pushed the dish away, resorting to strong coffee to fill the void in her midsection. She poured cream into her mug and stirred it, comforted by the familiar ritual. The coffee, at least, was good: rich with aroma, scalding hot and strong enough to dye shoelaces. Her spirits improved with every sip.

The gold watch pinned to Norah's deep lace collar gave the time as seven o'clock, so she was surprised to discover herself the last of the overnight guests. She was also grateful for a few more minutes of privacy. There had been precious little of it on the train and less on the stage. On the way west she had often found the presence of Mrs. Hay, the garrulous widow who had accompanied her as far as Santa Fe, to be a dire penance; now she reflected that the chaperonage of any respectable female would be infinitely preferable to the status quo.

Well, if Abner arrived this morning there would be no problems; but just in case he didn't, she explored alternatives while she broke her fast. The most logical solution would be to find some way to the Santa Magdalena Mission and Father Ildephonso. He was not only her godfather, but the orchestrator of her coming nuptials: it was dear Father Ildephonso who induced her to correspond with Abner Slade in the first place, and it would be Father Ildephonso who united them in the Sacrament of marriage.

Sounds in the lobby told her the clerk was now at his post. Norah quit the dining room and approached the hotel desk with the appearance of more confidence than she actually felt. Her questions proved as unavailing as they had been the previous afternoon.

"No, ma'am. Mr. Slade ain't checked in yet, nor sent no messages, neither."

"Then perhaps you might help me arrange some method of transport to the Santa Magdalena Mission?"

The man scratched his head with the end of his pen. There was a peculiar expression on his face, a rather sly and unpleasant smirk. "Well, Sergeant LeBeau, he stopped by earlier. Said to tell you he's already made arrangements."

"What sort of arrangements?" Norah's voice was dangerously calm.

The pen dug a little deeper into his pink scalp, and the smirk became a leer. "Don't rightly know, ma'am. He just said for you to sit tight and he'd come by."

Anger at the Scout's high-handedness flamed in her cheeks. "You may thank Sergeant LeBeau most sincerely. However, I will contrive without his intervention! Kindly inform me how I can get to the Mission as soon as possible."

"You can probably rent the smithy's wagon, but it's a long drive in the hot sun, and not one for a lady what don't know the countryside." He looked doubtfully at her hands, so small and white and uncallused. "Can you handle a pair?"

Norah flushed, hiding her complete mortification beneath her plummiest tones. "No. I cannot. I am afraid my education did not run to such things."

"Then," said a deep male voice behind her, "what *did* your education run to?" LeBeau ambled up to her side. The gray eyes were mocking, the resonant tones eloquent with disdain.

She felt surprise and a keen sense of disappointment at his manner. What had happened to the man who'd rescued her so gallantly yesterday and then kept his silent vigil? Either he had changed overnight, or she had completely misread his character. *Why am I constantly defending my actions with this man? He has no right to intrude in my business.* She fumed, rising like a trout to his bait.

"What I learned, if it is any concern of yours, Sergeant LeBeau, which I highly doubt, were all the things that are required of a well-informed woman in today's society." She took a quick breath and went on. "History. French and Latin. Deportment. Philosophy and Literature. Mathematics. Watercolors. Geography and Use of the Globes."

LeBeau smiled lazily. "Well now, that won't get you to Santa Magdalena, will it? I rest my case."

It seemed that he was determined to be rude. Norah could be equally scathing, in fact would derive great pleasure in delivering a stinging rebuke under the circumstances. "If you will excuse me, Sergeant, I was addressing this *gentleman*." She pointedly turned her back to him. Rudeness had always been a cardinal sin in her book, but she felt justified at the moment. "Where might I find the smithy, sir?"

Before the clerk could answer LeBeau did. "If you don't want to go to the Mission, just say so; but I thought you did."

She whipped around to him. "Yes, I do! Father Ildephonso is an old friend, and I know he'll let me stay until...until Mr. Slade arrives. Now if you will excuse me, I am making arrangements for my transportation, and I'm sure I do not require your permission to do so."

"That may be, but you'll never get all the way to Santa Magdalena on your own. In fact, I doubt you'd even get halfway there. You'd be just one more set of bones for the coyotes to fight over. Not a very pretty way for a pretty lady to end her journey."

Norah blanched, knowing he wasn't merely trying to frighten her: he meant it. While she hesitated the harsh lines of Le-Beau's face softened, and she glimpsed the man she had seen the night before.

LeBeau wondered angrily what there was about this woman to make him feel so damned chivalrous. She was engaged to Abner Slade, and he had decided during the long night that he would not involve himself in her affairs; yet here he was again. She was still making up her mind when he spoke.

"I'm going to Camp Greenwood, which is a few hours' ride from the Mission, and I'll take you along if you like. We can be there by late afternoon. Captain Gartner and his wife will put you up for the night, and you can make arrangements to go to Father Ildephonso in the morning."

Norah ground her teeth. She hated to be beholden to him, but it would serve her purpose. "Very well," she said resolutely. "I would be exceedingly glad of your escort. When do we leave?"

"As soon as you're ready."

"Give me a moment to change into more suitable clothes." She turned to the clerk, all hesitation gone. "Please send the porter up for my trunk and bags in exactly five minutes."

A faint smile of approval touched LeBeau's lips and was swiftly gone. Miss O'Shea might be a soft Easterner new to the ways of the West, but there was no false coyness or unnecessary dither once her mind was made up. As she went up the stairs with a graceful sway, he was assailed by the same brooding images that had plagued him through the night hours. *Slade's woman!* He scowled and went out.

Norah came back down in less than the five minutes she had requested, the bemused clerk following with her luggage. They went out to the boardwalk and the glare. He set her things down, then went inside and closed the door against the growing heat. The slattern from the dining room came into the lobby, wiping her reddened hands on the soiled front of her apron, and rolled her eyes flirtatiously. Despite his years, the clerk was the only bachelor in Greenwood Junction.

"Sure is something strange going on here, Clarence! Comes in registered as one man's wife, claims she's single, and then leaves with another, bold as brass! And she acts like such a lady, too.''

The clerk shot her a speaking look. "Just what I allus say. You can't trust a woman." He shook out an old newspaper and began to read the front page. He knew every word by heart. The woman stamped her foot and flounced off to the kitchen.

The heavy duck canopy and her wide brimmed hat protected Norah from the worst of the direct sun, but the dazzling light reflected from every surface. They'd been traveling four hours, and the sun was now directly overhead. Heat surrounded them, radiating from the sandy soil, the hot rocks, the blazing blue-white sky. Already her hair was falling in dampened wisps along the back of her neck. LeBeau seemed impervious, but to her it was a foretaste of purgatory.

Dear God, when will we ever reach Camp Greenwood! She pushed a strand of hair behind her ear and tugged at her corset surreptitiously. While LeBeau drove the team with an ease born of habit, she was wishing for the hundredth time that she hadn't laced the corset so tightly. It was an effort to breathe. Rivulets of sweat tickled between her breasts, and the sharp stays poked into her unmercifully as they jounced along. Her black skirt was dusty, her starched white shirtwaist wilted, and her temper fraying fast around the edges.

Even so, she found the countryside fascinating. The landscape had changed dramatically once they left the flat and arid plain behind them. Weird shapes of blood-red and bright orange sandstone reared up around them like prehistoric idols pointing toward the bleached blue sky. Norah had never in her life imagined such a place. Fat cacti and gray-green succulents grew out of what seemed to her to be barren soil, and giant saguaro grew like ridged totem poles. Spherical juniper bushes dotted some sections, sending their pungent piney scent to tease her with memories of cool Northeastern woodlands. If not for the heat she would be enjoying the journey tremendously.

"Does it ever rain here?" she asked, more to break the silence than for information.

LeBeau glanced over at her, noting the rosy spots of color

on her cheeks and their underlying pallor. "Heat getting to you?"

"No."

Her lie was proven as a drop of sweat ran down her temple on cue. She was aware that her companion took some perverse satisfaction in her discomfort, and was determined to bear it with fortitude. Another drop followed the first. "I was just wondering if it is possible for a person to melt like a wax candle. By the time we reach the Army post, there will be nothing left of me but a puddle of hot tallow! *Does* it ever rain here?"

"Not often. But when it does the desert blooms overnight. It's something to see."

He glanced at her and saw another trickle of sweat trail along the curve of her white throat. In his mind, he followed the path of that trickle as it slid inside her bodice and coursed over the swell of her breast, down into the shadowy cleft.

LeBeau forced himself to think of something else. It was bad enough that he had offered to drive her out to the Post with him, but that didn't mean she had any right to dominate his thoughts. A quick look from the corner of his eye told him she couldn't take the heat much longer. Pulling off his red bandana, he handed it to her, then guided the wagon off the track toward an outcropping of ginger stone. There was a wide gap between the wind-carved buttresses, cool and deep, offering welcome shade. She sighed in thankfulness as he reached behind to grab the canteen.

"Here, drink some water." He held the vessel to her lips while she swallowed the warm liquid. "You don't have to be a martyr to prove whatever it is you're trying to prove. We'll rest here until you're able to go on."

Norah glared and pushed the canteen away. "I was not being a martyr. I will make it to Camp Greenwood."

"Yes. As a corpse." His free hand reached for her wrist and held it. "Your pulse is pounding. We should have stopped an hour ago."

"I am perfectly all right, Sergeant!"

Their eyes met as his fingers lingered on her wrist, and Norah's anger faded abruptly. Something occurred between them in that moment, some conduit opened so that the boundaries of their identities blurred and shifted. His blood flowed into hers, and hers pulsed through his veins with every beat of her heart. In that brief empathetic flash they became one soul, one nameless being. The horses whickered softly, and then it was over as suddenly as it had begun.

LeBeau's hand dropped, and Norah looked away, frightened and exhilarated by the experience. He took the bandana from her and poured water on it, careful not to touch her, and his eyes avoided hers. "Wipe your face and neck with this. It will help to cool you off. And it would also help if you'd take off some of those clothes, or at least those ridiculous petticoats!"

The fact that he was right didn't keep Norah's temper from spiraling upward again. She clenched her teeth and struggled to keep from snapping at him. Manners and common sense won out. "Very well." She climbed down wearily from her perch. "But you will have to turn your head."

"I'll do better than that, I'll go out in the sun and dry my shirt."

He leapt to the ground with an unquenchable energy that Norah envied, and walked into the sunshine. He needed to get away from her. She was everything he scorned: an Eastern tenderfoot, a white woman too soft and ignorant to survive in this harsh land. She belonged back in some safe and stuffy parlor, dressed in silks and satins and sipping tea with her friends. He stripped off his shirt and faced a harder truth. She was everything he most admired in a woman: spirited and determined, intelligent and courageous—and filled with a slumbering sensuality he longed to rouse.

She was untouched by any man. He was sure of it. He was also sure she would be passionately responsive in the arms of the right man. But it would be Abner Slade who would initiate her, teach her the secrets of a man and a woman. Slade with his blood-stained hands. LeBeau ground his teeth.

While he wrestled with his demons, Norah slipped hastily out of her underskirts. The temptation to rid herself of the abominable corset was almost overwhelming, but she could not overcome her scruples to do it. Instead she reached inside her bodice and loosened the drawstrings a bit. At least she could breathe now. She rolled her stockings down and wiped her legs with the damp bandana. It seemed rather intimate to cool her skin with the cloth LeBeau had worn around his neck. She hastened with her task. When she had arranged her clothes again she got back on the wagon.

"You can come back now, I'm dressed."

There was no answer. She called again. Perhaps the heat had gotten to him after all. She jumped down and hurried after him. The light was blinding, and it took a moment before she could see. LeBeau was standing twenty feet away with his shirt spread out at his feet. The muscles of his back and arms rippled beneath bronzed skin as he stretched the kinks out of them. He turned to pick up his shirt, already dry from the scorching rays, and shook it free of grit.

Norah watched him without moving. She had never seen a man's naked chest before. The strength and suppleness displayed, the interplay of work-sculpted muscle and sinew and bone were fascinating. Embarrassment warred with curiosity and wonder at the wholly masculine beauty of his body. She told herself that watching him was like marveling at a superb statue, but knew she was desperately trying to intellectualize the raw impact of LeBeau's virility. He wasn't a statue, a cold marble work of art to interpret and idealize. God help her, he was a living, breathing man!

LeBeau looked up and saw her then. His face, relaxed before, tensed into the hard planes and angles she had observed earlier. There was no sound. The world and all its creatures stood still. Time was frozen while their looks met and held. Then he came forward in quick, long strides, and he grasped her by the shoulders.

"Don't you have the sense to wait in the shade? I have half a mind to turn the wagon around and take you right back to town. I can have you in Greenwood Junction in time to catch the afternoon stage."

Heat, annoyance, and his half-naked nearness had already wreaked havoc on Norah's strained nerves. She lashed out in a fury of angry words. "I will not go back. Do you know what my life was like in Boston? The monotony of the same walls, the same people, the same conversations over and over and over again—and knowing every day, every year ahead will be the same, and that there is no escape…"

She wiped a strand of hair from her eyes and gritted her

teeth. "I will never return to that living death! You have badgered, berated, and humiliated me every step of the way, and you may continue to do so but I...am...not...turning...back!"

He glowered at her. "Is that what you think of the Territory, Miss Norah O'Shea? A change of scene to assuage your boredom?"

Before he could continue she tilted her head back defiantly. "Why do you want me to go back so badly? Why do you dislike me? I've done nothing to you."

His grip tightened, but he didn't answer. Instead he caught her to his hard chest. She looked up in surprise in time to see his mouth swiftly descending on hers. He clasped the back of her head with one hand, twining his long fingers in her hair so there was no escaping. Before the shock of his action had time to sink in, the shock of his kiss threw her into a state of total confusion. He tasted salty and male. His tongue touched the corner of her mouth, and it opened in surprise.

That small gasp was all the invitation he needed. Norah, who had never received more than a chaste peck on the lips or cheek, was helpless before his onslaught. When the kiss ended she was breathless with yearning, and before she had time to think he was kissing her again. They were sweat-slick, and her shirtwaist clung wetly to his chest. She was melting away, but not from the sun.

There was a scent of musk around her now, and a dampness between her legs. For a few dizzying seconds she was carried away by a growing urgency that made her bend to him, cling to him. His mouth lifted from the hollow of her throat, and he swore once beneath his breath. Before she was ready to relinquish the warmth of his embrace, LeBeau pulled back.

"Did that answer your questions?" His face was dark with desire, but anger at his own loss of control won out. He could forgive her for being soft and ignorant. Even for being Slade's woman. But he could not forgive her for the effect she had on him. He strode back to the wagon without a backward glance, putting on his shirt as he went. Norah followed, her self-esteem as bruised as her lips. Not only had she been ruthlessly kissed by a man who was practically a stranger, but she had not put up the slightest resistance. And he had been the one to call a halt.

She scrambled back in the wagon, and LeBeau started the team up again, driving through the short tunnel of rock until they came out on the other side. They passed a wall of orange stone, and then a wide plain stretched out before them. They rode for two hours, and not a word was said between them, but each was aware of the other's every move and breath and sigh. The strain in his posture and clenched jaw accurately mirrored her own emotions. Watching his hands on the reins, she remembered how they had felt upon her skin.

Although disquieted by his ability to awaken her senses, Norah had to be honest with herself. She had enjoyed being kissed by him. And if he had stopped the wagon and tried to kiss her again, she had no idea of what she might do. Prudence dictated an offended manner followed by a slap to his face. Norah was unhappily aware that she would not be prudent. Fortunately for her peace of mind, the uneasy silence held until the stockade ramparts of Camp Greenwood were visible in the far distance, as a faint brown smudge on the horizon.

"There it is."

Norah followed his pointing finger. It didn't seem impressive at first: it was half an hour before Camp Greenwood's outer defenses looked like much beyond a low wall of mud brick and upright matchsticks. The optical illusion dissolved as they drew closer, and she realized it was the immensity of the landscape that made the Camp seem so tiny in comparison. While she stared at it, a whirlwind of ocher dust formed and headed toward them.

"What on earth is that?" Did tornados or cyclones occur out here?

"Just a welcome party from the Post. They all want to see who my female companion is: there aren't many women in this part of the Territory."

The horsemen from Camp Greenwood thundered up amidst exuberant cries and flashing hooves that kicked up a cloud of dirt. Norah held her handkerchief to her lips, but the dust still clogged her nose and throat. Coughing slightly, she turned to the side and encountered a leering Apache brave. He leaned so close as he rode past that his red headband brushed against her bonnet, knocking it askew. She gasped as another figure took his place, this one a young Cavalry officer on a dun-colored mount.

"Welcome to Camp Greenwood, ma'am." He touched his Campaign hat. "Lieutenant Anthony Newcomb, at your service." He was past the wagon then, lost in the melee. The air rang with noise as the horsemen swirled around, and Norah marveled that they were able to avoid colliding with one another. Resisting the urge to clamp her palms over her ears, she smiled politely. Suddenly, as quickly as it had started, the ruckus ceased. Indians and troopers wheeled their horses about, riding hard for the open gates of the Camp.

LeBeau snapped the reins, and the wagon rumbled past the shanty town of crumbling adobe where the Camp followers lived. Two unkempt women of indeterminate age leaned over steaming laundry tubs in torn gingham dresses, wiping sweat from their eyes as they examined Norah and her fancy Eastern clothes with contempt. A scrawny child chased a fat rooster out of the way as LeBeau expertly tooled the conveyance through the entrance.

Excitement filled Norah as she looked about. Buildings of whitewashed adobe lined the inside walls of the complex. In the center of the wide Parade Ground, a phalanx of troopers was drilling under the stern guidance of an officer. There were soldiers and civilians here and there, singly and in clusters, attending to the daily business of the Camp. A long mule train with jingling harness pulled laden wagons toward the supply depot. There would be no afternoon tea rituals here, serving up freshly baked buns and stale topics of conversation. No dark sitting rooms smothered under lace antimacassars, no browning ferns hanging above matched sets of badly painted china figurines.

"Why, it's like a bustling town!"

LeBeau was amused by her enthusiasm. Camp Greenwood was a small outpost in a string of others along the areas of greatest unrest, housing only one company of Cavalry. The larger Posts had no need for defensive walls, but here, with the troop at less than three-quarter strength, other measures were necessary.

He drew the team to a halt before a small adobe building.

A uniformed soldier reached up to catch the bit of the near wheeler while a tall, heavily built man approached, one eyebrow raised in inquiry. His light blue eyes were startling in the deeply tanned face, which was framed by chestnut hair faintly streaked with silver. There was an air of authority about him, and Norah was not surprised to hear that he was Captain Gartner, commanding officer of Camp Greenwood.

LeBeau picked Norah's cloak bag off the wooden seat and leaped down. "This is Miss O'Shea, Captain. She was stranded in Greenwood Junction overnight, and I couldn't very well leave her there. Miss O'Shea wishes to go to Father Ildephonso at Santa Magdalena, so I brought her to you until other arrangements can be made." He turned away from Norah, as if washing his hands of any further responsibility.

"Welcome to Camp Greenwood, ma'am," the Captain said warmly as he helped her alight. "I will see that you get to the Mission in the morning; meanwhile, my wife and I will be delighted to have you as our guest."

There was a friendly expression in his eyes, tinged with just the right touch of concern. With his ready smile and intelligent, confident gaze, Norah suspected he would be a man of firm decision, leavened with a dash of humor. A man to turn to in times of trouble. She didn't know why that last thought had come to her, but she trusted him instinctively.

"That is exceedingly kind of you, Captain Gartner. I find myself in a most awkward position! My fiancé, Mr. Abner Slade, was to have met me in Greenwood Junction; however he has evidently been delayed and left no message for me. Since I could not very well remain at the hotel for an indefinite period, I decided to go to the Mission. Father Ildephonso has been my friend since I was a child."

As the hasty explanation tumbled out Norah felt herself blushing with mortification. It didn't help at all to see the difference in Captain Gartner when she mentioned Abner's name. There was a reserved look to his features now and the slightest stiffness in the set of his shoulders. She couldn't let it pass unnoticed.

"Perhaps you know Mr. Slade, sir?"

"Yes, I am acquainted with him. The Camp has had dealings with his company in the past." A small silence arose before

Gartner recollected himself and took her arm. He reached for her small cloak bag with the other.

"You must be tired from your journey. I'll escort you to the guest accommodations, and we can discuss arrangements later. We started an addition to the house, but I'm afraid it is nowhere near completion. Abigail—my wife—is resting just now. She is in the family way, and has not had an easy time of it. I hope you will forgive me for not bringing her to meet you now."

"Why, of course! I would not wish you to disturb her." She felt sympathy for Mrs. Gartner; carrying a child in the later years was often difficult for a woman, especially under the harsh conditions of life on an Army post.

"The guest quarters are just past our house."

She turned the way he indicated, around the end of another building and was astonished to find a small white frame house set in the shadow of the protective wall. Carpenter's fancywork trimmed the posts and overhang of the wide veranda and the peaked dormers set into the low-pitched roof. Open green shutters framed the long windows whose multiple panes reflected the sunlight in neat golden squares. It was the first completely wooden structure Norah had seen in the Arizona Territory. It appeared to have been uprooted from some green Midwestern lawn and deposited a few thousand miles westward on the stony soil of the Camp. She thought it looked charmingly incongruous to the military precision of the Army post, and wondered if she looked equally out of place.

"Why, Captain Gartner, how lovely! This is the first real home I've seen in days!"

He thanked Norah with a tinge of pride, guiding her to a low building of whitewashed adobe adjacent to it. The deepset windows were unglazed and fitted with louvered shutters to keep out the sun, but not the occasional breeze. Gartner opened the door, and she stepped in. It was many degrees cooler inside the thick mud-brick walls, and it took a moment for her eyes to adjust to the gloom. The long, low room held two large beds, two oak commodes, and a large clothes cupboard. A rope, stretched just below the ceiling, held a flimsy curtain that could be drawn back at will, separating the two halves of the room.

"I will send the striker over with some water so that you may freshen up, and a pitcher of lemonade. We received a shipment from Mexico a few days ago.'' He checked the time on his gold pocket watch. ''We dine in half an hour, but I'm sure it's nothing that can't be kept warm if you need more time. I will return to escort you whenever you are ready.''

''Please don't hold dinner back for me. I have ample time to prepare myself. And, since the house is just next door, I will come over when I am ready.''

A few minutes after his departure the striker came, a gangly young corporal named Harris who hadn't yet begun to shave. Norah thanked him and sent him on his way as soon as politeness could tolerate: she wanted to wash the grime of the ride from her skin and slip into some clean clothes. She shook the dust from her dress and hung it up in the scrubbed pine wardrobe, thankfully removed her eyelet corset, and felt twenty degrees cooler immediately. Putting on a light cotton shift, she stepped out of her knee-length pantalets and stockings.

Next she removed the pins and combs from her hair until it fell around her shoulders like a cape of black satin. As she reached into her cloak bag for her silver-handled hairbrush, a sharp knock at the door made Norah pause. She went to answer it, but in her haste to undress she'd forgotten to bolt the door. It swung inward, and a man's frame filled the opening.

Sergeant LeBeau, again! She took an involuntary step backward. ''I did not think to bolt the door.''

''This is an Army camp. I'd advise you to start thinking, and to keep on thinking until you leave. The exercise might do you good.''

She gasped, and LeBeau smiled wryly. Suddenly Norah was intensely aware of her state of dishabille. Belatedly slipping out of sight behind the half-open door, she tried to shut it, and caught a quick and unsettling glimpse of his face. A dark flush spread across the high cheekbones, triggering a response that telegraphed shivers over the surface of her skin. The incident on the way to Camp was obviously fresh in both their minds. She ducked her head back quickly, her heart beating so fast she was breathless. LeBeau's hand caught the edge of the door, a strong, square hand that kept it from closing.

''What do you want, Sergeant? I am trying to get dressed for dinner.''

"In that case, I suggest you let me in, Miss O'Shea. I've brought your baggage."

She goggled. Sure enough, she'd forgotten about her trunk and valises. Why did Sergeant LeBeau always happen to be around when she made a fool of herself?

"Just a moment." She peered around at him. His face had gone remote and impersonal, but the high color lingered beneath his skin. "I was... I am not... I must get dressed, first." The hand holding the door didn't move. LeBeau's expression had changed yet again. Now his gray eyes were sparkling with laughter, and Norah's temper rose. He had laughed at her enough for one day! "Will you please have the goodness to let me shut the door, sir?"

"Certainly. If you will have the goodness to let me remove my hand first!"

"Very well." She kept her lips firmly set in a disapproving line and stood back nervously. If he tried to force his way in, she would scream and arouse half the Camp! The door closed, tightly. She latched it and slipped on her clothes, but could only get the dress half done-up in back, since she hadn't taken the time to lace her corset properly. She checked her reflection in the mirror: respectable, if not too neat. Cautiously, she crossed the room and opened the door.

"You may bring my bags in now," she said with chill civility.

LeBeau nodded, picked up Norah's battered valise and her bandboxes, and set them just inside the room. He took one handle of the humpbacked trunk, and for the first time she noticed he was not alone.

An Indian grasped the other handle. He wore buckskin leggings and a dirty breechclout with soft knee-high moccasins like LeBeau's. A tattered shirt, which had been red velvet before the nap rubbed off, barely covered his barrel chest. He looked Norah up and down slowly, then grinned and said something to his companion in his own tongue.

She examined the Indian with a fascinated horror: among several necklaces he wore was a rosary of polished black beads, and dangling from a twisted silver chain were things that looked suspiciously like finger bones. She didn't look any closer. The Indian leaned forward and grinned at her. His right upper incisor was missing. Norah smiled back brightly while her heart did push-ups in her throat, but when the man leaned further, she retreated posthaste.

"Afraid of Indians, Miss O'Shea?" LeBeau said from just behind her. Norah jumped. She hadn't heard him move.

LeBeau smiled, rather unpleasantly. "Don't worry, Runs-like-Deer won't hurt you. He has no communicable diseases, and he doesn't attack white women. At least he hasn't, so far." LeBeau gave a short bark of laughter, and went out, the Indian following.

Norah shut the door, furious. She could not figure out why LeBeau intrigued her even as he angered her. All she knew was that he could disturb her dignity with a word, her complacency with a smile. Slipping the latch home, she hoped she would not have to put up with his mocking insolence again.

Dismissing him from her mind, she changed into her second evening frock of peach silk embroidered at bodice and hem with rows of forget-me-nots. Peach kid slippers, white gloves, and a spray of chiffon flowers completed the elegant toilette. Norah brushed her hair until it shone, then wound it at her nape in a simple knot. She hoped to make a good first impression: Mrs. Gartner might not take kindly to having an unescorted female guest thrust on her with no advance notice—particularly an unknown female who had been stranded without a word from her fiancé.

With a silent prayer for acceptance by her hostess, Norah stepped outside. Inside the thick adobe walls of the guest house she had been quite comfortable, but in the open the heat was intolerable. She felt as if she were inhaling flames with every breath. By the time she traversed the few yards to the front door of the house, her lungs felt scorched.

The striker admitted her, and Norah suppressed a groan of dismay. The house was hot, dark, and steamy. Not a breath of air stirred. Deep green velvet draperies smothered the heavy lace curtains that swathed the windows. Settees and side chairs upholstered in rose and gold brocade flanked the empty fireplace, ornate mahogany cabinets and tables crowded the walls and every surface was covered with photographs and knick-knacks and furbelows. It was, she thought, a perfect re-creation of any genteel home back East with one exception: there were no ferns. The delicate houseplants could not survive five minutes in the stifling heat of the room; indeed, Norah doubted if she would, herself.

A girl rose from the settee as Norah was announced. She was small-boned with thick molasses-colored hair and very rosy cheeks in a pale oval face. In her summer frock of seafoam muslin trimmed with pink ribbons, she looked like one of Norah's former pupils from Miss Emerson's Academy. Her warm brown eyes were shaded with thick dark lashes as she smiled shyly back at Norah, who assumed her to be the Gartners' daughter. Her greeting, therefore, came as a shock.

"Good evening, Miss O'Shea." She extended a delicate hand and smiled prettily. "I am Abigail Gartner, Captain Gartner's wife. We are absolutely delighted to have your company for dinner."

Norah's mental image of a forty-plus woman with wind-burned skin and tired eyes dissolved at the reality of the Captain's young wife. *Why, she can't be a day over seventeen!* Perhaps the Gartners' marriage had been arranged, much in the way of her own betrothal to Abner. Smiling, she took the small hand in hers. The girl's skin was hot and dry.

"There will only be four of us tonight," the girl continued. "But I've ordered a nice little supper. Nothing fancy, mind you, but good wholesome food."

Norah chuckled. "After the gray gravy and stone biscuits I was given for breakfast, I can assure you that good wholesome food will be a *most* welcome novelty. And I am most happy to make your acquaintance, Mrs. Gartner. You cannot know how relieved I am to be in your good hands. Thank you for your hospitality."

"Why, we frequently house travelers through the area, and the striker does all the work; so you see it requires no expenditure of my energies. However, you may give me all the credit if you wish, and I will accept it quite happily." The brown eyes twinkled merrily. "For my own part, I cannot tell you how excited I was when Charles informed me of your visit to the Post. I hope I can induce you to remain."

Norah returned her warmth. "I am eager to go on to Santa Magdalena. Perhaps Father Ildephonso will have news of my fiancé. Meanwhile, I thank you most heartily and will accept your hospitality shamelessly, Mrs. Gartner.''

The girl blushed. "Oh, please, if you don't mind, I should like it so much if you would call me Abigail.''

"And you must call me Norah.'' They chatted with the comfortable air of old acquaintances, and in a few minutes both were at ease in the other's company. Norah liked Abigail's gentle eyes, her sweet smile and refreshing manners: here was someone who might be a friend, despite the discrepancy in their ages. As married women they would share many interests, and the harsh life would strengthen their ties. Norah's spirits rose appreciably.

In the sidelights framing a cabinet's glass door she saw their reflections, her own face pale, but Abigail's still blooming with bright flags of color in each cheek. A dim memory tugged at her brain. Alabaster skin that seemed to glow from within, and cheeks like summer roses: now where had she seen that combination before? Then the thought was gone.

Captain Gartner entered, resplendent in his dress uniform. The candlelight glinted on the gold buttons of his dark frock coat with its braided trim. His warm smile could not conceal the flash of anxiety in his eyes as they sought his wife. "Ah, there you are, my dear. Good evening, Miss O'Shea. I hope you've brought a hearty appetite with you.''

Abigail's face turned toward her husband as he came forward, like a sunflower tracking the radiant glow from east to west through the summer sky, and Norah perceived her guess had been badly off the mark. *Why, it's a love match!* she thought with delight. *And they adore each other!* Her heart warmed as she watched them. *This is what I want, this is what I hope to find with Abner.*

Abner. Yes, she was formally and lawfully betrothed to Abner Slade. But it was another face, dark and aquiline, that came into her mind. The Gartners were both looking in her direction, and Norah realized a remark had been addressed to her. She rallied quickly.

"Oh, I beg your pardon. I was admiring the portrait of Mrs. Gartner.''

Love and pride showed on the Captain's face. "It was done

when Abigail was fifteen, and is a remarkable likeness, is it not?''

Norah's brief lapse went unnoticed as Gartner began discussing the painting. It showed an almost plump Abigail, in a full-length view against a background of dark green, which accented the whiteness of her skin. The features were youthfully rounded, the underlying bone structure blurred. The girl in the painting was pale, with none of the rosy blush that brightened Abigail's face now.

"A lovely portrait indeed, but I think the Western air must agree with Mrs. Gartner's constitution." Turning toward Gartner, Norah was again aware of that submerged current of anxiety in his manner. Perhaps, like most doting husbands, he was anxious over the pregnancy. Abigail was very young.

They were joined by Lieutenant Newcomb, the young officer who had ridden at the head of the informal welcome party outside the Camp. He was sandy-haired and pale-eyed, with a multitude of freckles visible through his tan, giving him a speckled appearance. A bushy moustache and long burnsides did nothing to offset his boyish face; and although his uniform was smartly pressed and of newer vintage than his senior officer's, he lacked the other's air of confidence and military precision.

"I am delighted to make your acquaintance, Miss O'Shea. I hope your stay at Camp Greenwood will be a pleasant one." He bowed over Norah's hand and held it a bit too long. His moustache tickled her fingers.

"Come, let us go into the dining room," Abigail said brightly, leading the way.

Newcomb took Norah's arm, and they crossed the hall. The dining room was decorated in a pleasant combination of light amber and deep topaz. A silver epergne reposed in state upon the long table, flanked by branched candlesticks of heavily chased silver. The delicious aroma of roasted beef and potatoes promised a well-prepared meal, and Norah's mouth watered.

Abigail was a relaxed and gracious hostess, and dinner was a fine affair, with Captain Gartner putting himself out to entertain the unexpected guest. Only the Lieutenant's admiring looks and pointed glances disturbed Norah's contentment. She was not used to being stared at while she ate, and wished he would occupy himself in some other way. As dessert of chocolate pudding and ladyfingers was served by the striker, Abigail steered the conversation toward plans for her guest's entertainment.

"We might arrange a picnic for the ladies in some picturesque canyon," Newcomb suggested.

"Oh, yes!" Abigail exclaimed. "And an evening of charades or possibly a musicale..." Her eyes danced with anticipation as she enumerated a score of likely treats for the delectation of her uninvited guest.

"Do not make these plans solely on my account! I mean to go to Santa Magdalena Mission as soon as possible," Norah explained. "Father Ildephonso was expecting me today, you know." Addressing Newcomb, she added: "This was to have been my wedding day. Unfortunately my fiancé has been unavoidably detained."

"Fiancé!" The Lieutenant's face fell. "Might I know the name of the fortunate gentleman?" He raised a crystal wineglass to his lips.

"Why certainly. I am betrothed to Mr. Abner Slade."

Newcomb's glass slipped and splintered against his china plate. The striker offered a clean dry cloth to blot up the liquid, but not before Norah saw the look Newcomb exchanged with Gartner. Evidently Abner was not well liked by them. A pity. She hoped this would not prove a barrier to her friendship with Abigail. A moment later the striker returned with a whispered message for the Captain.

"Sergeant LeBeau delivered the news of your arrival to the Mission. Father Ildephonso sends you his best regards. He has no news of Mr. Slade at present, and hopes you will avail yourself of the Camp's facilities as long as you wish." He smiled at his wife. "And Abigail and I sincerely hope you will do so. Since there are no other married officers on the Post, it is very lonely for Abigail, and I know she would be glad of your company."

"Oh, yes! It's been so long since I've had a chance to visit with another woman," Abigail said quickly. "Not since Colonel Boyle and Lieutenant Forest brought their wives from Camp Verde. And there is going to be a party for my birthday in two weeks! Oh, do say you'll stay awhile, Norah! You could still visit Father Ildephonso at the Mission whenever you like. Do say you will, at least until Mr. Slade arrives.''

Suddenly Norah suspected the Gartners of trying to foster a match between herself and Lieutenant Newcomb, and wondered why. They were obviously not aware that a formal betrothal, such as Norah had undergone, was considered as binding by the Church as an exchange of marriage vows. It was also plain that Newcomb was quite smitten with her, but she mistakenly attributed it to the scarcity of marriageable females in the area. If she stayed on, it might only encourage him, and that would be unfair. On the other hand, she would enjoy Abigail's company very much. Since it was what she wanted to do, Norah let herself be persuaded.

"If you really promise not to go to any trouble, I would be pleased to stay until I hear from my fiancé. I am sure I will hear at any time.''

"Then it's settled.'' Abigail smiled, her dark eyes bright with pleasure. "If you like we can drive out to the Mission the day after tomorrow.''

Captain Gartner set his fork down. "I will arrange for someone to escort you two.'' Dejectedly, Newcomb spooned his dessert: his duties tomorrow would take him in the opposite direction.

"Dearest Charles, that won't be necessary.'' Abigail smiled fondly at her husband. "Your men are on constant patrol between here and the Mission, and there has been no trouble with the Indians in months. We shall be perfectly safe: what could possibly happen in broad daylight?''

A cool breeze passed over Norah, bringing crops of goose bumps out along her exposed flesh. She looked up in surprise. The draperies and curtains hung still in the humid air, and the door and windows were firmly shut. She was eager for the coming visit to Santa Magdalena and had no fears for their safety. After all, Captain Gartner agreed the area was well patrolled by the Camp Greenwood troops. What *could* possibly happen in broad daylight?

3

A light morning breeze ruffled the sleeves of Norah's pink-checked gingham and Abigail's yellow muslin, making them flutter like gaily colored butterfly wings as the gig bowled along toward Santa Magdalena. To pass the time, Abigail delivered a running commentary on the fauna and flora of the area, with special attention to those that facilitated survival in the wilderness.

"If you were ever lost or separated from your party, knowing the properties of the various plants could keep you alive while waiting for a rescue party."

Norah made a face of comic dismay. "Abigail, I am not at all edified by your cheerily delivered bits of information. I have no intention of ever being out alone in this stony wilderness!"

"Direct your attention next to those round little cactus plants," Abigail continued, the sternness of her voice belied by her twinkling eyes.

Dutifully turning in the direction indicated, Norah confronted a cluster of dull green globules, more wrinkled and less appealing than prunes, nestled against the beige and rust-streaked ground. "Those horribly ugly grayish ones?"

Abigail shot her a look of laughing reproach. "Ugly is as ugly does! If you are ever lost in the open and in need of liquids you can eat the flesh of those plants for moisture. The inside is rather like a jelly." She waved to the same general location. "But the other round ones, the darker green, are poisonous, so one must be very sure which is which."

"I am not an apt pupil. They look identical to me." Norah shook her head. "Yesterday I was quite angry with Sergeant LeBeau for deeming my education inadequate for life in the Territory. I am beginning to suspect he was correct, after all."

"Oh, I shall help you. It will not take long to learn the basics. I should know, having been a complete tenderfoot myself less than a year ago." She pulled back upon the reins, slowing Dulcey's gait somewhat as they descended the gently sloping sides of an ancient riverbed, its contours softened by the erosion of centuries. "Most of my life I thought chamomile and peppermint tea were the only medicines that didn't come from an apothecary's shop. I've learned so much, though: Sister Thomasina, the convent's Infirmarian, is teaching me the use of plants in healing."

"Ah, but I am even less prepared than you were. I have never even driven a buggy—there was no need for it in the city, and of course Miss Emerson kept a groom and undergroom to look after the carriage and take us out for airings. And that is only the start of it: you shall have your work cut out for you."

Abigail urged Dulcey up the far bank. "And a more delightful task I cannot imagine." They reached the level plain once more and began to climb a long ridge. "Look! There is Santa Magdalena straight ahead!"

The tiled roofs and adobe walls of Santa Magdalena could be seen as faint lines of white and reddish orange just over the horizon, and Norah shaded her eyes with her hand as they neared. A bell tower came into view first as they crested the ridge and finally the church, the convent school and several whitewashed mud-brick buildings were spread out below, encircled by a protective wall. The heyday of the Spanish missions was long past, and Santa Magdalena was a relatively small complex, clinging precariously to the side of another dried riverbed, this one furred with stands of cedar and oak.

Glancing at Abigail, Norah noticed how flushed the girl's cheeks were, and once again a faint memory tugged at her. Where had she seen such a bright wash of color against such porcelain skin? And why did it bother her so? She shook the thought away.

As they reached the entrance Norah prepared to jump down and pull the bellcord, but one side of the iron-banded oak gate swung inward on well-oiled hinges. She kept her seat as the gig went through and saw a young girl shutting the gate behind them. She had large dark eyes, olive skin, and night-black hair that made a pleasing contrast to her white cotton frock; but it was the unearthly perfection of her face that attracted attention.

"Who is that beautiful child? Surely not one of the novices?"

"There are no novices here, only the three sisters and their lay cook. That is one of the students. Her name is Dove-in-Flight, and she is as willful as she is lovely." Abigail sighed and turned the gig toward the hitching post in the shade of the convent buildings. "Sister Cecelia swears she has grown a new line or wrinkle every day worrying about her. I tried to help her with her lessons, at the request of the kind-hearted nuns, who felt she might respond better to someone nearer her own age, but Dove-in-Flight would have nothing to do with me. They are hoping to find a good husband for her as soon as may be, but she has only a small dowry."

Norah looked back over her shoulder. The girl was truly beautiful, with delicately arching brows, and lashes so long they cast shadows on her high cheekbones in the strong sunlight. Her slim body was rounded in womanly contours, and from the piquant child's face, the secret, knowing eyes of a woman looked out.

"With women such a scarcity in the Territory and with such grace and beauty, surely the lack of sufficient dower will not be a problem? Some man will simply fall in love with her at first sight and never count the consequences."

"I hope you be proved right, Norah." She nodded to the right. "Over there in the corner is the convent and the convent school where young girls are boarded. After your reunion with Father Ildephonso, I will take you there to meet the Sisters."

Adjoining the convent and school was an outdoor kitchen, and on the other side of a tiny courtyard, a long building that was probably the infirmary. From across the quadrangle the church dominated the compound and, unlike the layout of most earlier missions, was inside the protection of the adobe brick walls, its main entrance facing into the square. Next to it stood a small, single-story building, which Norah guessed to be the rectory.

They crossed the main courtyard and under the lacy foliage of ancient sycamores, rolling to a stop in front of a long, low building. Behind the wrought-iron grillwork several girls sat upon wooden benches in the inner court. They were all brown- or copper-skinned with neatly plaited hair, and dressed in similar plain white frocks, but not one of them had the arresting loveliness of Dove-in-Flight. Norah looked for the girl, but did not see her among the other students. A thin feminine voice floated on the air, speaking alternately in Spanish and heavily accented English.

"*La leche.* The meelk. *El pescado.* The feesh. *Las cebollas.* The oneeyons. Now you geeve to me in Engleesh."

"The meelk, the feesh, the oneeyons," a chorus echoed dutifully. Norah and Abigail grinned at each other, biting their lips.

"That is Sister Thomasina giving the older girls their 'Engleesh' lessons. She is really the Infirmarian, but Sister Immaculata, the Mother Superior, has been ill with dropsy the past few weeks. You will meet her today if she is improved, and also Sister Cecelia, who is a general favorite. One cannot be in her company long without smiling, for she is as round as a drum and as merry as a grig. And her 'Engleesh' is worse than Sister Thomasina's." Abigail had a sudden inspiration. "Perhaps you can put your talents to work while you wait for Mr. Slade to return."

"The thought has just occurred to me, also. Unfortunately, I do not speak Spanish."

"Ah, but I do. Perhaps we can work in tandem." Abigail's dark eyes sparkled with excitement. "I would welcome the diversion. Since Camp Greenwood is such a small Army post and none of the junior officers is married, I have few social duties to perform. Teaching at the Mission would fill my time nicely—for a few more months, at any length." She smiled dreamily, thinking of the child she carried beneath her heart, her gift of love and devotion to Charles.

Norah was touched by the look on Abigail's face, the softening and inner glow that transformed it. Perhaps she would wear that same Madonna look herself in a few months' time. The thought warmed her. Convinced that Abner would arrive to claim her momentarily, she was determined to be a good wife to him. Never once would he regret their marriage, if she had anything to say about it. She wanted very much to have a child of her own, perhaps several, God willing. Filled with thoughts of a baby in her arms, the fears and doubts of the previous night receded from Norah's mind. And with them, the image of Sergeant LeBeau that had lodged there, uninvited.

Climbing down from the gig, she took stock of her surroundings while Abigail tied the horses to the hitching rail. There was an air of peace to the Mission compound, the serenity that comes of shared purpose, the timeless quality of a place half in another world.

Abigail straightened her hat. "Father Ildephonso must be in the church. Do go and seek him out, Norah, while I take these jars of preserves into the convent. After so many years of separation, there will be much you wish to say to one another alone."

"I wonder if I will find him much changed." Suddenly she was nervous. After her parents had been killed in a carriage accident, Father Ildephonso had taken a personal interest in the development of Norah's mind and character, becoming a second father to the orphaned girl. Neither time nor distance had weakened their bond; in fact, his nearness to Greenwood Junction had influenced her decision to accept Abner Slade's proposal of marriage.

As Abigail knocked at the sycamore-shaded convent door, Norah emerged into the sunshine, heading toward the church with light, eager steps. Her thoughts flew to the past when she had been a day student at Miss Emerson's Academy: rows of scrubbed pine tables with straight-backed chairs; rows of books lining the shelves, below-the-window seats; the hated uniform of navy skirt and starched white shirtwaist with the prim navy ribbon at the neck. Other scenes surfaced, more personal, more painful: the new girl at school, homesick and trying desperately to fit into an already well-established hierarchy; one of the assistant teachers ushering a frightened sixteen-year-old into Miss Emerson's office to hear the terrible news; weeping alone in the chapel, praying that God would intervene with some miracle and bring her charming mother and handsome father back to life again. There had been no miracle, but there had been Father Ildephonso, wise and patient and comforting, teaching her that faith and love and time would heal her heart.

The bell in the church tower tolled, a deep mingling of mellow copper and authoritative brass, recalling Norah to the present. Eagerly, she went up the two steps and opened the door. Inside it was cool, the dim interior filled with muted light and the lingering fragrance of incense. The red sanctuary lamp cast ruby stains on the altar cloth of white lace, and reflected from the tall gold crucifix and branching candelabra. There was the warm glow and the pungent smell of turpentine and beeswax polish from the carved benches and hard wooden kneelers, as there had been in the Boston chapel where Norah had heard Father Ildephonso celebrate the Mass so many times.

"Norah? Is that really you?" A large man stood near a side altar, where a candle in blue glass flickered before a small statue of the Virgin Mary. His auburn hair was tonsured, his wide shoulders covered with the brown robes of his order. As Norah turned he stepped toward her, moving with the quick springing step of youth for all his sixty years. She ran forward to meet him, and they embraced, then stood back to look at one another.

"Oh, Father! It is so good to see you again. You have not changed in the least!"

The priest took Norah's hands in his. Here she was, the daughter of his own heart, after nearly ten years. "Norah, my dear child! And you have not changed except to grow in grace and beauty since I last saw you." His eyes, black as juniper berries, were grave. "It is through me that you undertook the long journey to the Territory, and when I received your note and Captain Gartner's message yesterday... I hardly know what to say to you."

"There is no need to say anything, except that you are as glad to see me as I am you. Mr. Slade will surely show up soon." She cocked her head to one side. "Or do you fear that I have been jilted?"

"Jilted? Oh, no. Mr. Slade has been most impatient for your arrival. I trust no accident has delayed him. Of course there

has been trouble near Tucson, and the Apaches have been...
Not that I think anything has happened to him, you understand..." He spoke unthinkingly, forgetting that Norah was not
used to the way of life in the Arizona Territory. The words
trailed off helplessly as her stunned expression registered on
him.

"Apaches! Do you think...?" Her voice faltered. Knowing
that Abner traveled extensively on business, she had leaped to
the conclusion that business affairs were responsible for his
absence. Now, spurred by the priest's remarks, her thoughts
took a more ominous turn. "Oh, how selfish and heedless I
have been! Deeming Mr. Slade discourteous and careless in
mistiming his return, I have been rather annoyed. It did not
occur to me that there might be more serious reasons behind
his failure. The poor man may be injured...or worse."

"Now do not immediately imagine the worst has happened,
for there are many quite ordinary reasons a man might be detained in this wild country—a breakdown, an injury to one of
the horses, the necessity for an unexpected detour." He patted
her shoulder. "I'm sure there is a simple explanation. However,
in the event of anything untoward, you are not to worry, Norah.
I will make some provision for you."

If his earlier words had caused her to fear for Abner Slade,
his latest ones created a distinct uneasiness for herself. Norah
had given up everything to come west and marry: friends, familiar surroundings, the opportunity to join the faculty of a
small private school in the country. None of this had weighed
against the chance of a new and vigorous life with a husband,
the chance to have children of her own. Once the decision to
accept the proposal was made, she had thought her future secure. Now Norah saw the awkwardness of her situation: she
had little money, no job, and—very possibly—no fiancé. It was
frightening. The Gartners and Father Ildephonso were her only
acquaintances in the entire Arizona Territory.

No, she corrected herself. There was someone else: Sergeant
LeBeau.

As they walked arm in arm down the length of the aisle,
passing through cool umber shadows and warm amber patches
of light from the high windows, Father Ildephonso paused near

the confessionals. "Would you like me to hear your confession while you are here, my child?"

Earlier she thought she had banished LeBeau from her mind, and now she knew that she had only been deceiving herself. "No. I...I just made my confession a few days ago in Santa Fe." *And how could I tell you what is in my heart? That I am kept from sleep at night, tormented by thoughts and dreams? That my only sin is regretting the formal vows of betrothal I exchanged by proxy—and all because of a tall gray-eyed man I have known for two days' time?*

Side by side they strolled in silence to the main door and out into the courtyard, both wondering if they would have cause to rue the arranged betrothal that had brought Norah west.

The sun sat low in the afternoon sky when the two visitors headed back to Camp Greenwood. As they rolled over the seemingly featureless plain, Norah noticed that the wagon ruts became invisible on the stony ground. She turned to Abigail. "Not a single thing looks familiar. How on earth can you possibly find your way back to the Camp with no landmarks to guide you?"

"Have no fear, I have made this journey several times before, and know where I am going. And even if I could not, Dulcey would find her way back to the stable."

Abigail snapped the reins lightly, and the horse broke into a trot, covering the uneven ground easily. For all her youth and seeming fragility, she handled the ribbons with a firm competence Norah envied, and as they went along an idea grew in her mind. "Abigail, would you teach me to drive? I have never had the opportunity to learn. Indeed, have never desired it! But I can see it must be a necessary skill out here, because of the vast distances between places."

"I would be delighted to teach you, and there is no reason not to begin today, before you change your mind. Dulcey is a good little mare, not at all difficult. Closer to Camp there is a level stretch of hard-packed ground that will be ideal for your first lesson. I had mine at the age of ten. My father taught me to handle the ribbons when I was a mere girl."

"And of course, you are in your dotage, now!"

Abigail laughed. "No, but I have always been far older than my years, perhaps from being an only child. When I met Charles, he treated me as if I were six years old, but of course I immediately fell head over heels in love with him. He was so strong yet so gentle, so handsome, and distinguished, that I was bowled right off my feet. I was afraid he thought of me as a niece!"

"Well, it is evident he did not see you in that light, after all."

Abigail blushed. "As it turned out, he did not. Yet he held back, thinking himself too old for me and that I would make a match of it with one of the younger officers. Even when I realized his affections were engaged, it took a good deal of effort on my part to make him declare himself. To this day, I think he would have not said one word to me if I had not encouraged him in a bold and most unladylike fashion."

"You are trying to gammon me, Abigail!"

"Judge for yourself: the night before I was to travel on to San Francisco, I arranged for Charles to drive me home from a reception. I was afraid he would not speak up, but would sacrifice us both for what he thought was right. I realized then that he needed my assistance, so when we pulled up in front of the house, I compromised him by throwing myself into his arms in full view of the open windows. Then I promised to wed him to maintain his honor."

Norah saw the mischief lurking in the soft lines of Abigail's face. "Now I am positive you are leading me up the garden path."

"Well, just a little, perhaps. But I assure you, I was almost that shameless. If you have ever been desperately in love you will know how I felt. I was in a positive agony."

"Then I am thankful I have not had the experience!"

Abigail shook her head wisely. "If you truly feel that way, then you have *never* been in love."

Norah continued to thank Fate, but this time in silence. Her ideas of love between a man and woman had been gleaned from the pages of books, and were essentially idealized versions of Arthurian myth. A gallant knight, a fair lady, and fine flowing speeches had been her naive standard of courtship, and all romantic encounters ended chastely with a kiss. Her imaginary heroes had been as likely to win by their wits as by their swords, and she had assumed phrases such as "desperately in love" to be exaggerations of poetic license. Now the intensity she had just seen on Abigail's sweet features and the vague longings she had experienced since first meeting LeBeau informed her that she had been quite wrong.

She pulled her mind away from these cogitations and observed the way that Abigail drove the gig. They had not gone much farther when they came to a wide section of level ground running parallel to a rock-strewn area fringed with low-growing grasses. To the west a deep ravine cut the clay-colored earth, and on the other side of the sloping ground, balls of juniper sprouted at regular intervals as far as the eye could see. It looked a likely place for a first lesson.

"Here we are." Abigail quieted the horse. "See how I hold the reins? Loop them over once to keep a firm grip on them. That way you will have proper control over the amount of slack. A horse will sense if you are hesitant, and you must let it know that *you* are in command."

Norah took the strips of leather, looping them over her hands as Abigail had done. She was nervous and half expected the horse to bolt. "All right. Now what?"

"Try to keep the same amount of tension on each lead so we travel in a straight line. Good. Now, let out a little slack and snap the reins lightly in the air a few inches above Dulcey's back."

Taking a deep breath, Norah followed Abigail's instructions. The wagon lurched forward, and the horse trotted off at a spanking pace. She tried to slow it down, but sawed unevenly on the leads, and the gig turned to the right.

"No, Dulcey! Not that way."

Although Norah tried to straighten up, the result was that they rode in a large circle, coming back to where they had started the lesson. She pulled hard on the reins, trying to bring the creature's nose back to the left, and the beast stopped with a jolt. Norah grinned sheepishly at Abigail, who dissolved in whoops of laughter. They laughed until they had to wipe their eyes.

"Would you like to begin again, Norah?"

"Most definitely. I shall continue until I master the rudiments...or until Dulcey masters me! I hope you may be prepared to return to the Camp well after midnight."

Their roundabout path was repeated amid gales of laughter that left them both weak. The third time Norah managed to keep her hands up and the ribbons straight. Starting out slowly, she gained confidence as they went along, covering the distance quickly. A few more attempts at stopping and starting put heart into her, although her mouth was dry and her palms damp.

"This is not as difficult as I..." she began. The first words were hardly out of her mouth when things began happening so rapidly she had no time to sort them out. Dulcey veered toward the rocky area to the side, and Norah feared the animal would injure herself on the uneven ground. She pulled the reins and directed the horse toward the short growths of vegetation along the edge. A stone shot sideways from the iron-clad hooves.

Without warning there was a movement through the grass, and a grey and brown coil lunged upward, hurling itself into a straight line of menace. The snake struck at the horse's right foreleg, barely missing its target. Dulcey reared up between the shafts with a shrill cry, then fell back, head down and legs flashing out. The rattler, slashed almost in two by the sharp hooves, flew through the air, landing twenty feet away among the rocks. The reins were jerked from Norah's hands, but she didn't have time to feel the pain of the friction burns across her palms. In an instant horse, gig, and hapless passengers were plunging headlong across the plain as the frightened animal tried to outrace its fear. There was nothing for the two women to do but hang on tightly and pray.

A veil of brown dust surrounded them, stinging their eyes and lungs. They were bounced about until Norah felt black-and-blue, but her prayers were not for herself, they were for Abigail and her unborn child. "Please God, let them be safe! Don't let them be hurt!" She was unaware she spoke aloud, and her words were lost in the drumming of the wild hooves. She hoped the horse would run itself out, but they went on and on, the gig careening from side to side until it seemed it would surely overturn. In the distance she saw the ramparts of the Camp, and hoped they might be observed by the lookout.

A blur of red-brown streaked alongside Norah, brushing the

brim of her hat. A man on a large roan had joined in their mad race. Inch by inch the thundering beast and rider gained ground, bearing down on the runaway horse. There was nothing Norah or Abigail could do to help their rescuer. The rider's arm stretched out toward the bit, muscles bunched and straining. He reached for it, but the horse tossed her head and turned from the straight path she had been pursuing. Now Dulcey was headed for a steep ravine a few hundred yards off.

Even as Norah saw the danger, she recognized the fearless horseman. It was LeBeau who straddled the powerful roan, LeBeau who crouched suddenly over its neck, and then made an incredible leap onto the runaway's back. Grabbing the leads, he turned the carriage away from the very edge of the ravine and certain disaster.

The vehicle slowed under the guidance of his strong hand, and Dulcey came to a complete stop, head down, sides heaving with exertion. LeBeau dismounted and went to her head, running his hands over her neck and murmuring to her. Norah got down rather shakily and turned to help Abigail, while LeBeau continued to soothe the trembling beast, speaking to her in low, soft tones. Norah thought indignantly that he showed little concern for the humans involved in the near tragedy, as she went to assist her companion down from her perch.

"I am so very sorry! I would never have forgiven myself if you'd been injured," she said, reaching her hand out to Abigail.

"Are you all right, Mrs. Gartner?" LeBeau came up beside them and swung Abigail lightly down to the ground. "Sit down in the shade of the buggy. You are looking quite pale."

"I am fine, really I am," Abigail protested breathlessly, yet her face was like bleached flour, and she found her legs would not support her. LeBeau caught her around the waist and lowered her to the ground, then squatted beside her. He offered her a drink from his canteen, then handed it to Norah without even looking at her. All his attention was focused on Abigail. "Would you like me to ride on to the Camp, or do you think you will be able to drive back? If so, I will ride at the mare's head and go slowly."

"Yes, I can manage." She tried to stand, but was unable. Norah steadied her. "You do not look as if you can get to your feet, much less drive. I might be able to handle the gig for such a short distance—'' she began, but was ruthlessly cut off.

"You!" LeBeau said coldly, rising to his feet. "You aren't fit to handle a child's pony! That mare is the gentlest horse in the world, and what you did to make her bolt like that is beyond my understanding." The words were bitten off one by one, and there was a white line around his lips.

Norah's heart was still thumping erratically from the runaway, and now reaction ignited her temper. She jumped up. "It was not my fault! I did not do *anything*! And I am perfectly capable of handling Dulcey for the short ride back to the Camp and—''

His anger was more than a match for hers, but LeBeau had no time to analyze it. Lightning flashed in his eyes as he interrupted, his voice less carefully controlled than before. "The only thing I want you to do is this: get back in the goddamned gig and keep your hands off the goddamned reins!''

Norah was too furious to answer, and wheeled away from him, heading purposefully toward the gig. She had not gone two feet when he stepped in front of her, clamping his hands around her upper arms. "I meant what I said. You are not driving the gig back." His tone was that of an adult speaking to a particularly recalcitrant child.

Tears of humiliation stung Norah's eyes, and a passionate temper, held fiercely in check for too many years, exploded into a wild fury. "How dare you! Take your hands off me at once."

He made no answer, and his silence only served to fuel her wrath. Her breasts rose and fell with her rapid breathing as she tried to twist away from him. Still his fingers curved into the softness of her arms and tension grew between them, a smoldering fire sending out small licks of flame to engulf dry tinder. Any minute, any second, it would burst out in a roaring, all-consuming blaze.

There was a different look illuminating his eyes now, something Norah found frightening and strangely exhilarating. She was increasingly aware of the warm touch of his hands through the fabric of her dress, the place where his palm rested against her bare skin. All her senses seemed to focus on that one spot, bringing a surge of an emotion that had nothing to do with anything but the nearness of a man and a woman. She fought the sensation, the odd lightheaded feeling that mixed with her anger, diluting it, transforming it to something entirely different, and tried to pull away.

"You have no right to speak to me that way, no right at all! Who are you to presume to tell me how to act? You are neither father nor brother nor husband! Now take your hands off me at once!"

LeBeau's eyes hardened to chips of flint, sharp and unreadable in a face of stone. Norah thought he was going to speak again, but he only pulled her closer until she felt the heat of his body coursing through hers. He released her, thrusting her away so quickly that she was caught unaware and almost fell.

"No," he said coldly. "I am not your father or brother...or husband. Thank God! I leave you to Mr. Slade."

LeBeau lifted Abigail into the gig, then leapt onto the back of the sweating roan, and rode to Dulcey's head. He murmured something to the animal and stroked her nose, then turned and nodded to Abigail, who sat with the reins clenched tightly in her hands. Without even waiting to see if Norah had gotten into the gig, he started off.

She scrambled up and took a seat beside Abigail, trembling with rage and something more. As they neared the stockade the gate swung open, and Captain Gartner rode out to meet them. Abigail stopped, and her husband tied his mount to the back of the gig, then jumped up into the seat. He took the reins from her, and she leaned against him for support.

"Captain Gartner, I owe you my most profound apologies," Norah said breathlessly. "You have been so kind to me, and I am horrified to think of what the consequences of this episode might have been."

"Oh, no!" Abigail interjected faintly. "It was not Norah's fault. It was a rattlesnake that frightened Dulcey. I saw it strike at her and miss, and that is what set her off."

"No harm done in any case," Gartner said with calm authority. "But I think we had best postpone your expeditions for a few days. This has been a shock to both of you."

Gartner's kind words made Norah feel worse, and the disdain she read in LeBeau's tight-lipped features only added to her misery. Then her Irish stubbornness righted itself, and determination sparked in the blue depths of her eyes.

I will show him! He told me once that I didn't belong here, that I should go back to Boston. Well, I will prove him wrong. I will prove that I can do anything Abigail or any other woman in the Territory can do. She tied the strings of her bonnet more securely beneath her chin and folded her hands tightly in her lap.

They entered Camp Greenwood and proceeded directly to the Gartner's residence. The Captain helped his wife down, and after a second's pause, LeBeau came around to aid Norah. She would have preferred to get down without his assistance, but her limbs were quivering. She put her hands on his shoulders, unwillingly aware of the powerful muscles beneath his shirt as he caught her by the waist to swing her down. He lowered her slowly, and she had her first inkling of his great strength. The gray eyes were level with hers, and his mouth was compressed in a straight line.

Norah felt a sudden need to explain, to vindicate herself. "There was a snake. It frightened Dulcey."

LeBeau set her on her feet, but his hands lingered at the curve of her waist a moment. A picture of this woman, broken and bleeding beneath the sharp hooves, came unbidden to his mind, and he pushed it away, afraid to face the true source of his anger. She was nothing to him. She was Slade's woman.

His fingers tightened, and she made a faint sound of surprise. Instantly he relaxed his grip. She felt as soft and as fragile as a flower in his hands, and her woman-scent came to him, warm and fragrantly compelling. "What did you expect? You took the horse through the rocks and grasses where snakes hide from the sun's heat."

His tone had softened considerably, which made Norah feel worse: her ignorance of the West had been a factor in the near accident. It had been her fault, after all. "I didn't know... There's so much I don't know." She straightened her spine. "But I will learn. I will learn!"

The lines of his face became gentler. She had meant no harm, but her natural habitat was a gold and velvet drawing room, a silk-lined boudoir. "I told you before: this is no place for a woman like you. You could have killed yourself and Mrs.

Gartner with you. Go back to your people. Go home before it's too late."

"I have no people. And I have nothing to go back to. This is my home."

He took her hand, frowning. She blinked back the moisture that suddenly brimmed and threatened to spill down her lashes. "I am sorry I was so rude to you. This is the second time you have come to my rescue."

LeBeau smiled as he looked down into the earnest face tilted up to his. "The third, if we're keeping score."

She sniffled and then laughed, a low musical sound that made his heart beat more quickly. A sudden need to comfort and reassure Norah swept over him, to be followed immediately by a flood of raw desire. He was caught by her beauty and dignity, but even more so, he knew, by the self-spun web of his own loneliness. How long had it been since he had made love to a woman? And what would it be like to make love to *this* woman? He almost pulled her into his arms then, and the uncharacteristic impulse startled him. He stepped back, and his face resumed its unemotional mask as he faced the Captain.

"They should not be going out unescorted anymore. I've brought news from Limping Bear: quantities of adulterated whiskey were sold on the Jicarilla Reserve. Many died in great agony; the three survivors are blind. A war party escaped the reservation this morning, and until they find the traders responsible, I would not vouch for the life of anyone whose path they cross."

Norah listened in appalled silence as they mounted the veranda steps. It was obscene for this untouched and incredibly beautiful land to be the setting of recurrent violence and death. They went inside and the stifling air was unbearable after the outdoor freshness. The open windows and uninsulated wooden walls only served to trap the heat.

Gartner deposited Abigail on the settee and faced LeBeau. "You won't be tracking again until you receive that packet of information from Fort Defiance. I would like you to escort the ladies whenever they leave the Post until then."

LeBeau flushed and set his jaw. "That is not a scout's duty."

Gartner drew himself up slowly, and Norah could almost see the invisible mantle of authority settling over him. "I do not need you to instruct me, Sergeant, in General Crook's regulations regarding the duties of Army Indian Scouts.''

LeBeau stiffened, and the men squared off. ''I beg your pardon. *Sir*.''

''Apology accepted. *Sergeant*. Now, if you'll get off your high horse for a minute, I can tell you I am not ordering you as your commander—I'm asking you as your friend.''

Although Norah leaned over Abigail, fanning the girl's heated cheeks, she was aware of the tension in the room. Outside, a voice called, and then it was quiet. The tick of the mantel clock came loud and clear. LeBeau's reply was terse with suppressed anger.

''Very well. *Sir*.''

Silence descended on the room to be shattered a few seconds later by the sound of the front door slamming shut.

It was four days before Norah prepared to resume the aborted driving lesson. On the appointed morning, which was somewhat hazy and overcast, the buggy arrived in front of the guest bungalow. Dulcey, decked in red harness, stamped her feet and snorted impatiently, but Abigail was not yet in the conveyance. Norah, wearing a silk-straw hat trimmed to match her old peach-colored muslin, was bright-eyed and eager to start. She was determined to learn to handle the ribbons expertly, and daydreamed of giving LeBeau the go-by on the road at some future date, leaving him behind in a cloud of dust. And she looked forward to that day with relish.

A young corporal handed her up to the seat, blushing furiously at her thanks. Just as she settled her skirts about her, LeBeau appeared beside the buggy. He nodded at the striker, swung himself up, and had the reins in his capable hands before she knew what was happening. In an instant they were in motion, and she was thrown back against the wooden seat.

''What on earth…! What do you think you are doing, Sergeant?'' He ignored her, guiding the buggy around a mule team and avoiding a slow-moving private by a hairbreadth.

''Now I suppose you are abducting me!'' she said waspishly. ''Turn around at once. Mrs. Gartner is driving out with me this morning.''

"No, she is not. Mrs. Gartner had a restless night and sends her regrets. In any event, the Captain and I thought it better that you learn to handle the ribbons with me."

He snapped the reins, and Dulcey fell into a brisk trot as they barreled out through the open gates. Once clear of the lean-to shacks outside the stockade and their scattered inhabitants, he let the horse have her head. Norah fumed silently. There was little else she could do while the buggy was in motion, except hold on tightly as they jounced along the ruts at an alarming speed. When at last the pace began to slacken, her bonnet was over her right ear and her hair coming loose from its neat coil. Her temper was equally disordered.

LeBeau reined in at some distance from the Camp, but still within sight of the lookouts on the walls. Straightening her hat, Norah sent him a darkling glance. "I am relieved to see you have regained control of the horse," she snapped, sure she would be bruised from the rough ride. Her only consolation was seeing that her comment had pricked his pride.

He shot her an annoyed look from the corner of his eyes as his color rose. "I was never *out* of control. And you damned well know it! I was only taking the freshness out of her so you would have a better chance of handling her."

"Then it was a waste of your efforts and a sorry trial of my patience, for I have no intention of taking a lesson from you. I refuse to give you another opportunity to sneer at me, Sergeant; you have already had more than enough amusement at my expense."

Rearranging her chignon as best she could, Norah then folded her hands primly in her lap. A cool breeze flirted with the flounces on her dress and tugged a strand of hair loose at her nape. LeBeau turned to her and held out the reins. She stared ahead. "What a beautiful morning," she said sweetly. "Do you think it shall grow hot by afternoon?"

"Don't be a stubborn fool! Take the reins."

"And you, sir, are a high-handed bully!" *And,* she thought, staring at the fly hovering over Dulcey's rump, *you will learn that my stubbornness is more than a match for your arrogance.* She admired the view, hiding her irritation.

Minutes passed while the impasse continued. The baffled horse looked back over her shoulder quizzically, and puffed air through her nostrils. The cloud cover drifted away, and the sun beat down upon then. Norah felt her nose beginning to burn, but sat as still as if she were in church listening to a sermon.

"Very well," LeBeau said at last. "Some mules I've known take well to direction. Others have to be shown."

"Mules!"

He slid his arm around her narrow waist and pulled her closer so they were shoulder to shoulder. Transferring the reins to that hand, he put his other arm in front of her so she was encircled. "Now watch what I do," he instructed, and set Dulcey off once more.

Caught in his arms, feeling his body pressed against hers, Norah was even more determined not to give in. From time to time LeBeau murmured in her ear. It tickled. They drove around the stockade twice this way, while her ire grew with every passing moment. Once she heard a shout of laughter from the walls, and her face grew bright with embarrassment. She held herself ramrod straight and caught her lower lip between her teeth, which was a mistake. She bit it. Only an angry hiss gave her away, and she thought LeBeau had not noticed. He had, and was hard put to keep from laughing at her indomitable will, and harder put to keep from stopping this charade and kissing her instead.

His arms made contact with her breasts time and again and a scent of light cologne lingered in her hair. He was becoming aroused, and regretfully knew it was time to end the farce. As he started the buggy up and swung toward the gates, she smiled in triumph. Not a split second later he cracked the reins high in the air, and dropped them in her lap. She took them out of pure reflex as panic welled inside her chest. Her breath stuck in her throat in a hard, painful lump. They careened along in a horrible imitation of the runaway episode, and she pulled back on the ribbons with all her strength. It brought her to her heels, and she would have staggered when Dulcey stopped short if not for LeBeau's protective arm.

"Yes," he said, as if continuing his dissertation, "some mules must be shown. And then, if they perform acceptably, they should be rewarded in some way."

Goaded beyond endurance, she struck out at him with her fists, but he caught them in his hands and held them. The temptation was too much to resist. His mouth came down on hers swiftly, surprising them both. The kiss was brief but implacable and left her with no doubt as to who was in control of the situation.

He released her abruptly and took up the slack reins. She kept her face averted as they drove in past the high gates, blushing in mortification, knowing others had seen and probably misinterpreted what had transpired between them. He had treated her like a camp doxie, someone to laugh at and then fondle for everyone to see! When they returned to their starting place before the Gartners' neat frame home, Norah jumped down without speaking, catching the hem of her gown. Without looking she tore it free.

He alighted beside her, handing the reins to the striker, but she brushed past. LeBeau saw for the first time that tears sparkled in her eyes and caught on her dark lashes. He had not meant to upset her, and certainly had not had any intention of kissing her publicly. He put out his hand. "Norah... Miss O'Shea... I am sorry for..."

Knowing a flood of tears was imminent, she hissed at him like a scalded cat. "Get away from me. I may have to endure your escort on my expeditions with Mrs. Gartner, but I do not have to put up with insolence from such as you."

His face froze as Norah brushed past him. How many times, in how many different ways, had he heard similar words in the past? She was a white woman. A lady. And he was an Indian, masquerading as a white man. But not for long.

Soon Iron Knife would be moved to Tucson for his trial. He had been captured near the border and the Army had taken him across the line into the Arizona Territory instead of back toward the Comanche strongholds. They thought to avert an outbreak by doing so, not knowing that Quanah Parker had anticipated their action. When Iron Knife was transferred, Horns-of-Buffalo and his waiting band would swoop down upon the column and rescue him. And when Iron Knife joined with Quanah against the white man, then the real fighting would begin.

There was no place for this woman in his life—and as she had made abundantly clear, there was no place for him in hers. *Suvate.* So be it. "Good day, Miss O'Shea." He turned on his heel, but she was already in the house.

4

Norah kept busy in the weeks following her arrival at Camp Greenwood. Each Tuesday and Thursday she drove out to the Mission with Abigail, always accompanied by the taciturn LeBeau, who rode alongside the gig with civil indifference, speaking infrequently to Abigail, and to Norah not at all. Since the day of the runaway gig, he seemed to be evading places and situations that might place him in her company. She did the same, trying to avoid the meeting of glances that left her eyes dazzled and her mind reeling, the accidental touch that sent shock waves ricocheting through her body. As each day passed she found him as dangerously fascinating, as cruelly beautiful as the red and gold and umber land she was growing to love.

Now she sat in the shade cast by the Mission's bell tower, ostensibly listening to Abigail give instructions to the school-girls of Santa Magdalena. Although she tried to keep her mind on teaching, it seemed impossible. She had developed a sixth sense where he was concerned, something that made her incredibly sensitive to his presence. Today the wide set of his shoulders, the muscled expanse of bronzed chest revealed by his partially opened shirt, the careless grace of his every movement, seemed to be imprinted on the insides of her eyelids, for she saw them there every time she closed her eyes against the strong light.

''Miss O'Shea has provided each of you with a paperboard

with your name written in block letters. I want each of you to carefully copy your name, three times, on your slates.''

The sky was a delft blue dome above the walls of the convent courtyard, and the deep bass hum of pollen-laden bees accompanied the occasional soprano squeak of chalk against slate. Eight dark heads bent over eight little slates, but Norah's attention had drifted to the far wall of the complex, where LeBeau leaned with casual elegance. Her eyes flickered in his direction from beneath carefully lowered lashes, then back to the white-frocked students.

''I beg your pardon?'' Belatedly she realized that Abigail had been speaking to her in a low voice. A bee buzzed by the ruffled hem of her rose-sprigged dress, then hovered briefly over Abigail's yellow dimity, disappointed to find no nectar in fields of such promising color. Norah watched it fly off and find success in the dark red blossoms of the plant that vined along the covered arcade.

''...and although she is proud and willful, I truly think Dove-in-Flight could be the best of all the students, if only she would apply herself.''

The other students, whose ages ranged from eleven to fifteen, were still working on their assignment, but Dove-in-Flight sat cross-legged on the ground, weaving a coronet of blooms plucked from the fragrant vine. Lying beside her was the slate, its surface blank. Her delicate face was dreamy, her lovely mouth curved upward in a secret smile.

''Yes, you are undoubtably correct. She is bright, and her spoken English is quite good, but Dove-in-Flight sees no need to learn writing skills. Standing by helplessly while a good mind goes to waste, was for me, the most frustrating aspect of teaching.'' Dove-in-Flight had built an invisible wall about herself, and nothing Norah or Abigail or the nuns of Santa Magdalena said or did could penetrate that hard, crystalline barrier. Norah had been bruised more than once in trying.

Abigail brushed an inquisitive beetle from her skirts. ''There are times when I feel the students are merely humoring us.'' She gave a rueful grin. ''Now I understand how my mathematics instructors must have felt!''

A door opened beneath the arcade, and fat little Sister Cecelia bustled out, bearing moisture-spangled pitchers of cool buttermilk which she placed on the plain plank table. She looked around, then shook her head in chagrin. Only the stiff white wimple kept her several chins from wobbling. "Where has that child disappeared to? That's the second time she's slipped away today."

Norah knew which one would be missing, even before she inventoried the little group. Yes, the place where Dove-in-Flight had been sitting a moment ago was bare, except for a scattering of scarlet petals slowly drying in the sun.

Opening the ornamental grille, she saw a flash of white skirts disappear between the church and one of the outbuildings. "I see where she went. I will go fetch her." The sun was molten gold in the smelter heat of the central square, and before she had gone more than a few yards, Norah's forehead was damp and her cheeks red. There it was again, that wisp of muslin near the corner of the church. She crossed beneath the lacy branches of the sycamores and stopped to catch her breath. Well, at least the girl hadn't gone off on foot outside the Mission, as she had once in the past.

Another hundred yards and Norah rounded the corner to confront her quarry, then stopped dead. In the shadows formed by the church and the outer wall, LeBeau and Dove-in-Flight stood close together. His face was intent as he leaned forward, hers smiling and saucily impudent. Norah fought anger and a baffled helplessness; and below these emotions, like a dark river, ran a swift current of pain.

She wanted to flee, but forced herself to go on. As she drew near, she noticed LeBeau's hand was clamped possessively around the girl's arm. She wished that she could retreat, but LeBeau looked up and saw her, and she had no choice. She certainly did not want him to think she was spying on him. "Dove-in-Flight is not finished with her lessons, Sergeant," she called crisply, not meeting his eyes.

"I will return when I am ready, and not before," the girl said insolently. Turning her back on Norah, she continued her whispered dialogue with the Indian Scout.

LeBeau's skin darkened, as a slow flush spread across his sculpted cheekbones. He spoke in low tones Norah couldn't decipher, and released Dove-in-Flight, who stamped her foot and clutched at his sleeve. Her black eyes snapped with an-

noyance, and her mouth turned downward in a sullen bow. She
spoke aloud this time, and in English. Her words rang loud and
clear on the still air.

"I do not have to jump because that one calls me! She is
nothing to me. Who cares for her foolish lessons? This is much
more important to me. I will go back when we have finished
talking."

Suddenly Norah was moved by an almost desperate need to
reach out to the girl: it was an uncomfortably fey feeling, an
intuition urging her to intervene before time ran out. *Time?
Time for what? Or for whom?* She shivered and looked up.
Not a single cloud marred the perfect bowl of blue sky that
arched over Santa Magdalena, and the sun's rays were as
white-hot as before. As quickly as the sensation had come it
was gone. She directed her anger toward LeBeau.

"Dove-in-Flight is here to learn, not to whisper with you in
corners. I have enough trouble trying to keep her mind on her
lessons as it is, and I'll thank you not to encourage her to shirk
her studies! I have spent the last two weeks encouraging her
to apply herself: I might as well have spent the time banging
my head against an anvil!"

LeBeau gave the girl a shake. "You must do as Miss O'Shea
tells you. Go back to your studies."

Dove-in-Flight glared at him, then changed her mind as she
took stock of the stubborn set of his jaw. She turned in a whirl
of petticoats and pushed past Norah, almost knocking her off
her feet. LeBeau steadied Norah, then dropped his hands as
high color rose in her cheeks. She turned to leave, but he
reached out and caught her arm, and once again Norah was
reminded of his strength.

"Do not be too harsh with her. She is just a child," he said
abruptly. "And a very unhappy one. Surely you can see that?"

Norah pulled away. "You are wrong. Very wrong...or very
blind. Her actions may be childish at times, but Dove-in-Flight
is very much a woman! Surely *you* can see that!" She hurried
away and left him standing there alone.

When Norah returned, Abigail was moving from student to
student, checking their work. "That is much better, Felicia. I
can see that you have been practicing." Abigail moved on to
the next, but paused when Dove-in-Flight flounced down on a

wooden bench, scowling. Norah entered the courtyard and went to meet her with Sister Cecelia on her heels.

"Where was she this time?"

"Over by the church, charming Sergeant LeBeau."

The nun smiled with relief, and the movement of her plump cheeks shaped her eyes into little crescents of flesh. "Oh, Sergeant LeBeau. That is all right, then. She will come to no harm with him." She clapped her hands. "Now, young ladies, it is time for your daily visit to Mother Superior." Bustling about, she shooed the girls toward the convent door. They scurried off like excited chicks before a flapping brown hen.

Abigail lowered her voice, and they moved away. "Dove-in-Flight was brought here by her family because she is… ah…*easily persuadable*, was the term used. She ran away with a man, but was found and brought here. Her people thought a stay with the nuns might exercise a beneficial influence; and of course it is much easier to keep an eye on her here within the Mission walls."

"They can't expect to keep her here forever." Norah drank a glass of buttermilk and licked her upper lip. "She is a young woman now."

"No, but Mother Immaculata is hoping to arrange a good marriage for Dove-in-Flight. With the shortage of women in the Territory, I'm sure the loss of her…well, I'm sure they will be able to find a good husband for her. She is beautiful, and her family has finally been able to arrange a handsome dower for her."

Norah didn't answer. Remembering Sister Cecelia's reaction earlier, she wondered if the nuns considered Sergeant LeBeau a suitable husband for Dove-in-Flight. A sense of oppression settled over her like a gray pall. She was glad the lessons were done for the day.

"Perhaps I should have a talk with Dove-in-Flight," Abigail went on.

"Or perhaps Captain Gartner should have a talk with his Scout," Norah suggested with acerbity. "I realize the girl is of marriageable age, but surely—" She stopped short. How could she point out the disparity in age between LeBeau and the girl, without giving offense to Abigail, who was thirty years younger than her beloved husband?

Luckily, Abigail misunderstood her. "Why, Norah! Charles places a great deal of trust in Sergeant LeBeau, and I am sure he is a man of honor. In any case, I doubt Sergeant LeBeau has any thought of her, except as a charming child."

Norah's spirits seesawed upward once more. She was unwilling to attribute the swings of her moods to anything but the uncertainty of her position as the promised wife of a missing man; but even as she outwardly professed an eagerness for the day when Abner would come to claim her, it was harder every day to keep him in her thoughts. *When Abner comes and all this waiting is over, everything will be all right. I'll be myself again.* The thought echoed hollowly in her heart, like words spoken down a dark and empty well.

With a little shake, she brought her mind back to the present. "How are plans coming along for your birthday dance next week?"

Abigail's excitement brought fresh color against the translucent whiteness of her skin. "Wonderfully! Colonel and Mrs. Boyle have accepted. Miss Tooms, who is visiting them from San Francisco, will join them. Major McKendrick and his wife and two daughters have accepted also and will be bringing a 'dashing and unattached Major' with them: those are the exact words Mrs. McKendrick wrote in her acceptance note. After dinner several others will join us for the dancing."

She could not resist teasing Norah. "First Lieutenant Newcomb was most pleased to be asked to join our party. I'm afraid you have made a conquest there. If Mr. Slade is not quick enough in returning, he may find his fiancée snapped up beneath his very nose."

"I'm in no danger of being swept away by Lieutenant Newcomb! And in the eyes of the Church, a formal betrothal with exchange of vows is as binding as a marriage contract."

As she spoke, Yellow Basket, one of the younger students, ran out from the arcade and thrust a slate forward into her hand. Norah examined it with puzzled curiosity. It was certainly not part of the day's lesson. At the top, in exceptionally neat block letters, were the words "I Love You." Beneath it was written "Little Dove." She showed the slate to Abigail. "Did you write this, Yellow Basket?"

The girl only squirmed and giggled, twisting the white cloth of her skirt around her brown fingers. Dove-in-Flight stepped from beneath the arcade, a haughty expression marring the loveliness of her face. Her finely carved lips drew back in that strange, secret smile Norah had seen before, her black eyes opaque as onyx.

"Of course Yellow Basket did not write that. She is only a stupid girl." Dove-in-Flight snatched the slate from Norah's fingers and held it possessively. "I wrote those words."

"They are nicely done," Norah said with a pleased smile. "I am delighted to see you are making progress in your lessons, after all." She brushed back an escaped strand of damply curling hair. Perhaps the effort of encouraging the girl was not entirely in vain.

"I did not learn this from *you*," Dove-in-Flight said challengingly.

"Then who taught you?"

The girl looked down and away, not in embarrassment, but rather as if deciding how much she should reveal. Then her lashes swept up and her chin tilted. The dark eyes were proud and knowing, a woman's eyes where a young girls' should have been. "I learned this from a man who has taught me *many* things. From my lover. He calls me Little Dove."

She made an odd little expression and turned away, leaving Abigail prey to pricks of indignation, and Norah to stabs of speculation and doubt. They stared at each other a moment, then gathered their things and went out to the gig, not speaking until they were alone.

"I think Sister Cecelia may have reason for her concern," Norah said quietly. Abigail looked distressed, and did not reply.

LeBeau was waiting for them by the hitching rail, impervious as always to the scorching sun. He watched Norah, but she kept her head lowered, screening her too-candid blue eyes from his gaze. He helped Abigail climb up to the seat, but Norah got in quickly before he could assist her, almost slipping in her haste.

As LeBeau swung onto his mount his face was calm, but his thoughts were not. He knew Norah was upset, even though her face gave nothing away. She did not seem angry. It was more a sense that she had drawn inward upon herself, the way certain flowers closed their petals in the failing light, gathering into tight protective buds around their tender hearts. It bothered him to feel so attuned to her.

When they rode out through the gates he tried to see her face, but it was hidden by the brim of her straw bonnet. Well, it was none of his business. She was Slade's woman. There was no place in his life for her or anyone like her. Limping Bear's latest report had given him much food for thought: a plan was being set in force to free Iron Knife from Federal custody. Without a doubt the Army would be mobilized to hunt the fierce Comanche war chief, and the men of Camp Greenwood would be involved.

And then...and then I must make my choice. Quanah Parker and his band of Comanche had successfully evaded the Army once again and gone into hiding somewhere in Texas. When Iron Knife escaped, the Comanche would rally their allies for one last, desperate, battle for freedom.

He kicked the roan into a canter and forgot the present as he anticipated the ways his path might go in the future: to forego his heritage and live as one of the white men he despised—or to die with his honor intact, a Comanche warrior.

Norah, meanwhile, found herself trapped in the immediate past. *From my lover,* Dove-in-Flight had said. The words ran in circles through her mind. *My lover, my lover, my lover, my lover...* She remembered Dove-in-Flight and LeBeau standing so close, looking at one another with such intimacy. How could he! He was so much older, and Dove-in-Flight was only a heedless schoolgirl! It was no wonder her head was turned by his interest. After all, LeBeau was a very masculine and attractive man.

She put her hands to her eyes, as if to block out the images that filled her mind. Her stomach seemed caught in a vise. *My lover, my lover, my lover, my lover...*

"You are quite pale, Norah. Is it the heat?" Abigail's face was filled with friendly concern.

"I beg your pardon? Oh, yes. It is a trifle warm, isn't it? I'll be all right once we reach the Camp." Norah forced her eyes to stay open despite the sudden spears of light that reflected from some bright bit of rock along the trail; and although

LeBeau rode only a few feet away as they headed back, she didn't look at him once on the long ride back to the Post.

Norah's orderly new existence eroded quickly. First the weather changed. Hot winds blew in from the desert, sobbing and moaning, blowing up shimmering curtains of dust and sand that isolated Camp Greenwood from the rest of the world. An irritable restlessness struck man and beast, and Norah was not immune. The ill wind continued, sometimes with a shrieking sound that set her teeth on edge, other times whimpering until even those with the thickest of skins seemed flayed to raw nerve endings. Few ventured from the shelter of the stockade, and by Thursday a number of disturbing events had broken through the calm surface of life on the Army post, like jagged rocks suddenly showing their teeth beneath the waters of a once-placid harbor.

It had all started the previous Sunday, and each separate incident was of more dire consequence than the last. On Monday a fight broke out in the mess hall. Private Peterson was severely injured. On Tuesday two men deserted in the morning and were brought back in manacles by late afternoon. The Captain ordered them to be whipped, and the crack of the lash went on long after the cries had faded. Abigail went around the house with red-rimmed eyes, and Gartner's jaw was locked in stony position. Norah felt the strain between them and worried over their rift, caught between the unhappiness of her friends.

On Wednesday affairs accelerated: a mad dog was shot outside the gates; Medallion, the Captain's favorite horse, broke a leg and had to be shot; and Private Peterson succumbed to a lethal infection, all before midday. On Thursday the winds died, and people stirred forth again, but the edginess of several days' accumulation did not abate. There were scattered arguments and fistfights, but activities beyond the Camp had been peaceful. Gartner was coaxed into letting the women visit the Mission again, and both Norah and Abigail left with the relief of persons newly escaped from a madhouse. LeBeau was off the Post, and another trooper was assigned to accompany them. Not long after they left for Santa Magdalena with a young corporal, bad news arrived from the west and south: an entire family heading for the shelter at Camp Verde had been slaughtered by marauding Apaches, and Iron Knife, the fierce Comanche war chief, had escaped from Federal detention and was heading toward the Mogollon Rim. Gartner ordered a party of men to Santa Magdalena to warn Father Ildephonso and to escort his wife and guest back posthaste. Not long afterward twelve soldiers were stricken with food poisoning after eating stewed chicken.

Into this uproar, just before sundown, LeBeau came riding in the Devil's own temper. As he spurred his horse through the open gates he saw, not the activity of the Army post, but the face of Samuel Blackwing in the Navajo's last moments. It had been hard to distinguish the words through lips blue and twisted in agony, but Samuel's words might be the only clue: *"El gato."* The cat.

LeBeau strode to the Captain's quarters with a curt word for the sentry, and found Gartner pouring over a dispatch from headquarters. By the deep creases in the older man's forehead, he knew the news was not good. Gartner looked up and grunted, shoving the papers aside. "Any trouble on the way in?"

"No new tracks in the area. Another cache of tainted whiskey has been traded, this time to the Navajo living near the arroyo they call *Rio del Muerto.*"

"Did you get there in time to see anything of the culprits?"

"No. I got there in time to witness the death throes of an old woman and two young men!" Each word was dipped in bitterness. "They died before they could tell me anything. Whoever is responsible is also clever, conducting normal business for the most part, then unloading the lethal cargo for turquoise, silver, and hides. Each time the drop-off is made to an isolated group, and the traders take their booty and slip away."

"Well, I'm glad you're back, Sergeant. A prisoner taken near the Texas border last May has escaped and is known to be heading this way." His fingers drummed the desktop while he watched the Scout.

LeBeau cast him an assessing glance. Not by the slightest flicker of emotion did he show that he knew what was coming—in fact, he had heard it through the Indian grapevine long before the first Army dispatch had been sent out.

"A dangerous man, I take it."

"*Very* dangerous. The one the Comanche call Iron Knife. He and his henchmen killed two Federal Marshals during the escape. Word has it he's planning to rendezvous with members of Quanah Parker's band somewhere up on the rim. They'll gather as many people as they can and then ride back to the Panhandle when things cool down. In the meantime, he'll be stirring up all the braves on the reservations."

Gartner wiped the back of his hand across his forehead. "We can't put up with another insurrection! If there's sufficient outcry in Washington, they'll order enough troops and powder to blast every last Indian off the face of the Territory. You know how I feel about that. Good God Almighty, I don't want another Sand Creek Massacre here! I can't let it happen. And the only way to prevent it is to have someone go after Iron Knife and bring him in."

LeBeau understood. Gartner was giving him the opening to volunteer, which was neither normal procedure nor the Captain's usual method. He stared hard at his commander, trying to read the lines of his face. Gartner was too good an officer to give anything away intentionally, but a telltale wave of dull red crept up his cheeks.

So, LeBeau thought. *He has guessed at my background and wonders where my loyalties lie. Well, where do they lie? With the life I've chosen, or with the life I left behind?* His face settled in somber lines, and his eyes became black glass, hiding any emotion.

From the first he had always known that the day would come when his Comanche blood was brought in direct conflict with his white man's identity. Iron Knife was of LeBeau's people, a symbol of the last efforts of resistance against the crumbling red universe. And he was even more than that to Gartner's chief Scout: Iron Knife was kin. The seconds stretched out while LeBeau examined his heart, but there was really no need. He already knew the answer. He looked straight at Gartner and spoke deliberately.

"If you are asking my opinion, then Sergeant Wattles is the man for the job. He's a good scout, and his men are the equal of mine." His eyes met Gartner's steadily. *I will not fight against Iron Knife. My hand will not be raised against him.* Although the words were unspoken, they hung in the air between the two men as clearly as if they had been proclaimed aloud.

Gartner sighed and sat back. His suspicions of LeBeau's Comanche blood had been right then. Well, Billy Wattles *was* his best man—after LeBeau. Again his fingers tapped a rapid cadence on the desktop. He had always sensed a fine line separating an order LeBeau would take and one he'd turn his back on, court-martial or no. He also knew that his Scout operated with his own set of rules and restrictions: that they had so far overlapped with Army discipline was almost more than the odds could bear. He didn't press the issue.

"Yes," he said slowly, giving LeBeau a level look. "I agree that Wattles is the man for the job...in this case." He picked up a sheet of paper filled with lines of angular handwriting. "You heard about the massacre of the family in the Verde Valley?" Another sigh. "I will be relieved when Abigail and Miss O'Shea return from the Mission."

LeBeau leaned forward and placed his hands on the desk. "They are out there now? How long have they been gone? Who is with them?"

Gartner was struck by the intensity of his concern. "No need to worry, I sent an escort party to bring them back."

"I'll ride out to meet them." He had arrived hungry and saddle-weary, but new energy surged through him with the spurt of adrenaline that had followed the Captain's statement. LeBeau bounded to the door with a curt gesture that sufficed for a salute.

Flying over the roan's back, he raced off without a pause, but when he drew near the gig was already at the gates. Something had happened. Even at this distance he could discern the grim faces of the soldiers and the agitation of the women. A trooper drove the gig, his horse tied on behind. Norah leaned over Abigail, who lay against the seatback.

LeBeau rode up to the burly Sergeant riding point. "Trouble?"

"You name it, we got it. Miz Gartner's took ill, there's a mutilated body on the trail from the Mission, and to top it off, there's a missing girl. One of them Indian students the Sisters took in. She's been gone since day before yestidy," he rattled on, oblivious to the change in LeBeau.

"At first they thought she upped and wandered off into the countryside and got lost. Now one of them orphan gals claims she saw the girl outside the Mission walls, talking to a man on a black horse. The priest is afraid of foul play, but it seems it ain't the first time she's gone off with a man. Bet a month's wages some fellow offered her a few trinkets if she'd run off with him."

"Her name! What is the girl's name?"

At LeBeau's hoarse cry Norah looked up from ministering to her friend. It sounded as if it had been ripped from the fabric of his soul. His face was white as a winding sheet, the bones standing out sharply, while his eyes were vacant of all emotion, blind and blank. The Sergeant scratched his chin, trying to remember the name of the missing student. LeBeau urged his horse forward with an impatient oath, and Norah shrank back a little as he reined in by her side. He reached down and grasped her arm, bruising it to the bone. Her mouth dropped open in shock: Death stared back at her from his dilated pupils.

"Dove-in-Flight," he said harshly, and it was not a question. The pain etched on his features mirrored the pain in Norah's heart.

"Yes." Her lips were so numb with fear she found it hard to form the single syllable. He let her go, and she rubbed her arm, trying to increase the circulation that seemed permanently blocked.

LeBeau wheeled the roan and rode out through the gates at a thunderous gallop, disappearing into the dry fogs of dust that lay across the land. The trooper drove the gig to the hitching rail outside the Gartners' house, while Norah bent protectively over Abigail. "We are home, dear. Let us get you inside and out of this terrible dust."

Abigail only looked at her with frightened eyes as another paroxysm of coughing shook her. It had started on the way back from the Mission, and worsened rapidly. She coughed again, a deep rasp followed by a bubbling, liquid sound. Crimson spots appeared on her lace-trimmed handkerchief, growing like evil flowers.

Then Norah understood. Memory flooded back, and she felt cold: Miss Elphinstone, one of the teachers at the Academy, had suffered from Consumption, the dread disease that ate away the delicate tissue of the lungs. Miss Elphinstone had died on her twenty-first birthday from a fatal pulmonary hemorrhage. The roses that brightened Abigail's cheeks were not the blush of health but the bloom of death.

With realization came shock and overwhelming sorrow, and then a terrible, helpless rage. *No! Dear God, no! Not Abigail, so much in love, with all her life before her! And the baby...*

Abigail saw Norah's horror and pity as she recovered her breath. "No, no! It is nothing.... Just a little problem I...have with my chest...from time to time. I shall be quite...all right... in a moment."

The Captain came up to them, took one swift glance at his wife, and picked her up in his arms. "You have been overdoing it again, my dear," he said with false heartiness. "It takes time to adjust to this climate, and you have not yet adapted completely."

He carried her into the house, placing her gently on the velvet chaise in the drawing room. With his own handkerchief he tenderly blotted the perspiration beading her upper lip, and called the striker to fetch a cooling drink. His actions were calm, but there was fear in his eyes, and that frightened Norah more than anything else: Charles Gartner was not a man accustomed to that emotion.

He smiled at Abigail, but his eyes were haunted. "I think you had better stay on the Post until this infernal dust subsides, even if we do round up those renegades."

"You are...right, dearest. I shall rest...all day tomorrow." Abigail's voice was still slightly breathless, but she attempted the distraction of light conversation. "Norah... I expect you to...put your foot down with me if I try to persuade you to...go junketing about with me until...after the party. I must be full of...good spirits for my birthday dance, and—" She broke off and choked as another spasm overcame her.

The Captain's handkerchief now sported a crimson center, and Norah knelt beside them. Abigail raised her hand in a strange defensive gesture, as if waving away any questions or commiseration. "I am truly all right...."

It took all of Norah's courage to refrain from speaking, but the silent pleading in her friends' eyes could not be ignored. It was evident that they knew the diagnosis and prognosis of Abigail's disease; and if carrying on the pretense that it did not exist made life more bearable for them, Norah would be the last to deny them that frail comfort.

She turned away and busied herself gathering pillows to support Abigail's head. Although warm sun filtered through the opened drapes and the lace-curtain panels, she felt chilled through and through. She arranged the pillows and then went to stand by the window in a patch of golden light. It didn't help.

She parted the curtain as if she were looking out, but her eyes were blinded by glistening tears. Listening to another episode of coughing, she devoutly prayed that Abigail would be recovered enough to enjoy her birthday party.

It might very well be the last one she would ever have.

5

Colored lanterns were strung inside the huge tent, and within the red and blue and orange globes small flames danced like fiery moths. The fiddlers stood on the small dais at one end, running their bows lightly across the strings as they tuned up, and dashing Cavalry officers in full dress uniform hovered over ladies who shimmered in a rainbow of silks and satins.

"It's a fairyland!" Abigail exclaimed delightedly, clapping her hands.

"Yes, and tonight you are Queen Titania." Colonel Boyle smiled at his hostess. A stocky man with silver hair and a matching fringe of moustache, he had eyes as bright and alert as a hawk's. "It is your birthday, my dear, and we are all at your command."

Abigail was indeed lovely in her gown of apricot and cream silk and had rebounded miraculously from the exacerbation of her illness. Looking at her now, Norah found it hard to believe anything was wrong with her health; yet she had seen the scarlet patches upon Abigail's handkerchief and had heard that ominous wracking cough.

Norah sat on the Colonel's other side, resplendent in a red silk creation that made her hair shine as dark as a blackbird's wing against the whiteness of her skin. Around her neck she wore a locket with seed pearls on a black velvet ribbon, and she had taken great care in pinning her heavy tresses in a new and becoming style. Her eyes scanned the tent, but there was no sign of a tall, gray-eyed Sergeant of the Indian Scouts. She tried to pretend to herself that it didn't matter, but was guiltily aware that every effort taken with her toilette had been made with one object in mind: to impress LeBeau.

A shadow fell across her, and Norah's heart fluttered. Turning, she hid her swift disappointment as First Lieutenant Newcomb bowed. He was a chivalrous young man, sandy-haired with light blue eyes filled with admiration now, and appeared to have no faults that she could determine, except perhaps his embarrassing anxiety to please her. She had already been on the receiving end of several jocular comments caused by Newcomb's devotion, and tried to treat the situation as casually as possible.

"Miss O'Shea, I beg you will grant me the honor of escorting you out for the first dance."

"By all means, if you have no regard for your feet, Lieutenant! I must warn you I have not danced since my graduation from Miss Emerson's Academy, when the young men of St. Cyril's came en masse to our Senior Ball. During the first dance I trod so violently on my partner's feet that he cried out, and I spent the rest of the evening hiding behind a potted palm."

"Then, ma'am, I can only assume your partner was a clodpole, and did not know how to guide such a graceful dancer, for you are lighter than thistledown on your feet."

She twinkled demurely up at him. "I only hope, sir, that I am that light on *yours*!"

He took her hand in his large freckled one, holding it as if it were an eggshell subject to imminent breakage, and conducted her onto the dance floor. The surface of smooth-sanded boards had been waxed to a mellow glow. Now it shone in the light of the suspended lamps, inviting the dancers to try their steps.

As the Lieutenant guided her around the tent, Norah saw that Colonel Boyle, as the ranking officer, had led Abigail out for the first set. The steps of the dance brought them into two long lines. Abigail, her cheeks feverishly flushed, came down the center of the set with Colonel Boyle. Next Captain Gartner followed, escorting the Colonel's wife, a pleasant but outspoken little woman of firm convictions, dressed in olive-green satin. Norah found herself watching the Gartners as her feet went through the intricate pattern without missing a beat. Even in the midst of the dance, their eyes sought one another, exchanging loving glances. Norah felt a pang of unease. It seemed cruel and unfair of Fate to have brought them together, and then dangle such a terrible threat over the happiness of their marriage.

"I don't think you heard a single word I've said, ma'am." Lieutenant Newcomb's eyes reproached Norah as his arm tightened slightly on her waist.

She smiled up at him mischievously, while her mind scrambled to catch the echo of his words. "Of course I have, Lieutenant. You said that my eyes are like stars and I am as light on my feet as thistledown, is that not right? And how very immodest of me to repeat it!" Her partner blushed with gratification and swung her around on his arm. It was not just a lucky guess on Norah's part: he had told her that three times since they had taken the floor.

She tried to keep her mind on his pleasantries for the rest of the number. Lieutenant Newcomb, who had been becoming progressively more possessive since he'd partnered her at dinner, was less than pleased when Major Van Hever claimed her for the next. Van Hever was a blond giant with a guardsman's thick brush of a moustache and hazel eyes that always held a smile. As he swept Norah into a waltz she caught a glimpse of Newcomb, glowering from the sidelines.

The Major smiled down at her boldly. "I believe the good Lieutenant is going to call me out before the evening is through, but it will be well worth the price of a waltz with you. You waltz as delightfully as you look, ma'am."

Norah peered up at him and laughed as they spun past the other couples. "As for you, sir, your compliments are as smooth as your dancing."

"I speak God's truth, Miss O'Shea, and only a peg-legged pirate would have difficulty dancing with someone so graceful as yourself."

"Are there Irishmen in your lineage, Major?"

He gave her a laughing yet hopeful look. "Would some Irish blood do anything to advance my suit?"

"Alas, you are too late. My hand is already claimed."

"Only your hand, fair lady? Not your heart?"

"I have given my word in a formal betrothal, Major; and that is far more binding than if I had merely given my heart."

For a moment his face was sober, the flirtatious manner gone. Norah had a brief glimpse of the man behind the dashing facade, lonely and a little wistful. It seemed that Arizona Territory was filled with men eager for feminine companionship, while her acquaintance in Boston was primarily that of women hoping to find a husband before permanent spinsterhood became their lot in life: what a tragedy that they would, in all likelihood, never find one another!

They whirled around and around beneath the lanterns. Norah was enjoying herself tremendously, letting the years roll back until she felt eighteen again. When was the last time she had been this lighthearted and gay? When was the last time she had danced with a man? It was exhilarating to feel young and carefree once more, with no thought in her head other than to savor the moment.

The music ended and Norah, pleading the heat, took a chair on the sidelines while the Major went in search of a cooling drink for her. From the corner of her eye she saw First Lieutenant Newcomb bearing down in her direction with single-minded determination, and she allowed Captain Mitchell to lure her into another country dance. When the set ended she managed to sit between Abigail and the Colonel's wife, knowing Newcomb would have to ask one of them to dance out of common courtesy, before he could partner her again. With them on the sidelines was Miss Tooms, the Boyles' guest. Although the lady was every day of forty years, she dressed and wore her hair in the style of a very young girl. The fashion did not suit her, nor did the gown of heavy puce satin, which gave a decidedly sallow tinge to her complexion.

Suddenly Mrs. Boyle sat upright, surprise written in every line of her face and a patent admiration in her amber eyes. "Who is *that*?"

Norah looked up swiftly. LeBeau stood just inside the entrance, surveying the room. He wore a regulation dress uniform and looked devastatingly masculine. Her heart began to race wildly, and her palms were suddenly damp. She wiped them with her lace handkerchief and pretended to be looking at something across the room.

"Oh, I am *so* glad he has come, after all," Abigail said with quiet warmth. "That is Sergeant LeBeau, one of the Indian Scouts attached to the Camp. He is a particular friend of my husband's...and of mine," she added hastily, seeing the prunes-and-prisms expression on Miss Tooms's angular face.

"How very odd, to be sure," Miss Tooms murmured with disapproval.

Norah thought Miss Tooms looked exactly like a horse, and not a particularly well-favored one, at that. She did not like the woman, finding her manner condescending and her high-pitched voice irritating. It severely taxed her manners to repress a stinging reply to Abigail's guest, but the Colonel's wife, being a cousin of Miss Tooms, was under no such restrictions.

"Tosh!" Mrs. Boyle said dismissively. "This is Arizona Territory, not West Point."

Abigail filled the void that followed. "Exactly, ma'am! Sergeant LeBeau saved the lives of Miss O'Shea and myself a few weeks ago, when the horse pulling our gig bolted. It was most providential that he was nearby, and able to ride to our rescue. I invited him tonight, but he declined, saying it was not seemly for him to mingle socially with the commissioned officers and their families. Charles promised he would change the Sergeant's mind."

The music stopped, and Norah observed LeBeau coming toward them. He crossed the now empty dance floor without the smallest sign of knowing his arrival had caused comment, but she thought his color was heightened as he drew near. There was not a woman in the room unaware of his presence, from Cora Boyle to the seventeen-year-old twins of Major McKendrick from Camp Verde. Backs were straighter, smiles sweeter, and voices raised in tinkling laughter.

Then he came into Norah's line of vision, and their eyes met briefly. She was the first to glance away. She was sure he meant to ask her to dance, but LeBeau ignored her, bowing to his hostess as the musicians struck up again.

"I've come to claim my dance, ma'am." He held out his hand and Abigail rose, smiling shyly.

"I am very pleased that you have joined us, Sergeant LeBeau." She placed her hand on his arm, and they went off to take their places for the country dance now forming.

"Well, I can hardly believe my eyes," Miss Tooms announced with icy rigidity. Censure scored deep creases from her pinched nostrils down to her tightly tucked mouth. This was *not* how things were done in St. Louis! "I'm sure I've never seen a sergeant dancing with a captain's wife before. And an Indian Scout, at that."

"Indeed?" Mrs. Boyle lifted a cool eyebrow at her cousin. "Perhaps you've not attended enough dances then, Hannah." She turned with a comment to Norah, leaving Miss Tooms to stew in her own vinegar.

Norah hardly heard their interchange. She had hoped that LeBeau would ask to stand up with her next, but she was squired first by Captain Gartner and then by Colonel Boyle, who regaled her with naughty stories of his youthful days. While she smiled and made the proper responses to her partners, her eyes scanned the room, looking for one man. At last she realized that all her gaiety and sparkling glances were wasted. The only audience she wanted was not there: LeBeau had waltzed with Abigail and left.

Suddenly the music didn't sound as lovely, and the colored lanterns lost their enchantment. Norah sought refuge on the sidelines, and Abigail came to sit with her. The heat was unbearable, her feet hurt in their dainty silver slippers and her head ached abominably.

"How very warm it is in here!" Abigail fanned herself, then glanced shyly at Norah. "I am sorry to see that Sergeant LeBeau has left so early. I thought he would surely lead you out for at least one set, Norah."

"Oh? I did not! He has never distinguished me with any particular attention. Except for incivility!" Norah corrected coolly. Her head was throbbing in earnest. She was angry with herself for indulging in all sorts of foolish fantasies, letting a few careless words and glances grow to ridiculous proportions in her own mind. How LeBeau would laugh at her if he knew!

"But..." Abigail flushed and bit her underlip. "You must pardon me, but I had thought... Perhaps he will return in a moment."

Norah stood up abruptly. "Excuse me, Abigail. I have the headache and require some fresh air."

Mentally cursing herself for a coward, she fled into the darkness outside. Necklaces of constellations adorned the black velvet sky. Across the way, two troopers jigged to the music issuing from the tent, their arms locked together as they kicked their booted heels and spun around. From another direction the muted sound of a penny-whistle floated on the ocean of warm air, bringing the plaintive strains of a familiar Irish ballad to Norah's ears.

Without warning she was terribly homesick for the cozy little world she had left so blithely behind, forgetting the loneliness and the sense of life passing by that had made her reach out for adventure with a child's greedy hands. Boston. Miss Emerson's Academy. She closed her eyes, pretending she was back in her own spartan room on a summer's night, listening to Mr. Donophan play his whistle. In a moment she would go to the window and watch the yellow moon rise high above the maple and elm trees. There would be no worries, no cares. She would stand there, invisible in the darkness, brushing her long hair and twining it into a fat braid to hang down her back....

Had a fairy godmother appeared just then, complete with magic wand, she would have wished herself straight back to Boston.

"Miss O'Shea?"

Norah recognized First Lieutenant Newcomb's voice from within the tent behind her. He was a fine dancer, an eager conversationalist, and an attentive escort, but she had seen the earnestness in his face, the increasing warmth in his eyes when they rested on her tonight. She was in no state of mind to receive an impassioned and unwanted declaration of love, and fled into the shadows. Rounding the end of the tent, she darted into the gloom alongside the guest quarters, seeking to be alone. It was black as pitch, and Norah ran smack into something. The wind was almost knocked from her, and it was that fact that kept her from crying out in terror, for she was ruthlessly pinned against a man's hard body.

"What the hell...!" a deep voice rasped in her ear.

The moon rose over the stockade, sheathing the world in silver. It was LeBeau who embraced her so tightly, in instinctive reaction to their collision. The irony amused him: coming out of the tent to wrestle with his private devils and turbulent thoughts, the last thing he wanted was to find his arms around the woman who was the cause of them. Yet he didn't let her go.

Norah could feel the drum of his heart, slower and steadier than her own. The light frosted his hair, turned his gray eyes to quicksilver. His scent was all around her, smelling of pine and leather and man. She could not have spoken if she'd wanted to, and only his strong arms kept her erect on knees that were weak and trembling. The muscles of his arms tensed, pressing her closer against his chest. For a moment she longed to rest her cheek over his heart, lose herself in the shelter of his embrace. Then she realized the impropriety of the situation, and struggled until he released her.

"What are you doing out here? Why did you leave the dance?" he asked without preamble.

"I...I just came out for a bit of air." She stepped back and tried to reclaim her composure. "I did not mean to wander so far from the tent." Her heart was hammering against the silk bodice of her dress and in the pulse point at the base of her throat. She was thankful for the soft shadows of the moonlight as she glanced up at LeBeau. Still nettled because he hadn't danced with her, she said the first thing that came into her mind.

"Why did *you* leave so early, Sergeant? Surely you cannot have danced more than once before leaving."

His mouth twisted into an odd smile. "Dancing is only an excuse for a man to take a woman he desires into his arms. Nothing more nor less." His eyes were dark now, darker than the shadows that closed in as clouds from the north blanketed the moon. "I am not the kind of man who needs such an excuse when I want to take a woman in my arms."

Norah could think of no reply. He came a step closer until mere inches separated them and she could feel his breath stirring her hair.

"You should not be out here alone. This is an Army post, Miss O'Shea, and you are a beautiful and desirable woman. Although the men of this command are well disciplined, they are still men. I would advise you not to walk around at night unescorted. It might not be safe."

"You are being ridiculous! And I am perfectly safe with

you,'' she answered, attempting a bantering tone out of sheer nervousness.

Instantly she was in his arms, her breasts crushed against the hard expanse of his chest, her hips brushing his thighs. His face came down to hers, and his breath misted her skin. Alarm shot through her, mingling with the erratic voltage that rippled outward from some central and primitive nerve point.

"*Are* you safe? *Are you?*" His eyes shone with hot silver light.

LeBeau's hands roved over her back, pressing her ever closer, and Norah felt the power of his thighs, the hard proof of his masculinity against the softness of her own flesh. A field of electrical excitement began to throb around them, increasing with each second. The heat of his body warmed hers, but it was the dark desire in his face that ignited her own blood, that sent it singing through her veins and roaring in her ears.

He saw the bounding pulse at Norah's throat and felt her sway against him. His embrace was an iron band, threatening to cut off her breath as his face neared hers. "How safe do you feel now?" he asked hoarsely.

She trembled in the strong circle of his arms, but shook her head. No, she didn't feel safe, but neither did she fear any harm from him. She feared only herself and the newfound desires that whirled through her, rousing wild and unnamed longings whose existence she had never dreamed of till now.

"I am not afraid of you," she whispered.

He searched her eyes and saw she spoke the truth. An ache rose inside his chest, filling it to overflowing, and in the back of his mind a part of him felt despair.

If she had screamed or fought or fainted in the accepted fashion of maidenly behavior, he could have laughed and thought her a fool. If she had wantonly returned the embrace, boldly molding the womanly contours of her body against his, he would have thrust her away and left without a backward glance. But she was not like any other woman he had ever known, and so he held her, inhaling the sweet scent that was peculiarly hers and wanting her desperately. His hands explored the contours of her back and the flare of her hips.

"Damn you!" he cried softly, knowing it was he who was

damned. This was not in his plans, this terrible longing, this agony of need.

Norah lifted her eyes to his and drank in the stern beauty of his face, the clean austere lines etched in black and silver by the moonlight. Magic had touched her. Magic and moonlight and madness, she thought, smiling up at him. She wanted to reach up and outline the proudly arching cheekbones with her fingertips, to place them next against his lips and trace their firm curves.

LeBeau regarded her gravely, and the ache in his chest moved downward to settle in his loins. The rustling silk of her dress was cut low in front to show off her shapely shoulders and bosom. He imagined pulling the fabric down to free her curving breasts, and felt her nipples tighten beneath the thin fabric, as if she shared his vision. He imagined the way she would look with her fragrant hair spilling down over her nakedness, and she reached a hand up to touch the clasp that held her hair in a loose tumble of curls. He took a sharp, quick breath.

Her face was soft and dreamy, the face of a woman awakening. Her eyes watched him from beneath her half-closed lids, and her lips were moist and slightly parted. "Why are you looking at me like that?" she asked in a voice that was barely audible. "What are you thinking?"

"I was thinking how you would look with your hair down. I was thinking..." He stopped, and a shudder ran through his body.

Norah waited, carried away by her emotions, far beyond reason or self-preservation. There was no shyness in her, only the need for his touch. LeBeau's hand rested near her breast, and she brushed against him, feeling his palm curve and close over it in an act of intimate possession. She shut her eyes, and his fingers tightened, caressing her through the fabric, and she stopped breathing. He slid his hand up to the low-cut neckline of her dress and slipped it inside, cupping the softness of her breast. Her breath came out in a long sigh as a shower of red-gold sparks burst upward from the base of her spine and exploded in her brain. Her blood coursed hot and bright through her veins.

As his callused fingertips lightly brushed across the sensitive tip of her breast she stiffened, suddenly frightened by the sensations that welled from deep within her. Instantly his hand withdrew. A murmur of protest escaped her lips, and she moved against him, needing the contact of his flesh with hers. Nothing else mattered. She was intoxicated by his scent, his touch, and the knowledge that he desired her. He cursed under his breath, then buried his face in her hair and groaned, wanting her with a fierceness that was new to his nature. Her eyes were dark as sapphires, the pupils widely dilated, and her lips moist and slightly parted, as if begging to be kissed. Did she know what she was doing to him? To herself? LeBeau cursed silently, warring with himself until a lifetime of rigid control won out.

"Little fool!" he whispered, holding her away from him. "You are playing with fire, and fire burns! You are too innocent and inexperienced to control your own passion, much less mine!" Her arms wound around his neck. She was supple and pliant in his arms, swaying against him as if she had no will of her own. "If we were anywhere else I would take you here and now, knowing that it's what we both want."

He lifted his head, and the shadows of the stables beckoned. No one would see them, no one would hear them. He could hold her naked in his arms while he explored all the wonderful secrets of her body he had known only in his dreams. Her arms tightened around his neck, and he swept Norah into his arms. Carrying her into the stable, LeBeau lowered her into the clean straw, covering her with his own length. His strong hands molded her breasts, caressing them through the silken bodice, and she arched upward eagerly.

His mouth found the hollow beneath her soft throat and moved lower, seeking her breast. A liquid, melting sensation spread outward and upward from her loins, and she sighed with pleasure, knowing she had neither the strength nor will to make him stop. She had lost the ability to think, to reason, and the habits and teaching of a lifetime evaporated beneath his touch and her own desperate longing. When he lifted his head she tangled her fingers in his hair and tried to pull him back, but he flung himself away from her with an oath. His breathing was ragged and his eyes half mad.

He still wanted her. God, how he wanted her! But even in his heat he realized it would mean her ruin. "Straighten your

dress and get back to the dance. Hurry, before they come looking for you!''

Norah stared at him, unable to believe what was happening.
She was dazed with sensation and confused by his sudden
change. One moment LeBeau had cradled her in his arms, filled
with passion and tenderness; the next he was raging at her, his
face twisted with something that might be anger or pain. She
sat up, clutching at her falling hair and her skewed bodice. The
touch of his mouth was still warm upon her breast, and she felt
rejected and betrayed. ''What is it?'' she gasped. ''What is
wrong?''

He shook his head slowly, like a man in the toils of a dream.
Or a nightmare. ''Who are you, what are you, that you haunt
me so? I have not known a day's peace since we met! I wish
to God that Slade would come and take you away. I wish to
God I had never set eyes on you!''

Norah felt as if he had struck her. ''Why? I don't understand.''

LeBeau stood a few feet away while she struggled to her
feet. He picked a piece of straw from her hair, snatching his
hand back quickly. She was trembling violently, and her eyes
were wild and frightened. The need for her still burned in him
like a torch, and he didn't dare touch her, or it would ignite a
blaze he had no hope of keeping in check.

How could he make her understand? He was a man sprung
from the soil of the Territory, a man who could sleep on the
hard ground and live alone in the wilderness, a man of few
words and many passions and an uncertain future. There was
no room in his life for this woman.

''Why? I can think of a thousand reasons. You are a woman
used to feather beds, linen sheets, and soft words! A woman
whose life is bounded by the precepts and opinions of others.
My God! I would have ruined you if we hadn't stopped, and
still you ask me why?''

His hands clenched at his sides. ''You deserve something
better than a heated coupling in the straw, and that is all I can
give you. There can be nothing more between us. Ever! Go
back to your silks and perfumes and fancy lieutenants.''

Norah half lifted her hand, but he turned and stalked away
until he was only one more shadow among the others, and she

was alone. She felt lost in a nightmare, shamed by her behavior, and even more by LeBeau's rejection. He had stopped before matters got out of hand, but Norah knew she would never be the same. She had taken one taste of the forbidden fruit, and the days of her womanly innocence were over.

Leaning against the side of the stall, she tried to make sense of it all. She was too stunned to weep. Footsteps outside made her aware of the consequences of discovery, and she stood upright. Although it would be torture to face Abigail's guests and make small talk, Norah knew she must at least bid her hostess good-night. Making sure her hair was properly pinned, she straightened her dress and brushed off the clinging bits of straw. She slipped back into the tent, to be greeted quietly by Abigail.

"Oh, there you are, Norah! I was about to send Charles to look for you. How is your headache? Would you like one of Dr. Porter's powders for it?"

"Thank you, but it is no better. I believe sleep is the best remedy for me." She was desperate to be alone and away from the noise and chatter and from Abigail's too-noticing eyes. The thought of smiling and carrying meaningless conversations was intolerable.

"I will make your excuses then," Abigail said softly. Although she saw that Norah was pale, she did not think her indisposition had a physical cause. Dr. Porter's patent powders might not help, but sometimes a good cry in a darkened room was the best medicine of all. "Do go and lie down now."

Norah gave her a quick embrace and hurried out into the night, leaving the disconsolate Lieutenant Newcomb in the clutches of a triumphant Miss Tooms. Her thoughts were all jumbled together, revolving upon one another chaotically, and she welcomed the privacy of her room. As she shucked off her silk gown in a crumpled heap, she thought that Abigail had an uncanny perception for her age. *She certainly was not taken in by my excuses!*

It was good to be alone. She needed to think. Surely the emotions she had seen on LeBeau's face were not products of her imagination? During that long moment in his arms, she had been certain that the attraction was not only mutual, but deep and genuine, and would willingly have yielded. She had never suspected the depths of her own sensuality, and the knowledge shocked her deeply.

Her eyes fell on the leather-framed picture of Abner. Was it the recollection of her betrothal that had caused LeBeau to change so abruptly? She flushed with chagrin to think that he had remembered what she had not. At last she put on her night rail and climbed atop the mattress, knowing sleep would be long in coming. Watching the pale bars of moonlight upon the ceiling, she wondered if LeBeau would have acted differently toward her if she were not an engaged woman. Would he court her as assiduously as Newcomb did if circumstances were changed? If, for instance, Abner never returned to claim his bride?

The last thing she heard that night was the sound of the penny-whistle, playing a Welsh lament for a lost lover. The first thing she heard the next morning was that Abner Slade had arrived in Camp Greenwood two hours after sunup, inquiring after his intended bride.

6

Norah paced back and forth across the floral carpet in the Gartner's sitting room, trying to control the trembling of her hands. Her skin was damp with nervousness, her starched white sailor collar wilting above a shirtwaist of rose and white stripes. The confused emotions aroused by her great attraction to LeBeau were nothing to the chaos she had felt since hearing of Abner's arrival. So many weeks had passed, so many things had happened since she arrived in the Arizona Territory, that everything connected with her betrothal and proposed marriage had taken on the quality of a half-remembered dream.

A knock sounded on the paneled door, and she started. Quickly she patted her hair into place, but the wayward tendrils curled around her face in dusky ringlets. Attempting a poised smile, her lips quavered and she had to clamp down to keep them steady. Abigail stepped in. "Mr. Slade is coming up the walkway. I thought I would let you know." The tip of her tiny nose was reddened, and the rims of her eyes were swollen.

Hastening to her side, Norah clasped her friend's hand. "Dear God, has there been more trouble?"

"Yes. Another ranch was attacked. People we know...the Hazlitt family... It was very bad."

Although wrapped up in her own problems, Norah was still aware of the terrible events moving outside the high walls of Camp Greenwood, for word spread from soldier to soldier more quickly than gossip at a church social. The entire Post buzzed with the news: the war party of Apache braves had attacked the morning stage, leaving no survivors; Iron Knife had reportedly been seen a dozen places, all of them too widely separated for truth; and two Mexican girls had been kidnapped from a spread down near Tucson. The whole Territory was in an uproar, and General George Crook was mad as hell, and on his way to Camp Greenwood.

Abigail bravely blinked away her tears. "Sergeant LeBeau left with his band of scouts during the night. Lieutenant Newcomb is taking a large party out this morning...." Her voice dissolved into a quickly stifled sob. "Major Van Hever is dead of wounds suffered in this morning's skirmish."

Norah's stomach lurched. Major Van Hever with his guardsman's moustache and laughing, lonely eyes. He had been so vital, so full of life, that she could not quite believe it. Wordlessly she put her arms around Abigail's shoulders.

"Oh, Norah! It is so terrible. Last night the men were laughing and dancing with us, and...and who knows how many of them will not return?"

"Charles will be safe. You must not worry." But what of LeBeau? Dead or dying even now, out in the blistering sun? She could not bear to think of it.

Abigail rallied, lifting her chin. "I will be all right." She gave Norah a watery smile. "I am a soldier's wife. It is just that I have been one such a little while..." Both stopped, hearing voices on the porch. "That will be Mr. Slade now. I shall slip away and let you greet him in privacy."

She was gone in an instant. Norah hurried to peer out through the open spaces of the lace curtain while her heart fluttered. There was barely time to observe a figure in a tan suit and newly polished boots. She crossed the carpet and stood waiting, with her back to the mantelpiece.

The door swung open again, and a man stepped over the threshold. There was no need for the formal introduction. Although he looked much older than his thirty-six years, Norah was by now familiar with each line and feature of his face, having studied his portrait a hundred times. His skin was deeply weathered, but he was as handsome in person—and as ruthless appearing—as in the photograph he'd sent her. Tall and well built, he had the thick-muscled type of body that often ran to fat in later years. Flaxen hair fell in waves over a high forehead and heavy-lidded eyes of a curious tobacco color inventoried Norah from head to toe, with bold appreciation of her womanly attributes. Dull color swept up over her throat and face under his protracted scrutiny, but she stood her ground with head held high. It was not an auspicious start to their relationship: she was not used to being examined like a horse or cow for sale.

The inspection finished, he smiled in evident satisfaction, then crossed the room in her direction and bowed. "My dear Miss O'Shea, I am Abner Slade, at your service."

"How do you do? We have feared for your well-being these past weeks."

She managed a smile and gave him her hand. He took it in his, then bent to press a kiss on it. His mouth was hot and moist against her skin, and she almost pulled back as his lips lingered. The gesture seemed too intimate, and she had a strong urge to wipe her hand. Unconsciously she compared him with LeBeau, noting that his nose was proud rather than patrician, his mouth stubborn rather than firm, his air aggressive rather than commanding. And his eyes...his eyes were not the changeable gray of a stormy sky.

"I trust that you have not been too uncomfortable here?" He looked around Abigail's parlor with open disdain. "I have in mind to build you a house three times the size of this one, and fill it with every elegancy at my disposal. As the wife of a wealthy man, you will have the luxuries that few women in the Territory can command. You must invite Mrs. Gartner to spend some time with us in the future."

Amazed by lack of any explanation for his prolonged absence, Norah now was equally taken aback by his boasting. Slade saw the surprise she was unable to hide.

"I'm proud of my success, ma'am! My Pa died when I was nine, and I went to work in a dry-goods store to make ends meet. I came here from Kansas City with ten dollars and a broken-down horse, and parlayed them into a flourishing business. There's not a man in all of the Territory who doesn't know of me, and in time there won't be a man or woman in the entire West who doesn't know the name of Abner Slade."

He was certainly the very picture of success in his well-cut suit, Norah thought, trying to overcome her initial dismay. The gold belt-buckle plate and heavily chained hunt-case watch that hung from the pocket of his gold brocade waistcoat were perhaps too ornate to be in the best taste, but they certainly proclaimed his status for all the world to see.

Sunlight slanted off the large signet ring on his left hand. For the first time Norah noticed the wide bandage beneath his left shirtcuff and along the fleshy part of his hand. "Oh, you have been injured! I feared some misadventure had befallen you, and see my apprehensions were not without foundation."

Abner glanced down and then away. He seemed annoyed, and a rush of blood darkened his face. "A scratch! Don't be concerned about it." He thrust the hand into the pocket of his coat and smiled at her with considerable warmth. He came a step closer and put out his hand to touch her face.

"You are very like your portrait, but more beautiful than I expected," he said with gratification. "I am a rough man, Norah. Everything I have, I've earned for myself. When I was struggling to establish myself, I promised myself that one day I would own three things: a successful trading business, the biggest cattle empire in the Territory, and a beautiful, educated wife."

Being counted in with his material possessions did not sit well with Norah. "Sir, you will not own me!" she chided softly. "I will be your wife, but I will be no man's possession."

Again Abner's hand fell to her shoulder, and he leaned down from his height. "Let me choose my words more carefully: you, my dearest Norah, will be the jewel in my crown. I shall be the most envied man in the Territory."

His attitude did nothing to calm her agitations, but it was too late for second thoughts now. "Won't you be seated, Mr. Slade?" She backed away, indicating the velvet side chair. He smiled and dropped his hand, though it was obvious that he was humoring her mood. Norah perched on the settee, and he sat down beside her, so close that their shoulders and thighs were in contact. There was no room for her to move away.

"Why call me 'Mr. Slade,' my dear? Surely you are not afraid to call me by my given name, for I have a strong desire

to hear the sound of it on your sweet lips." His thigh exerted
subtle pressure against hers.

"Would you care for some tea...Abner?" Before he had
time to answer she filled a china cup and offered it to him,
placing it between them like a small porcelain shield.

He took the saucer and held it slightly away from himself,
as if not quite certain what to do with it. From the strong odor
of spirits on his breath, Norah suspected that tea was not his
usual afternoon drink. She poured a dollop of milk in hers and
waited for him to make the next move.

Abner set his cup of tea on the side table and placed his
hand on her knee. "Matters have been delayed long enough. I
see no reason why we should not be married tomorrow."

His words echoed through her brain like cannon shot. Norah's cup rattled against the china saucer, and she put it down,
ignoring the hot fluid that dashed over her fingers.

"So soon!"

"Soon? Why, we have been engaged for eight months! Tomorrow is not too soon at all." He rose to his feet, then reached
out and pulled Norah up to face him. "Not when my every
waking hour has been given to thinking of the moment when
I can truly make you mine!"

There was a look of hunger, a sudden flaring of desire in his
eyes, but it was not at all like the expression Norah had seen
on LeBeau's face. This was something different, something
darker and frightening. He grabbed her roughly to him, pressing hot kisses on her lips, her throat, the white swell of bosom
above the bodice of her dress. His mouth was moist against
her skin, his hands insistent as they skimmed over her neat
waist and moved upward to her breasts.

"It will be difficult enough to wait one day," he said
hoarsely. "I can hardly bear to wait another minute to possess
you."

His fingers touched the bare flesh above her modest neckline,
dipping beneath it, ruthlessly tugging the fabric downward. Norah pushed him away with all her might, forgetting how very
different her reaction had been the night before, when another
man had done the same. The seam of her bodice ripped in a
short staccato burst, and he pulled the fabric down, exposing

the top of one breast. She was angry and terrified, afraid he would force himself upon her there in the Gartner's parlor.

"Let me go! How dare you!" She yanked herself out of his embrace and covered her bosom, glaring at him in a fury. "How dare you maul me in such a way!"

"You are a woman, Norah, and know nothing of the strength of a man's passion. You are mine now, and I have little patience with maidenly reserve." He advanced on her with a mocking smile, and pinched her chin in his fingers. "And you *are* mine. Get that into your head right now!"

She struggled, and odd gold lights seemed to glow in the depths of Abner's eyes, as if it excited him. She forced herself to go still, and his mouth came down on hers so hard that her lips were bruised against her own teeth. And this was the man she had sworn before God to wed.

There was a sharp rap at the door, and Abner released her, smiling as she moved away. He'd gotten himself a regular spitfire beneath that fragile, ladylike facade. The combination aroused him so that the mere thought of taming her was almost a physical pleasure.

Captain Gartner entered. "Father Ildephonso asked me to send a messenger as soon as you have completed your arrangements for the wedding. There's a party headed in that direction, so I thought to check with you now."

His eyes swept over the little scene, and his jaw tightened. Norah blushed fiercely, knowing he had seen the tear in the bodice of her gown. While the men exchanged cool greetings, she stood silent. Her lips tingled and felt swollen. She wondered if it was noticeable.

"It is all taken care of: we will be married tomorrow morning," Abner answered.

Gartner glanced at Norah. She felt breathless and trapped, as if the life were being squeezed out of her. "If you please, I would like to wait...a week or two before we are wed. Until we know one another a little better."

"We were to have been married a month ago, my dear, upon your arrival. I see no reason for further delay. With the unrest in the area we had best make the journey to my ranch as soon as possible, for it will only get worse as time goes on."

She felt a desperate need for more time, yet had no legitimate excuse for postponing the marriage. Things were not at all what she had expected but what choice had she? Their betrothal was as legally binding as a marriage, in the eyes of both the Law and the Church. Boston might as well be at the ends of the earth now, for Norah had burned her bridges behind her. She was penniless and friendless, except for Abigail and Charles Gartner. Her interlude with LeBeau had been nothing but the wishful product of her romantic imagination and his own boredom. Or perhaps a need to humiliate her. Certainly he had made his feelings plain enough: *"There can be nothing between us. Ever!"*

Abner slipped his arm about her waist. "Tell Father Ildephonso we will be married at ten o'clock tomorrow."

Gartner glanced at Norah for confirmation. "Tomorrow," she repeated, and her voice was only a whisper.

Norah shifted impatiently on the hard bench in a small room off the church vestibule, while Abigail applied the finishing touches to her coiffure. Next the wreath of white satin leaves and long point-lace veil were set upon her black tresses and pinned in place.

"Oh, you are such a beautiful bride! Wait until Mr. Slade sees you." Abigail chattered nervously. This was not the wedding she had planned in her mind for Norah. Not with Abner Slade cast in the role of groom.

The bride stared at her hands, folded tightly in her lap. Norah had not slept at all, and the long drive to the Mission had been made in a haze of emotional and physical fatigue. This trip to Santa Magdalena had been totally different from the others, for a heavily armed party had surrounded them on the way. There had been another, greater, difference. This time Abner had been present. And LeBeau had not.

He had gone with his men on the trail of the marauding Apaches, and the knowledge that their paths would never cross again was like a lead ball in the pit of Norah's stomach. A thousand times she had tried to turn her mind from the Indian Scout, but it was no use. How could she go through with this marriage to Abner when her thoughts and barely defined longings revolved about another man? How would she ever survive this inner turmoil that threatened to tear her apart?

"Now," Abigail commanded. "Tilt your head up so I can fix this last little piece."

Norah obeyed, and as she looked up she spied a small statue of gilt and painted wood in its foot-high niche. It was a graceful Madonna, cradling the Infant in her arms, and it reminded her of the larger one in the Boston chapel where she had exchanged her proxy vows. The image seemed to be smiling serenely down at her in perfect understanding. In the Boston chapel she had prayed to have the strength and courage to be a good wife and, God willing, a mother. Remembering that prayer now, she vowed again to do her best to fulfill her obligations to Abner. She would bury her guilty secret beneath the weight of duty, and in time she would forget her foolishness. Suddenly Norah felt a sense of peace settle over her, and was comforted.

Sister Cecelia jiggled in, a smile bracketing her white teeth and forcing those multiple chins into horizontal pleats above the starched throat of her wimple. "Come, children. Everything is ready to begin."

Norah rose, and her gown of white organdy and Brussels lace rustled softly. It had belonged to her mother. Inwardly she saw herself as one of a long line of brides stretching far beyond her mother and grandmother into the mists of antiquity. And someday there would be another line of women, daughters of her daughters, going forth to meet the future on their own wedding days. She smiled, and some of the color came back into her cheeks. "And I am ready to begin, also."

As they stepped into the vestibule, Abigail reached up to pull the short veil down over Norah's face, and gave her an encouraging smile. "That is much better: earlier I feared you were ready to bolt!"

"Wedding nerves. Nothing more."

There was a blur of movement on the altar as Father Ildephonso came out from the sacristy, resplendent in the white brocade vestment worn for weddings, christenings, and other joyful occasions. Yellow Basket straightened the lacy train, then hurried to take her place before the bride. The girl stood triumphantly, carrying a basket of yellow silk roses that matched the sash of her white dress. She was delighted to take part in the ceremony, and only wished Dove-in-Flight could see her now: but she had run off with her lover and never returned. Father Ildephonso took his place facing the bride down the sunlit aisle, and the girl had no time for further regrets.

The tones of the organ began, low and soft at first, then rapidly swelling to fill the nave with glorious sound as Sister Cecelia's plump fingers swept over the keys. Abigail pressed Norah's hand once, then hurried to take her place in the pew at Captain Gartner's side. Norah's feet began to move, and she found herself halfway down the aisle without remembering how she had gotten there. The events became a waking dream, fragmented into discreet images: Grandmother O'Donnell's ivory rosary twined through her own fingers, the silver crucifix on the end swaying with her movements, catching the errant sunbeams; Father Ildephonso looking solemn and proud; the gilt-trimmed statues, the branches of beeswax candles, the embroidered linens and gem-crusted chalice shining in front of the tabernacle. And at the altar rail, Abner waiting. He took Norah's hand firmly in his and said his vows in a sure, steady tone. She heard her own voice, high and clear as a crystal bell, repeating the words. The ring was on her finger, the troth plighted, and she was Mrs. Abner Slade.

And as the marriage bells tolled, LeBeau rode toward Camp Greenwood. He was bone tired and covered with dust. Approaching the gates, he saluted the lookout. "What's going on at the Mission, a funeral?"

"Naw. A weddin'. Abner Slade and Miz Gartner's houseguest tied the knot."

LeBeau turned to stone. "Married." He pulled his horse about so sharply it reared in protest. No sooner had its hooves touched the ground than he kicked it into a gallop, riding away from the singing of the bells like a man possessed.

Time blurred, compressed, and shifted. By sunset Norah was back at the hotel in Greenwood Junction, preparing for the last night of her maidenhood, the first of her married life. Mrs. Beasley's round red face beamed happily as she laid out the fine lawn nightgown and peignoir for Norah. "Anything else

I can get for you, Mrs. Slade? A bite to eat? You must be feeling a bit hungry from the long ride into town.''

"No. Thank you. I couldn't eat a thing." It was true. Norah knew anything that went down would inevitably—and immediately—come back up. In a few moments she would be truly alone with Abner for the first time, and although he was now her husband, he was still practically a stranger.

"All right. I'll have Cletus bring up some cans of water for the hip bath as soon as he's done rubbing down the horses." Still beaming, she nodded and backed out the door, closing it quietly.

Norah set her silver-backed brushes out on the dresser. The mirror above reflected the same bed of tarnished brass she had slept alone in four weeks ago. It looked enormous. And tonight, she would sleep there next to Abner. Her stomach tightened at the thought. Taking the brush, she perched on the edge of the high bed and pulled out the pins that held her hair in place. The shining mass spilled over her shoulders, falling far below her waist. She began brushing it with long strokes, more out of nervousness than need, for her hat and its dust veil had kept it clean.

The door flew open with a bang, and the brush clattered to the floor. Abner entered, but stopped as he caught sight of her. He was smiling, but the look in his eyes sent a frisson of fear up her spine. Without bothering to close the door, he crossed the room and loomed over her, dark color suffusing his face. Reaching out, he gathered handfuls of her hair in his hands, letting them slide across his palms like lengths of silk, while she watched him, wide-eyed and frightened as a doe.

"Oh, yes!" he said slowly, "I think we have made a good bargain, you and I."

Before she had time to think, he was pressing her back on the mattress, bearing her down with the weight of his body. The breath was almost knocked out of her, and she had no strength to even speak. Abner's hands pawed at her bodice while his mouth fastened on hers. His lips were wet, and there was whiskey on his breath.

The door still stood open wide to the hallway, and the sound of footsteps brought Norah's paralyzed senses to order. She gasped for air and pushed at his chest without effect. A shout of rough masculine laughter was followed by bawdy comments as the two travelers passed their room. "Hey, friend! Need any help wrestling that heifer?" one called out.

Cursing, Abner got to his feet and slammed the door, driving the bolt home with terrifying finality. Norah jumped up and stood with her back to the window, trying to control the situation and maintain some semblance of dignity. Abner's actions were outside both her experience and her expectations. He came toward her purposefully. Little gold lights glowed like sparks in his eyes. "It will be easier for you if you don't fight me. I don't want to hurt you. And in time you will come to enjoy it, I promise you."

She stepped back and bumped into the low wooden sill as he advanced. "I've waited months for this, Norah! I am not a patient man, as you have just seen. Perhaps I was carried away for a moment. You're a lady. I like that." He smiled again, the same unpleasant smile that had sent a chill up her spine earlier. "But lady or not, you are my wife, and your chief duty is to please me!"

"I am prepared to do my wifely duty, Abner. But I am not prepared to be publicly mauled on my wedding day!"

He grabbed her and pulled her close, planting a hard kiss on her unwilling lips. His tongue darted out and ran along her lips, but she didn't understand and resisted. His hands encircled her upper arms painfully. "Open your mouth!"

Norah was confused and frightened. "What? I—"

That was all it took for his tongue to slip inside. It filled her mouth, hot and moist and tasting of stale tobacco and alcohol. She was afraid she might gag, but reminded herself that this must all be part of being a wife. His fingers dug into her flesh, and his tongue probed deep until she felt she might suffocate. *Dear God, will it never end?*

She was stiff and awkward in his arms, and Abner's mouth came free of hers. He eyed her in frustration. "Kiss me back," he commanded, and proceeded to invade her mouth again.

Kiss him back? Norah thought distractedly. What in heaven's name does he mean by that? Then his fingers were fumbling at the front of her blue traveling dress, undoing the frogs that held her jacket over the shirtwaist. He slid his hand between the buttons of her shirtwaist, only to be frustrated by the iron-hard stays of her corset and the heavy cloth of the corset cover.

"Take those damn things off! How can we do anything with these infernal layers of clothes in the way!" He was breathing heavily, and the veins stood out on his temples. "What are you waiting for?"

Norah made a last attempt to salvage her wedding day. "This is not how I anticipated we would begin our married life, Abner! I would... I would like my bath first...and to change into my nightclothes to make myself ready."

After a pause his grip slackened. "Ah, yes. You women all like your little romantic trappings, don't you? Candlelight and soft silky gowns." He looked at her hard. "You want to play the innocent little virgin scene. Very well, I'll play along. This time. But from now on, I'll expect you to be ready when I am!"

A thumping at the door heralded the arrival of her bathwater. Abner laughed harshly and released her. "I've got some business across the street. I'll be back in a while. Get yourself all fancied up."

Norah held her breath until he left the room and the porter brought in the steaming cans. When he was gone, she locked and bolted the door, wishing she could keep it that way. She disrobed and stepped into the water, washing away the fatigue of the journey in the warm, scented water. She could have soaked in the tub for an hour, but fear that Abner would come back and find her there made her hurry.

Toweling dry, she put on the long-sleeved gown of sheer lawn and quickly buttoned the sixteen tiny mother-of-pearl buttons that closed the front. As she moved, Norah caught a glimpse of herself in the cracked mirror over the dresser. The white lawn was so fine it was almost transparent. She had never even seen herself naked, and was almost embarrassed to look. Without the corset and stays that had been so hideously uncomfortable on the journey, her waist was still narrow, her breasts round and full beneath the gauzy fabric. She scurried toward the bed and climbed in, pulling the sheet up to her chin.

Footsteps came along the corridor outside her door, then continued to the end of the hall. A long sigh of relief escaped her. Closing her eyes, she lay rigid upon the bed while seconds stretched into minutes and the minutes ticked steadily by. Where was Abner? At last lack of sleep the previous night and the day's toll of emotions caught up with Norah. Her breathing became soft and regular, and she drifted into a light slumber.

Wakefulness and terror came together in the darkened room. The smell of whiskey and stewed onions filled the air. Norah remembered where she was. And why.

"Abner?"

"'S me, swee'heart. Your lovin' husban'."

The mattress dipped beneath Abner's weight as he groped for her. His hand found her thigh, gripped it painfully, then pulled the gown up over it. His hot palm fell against her bare flesh, and she tried not to shrink away. His other hand reached up to fumble with the neck of her gown, and found the sixteen little pearl buttons, sewn on with loving care and fastened earlier with desperation. They were too tiny for him to deal with in his haste. He swore in frustration, words that Norah had never heard before. Now both hands were at the neck of her gown, and he wrenched the fabric, tearing it away to expose her breasts. Buttons popped and fell dancing to the floor.

"Abner, are you mad?" Norah pushed at his chest and felt the brass buttons of his waistcoat, the roughness of his suit. He was still fully dressed. Her eyes were more accustomed to the darkness now, and she saw him outlined above her. "Abner, please…you're hurting me."

He cuffed her angrily. "Then hold still, damn you!"

He sprawled across her, his mouth hard against the softness of her breasts, while he rooted blindly like a mole. There was no gentleness in him as he tugged and suckled, and Norah could hardly bear it. This was not how it was supposed to be! In the stable with LeBeau, she had experienced one brief taste of the pleasures of physical love. There would be no such wonders to discover within her marriage bed, and she uttered a small sound of despair. As if spurred on by it, Abner worked the hem of her gown above her waist, ruthlessly seeking the intimate spaces of her body.

There was something hard against the inside of her thigh and then between her legs, as Abner entered her without warning. She was not ready for him, and the breaching of her maidenhood was a waking nightmare, a plunging, painful reality smelling of sweat and whiskey and something new. Norah thought she'd been rent asunder. When he was done, panting and gasping against her, she felt bruised and violated.

Abner fell asleep, still half atop her. She was afraid to move, afraid that he might wake and start again. When the cramping in her right leg and arm became intolerable, she eased herself slowly from beneath his bulk. It hurt to move. She stood up, and her legs shook. Limping to the window, she pulled the torn lace curtain aside. Greenwood Junction looked the same in moonlight as it had on her first visit, when LeBeau had kept watch down below in the street. Her hands fisted at her sides. How could the world seem the same, when she was not? When everything was so horribly different now?

Letting the curtain drop and the tears fall hot and fast, she stuffed her fist in her mouth to silence the sobs. She sank down to the floor, her back to the wall, and curled up in a ball of misery. After a while the tears were done. Her eyes felt dry and full of sand. She would have to make the best of the life she had chosen, as other women had before her. There was no other way.

After a while Norah rose and bathed in the cold water of the hip bath. Although she washed and scrubbed, when she stepped out she still felt soiled. Walking to the window, she peered around the edge of the curtain again. The street was as empty as she felt inside.

7

The buggy passed over a rough patch of ground, and Norah winced. The morning had brought a repetition of the night's events, and she was so sore she could hardly sit. Beneath the spreading skirts of her blue traveling suit was a small carriage blanket. She wished it were a feather pillow. Holding rather vague notions about marital relations, she wondered how frequently Abner meant to demand his conjugal rights. She righted her chip-straw bonnet as they drew to a stop at the edge of the sudden drop-off.

"There it is. The beginning of my empire!" Abner slowed the team as they approached a vantage point on the high ridge. "Well, what do you think of it?" He looked out over the land with great pride.

Below them was a shallow, sprawling valley, cut diagonally by a narrow stream. It was the first open water Norah had seen since arriving in Arizona Territory. It had its source in a small spring, close to the main buildings, that fed a deep limestone sinkhole. A long, low house of adobe stood nearby in the lacy shade of several ancient sycamore trees. There were clusters of barns and sheds, and wagons sprawled around them, and a number of men were busily unloading goods and shouldering them into one of the barns.

"I had no idea your holdings were so large," Norah said, trying to comprehend the vastness of the ranch that was her new home.

Abner laughed. "This isn't the half of it! I own everything from here to the horizon and beyond." He turned to her, and the same possessive look was in his eyes as when he had surveyed his land. "I am going to be the most successful man in the Territory. That's why I need a woman like you to smooth out my rough edges, show me the way to go properly in society."

She looked at him in pleased surprise. It felt good to be needed and not as just the icing on Abner's many-layered cake. Things would work out. She'd find a way. "I will do my best to be a good wife to you, Abner."

"Yes," he went on in satisfaction. "A successful man needs a wife who's pretty and educated, one that every other man can look at with envy." He snapped the reins, and the carriage jerked forward to begin the long descent, and Norah knew he hadn't even been listening.

A short time later they rode through the entrance, beneath the wooden sign that bore Abner's emblem of a rampant mountain lion. As they pulled up before the house, she noted the same insignia burned into the sides of the wagons. The shuttered windows of the adobe house were closed against the afternoon glare, giving the place an unwelcoming aspect. Norah refused to be daunted. Abner helped her alight, and escorted her to the door, emblazoned with the same mountain lion insignia. She half expected to wake up in the morning and find the same mark branded on her rump.

The door swung inward on silent hinges, to disclose a thin dark woman in her twenties. She wore a bleached cotton blouse and skirt and a frown. Shoulder-length hair, straight and dark, was caught back with a soiled red ribbon. Her feet were bare. Both the clothes and feet were in need of a thorough washing; still Norah admitted the woman would be presentable, even attractive, if she were clean and the snarls were combed from her hair.

"This is Elena. She does the cooking and cleaning." He gave the servant a slight nod. "Say hello to your new mistress."

"*Buenas dias*, Señora Slade." The woman sketched a scant curtsey, her eyes black as sloe berries. Slyly appraising Norah, she stepped aside for them to enter.

"Thank you, Elena." Norah smiled. Her smile was not returned.

There was a strong smell of garlic on Elena's breath when she showed her yellowed teeth, and a faint whiff of pine needles underlying it. At first Norah couldn't name that hint of evergreen, then she remembered the sleepy traveling man in the train on her way west, and identified the pungent scent of gin. A housekeeper addicted to drink could be a source of trouble. She would have to keep an eye on Elena.

She waited to see if Abner planned to carry her over the threshold, but Elena had halted him on the doorstep. Norah stepped inside the dimly cool interior, pausing at Elena's words.

"There is trouble," the woman said in low rapid Spanish. "Kincaid wants to see you immediately."

Abner cursed, and Norah turned back in time to catch the look the housekeeper shot her way. Neither Abner nor Elena knew she understood a good deal of Spanish because of her time spent teaching at the Mission. Instinct kept her face carefully bland, and she continued to look about, as if examining the room. Abner took the other woman by the arm, and they moved out into the yard, but the wind carried their exchange to Norah's interested ears.

"That one," Elena asked tartly. "Does she know?"

"No, and hold your tongue! She is not to know anything. Tell Kincaid I will be along in a few minutes."

Elena's reply was too muffled for Norah to hear, but one word came through clearly: *LeBeau.* Abner's hands hooked over his belt. "Don't worry about him. I'll take care of it."

Abner came inside alone, looking angry. "Elena will show you around the house. I have some business to attend to."

"Is anything wrong?"

"No. I have to ride out to the south valley and check on a problem with the cattle. I'll be back by suppertime. But first there's something I have to show you."

Taking Norah by the arm, he led her to an engraving hanging above a storage chest. It depicted a large house with soaring gables, fanciful turrets, and a multitude of bay windows. In Boston, it would have been perfect, but in Greenwood Junction it was an anomaly. Norah could picture the relentless sun pouring through those tall windows until the house was an inferno.

"It is not, perhaps, as fine as what you are used to, but by next year we will have a *real* house like this one. I said you would be the jewel in my crown. A rare jewel deserves a proper setting."

It was difficult to conceal her dismay. "It is beautiful, Abner. But so is this house, and it is large enough for our needs." *And those lovely, thick adobe walls keep that infernal heat out!*

"You don't understand. I haven't explained everything yet. When I was a poor boy in Kansas City, I worked for Felix Gentry. This is a picture of his house that I just bought at auction. It used to hang above his desk." Abner's lips curled. "Felix Gentry worked me like a dog, and treated me like dirt! I used to fall asleep promising myself two things: that one day I would have a place that would make his house look like a hovel in comparison; and that I would ruin Gentry if I ever had the chance."

His tobacco-colored eyes lit with satisfaction. "When our new house is built, I'll have made good both my promises!" His smile sent chills down Norah's back. "Last April, after sustaining severe business losses, Felix Gentry went home to his fine, three-story house, sat down in his fine, damask-covered library, drank a bottle of hundred-year-old brandy... and put a bullet through his brain."

His tongue touched the corner of his mouth, as if tasting his victory. Then he pulled out his pocket watch and checked the time. "I'll be back by suppertime. Elena will show you over the place."

Norah stared at his retreating back, shocked by his intractable bitterness. He had purposely set out to ruin Felix Gentry, and now found pleasure in feeling responsible for the man's suicide. She found such single-minded cruelty terrible to contemplate in anyone; in her husband it was intolerable. The polite letters she had exchanged with him during their long-distance courtship had never given the slightest hint of such traits. What kind of monster had she married!

"I will show you the rest of the house," Elena said from behind her, and walked away without waiting to see if Norah followed. All her deference to her new mistress seemed to have vanished with Abner, and her voice was ripe with disdain.

After hesitating a second, Norah crossed the clay-tiled floor in the housekeeper's wake, looking about the main living area for more clues to her husband's personality. She wanted no more unwelcome revelations. The room was rectangular, perhaps twenty by thirty feet, and dominated by heavy pieces of furniture in the Spanish style. It was also in need of a good cleaning. In ordinary circumstances Norah's housewifely instincts would set to the task of making it more livable, but this was not an ordinary circumstance.

There was definitely a problem Elena had said, which Abner did not want her to know about. It seemed odd, but then some men did not deign to discuss any business with their wives, she thought. Or was there some more ominous reason?

Elena proceeded across the floor in small, quick steps, as if impatient of her task, and Norah had scant time to survey the rest of the room as she followed. An ornately carved chest of black wood loomed in one corner, and a dresser of the same type stood beneath one of the small, deep windows. There was a second pair of shutters on the inside of each window, braced with iron for strength, another reminder that life in the Territory was still untamed.

A scrubbed trestle table with long side benches and two high spindle-back chairs stood beneath the other window, flanked by tall chests carved and painted in dull russet and trimmed with ocher. The walls and ceiling were whitewashed in between the darker beams. To the back, a narrow room ran half the length of the living area. Elena threw the door open. "Señor Slade's office."

Much of the room was visible from the center doorway. The corner was filled by a big oak desk. Two leather chairs faced each other over a checkerboard, and a table with a decanter stood next to it. Framed maps covered the opposite wall, and a double row of books filled two shelves. Norah stepped forward, but Elena's arm shot out to bar the way.

"No one enters this room. It is the *señor*'s orders."

"Like Bluebeard's tower?" It was evident that Elena was testing her new mistress's authority. She was also severely trying her temper.

"I do not know who you mean," Elena said abruptly. "But no one enters this room except the *señor*...and me. The *señor*, he trusts me. And he is very good to me." She sent another sly look at Norah from eyes that hinted of clandestine knowledge. Her head tilted to the side, and her full, sensual mouth opened in a small smile.

Angered by the woman's attitude, Norah immediately entered the room, resolved not to be cowed. She took her time examining the books, one by one, tried out both chairs, and pulled back the curtain to admire the view. Elena stood in the doorway, her face stubborn and angry until Norah tired of her game of strategy. She went to the big desk and drew her finger through the dust that coated its surface.

"The next time you are in this room, Elena, which will be immediately after the midday meal, you will bring a dust cloth and mop and set it to rights." She held her back straight and brushed past the housekeeper, heading for the far wall. "What is in here?"

"The bedroom," Elena said sourly, following her inside. This room was square and dark, containing a high bed with a plain headboard, a single dresser and one ladder-back chair. There was no window. Norah didn't think she could sleep in a room without a window. Already the air seemed close and stale. Then she saw that there was one behind the dresser, boarded up. She would ask Abner to move the dresser away. Discovering a reinforced wooden door on the far side of the dresser, she opened it. Warm sunlight fell on her, banishing the gloom. She looked a question at Elena.

"In case of attack," the woman said with a small, satisfied smile. "That way no one can get in, but you can get out. Or maybe not. Who knows?" She watched for Norah's response, and appeared disappointed when none was apparent.

"If you are trying to frighten me," Norah announced calmly, "you are wasting your breath! If I were the type of woman to be afraid of bogeys, I would not have come west in the first place!" She opened the cupboard and inspected it for storage space. "There is considerable dust in here. I will wait to unpack until after you have cleaned it."

There was a muffled sound behind her, a Spanish expletive she did not understand. When she turned Elena was by the bed, and her smile had returned. She looked like a sleek cat, remembering countless dishes of cream. "You will like this mattress, *señora*. It is comfortable." She stroked the coverlet as if she were stroking a lover. "Very comfortable."

Everything became extraordinarily clear to Norah then, like moisture evaporating from a mirrored surface to reveal a hard, bright reality. She understood the reason for the woman's hostility: Elena had been Abner's mistress.

She made a valiant effort to rationalize her new and unwelcome knowledge. The Arizona Territory was a God-forsaken place, and women were scarce: if Abner had succumbed to loneliness, like many another man, and turned to his housekeeper for comfort, who was she to judge? The past was better forgotten. The important thing to remember was that she was his wife now. Wasn't it? Over the dull thud of her heart Norah heard her own voice come out with the same quiet authority she had used as a schoolteacher.

"I neither know nor care what your standing may have been in this household prior to my arrival; however, you may be certain that the situation is now considerably altered. If you have any thought to the contrary, it might be best for you to leave immediately."

Elena licked her lips nervously. "I do not know what the *señora* means."

Norah gave her a shrewd glance. "I think you do. I think we understand one another perfectly well: there will be only one mistress in this house—myself! If you wish to remain as housekeeper here you will have to earn your keep. I will be fair with you, but if things are not done to my satisfaction, you may expect me to make some wholesale changes. And now, I will inspect the premises on my own, so that you may get started on sweeping away this dirt and dust."

Elena left in a fury, but was cagey enough to keep quiet about it. *You will not last long here, my fine fancy señora. He will tire of you and you will learn fear. One day soon you will run back to where you came from like a frightened mouse. And then I shall be the mistress here.*

Norah sat on the edge of the bed, brushing the dust from her hands. It had been a most instructive day thus far. The sun was still high in the sky, and she had already learned several important facts: the raptures of love were nothing but poetic propaganda; her husband was brutal and callous, and her housekeeper had preceded her in Abner's bed. Well, she had chosen this life, and she would diligently apply herself to being a good wife, and make what she could of it.

The odor of roasted chicken wafted on the air, and her stomach rumbled. She decided she was becoming hardened by life in the Territory. Scant weeks ago such revelations would have sent her into a catatonic state; today she found herself wondering when lunch would be served.

After two months of marriage to Abner, Norah was a different woman than the one who had left Boston with her life before her. The abolition of her innocence, begun on her wedding day, seemed complete: love did not necessarily follow an exchange of vows, life was not a fairy tale, and Abner bore no resemblance to the heroes found in the deckle-edged volumes of Henderson's Lending Library.

She discovered other things as the days wore on, among them that she had the courage to endure a physical relationship that was increasingly distasteful, and an emotional one that was barren of hope for improvement. She also discovered that she was pregnant. The first week in September Dr. Porter made a housecall, and his examination confirmed Norah's hopes. She was jubilant. A child, a child of her own! Not even Elena's sour looks and sly insinuations were enough to dampen her spirits.

When Abner returned from town he came immediately into the bedroom where she was resting. "Well, what did Porter say?" he asked curtly.

She sat up and smiled with sudden shyness. "Dr. Porter confirmed that I am with child. Oh, Abner! We are going to have a baby!"

"He's sure?" Abner's face was alight. "That is good news indeed!"

Norah's heart warmed to him. A man who loved his children might learn something of tenderness in time; Abner's hatreds, fed by years of poverty, might one day be conquered. She could still build a life from the wreckage of her dreams. "He was most definite! It will be sometime in late April or May of next year."

"That's wonderful!" A sudden thought brought a frown to his face. "But what of the spotting?"

Norah blushed. "I am to stay off my feet for a few days and...and...we are to abstain from...intimate relations until the bleeding stops completely."

She was terribly concerned about Abner's reaction. He was insatiable in his needs. He was also still heedless of her discomfort and frequently rough in seeking his own satisfaction, as proved by the many small bruises hidden by her clothes. Although faint, they were a constant reminder of the volatility that underlay his passions.

"That won't be a problem." He ran his fingers down her arm and smiled. Yellow lights flared in his eyes. Norah tensed. She had learned to mistrust those strange smiles of his.

Abner laughed, and caught her face hard between his palms. "Why do you look at me like that? I won't do anything to harm my son. A man needs a son. And I need an heir for my empire!"

Disappointment brought tears to her eyes. Abner had not been thinking of the baby as a child to love and raise, but as a tool, an extension of his personality to further his power. She was relieved when Elena came silently into the room behind him.

"What is it, Elena?"

Abner whirled on the woman. "What do you want? I told you I won't have you sneaking around like a cat!"

Elena lowered her eyes, but her expression was one of sullen enjoyment. "*Señor*, Kincaid has sent for you," she announced in her rapid-fire Spanish. "He is in White Horse Canyon—the section above the Devil's Tongue, and requires you at once."

"Damn it, can't the man handle anything without me! What is it this time?"

"Some Indians have been nosing around up there. He thinks they are looking for the girl."

Abner's face was ashen when he turned to Norah. "Don't expect me back till nightfall." Without another word he was out the door, shouting for his horse.

Norah realized Elena was observing her intently. She pretended she hadn't understood the conversation. For some reason it seemed important not to let on. Day by day she was becoming more aware of a mystery about Abner and his business affairs. But *"the girl"*? What girl? "What has happened, Elena? Has there been an accident?"

The woman merely shrugged, apparently satisfied, and Norah picked up her sewing basket from the bedside table, then became aware that Elena was still watching her. She looked up.

"Did you wish to ask me something?"

Elena's upper lip curled. "Do not be so sure about the child, *señora*. Many things can happen between now and the springtime."

Norah gasped as if she'd been struck. "Is that some kind of threat?"

"Of course not. But this is a wild and lonely place. I only give you a warning." She was enjoying herself, and it showed. "A bad fall, a fever perhaps, a sudden fright... I only say to you, it is very early yet. Do not be too sure."

Suddenly Norah was frightened. There were certain herbs, certain medicines that could cause a woman to miscarry. Would Elena stoop to such things? "I will mention your... 'warning'...to Mr. Slade. Should it turn out to be in the nature of a prediction, he will remember what I will tell him. He wants this child very much."

Elena shot her a look of pure venom. "Don't worry, *señora*. You have nothing to fear...from me." She always backed down from a direct confrontation, but with every retreat her animosity grew.

Norah selected two lengths of soft flannel and a piece of muslin on which to trace and cut out patterns for the baby's layette. She was tired of lying abed, and went into Abner's office. The room had become her favorite place to sit, in defiance of Elena's proclamation. If Abner disliked it, he made no mention of the fact. Ensconcing herself in the big leather chair, she contemplated the pieces of flannel, wondering which was best suited to what article of clothing: gowns or jackets, short coats or bonnets, sacques or blankets? *How I miss Abigail! She could advise me on these fabrics. Perhaps I shall take*

*them along when we go to Camp Greenwood for the Jamboree
next week, and have a consultation.*

The colored cloth dropped to her lap. She could never think
of Camp Greenwood without thinking immediately of Sergeant
LeBeau. Would he be there for the races, or was he out in the
wilds somewhere? Did he ever think of her? Did he wonder
what had happened to her, just as she did of him?

Picking up her cutting shears, Norah began to follow the
lines she had traced in the yellow material, envisioning the final
product. She had cut out the front of a little gown when men's
voices came through the open window. One in particular
caught her ear.

"Tell Slade I'm here. I'm sure he's been expecting me for
some time."

Norah jumped to her feet, unable to slow the trip-hammer
rhythm of her heart. She knew that voice as well as her own.
It still haunted her dreams. Not able to decide if she should go
or stay, she suddenly found herself outside in the bright sunlight.

LeBeau stood between two of Abner's ranch hands, as
darkly handsome as ever, eyes wary and hot with anger. He
wore the same faded regulation trousers with an equally faded
blue shirt. His hair was longer, his face leaner and more dangerous than before. There was a large knot of injured flesh
swelling near his temple. He attempted to free himself at the
sound of her approach, fighting against the arms that held him;
but when he saw Norah he became as still as stone.

"Sergeant LeBeau!" She turned to Francisco, one of the
new hands. His face was bloodied, and he held a gun to the
Scout's ribs. "What is going on here?"

"We found him nosing around in the long barn, *señora.*"

"Release him." Norah hurried toward them, but the men
looked at each other and back to her again in confusion. "This
man is a friend from Camp Greenwood," she said indignantly.
"Release him at once."

"But *señora...*"

"That was an order, not a request!" Reluctantly they did as
she commanded. They shuffled their feet uneasily, and Francisco dabbed at his cut cheek. Norah ignored them. "Come

into the house, Sergeant, and you may tell me why an Army Scout is found hiding in one of my barns.''

''Thank you, but I must decline your kind invitation. I have business with your...husband,'' he added brusquely. There were so many things he wanted to say to her, yet her marriage hung between them, an impassable barrier. He saw the shadows beneath her eyes, heightening the color of her irises. Not a day went by that he didn't remember that open blue gaze and curse himself. He did not want to figure in her memory as a man so barbaric and uncontrolled that he had almost tumbled her in the stables like a common whore.

Norah's face, so pale before, burned with embarrassment at the recollection of their last meeting. She took refuge in her role as hostess. ''Would you care for some refreshment? A glass of cider or ale?''

''No.'' He couldn't swallow anything that belonged to Slade. Did she have any idea of the villainy her husband committed? Was she aware of his activities, or just another victim? ''I am here to see your husband on an urgent matter. He has been expecting me for some time. Where can I find him?''

''He is not here. I do not expect him back until tomorrow. He was called away. I cannot recall the name of the place.'' She crinkled her forehead. ''Ah, yes. White Horse Canyon.''

The change in LeBeau was frightening. His face was frozen into hard lines, his mouth stretching in a grimace. He looked inhuman, a statue cast in bronze, with fearful crystal eyes. She recoiled, and his hand shot out to take her wrist. Norah cried out, and he looked down. His fingers had curved over an area of skin stained by fresh bruises. Turning her cuff back, he disclosed another, fading and yellow.

''How did you get these?'' he asked in a low rough voice.

Flushing, she lowered her lids. ''I don't know. I bruise easily.''

He lifted her chin with one finger, searching her eyes. ''Don't lie to me. Did he do this to you?''

What right did he have to ask? He had rejected her, and rightly so, for she had belonged to another man, as much then as she did now. And there was the baby to live for, plan for. ''I cannot conceive of what possible interest my private life would hold for you, Sergeant LeBeau.''

Grinding his teeth, LeBeau dropped her hand. She was right. He had no business interfering in her life unless he had something better to offer her. And he had nothing to offer. Francisco and the other man watched their conversation from the shadow of the barn entrance. "I had better be on my way before your men have second thoughts about me."

He paused. "Have you ever seen your husband wear a gold ring? A ring with a mountain lion engraved on it?"

"The only ring my...Abner wears, is his wedding band. Though what business that is of yours either, I do not know!"

He grasped her shoulders and examined her closely. "Swear to me!"

"You are being ridiculous!"

"Very well." He straightened and released her. "There is nothing more to say, is there? Tell your husband I will be back soon to settle my business with him—for good!" LeBeau whistled, and a gray gelding came running from its place behind the stables. He vaulted onto its back. "Good day, *Mrs. Slade.*"

Norah did not go inside until the sound of his horse's hooves faded into the distance. Then she gathered her skirts and hurried to the bedroom. If Abner did have such a ring, she knew where it would be. She shut the door and went to his bureau. Taking out the carved wooden box from the top drawer, she lifted the lid. Lined with burgundy velvet, the upper tray held his best gold pocket watch, assorted shirt studs, and an ornate gold knife. In the lower tray she found a rose-gold chain, four cufflinks, and a circle of crushed velvet. It had been formed by the pressure of a heavy ring. There was no way of telling what the ring had been like, except for its diameter, clearly marked in the cloth. Why had LeBeau been so interested in Abner's ring?

A hinge squeaked. Replacing the jewelry box, she ran to the door and flung it wide. There was no one there, but she knew Elena had been spying on her.

Night came, but Abner was delayed. Norah sat by lamplight and cut out the baby clothes until her eyes were too weary. Yawning and stretching, she readied herself for bed, and was in a deep sleep when he arrived. It was past midnight. Still tangled in strands of sleep, she struggled upright. "What...? Oh, Abner! How you startled me!"

Whiskey fumed his breath, but underlying was another odor. Perfume, sweet and cloying. He'd been to Greenwood Junction. To Mercy's place. Norah had never seen the woman, but she knew her scent. The only thing she hated more than Abner's rough advances was having him come to her straight from Mercy's bed. At least the pregnancy would give her some respite.

She lay back on the pillow, trying to decide whether to tell him about LeBeau's visit now, or wait till morning. *I'll wait*, she decided. *There's no sense going into the whole thing tonight, especially when he's been drinking.* The night air was cool, and she burrowed under the covers. In a few minutes she was half asleep again.

Abner grunted and pulled his boots off. They clunked on the tiles, and a moment later his belt buckles hit them with a low metallic sound. Norah was barely aware of him as sleep lulled her. Then he climbed into the bed and reached impatiently for her. His hand grasped her breast through her nightgown as his mouth rooted wetly against her. He tugged her gown upward, and she came fully awake.

"Abner, we must not..."

His mouth left moist snail trails across her abdomen as his hands slid inside her thighs, forcing them apart. "Don't be coy with me. I'm not in the mood for it." He tried to thrust into her but Norah twisted away.

"Abner! Remember what Dr. Porter said! The baby..."

His frantic motions ceased. "I forgot."

She relaxed, expecting him to roll off her. Instead he laughed, and Norah's throat clogged with fear. "Ah, my innocent little wife! There is more than one way to skin a cat, as you will discover." Gripping her shoulders cruelly, he twisted her around. His voice was hoarse with excitement against her ear. "I see I have neglected your education. You do have so much to learn. And how I shall enjoy teaching you!"

8

Outside the walls of Camp Greenwood, the September Jamboree was in progress beneath a hot copper sun. It seemed to Norah that half the Territory must be congregated on the wide, flat plain for today's races. The women sat in the shade of a tent provided for them, waiting for the next group of riders to thunder by on their way to the finish line. Today, in deference to the heat and glare, they were all dressed in white or ivory, even the Colonel's wife, who usually affected the more somber colors suited to her age and station.

Mrs. Boyle, wife of the redoubtable little Colonel, sat on Abigail's right hand with Miss Tooms, her lingering houseguest, just beyond. Norah was on the other side, and heartily thankful for it. She liked Cora Boyle, but found her cousin intolerable.

Between races, as now, the other women worked at their embroidery, an occupation highly befitting a lady. Abigail, holding her hoop with trailing silks above her gravid abdomen, set precise stitches into a layette sacque of lightweight flannel: Norah, entranced with the barbaric spectacle of powerful beasts and expert riders, sat idle with her hands in her lap.

"It is *so* good to have you here with me again. I only wish I could persuade you to stay past the end of the week."

"You cannot know how sincerely I wish the same!" Norah replied with more asperity than she had intended: ten weeks of wedded life had been more than ample time to learn the cruel twists and turns of Abner's personality and habits.

Placing her embroidery aside, Abigail leaned toward her and spoke softly. "You do not look in good health, and I was concerned when you first arrived; however, seeing your lack of enthusiasm at the breakfast table, I concluded that you might find yourself in the earlier stages of an 'interesting condition.'" She dimpled. "How well I remember those first few months, when the very thought of food was revolting."

For the first time in weeks, Norah smiled spontaneously, and was unable to hide the sudden glow in her eyes. "You have guessed my secret! I meant to tell you when we were alone, but there has been no opportunity for a private coze. Abner will be going down to Mexico in November. If you like, I will stay with you from then until your baby is born."

"I should like that very much. The closer it comes to my time the more I realize how comforting the presence of another woman would be. Charles wanted me to go to Santa Fe for the lying in, but of course I would not leave him. And now Doctor Porter says I must not travel at all."

Seeing the smudges of exhaustion beneath Abigail's nut-brown eyes and the dull limpness of her once shining hair, Norah was doubly glad Abner had decided to come to the annual Jamboree. Abigail's small body had dwindled as her belly had swelled with child. She looked to be all eyes and bones, except for the advanced state of pregnancy that mounded her dress. The permanent flush had ebbed from her cheeks, and her skin had the translucency of fine china held up to the light. Her worried thoughts were interrupted by a flurry of activity at the other end of the course.

"It must be time for the next race." She peered toward the starting line. There was little to be seen down the length of the course except the clouds of glinting soil churned up earlier by the flashing hooves. A cry went up in the distance, and she rose to her feet. There they came, dashing over the hard-packed surface in veils of shimmering dust. A single dark shape emerged from the cloud, and Norah's heart drummed out a fast tattoo against her ribs as she recognized the heaving roan and its bronzed rider. They had won the big race the day before, but then the red gelding had worn a metal harness, and the man

astride it had been outfitted in the garb of an Indian Scout. This
time LeBeau rode bareback, the rippling muscles of his naked
chest and arms glistening with sweat.

Below the waist he wore buckskins and knee-high moccasins, rolled down at the top; above the waist he wore only a
piece of turquoise dangling from the thong about his neck. *He
looks as wild and fierce as any of the Indians*, Norah thought.
He is magnificent!

Sweeping past the tent, he dropped off one side of his mount
until his feet touched the ground, then vaulted up again as the
roan hurtled along. He repeated the maneuver from the other
direction. Swinging under the horse's belly and up its other
side, he crossed the finish line two lengths ahead of the rest,
drawing gasps from the watching women for his show of
equestrian skill.

"Did you ever see the like?" Abigail exclaimed.

"There is not another here to compare with Sergeant Le-
Beau," Norah agreed. "How splendid a rider he is!"

Miss Tooms gave her a look that combined astonishment
with censure. "I was not aware you were acquainted with any
of the troops, Mrs. Slade," she said in a shocked tone.

Abigail intervened with the adroitness of a good hostess.
"Perhaps you have forgotten that Sergeant LeBeau attended
my birthday dance—at my personal invitation. And of course,
he saved our lives one day when Norah and I were out in the
gig. He escorted us to and from Santa Magdalena for several
weeks after that."

Miss Tooms gave one of her unpleasant sniffs. "I am glad
to hear Captain Gartner's scouts are doing something more than
mingling with their filthy Indians! Why at Camp Verde they
are excused from all regular tasks." She knotted a thread and
cut a new piece of floss. "I fail to see why these Indian Scouts
are allowed to dress in such uncivilized fashion. Half naked
like savages!"

Mrs. Boyle eyed her houseguest with weary distaste. The
Colonel had reminded her pointedly that guests, like fish, became overripe in time; unfortunately, Miss Tooms, a third
cousin of Cora Boyle, hoped to acquire a husband in the
woman-scarce Territory. She showed as much sign of moving
on as did the mountains to the north.

"Those are General Crook's orders, and the Colonel agrees! The Indians that track with our scouts do not approve of uniforms. They cannot respect a leader who shows no individuality in dress, and that is why the General allows such latitude."

The explanation did not satisfy Miss Tooms. "Personally, I find it disgusting and unchristian for a white man to go about half-clothed like painted pagans. Why, look at that man over there, Mrs. Gartner! It is hard to distinguish whether he is a scout or one of the Indians."

"Well," Abigail replied coolly, "that is considered an advantage. And I believe many of the scouts are part Indian, themselves."

"Is Sergeant LeBeau Indian?" Miss Tooms asked, intrigued despite herself. "I had supposed him to be French, from his name."

"I doubt that Mrs. Gartner has taken the time to investigate the backgrounds of all the men assigned to Camp Greenwood, Hannah!" Mrs. Boyle said pointedly. "It is not her business to do so. And I would advise you not to concern yourself, either."

Miss Tooms turned an unbecoming red and fanned herself vigorously. "Personally, I *am* concerned to find us almost surrounded by these rag-tag Indians in their heathen clothing. Bits of bone and feather and animal hides! Savages!"

"Do you think them so different from us?" Norah asked with dangerous civility, fingering her long strands of ivory beads. "If you are judging by clothing alone, why your bonnet is decked with the plumage of some exotic fowl, and my own necklace is carved from the tusks of animals." She eyed Miss Tooms's hair brooch, formed from braided locks of the woman's deceased parents, but refrained from pointing it out as another example of her strange adornment. The spinster flushed unbecomingly, well aware of her intent, and went back to her needlework.

"One thing is sure," the Colonel's wife added. "No one else comes near them in daring horsemanship, except for that handsome Sergeant LeBeau. I do admire a man who sits a horse well!"

Abigail, ever the good hostess, broke in with a soft question, and the conversation drifted back to everyday matters, each taking turns like the players in a poker game. Abigail mentioned a new recipe for gammon, and Hannah Tooms raised her with a description of the shop in Philadelphia where she had purchased her tortoise combs. Mrs. Boyle added to the pot with the information that she had ordered several els of serviceable gray worsted, and had they heard that the oldest McKendrick daughter was engaged to Lieutenant Mitchell.

Norah had lost interest, and declined to ante-up. Her eyes followed one horse, one rider. LeBeau rode slowly along the sidelines, back toward the starting line, stopping now and then to accept congratulations from the onlookers. He was a magnet, attracting her eyes, attracting her thoughts. She was embarrassed by her continued fascination with him, but helpless to do anything but avoid him.

It's only that he was kind to me when I arrived in Greenwood Junction. And he is so very different from anyone I have ever known, she told herself unconvincingly. *And because a woman never forgets the first man who kissed her.*

LeBeau felt Norah watching him and slowed the roan. While seeming to ignore her presence, he had been acutely aware of her every movement from the corner of his eyes. He looked at her fully for the first time. Gray eyes met blue in a flare of sparks, a silent sensual acknowledgment of the attraction that still existed between them. Norah felt as if all the world could read her thoughts, and she glanced away immediately.

He watched the color creep into her cheeks, but without any feeling of satisfaction. She had intruded on his dreams last night, a shadowy and desirable woman, tormenting his thoughts and making sleep impossible; but now in the glaring afternoon light he thought he saw her more clearly. There was a womanly ripeness to her body that had not been there before. Even the way she looked at him was different, the look of a woman assessing a man. There was a new knowledge in her face and in her bearing. LeBeau was familiar with the white man's story of the first people: did Eve wear that same expression after tasting the forbidden apple?

She was no longer the fragile and frightened woman he'd helped in Greenwood Junction. No longer innocent of the sleeping sensuality that lay just below her quiet surface. She looked his way again, and he saw the reflection of his own hunger in her face. He smiled, singling her out with a mocking bow. His mouth twisted into sardonic lines. Another white woman, he sneered mentally, wondering what it would be like to lie with a soldier...or an Indian. Did she know he was Comanche? Would she care if she did? He swore softly under his breath. She was always in his thoughts, materializing in front of his mind's eye like a persistent ghost; and at night she was beside him in his bed, a specter of what might have been.

Damn her! He nudged his horse into a trot.

A man stepped in his path. Abner Slade. "I'll thank you not to insult my wife with your attentions, half-breed." Abner's eyes were narrowed to slits. He had seen the exchange of glances between Norah and the Scout. Was LeBeau the reason his wife shrank from his touch? Had there been something between them during the weeks he was detained in Mexico? Had LeBeau been there first? A red rage misted his vision.

"I'm talking to you, and you'd better listen. If I see you talking to my wife or bothering her, I'll put a bullet through you!" LeBeau turned the roan aside with a touch of his knees. It was as if he had not heard the other man. Abner moved in front of him again.

"What's the matter, *Sergeant*, have you spent so much time with your savages that you can't understand English anymore? Is that why you're dressed like a damned red Indian today, instead of a soldier? Reverting to your own kind?"

His diatribe was attracting keen-eyed observers now, and the continued silence of his intended victim added to his ire. LeBeau sat motionless on the sweating horse, staring straight ahead as if Abner did not exist. He fully intended a confrontation with Slade, but not now, not here in front of so many witnesses.

"Answer me, damn you!" Frustrated because there was no harness he could take hold of, Abner reached out and grasped at LeBeau's foot. For his pains he received a sharp kick to his wrist that sent a spear of agony lancing up his arm. Before he had time to do anything but cry out and cradle his injury, LeBeau had dismounted and was upon him. His hands curled around Slade's throat and tightened until his air rattled out in a strangled croak. "I can't breathe...."

"This," LeBeau said softly, "is how Samuel Blackwing and

the others must have felt when your poison worked its evil. Does it surprise you that I know? I suspected long ago that you're behind the tainted whiskey being sold to the reservations.''

''You're insane! You have no proof—'' His breath came in a harsh whistle, and he could no longer speak as the long fingers applied increasing pressure to his windpipe.

''No proof that would convince a white man's jury...yet! Your trail has been well-covered, Slade. But tomorrow, when my enlistment is up, I'll be able to follow my clues. And then I'll get enough evidence to hang you.''

Abner struggled to reply, but could not. His vision dimmed. His face grew crimson with engorged blood, then purple, and his tongue protruded. The pressure in his head was unbearable, but still the relentless fingers tightened, crushing the breath from him until his eyes started from their sockets.

Captain Gartner stepped between them. ''What the hell do you think you're doing, Sergeant? Give over!''

LeBeau lifted his adversary off his feet, shaking him as a terrior shakes a rat. He released Abner abruptly, dropping him into the dust. ''I have a score to settle with Mr. Slade,'' LeBeau said in deceptively soft tones. His eyes were cold steel.

''Well, settle it tomorrow when you're a private citizen again,'' the Captain ordered. ''You're one of my troopers, LeBeau, at least until tomorrow, and you're still under my command till then.''

He gave Slade, who was coughing and clutching his neck, a hard look. ''What the two of you do away from the Camp is your own business, but when it happens on my ground, it's my business. There may be bad blood between you two, but I won't have you conducting a feud on my Post. Especially in front of the ladies!''

LeBeau's jaw was rigid. ''Very well, Captain.''

With a careless salute he leapt onto his horse. Although his features were impassive as he trotted to the sidelines, his blood ran hot. He should never have let that scum-of-the-earth goad him into losing his temper. Well, it was under control now. He would take care of Abner Slade—but all in good time. Dismounting, he began to rub down his horse.

Meanwhile Abner followed Captain Gartner toward the

ladies' tent, ranting all the way. "I want that man court-martialed! I just asked why he was dressed like a damned Indian." He hurried to keep up with the other's pace, nursing his aching wrist. "LeBeau attacked me for no reason at all."

"You started this entire episode," Gartner replied curtly. He was in no mood to humor Slade in his grudge with LeBeau. Slade might be an important supplier of leather and tinned goods in these parts, but there was something about him that made Gartner's skin crawl. "If the ladies weren't present, I would have left the two of you to finish it. I don't know what started the animosity between you and my best scout leader, but I'll say this: I've never known LeBeau to act without just cause."

He lengthened his stride, leaving Slade behind in his desire to check on Abigail. The heat did not agree with her constitution. How relieved he would be when she was safely delivered of the child! Much as Gartner would love to have a son or daughter, he would have preferred to spare Abigail the risks of childbirth at all.

The thought of any danger to her was like a cold fist closing over his heart. She was precious to him, and many a night he would lie awake just for the pure joy of watching over her as she slept. In the past month his vigils had taken on a different aspect: he watched to make sure she was still breathing. His recurring nightmare was that he would awaken one night to find her lying dead in a pool of blood.

He quickened his pace and reached the tent with Slade on his heels. "Well, ladies, how are you enjoying the races and trick-riding?" His greeting encompassed them all, but his eyes were only for his young wife. She looked thin and wan except for her distended abdomen. "Are you feeling the heat, my dear?"

"Oh, no, it is so exciting! I'm enjoying myself, truly I am." She raised her eyes to her husband's face and the love between them was there for all to see.

Norah was struck with a bolt of envy at their undisguised affection. Her life with Abner was free of want and filled with the comforts his profits could provide, yet that could never make up for what the marriage lacked. Abner's need for success and hers for love were separate languages that neither could translate. *We are like two people standing on opposite cliffs, shouting into a high wind and unable to hear each other.* In the next instant all thoughts of her marriage were driven from Norah's mind. Abigail had fainted.

The Captain caught his wife before she fell from her chair, and Norah rushed to assist him. In her swoon, Abigail looked even younger than her eighteen years, the thin bones of her face sharp beneath their fragile covering.

"Get the wagon," Gartner shouted, and a private ran off to fetch the vehicle. While Mrs. Boyle fanned Abigail, Norah dampened her handkerchief with water and dabbed at the gray little face. When the vehicle pulled up, Mrs. Boyle and Miss Tooms followed in the Colonel's carriage while Norah sat beside the stricken girl and held her hand. They were at the house in a matter of minutes, and Abigail had still not roused from her swoon.

Gartner carried her to their rose and white bedroom. It was a cheerful room, not the scene for an impending tragedy, Norah thought, drawing back the white spread and embroidered linen topsheet. He placed Abigail on the bed, and the Colonel's wife bustled in and took charge. "Leave us for a while, Captain. We have work to do here."

A good officer knew how to take orders as well as give them. Gartner leaned over to kiss his wife's pale lips and left Mrs. Boyle in command of the field. He paused in the doorway. "You will call me immediately, when she rouses?"

He looked beseechingly at Norah, but Mrs. Boyle answered first. "She will be coming round any time now, Captain Gartner," she said stringently. "You go pour yourself a glass of brandy while you wait."

"Go," Norah added, placing her hand on his arm. "It is probably only the hot sun. We will loosen her stays to make her more comfortable, and that should help considerably."

Miss Tooms frowned disapprovingly as he left. "Need you discuss a female's intimate apparel with the Captain in that fashion? I am an unmarried lady, after all!"

"You do not need to remind us of *that*, Hannah." Mrs. Boyle smiled dryly as she placed a hand on Abigail's distended abdomen. "And there is no need for false modesty. Captain

Gartner has been married for over a year. I am sure he is quite familiar with women's undergarments.''

Miss Tooms was not soothed. "There is no excuse for indelicacy in front of a gentleman."

"Well, things are about to become more indelicate," the Colonel's wife announced. "I think you can best assist me, Hannah, by ordering some water put to boil and requisitioning a quantity of clean flannel; for if I am not mistaken, Mrs. Gartner is about to deliver her baby."

Miss Tooms left the room hurriedly with the air of one making a narrow escape. Norah helped loosen Abigail's corset, then checked her patient's pulse. It was rapid and weak, a sure sign of shock. "Her pulse is quite thready." Pulling back the sheet, they lifted Abigail's petticoats. They were saturated with blood.

Mrs. Boyle clucked her tongue sadly. "Send for the surgeon at once. She is hemorrhaging. She is losing the baby."

Norah whirled toward the door and down the steps, nearly colliding with Abner at the bottom. Without thinking, she pushed past him and hurried into the small drawing room. "Captain Gartner, you must summon the surgeon. Abigail is bleeding and Mrs. Boyle thinks...thinks the baby—" She stopped. How do you announce the end of someone's dreams to them?

Gartner's face drained of color until it was as pale as the small one in the bed upstairs. His features seemed to crumple for a moment, and in that brief span of seconds he looked his age and more. Then he straightened his shoulders. "Thank you." He went to the hallway and called out, "Corporal! Bring the surgeon here, on the double! Mrs. Gartner requires him urgently."

Norah climbed the stairs slowly, knowing already what would come to pass. She grieved in her heart for the young mother and her husband, and for the child that would never live to draw breath. Outside the bedroom she stopped to dash the tears away, calmed herself, and went in. Mrs. Boyle looked up and shook her head gravely. Abigail lay beneath the sheet like a marble effigy, and the room was filled with the hot metallic scent of blood.

The Post surgeon came and did what he could, which was precious little in the circumstances. Abigail was in some discomfort when she awakened, and much distressed. Had this been a normal birth, the pain of labor would have been mitigated by the joy of delivering a healthy child. But this was not a normal birth, and a funereal pall hung over the sickroom.

The surgeon administered laudanum drops in a glass of water, leaving instructions to repeat the dose during the night, if necessary. When labor began in earnest, Abigail gritted her teeth and clung to Norah's hand until it tingled and went numb. By evening it was over, and Abigail wept quietly against the pillows, her brown hair spread over her shoulders like a mourning shawl.

"It was a boy, wasn't it?" she said to Norah later while her tears dried upon her face.

"Yes. I am so sorry...so sorry." Norah clenched her jaw as she chafed Abigail's cold hands, trying to control her own emotions for the sake of her friend.

"I wanted so much to give Charles a son!" Despite her weakness, she insisted on sitting up against the pillows when Captain Gartner was at last allowed in to see her. Norah caught Mrs. Boyle's attention and nodded toward the door. They slipped out, leaving husband and wife alone together, but not before they heard Abigail's brave words: "There will be other babies, Charles. Strong, healthy children...."

As they went down the stairs Norah felt a sudden chill run along her spine, and she knew, without knowing quite how, that there would never be another child for Abigail and Charles Gartner. Later, in the stillness of her own room while Cora kept watch at Abigail's bedside, Norah was unable to sleep.

LeBeau, too, was wakeful. He unbound the thong that kept his hair restrained and raked his long fingers through it. In a few hours he would be gone. Everything he owned was rolled up in his saddlepack, ready to go. He got up from his pallet and went outside, squinting at the sliver of new moon that hung like a yellowed cheese rind against a black sky.

Someone sidled up to him. LeBeau didn't turn. He recognized the sound of those footsteps and the man's individual scent. A seam-faced Indian of indeterminate years stood next to him, dressed in a disreputable plaid shirt and new buckskin leggings. He was exceedingly fit, and few could have guessed his true age, for he looked much younger.

LeBeau did not ask how the newcomer had gotten into a Camp supposedly secured for the night. "What news do you bring, Limping Bear?" he asked the old man in the Comanche tongue.

"Two suns ago near Santa Fe, Horns-of-Buffalo and his men rescued Jumps High and Turtle, the Kiowa war chief. Much blood was shed and many horse soldiers were killed."

"Where are they now?"

"Heading this way, toward the canyon camp. We will have a large party when it comes time to join Iron Knife." He paused and his eyes skittered away from LeBeau's face and focused on something in the darkness. "I have other news, not good. See what I have brought you."

He held out his hand, and LeBeau pivoted silently to face him. A small copper disc, incised with the symbol of a flying dove, hung from Limping Bear's hand by a thin grosgrain ribbon. LeBeau's breath hissed on a sharp intake of air. The last time he had seen the ornament, it had rested against Dove-in-Flight's breast.

"Where did you get this?"

"A trader on the Santa Fe Trail. He won it from a man in a game of euchre. That man, he traded for it with a Navajo at the Blackwater Mission." Limping Bear made a brief facial twitch in the direction of the stables. "The Navajo, he stole it from the man who sold you that red horse."

"*Slade!*" LeBeau's hand closed over the copper disc and the lines of his face hardened into granite planes. Although the disc was still not enough proof to bring before a jury, it was enough for him. The last doubt was gone, and with it the last hope. Dove-in-Flight was dead.

LeBeau turned his face away. A falling star blazed whitely against the western sky. He did not see it. The breeze ruffled the strands of his shoulder-length hair. He did not feel it. For a time he felt dead. Cold and dead. He closed his eyes tightly, trying to blot out the nightmare images that rose in his brain. *Little Dove! Little Dove!*

A spasm of agony gripped LeBeau, as if his heart had ruptured and bled into his chest cavity from the violence of his

emotions. It was only because of that pain that he knew he was
still alive. It spread slowly outward, and with it came a warmth
that changed into a burning, caustic heat. Hatred poured
through his veins like acid, eating away the thin gloss of civilization that held his passions in check. His hand curled around
the piece of cool, smooth copper. "I will keep this."

"You have the look of death in your eyes, my son," the old
man said in low tones. "I will be with you in this."

"No!"

His voice was a harsh whisper and a sentry, prowling his
watch, looked in their direction. LeBeau and Limping Bear
melted into the inky pools of blackness formed by the right-
angled barracks wall, and remained motionless for several
minutes. Satisfied that he had only heard a trooper muttering
in his sleep, the sentry continued on his rounds. When he was
gone, LeBeau spoke rapidly in the Comanche tongue.

"Take this message to Horns-of-Buffalo: I will discover how
the man called Abner Slade came to have my gift to Dove-in-
Flight, and he shall answer to me. *To me!* No other hand shall
touch him!" LeBeau's gray eyes darkened until they looked as
black as his companion's.

Limping Bear's eyes glimmered like nuggets of coal.
"Horns-of-Buffalo says that many hands finish a task swiftly."

Abner Slade and his kind had taken away everything LeBeau
had ever valued, destroyed everything he had ever loved: his
way of life, his peace of mind, his mother, and now, Dove-in-
Flight. "Tell Horns-of-Buffalo this also: the trap that is most
carefully laid is the one that is most deadly." The smile that
curved his mouth upward was chilling.

"Do you know where to find this one called Abner Slade?"

"He rode out earlier today, heading across the plain past
Pointing Rock. Pick up his trail and leave me signs along the
way. I will catch up with you before sundown." He smiled
grimly. "Well before sundown!"

The old man nodded and seemed to dissolve into the moonlight as soundlessly as he had appeared. LeBeau remained
where he was, tears of rage blinding his eyes. The moon rode

high in the sky, and still he stood there, holding the disc so tightly that the sharp edge cut into his palm and blood ran down between his fingers.

He did not even notice.

9

The bugler called reveille at 5:30 A.M. The morning was gray and bleak, the sun only a promise as it sent thin rays above the crack of the horizon. An early chill had come down out of the northwest, dropping the temperature low during the long night and prophesying a cruel winter. While Norah slept in the big armchair beside Abigail's bed, a meeting took place in the Captain's office.

Captain Gartner had not slept, but his chin was clean-shaven and his back straight as he sipped his morning coffee and argued with LeBeau. Death came frequently to harvest the inhabitants of the Arizona Territory, but life continued. At least the surgeon had been able to save Abigail, and she was all that mattered to him: he knew that now, more than ever. Despite his personal sorrows, he was still the commander of the Camp, and he did not default his duty.

"Ten dollars more a month," he repeated. "But only because you're my best Scout."

"I have things to do, and I can't do them in the uniform of the U.S. Cavalry," LeBeau said quietly. The copper disc that hung upon his breast glinted with the dull morning light, and his gray eyes were hooded, his face reserved almost to the point of blankness.

"Ten dollars more, and a one-grade increase in rank. I've already talked to General Crook, and he'll sign for it."

"No, thank you, sir."

The Captain sighed and rubbed his chin, as a reluctant grin eased lines of care from his expression. "I see that you mean it. You've never stuck to protocol in addressing me before, have you, LeBeau?"

"No. A scout has to maintain his pride with all you West Point fellows, somehow, sir." LeBeau looked at the Captain, and slow smiles spread over both their faces.

"I think it's time for a compromise, then. I'll grant you a leave of absence if you'll sign on for another hitch when the leave is up. All other offers will hold good, too. That's the best I can do."

LeBeau hesitated. He had no intention of coming back, but Gartner had been more than his Captain, he had been a friend. He saw how important this was to the older man and pondered his decision. "I can't answer for myself six months or a year from now. You grant me the leave of absence, and I will decide whether or not to re-enlist when the time comes. That is the best *I* can do."

Now it was Gartner's turn to be silent. His fingers tapped the top of the desk. At last he sighed. "All right. I'm not happy about it, but I realize I can't sway you. Good luck to you."

He offered his hand, and LeBeau gripped it. "And good luck to you, too." He grinned. *"Sir."* With a wave of his battered hat, he strode out into the new day.

Before the yellow ball of sun rose over the rim of rock to the east, LeBeau was on his way. As the Camp gates were swung wide he rode through, never once looking back. He wore buckskin breeches and a shirt of faded blue cloth along with his campaign hat and Army-issue boots; and he wore the copper disc with the bird symbol that Limping Bear had brought him around his neck on a slim leather thong.

Everything he owned was either on the prancing roan or on his own back, except a trapping cabin his father had built in the mountains far to the north and west. LeBeau had no intentions of ever claiming that legacy. He was turning his back permanently on the white man's way of life, and returning to his people.

He was going home, or rather to what was left of it: in the Texas Panhandle, Chief Quanah Parker's people had been joined by some Kiowas and a few others in evading the greedy hand the Great White Father held out to his Red Children. Iron Knife would be joining Quanah Parker, and they would ride together into the last battle for their freedom and heritage.

But first, he had a score to settle, deaths to avenge. He was certain beyond doubt that Slade was behind the adulterated firewater that had killed many Indians; and in his heart he had known for some time that Dove-in-Flight was dead, but had not been able to face that terrible truth. Now he had even more reason to hate Abner Slade.

Instead of turning east toward New Mexico Territory, he would ride west a while, then south, to pick up Limping Bear's trail. His only regret, as the horse picked its way through a rock-strewn section, was that his anger had led him to tip his hand to Slade about the poisoned whiskey, for now he would be on his guard. Well, no use repining. He had other things to take care of now.

First he would stop in Greenwood Junction. He had promised to say goodbye to one of Mercy's girls before he left, and there was a trinket in his shirt pocket for her. He would rather not make the detour, but Maria was a nice girl, he thought, and she had saved his life once. Besides that, a promise was a promise, and when he gave his word, he kept it. The day warmed as he rode, but an underlying nip in the air foretold that the hot summer had run its course. The climate in the valley would remain mild, but up on the plateau and in the mountains winter's chill breath would already be shriveling the plants and sending the animals into their nests and burrows.

He rode into town just as the stage pulled in, and that made him think of Abner Slade's wife. She had invaded his mind, waking and sleeping, from the day that they had met, and he was glad he'd left Camp Greenwood. Since she had arrived there, his obsession with the woman had grown worse: he had found himself watching her, keeping track of her movements against his will. With a quiet oath LeBeau slid from the saddle.

He hitched his horse and strode into Mercy's brothel, creating quite a stir among the unoccupied ladies of the place. He glanced around the parlor; the fat-legged piano hidden beneath a flowered and fringed cloth, the heavy furniture covered with glasses and half-filled decanters, the cheap gee-gaws all met with a disdainful look. Women in various stages of dishabille sat or lounged around the room, waving fans of silk and paper and painted chicken skin to cool their sweating faces.

"Will you look who's here, girls!" The skinny blonde lounging on the brown velvet divan had applied several coats of blacking to her lashes, and it had melted and run down beneath her eyes. She was not a favorite with the other girls, and none had bothered to tell her to repair her face. She tried a provocative smile at LeBeau, unaware of her bizarre appearance. "Thought you'd left town permanent, Sergeant."

Mercy came from the back room, rustling as she walked in a tight gown of bottle-green fabric that made her hair seem the color of fox fur. Her eyes looked the same color in the light that filtered through the heavy gold draperies at the tall windows. "Looking for 'Paches, Sergeant? I reckon that's the only reason you'd come in to my place." Nervous titters of laughter followed her sally.

"I'm here to see Maria," he answered coolly, hiding his disgust at the musk and civet smell that emanated from Mercy. More than one painted face showed disappointment at his reply.

"So that's it! You have an eye for the young 'uns. Well, if I'd known that sooner, you and I might have done some business, Sergeant. But around here, even talking costs money."

He took a silver coin from his pocket and threw it at her. Quick as a cat, she caught it in one greedy paw. "Maria! Customer! Get a hustle on."

This time LeBeau didn't bother to hide his feelings. He turned his back on her and strode out to the stairway. A girl came running down the steps in a flurry of petticoats and a cloud of heavy fragrance. She was small and pleasingly rounded, with a child's artless face beneath the carefully applied rouge and lip pomade.

"Ah, I knew you would keep your promise," she said, laying a plump hand on LeBeau's arm. She saw the expressions on the other faces. "Let's go up to my room where we can be undisturbed." Her eyes were hopeful. She had never yet been able to get him into her bed, but perhaps now...

"I can't stay, Maria."

Her face fell. "Well, at least let us talk in private." Perhaps he would change his mind when they were alone.

She turned toward the stairway and gestured for him to follow. Reluctantly he fell in alongside her, and they mounted the steps in silence. She led him down the left corridor, stopping at the third door on the right and flinging it open. It was a small room with a large bed and not much else in the way of furnishings, except for the washstand and the ormolu mirror above. Here and there were a few attempts to personalize the surroundings: a bright Mexican rug, a chipped pottery vase, a blue and green peacock feather thrust into the frame of the looking glass. There was a rag doll with hair of yellow yarn on the plain white counterpane covering the bed: it was worn and faded but appeared to be much loved.

LeBeau surveyed the room with sadness. He examined Maria's face as she smiled up at him. "How old are you?" he asked softly.

"Nineteen," she said quickly. Too quickly.

He took her chin in his hand. "How old?"

Something in his expression made her tell him the truth. "F-fourteen last month."

LeBeau cursed long and fluently. "Why are you here? Who brought you to this place?"

She shrank before his wrath. "My father…sold me to a man… There was no money, no food at home. Here I am well fed, and I have my own bed. It is not so very bad."

"Isn't it?" The gray eyes regarded her for a long moment. He shook his head.

Maria threw her arms around his waist. "Let us not talk of things past. I have wished that you would come up to my room with me, oh, so many times! You do not really mean to leave now, do you?"

"I brought you something," he said to change the subject. Her attention was immediately diverted as he removed the pretty bangle from his pocket and held it out to her.

Maria took the necklet with a small cry of pleasure. "I have only had one present before," she said, clasping it about her throat. She ran to the mirror and preened, tilting her head to one side, her reflection eyeing him coyly. She laughed and opened a small box on the washstand, taking out a bracelet of shell inlaid with squares of iridescent abalone and slipping it on her wrist. "Do you like it?"

Instantly LeBeau's long fingers reached out and curled around her arm. "Where did you get that?"

"From a man. Are you jealous?" She tried to dance away, flirting with her long lashes. Maybe LeBeau would stay with her after all. Then she saw the look in his eyes, and knew the emotion that hardened and darkened them to slate was not jealousy.

"Was that man Abner Slade?" He didn't even need to hear her reply. It was written all over her. He dropped her arm, not realizing he had bruised her flesh. If there had been any trace of doubt in his mind that Slade was implicated in Dove-in-Flight's disappearance, seeing her bracelet on Maria's arm had removed it completely. He went toward the door.

"How did you know?"

She stared at him. He was like some terrible idol carved in stone, his features twisted into a terrifying mask. Then LeBeau opened the door and went out. Maria crossed herself hastily and ripped the bracelet from her wrist. Although she didn't know why, she felt that someone would die because of it. "I think I do not like this anymore," she told herself as she put the piece of jewelry away. "I will give it to Amalia."

LeBeau went out into the hot and dusty street. He untied his horse and was about to get into the saddle when the blacksmith called out to him. He led the roan by the bridle as he went toward the shed at the far end of the road.

Several naillike spikes protruded from the smithy's mouth, like ugly metal teeth. He removed them and put down the piece he was repairing. "Heard tell yer done with the Indian Scouts."

LeBeau nodded. He saw no reason to advertise his arrangement with Gartner.

The other man wiped his hands on his leather apron in a nervous gesture. "Well, there's something you should know. Abner Slade—him that sells the leather goods—seems he had a horse stolen. Or so he says. A roan gelding, seventeen and three-quarter hands, with an X-bar-X brand on the rump and a half-moon scar on the left fetlock."

The roan whickered softly and swished his tail from side to side. LeBeau looked from the horse to the smith. His voice was a lazy drawl, but every muscle in his frame tensed. "And have you seen a horse that matches that description?"

"Nope." The smith picked up an iron bar and put the end over the fire to heat. "Just thought I'd mention it to you."

LeBeau nodded. "I appreciate the information." He swung into the saddle, and the roan gelding with the X-bar-X brand and the half-moon scar cantered easily away with its rider. Once out of the little town, however, LeBeau kicked the horse into a gallop, anxious to keep his appointment with Fate.

As he rode on, LeBeau's thoughts took a course he didn't like. He found himself thinking of a woman, a woman with skin like fresh cream, hair like a black velvet night, and eyes the color of the pale turquoise from Lost Canyon.

He wondered what would happen to Slade's wife when her husband was dead, as he soon would be. He wondered if she would pack her things and go back to wherever she came from. He wondered again why he cared.

"Damn the woman!" he said aloud, and the roan pricked up its ears. Resolutely, LeBeau put her out of his mind.

He reached the point where he thought to pick up Limping Bear's trail by midafternoon, but there was nothing to indicate the Indian messenger had returned this way. He circled the area before going on, moving through the mesquite and round junipers until he came to the scraggly cedars that rimmed the edges of the creek. The water was low, no more than a trickle now, but he had seen it roaring with the torrents of the spring run-off, washing away trees and rocks and any creature unfortunate enough to fall into the churning maelstrom of rushing brown waters.

His search was rewarded. Off to the left he found the marks of Limping Bear's moccasins. He dismounted, hiding his horse in the bushes. Limping Bear had done the same, it seemed, then doubled back and ridden off toward a wooded canyon that slashed deeply into the earth about a mile ahead. The breeze riffled the branches above. Suddenly he smelled cedar, and with it came the scent of danger. There was no sound, no moving thing in sight to trigger his instincts, and yet there was no doubt in his mind. Then the light shifted, and the feeling passed.

There was something scuffed in the reddish dirt at the base of a tree. They would have looked like random marks in the sand to any other man, but LeBeau recognized the code that he and Limping Bear had devised long ago. The message was of two men on horseback, and above that symbol, a bird in flight. Abner Slade was on the trail ahead, and he was not alone. Thus warned, LeBeau continued on his way, leaving no footprints as he stepped over the rocks, and circled back to his steed. He would catch up with Limping Bear by nightfall.

The rest of the afternoon was quiet, and eventually he approached a vulnerable point, a crest of rock that overlooked a wide valley on the left and a deep crevasse on the right. For a matter of seconds he would be silhouetted against the sky before plunging into the relative safety of the oak and aspen cover. Limping Bear had come this way with no signs of trouble: there were his tracks in the red earth and dried needles and leaves alongside the limestone platform.

LeBeau emerged from the screen of brush into the full sunshine. The rays were bright in the open, and the copper disc that dangled against his bare chest seemed to brand his skin. He felt a presence around him, heard ghost whispers of warning. He looked around but saw nothing.

He came out on the rim into bright golden sunlight. LeBeau felt the shot before he heard the ricochet from the rock, or the sharp crack and dull echo of the report. He was unseated from the force of it, and his horse reared dangerously above him. He rolled out of the way. The bullet had hit the copper disc at an angle and deflected to his shoulder, just missing his left lung. LeBeau cursed and stuffed his wadded bandana against the wound, vainly trying to stem the crimson flow that stained his blue shirt. He was bleeding heavily. The horse shied again, and he raised himself to grab the rifle from his pack, knowing the animal's body would shield him. Another shot shattered the air, striking the limestone ledge behind him, making it ring discordantly, like the strings of an untuned harp.

He threw himself sideways, then scrabbled away down the path, zig-zagging into the woods. The blood was streaming from his arm now, and his hands were slick with it. He hid in a small eroded hollow beneath the roots of an oak and waited for the enemy to show. From the direction of the rifle fire he knew that there were at least two of them. As he waited, a wave of nausea and dizziness rolled over him, carrying him almost to unconsciousness on a tide of pain. He mastered the sensations and rolled into the wound, hoping his weight would help to staunch the bleeding. A sea of agony crashed down on him and mercifully, he lost consciousness. After a time he came to, and heard the sound of voices. He recognized one.

"That'll teach that goddamned half-breed to steal a white man's horse," Abner Slade was saying to his unseen companion. "The sumbitch must've fell down the bottom o' the ravine!"

"Well, the buzzards'll finish what's left o' him," the other replied in a gravelly voice. "No one never made it out o' the Devil's Chimney alive." He cleared his throat. "Now, just give me that there five dollars ye promised, I'll be on my way to Greenwood Junction, and not a word said t' anyone."

Stealthily LeBeau reached for his rifle. If he could only get that bastard in his sights! The effort cost him too much, and black holes appeared in his vision, growing until they blotted everything else out. When he came around again his attackers had gone, taking the roan with them. He gritted his teeth in angry resignation. *Not here then, and not now, Abner Slade, but soon. Soon.*

When the stars came out, Limping Bear found him. Hatred and the need for vengeance had kept LeBeau alive. His shirt was glued to his skin by the dried blood. He was weak, but the bleeding had stopped, and his brain was clear.

"We must not stay here," Limping Bear told him as he bandaged his comrade's wound. "This is an evil place, and it is better to travel in the dark and take our chances with the ghosts that roam at night, rather than remain."

LeBeau nodded agreement, remembering the psychic whisper he had heard. There was something in the atmosphere of this place that wasn't quite right. He rode postillion behind the other man for what seemed like endless hours. Before dawn they stopped, and he almost fell from the horse while dismounting.

"Wait quietly. I will bring you a horse," Limping Bear said, making a place for the injured man to rest.

LeBeau slept a short time, and woke when Limping Bear returned. He got on the horse the old man had stolen for him, and they continued their interrupted journey, circling the perimeter of the valley.

Every movement sent hot blades stabbing into his shoulder,

but LeBeau gritted his teeth and rode as swiftly as possible. When they came to a certain spot in a place that overlooked deep gorges and high-walled canyons, he pulled his mount to a halt.

"Wait here. I will not be long." He slipped from the saddle and made his way over the broken ground. He was lightheaded but walked with a sure tread, for he knew this place well. There was a cave hidden just a few feet away.

LeBeau went into the cave. He took off the dirty campaign hat, the faded shirt, the leather boots and belt. He levered up a flat slab of rock, although it cost him much effort. Beneath the stone was a large package wrapped in an oilskin. Inside it were a buckskin shirt, soft moccasin boots, and a suede talisman pouch. He put them on, chanting under his breath as he did so. Then he took everything but the Army field boots, wrapped them in the oilskin, and hid them in a depression beneath the flat slab of rock along with his separation papers and his gold watch. One day he might want them, but he had no use for such things now.

He stood up carefully, holding his injured shoulder. When he came out of the cave, Limping Bear saw the difference immediately: Sergeant Roger LeBeau of the Camp Greenwood Indian Scouts had gone into the cave and a Comanche warrior had come out.

The old man raised a hand in salute. "Welcome back, Storm Caller, Rider-of-Storms. Welcome back."

The man who had been LeBeau made no answer. None was needed. He mounted his horse and the two Indian warriors rode off into the night.

10

Abigail Gartner recovered from her miscarriage with Norah's gentle nursing. Now, after three weeks, Norah was back home in her own bed, wondering if her pregnancy was doomed to end as Abigail's had. The spotting had begun the day of her return from Camp Greenwood, becoming heavier each day. She patiently endured Dr. Porter's examination and awaited his verdict.

He was a faded, earnest man with a sandy small moustache that matched his thin hair, and Norah trusted him. He wiped his hands on the towel and arranged his spectacles more securely on his nose.

"I am sorry, Mrs. Slade, but I can neither offer assurances that you will carry the child to term, nor guarantee that a subsequent pregnancy will be more successful. Only time will tell."

He cleared his throat and looked away from her white and distressed face. "I will give you a tonic and a list of precautions to follow. Meanwhile, you are to stay at bedrest and avoid all excitement, and…ahem…all the other strictures I gave you on my previous visit."

"I will do my best."

Dosing Norah with a vile-tasting brown medicine, he left the bottle on her bedstand and closed his bag. "If you do begin to bleed again, I think we would be wise to let it take its course: I fully believe that there are times when Nature knows best.…"

Norah nodded and tried to form a brave smile, but tears brimmed over and spilled down her face. She understood what Dr. Porter was saying: there was something very wrong with the pregnancy or with the baby itself.

"Thank you, Doctor."

He went out, closing the door behind him. Norah expected Abner to come in, but the door remained shut. After a time she became drowsy from the medication, and slept.

She awakened with a ravenous thirst, but the pitcher on her bedstand was empty. Ringing the small brass bell Abner had provided was useless. Elena was either outside, or was not bothering to answer. Lately she had taken to disappearing for long periods in the afternoon, and Norah suspected the woman of slipping out to be with one of the ranch hands. Elena was not the kind of woman to remain long without a man.

Norah got out of bed unsteadily and wandered through the house. Neither Abner nor Elena was there. She dipped some water from the stone jar they kept filled for that purpose. It was refreshing and cool. As she took another drink, an erratic pounding came from the entry door.

As quickly as she could, Norah crossed the tiles and opened the door. A young man leaned against the jamb, pale and sweating. His lips were blue and swollen, and she scarcely recognized him at first.

"Francisco! What is wrong? Are you injured?" There were no signs of blood on his clothing or about his face that she could see.

He wavered on his feet and Norah reached out to steady him. "*Señora Slade…por favor. Agua, por favor!*" Francisco fell to the floor writhing and clutching his abdomen. His face had taken on a ghastly hue, and bits of foam clung to his lips.

"Where are you hurt? Tell me!" Norah knelt beside him, horrified and bewildered.

"*Poison…Almirez…the barn…the long barn…*"

She ran to fetch the water he'd begged for, but by the time she returned there was no need. He lay as he had fallen, his body twisted at the waist, his face contorted, the eyes vacant as his last breath came out in a final sigh. *Such a tiny sound for a soul escaping*, she thought in horror, dropping the dipper. Water splashed across her bare feet and on the chest of the corpse. She knelt and closed the eyelids over the blank eyes, then stood up, shivering violently with reaction.

She had only seen the face of Death once before, when the consumptive teacher had died at Miss Emerson's. That demise had been peaceful and unthreatening. Francisco's agony and death were obscene. She turned and ran, calling for Abner. It seemed to take forever to get to the doorway. The ground was hot and stony on her bare feet, but she didn't want to waste the effort in going back.

There was not a soul in sight. She remembered that Francisco had said the name of Almirez, another of the new men. A terrible thought grew in her mind. Perhaps all the hands were dead or dying! Was it food poisoning? What could they have eaten?

And where was Abner? He said something about a repair in the bunkhouse. Late sunlight struck the door handle of the building as she made in that direction. Twice the gripping abdominal pain came back and she had to rest, but this was an emergency! Norah forced herself to go on, and when she reached the bunkhouse she heard a man's voice. Abner's voice.

"Oh, thank God! Abner, come quickly! There has been an accident—"

She flung the door open without thinking, and what she saw there was burned into her brain. Even with the windows shuttered she could clearly see the spartan bunks, the family photos and girly posters on the walls. And in the lower bunk facing the door, Abner and Elena lay coupled, their naked limbs entwined and filmed with sweat.

Norah was speechless with this new shock, and could only stare. For a moment Abner was frozen with surprise, but Elena smiled in lazy triumph. He leaped up and grabbed his trousers. "What do you mean by spying on me? You're supposed to be in bed."

Elena rose to her knees and stretched, her hands clasped behind her neck. Her body was lean and supple, with small pointed breasts. She showed triumph, not shame at having been caught in adultery with her mistress's husband.

"She is jealous, no? Because she cannot keep her man satisfied."

Norah took a step back, collided with something, and fell

heavily. Pain tore through her again, and she gasped. Elena laughed at her clumsiness. Abner wheeled on his paramour. "Shut up, you bitch, and give me a hand with her!" He bent to pull Norah up.

She flung herself away from him. "Don't touch me! Don't either of you touch me!"

She sat up against the wall and faced him. "Francisco is dead! He came to the house and said something about poison...and the long barn. I think Almirez might be stricken also."

Abner clenched his hands and cursed violently. "I told them to stay out of there!" He put his boots and shirt on hastily, then looked at Elena. "Take the *señora* back to the house and get her into bed. Can't you see she is ill?"

"I am not her servant! You cannot expect me to be a nurse to your wife! She bears your name, but I am the one who warms your bed." Elena faced him angrily, her naked body gleaming in the dim light.

Abner grabbed the woman's arm and shook her. "You! You are nothing but a slut, and you'll do as I say. Norah is my wife. Never forget that she bears not only my name, but my child— and if you do anything to harm my child, you will be more sorry than you can even imagine!"

"What will you do, kill me, too? I am not a young girl to be lulled by your soft words like that other one. It will not be so easy to dispose of me!" Fear lurked behind the defiance in her voice.

Abner's face was a mask of rage, and webs of veins swelled at his temples. "Cross me, and you will see!"

He flung Elena from him and went out. The woman curled her lip and followed Abner through the door, pulling on her blouse and skirt as she went. Norah struggled to her feet and sat down on one of the other bunks, burying her face in her hands. She was physically ill, less from the threatened miscarriage than from the day's ugly revelations. Even the knowledge that Abner had lain with Elena was nothing in the face of the death of two men, and now Elena's words. What had she meant? Norah stood up dizzily. There was only one way to find out. She would have to confront Abner.

Halfway to the long barn a shaft of pain ripped through her

abdomen. She reached for the edge of the wagon that stood between her and the barn, but fell forward into the dust, trying to break the fall with her out-thrust hands. A spreading blackness ate away at the edges of her vision, and Norah closed her eyes. She lay there, sweating and clammy, while waves of nausea surged through her. Two men began shouting near at hand, and at last their words penetrated her numbed mind.

"And I say it's *your* fault, Mr. Slade. You can't blame me. They found the poisoned swill you've been selling to the Indians and drank it before I knew anything about it."

Norah opened her eyes. Through the spokes of the iron-banded wagon wheel, she saw Abner and Joe Kincaid coming out of the long barn. Kincaid's face was ruddy above his thick buffalo neck, and his black eyes were wary. Abner's hands were fisted at his sides, and impotent fury was written in every line of his body. She saw his hand steal to his side, but his gun and gunbelt still hung in the bunkhouse where he'd left them.

"Shut your goddamned mouth, Kincaid! I don't know what the hell you're talking about."

"I'm talking about the one-hundred-proof 'eye-wash' you've got in them barrels that have the X-bar-X mark on them, instead of your puma brand. There's stacks of 'em in the long barn. I just smelled that stuff, and if there ain't shellac thinner or something mixed with it, I'm the King of England! And that's the stuff what killed them Apaches and set them others off killing and raiding. You're behind it all, aren't you?"

"You're out of your mind, and I don't take that kind of talk from anyone. Get out of here. Get off my land!"

Abner's low growl held loathing and a tremor that Norah realized was fear, not merely anger. She didn't want to believe the man's accusations, but there was a ring of certainty to his voice. She sat up, but had to put her head against her knees and wait for the world to stop spinning. The pain in her abdomen had turned to a deep, persistent ache.

"Yeah, I'll get off your land. If you really want me to," Kincaid huffed. "And I'll go straight to the Federal Marshal in Tucson."

Abner's eyes narrowed. "I wouldn't be too hasty if I were you."

"Yeah?" The man stepped back. "Why not?" There was a challenge in his manner, but he still gave ground.

"Let us just say it might be worth your while." Abner's voice flowed like silk. "You're a bright fellow, I can see that. You're wasting your talents as a ranch foreman. I need someone with your qualities in my…other business dealings. Why, I need someone like you so badly I'd be willing to pay a good bonus if you'd start right away. A very good bonus."

Norah's body quivered with the outward signs of the revulsion that filled her soul. She had lived with Abner as man and wife, and she carried his seed within her. The seed of a murderer. Without warning, another sharp ache radiated from her spine to her abdomen, like a knife twisting deep in her womb. She knew with a woman's instincts that she would not give birth to a living child from this pregnancy. Even Abner's own child repudiated him.

Kincaid cleared his throat. "All right, you got a deal. But I won't sell no poisoned whiskey to no Indians."

"You won't have to. I take care of that myself. Just remember that Francisco and Almirez would still be alive if they hadn't meddled in my affairs. Greed and curiosity killed them."

Abner started walking again. "It's a good thing the other hands are on the far side of the valley today. In the morning I'll want you to get those barrels moved out. Take them up to White Horse Canyon and hide them in one of the caves." There was a pause.

"First, we'll bury the bodies. I'm leaving for Tucson tomorrow. We'll give out that Francisco and Almirez went with me. When I get back I'll say we were ambushed by Apaches; that the two men fought bravely, but we were outnumbered."

Kincaid's voice was hesitant. "Almirez is still alive."

"Take care of it. I don't want any witnesses."

"Right."

They came around the wagon, hashing out the details of moving the barrels, and then Abner saw Norah, lying face downward on the ground. He swore and knelt down beside her.

"Norah? Are you in pain? Is it the baby?"

Through the haze of anguish she heard his voice, saw his hands reach out to lift her.

"Don't touch me! I meant what I said earlier. Don't ever touch me again!"

Ignoring her outburst, Abner picked her up and carried her into the house.

It was difficult living in the same house with a murderer. Every day Norah's physical strength increased, and with it the desire to escape from her nightmare marriage. Life in Boston had been a purgatory of boredom, but life with Abner had become Norah's hell. At least he slept on a cot in the spare room, while she occupied the bedroom alone. She had not lost the baby yet, and that was the only reason for his forbearance. The obsession for an heir to his business empire had taken deep root in his mind, and was far stronger than his lust for his wife. Abner talked of a son with single-minded certainty, but Norah knew in her heart that it was only a matter of time before she completed her miscarriage. Her abdomen was almost back to normal now—the baby was not growing and she felt no spark of life within.

She could not go on this way. She had hoped by now to hear from a friend who had been a fellow teacher at Miss Emerson's Academy. Norah had written to Belinda shortly before her marriage, but no reply had arrived. Surely she would hear from her any day. Propped up on pillows in her bed, Norah drafted another letter to her friend, asking for assistance in finding a position at some select school back East.

Miss Belinda Gregory
Mount Holly Academy
Oakville, Massachusetts

Dear Belinda,
While I have found the Territory to be most fascinating, I am unable to remain here for reasons which I cannot go into at this time. After careful consideration I have decided to return to the Boston area in the immediate future. Meanwhile I am hoping that you can apprise me of an institution seeking a teacher of my qualifications. If you know of any such post available and would put my name forward for consideration, I would be deeply in your debt.

Enclosed are my references from Miss Emerson's Academy and a personal reference from Father Ildephonso.

I hope this letter finds both you and your dear mother in good health, and I send my fondest regards, as always. I will look forward with sincere pleasure to the day we meet again.

She reread the note, adding a brief closing and her maiden name. It would be easier that way, and no questions asked. Carefully folding the paper, she placed it in the addressed envelope as the drum of hoofbeats came through the window. Norah got out of bed quickly and went to the open window. One of the hands was riding past the house, and she knew he was heading for Greenwood Junction. Abner had gone there yesterday, but she had not dared entrust her letter to him.

"Mr. MacPherson?"

The man brought his mount to a halt near the window and touched the brim of his hat. "Morning, Mrs. Slade."

Norah stood on her tiptoes and leaned forward. "Are you going to town? I am afraid I forgot to give Mr. Slade this letter to take to the Post Office, and was wondering if you would be so kind as to deliver it for me."

"Sure thing, ma'am." He tipped his hat, took the note from her hand, and placed it inside his vest.

"Thank you kindly," she said, unaware that she was beaming at him, positive she had found a way of escape from life with Abner.

The hopes that grew in her bosom with the dispatch of the letter had little time to flourish. Two days later, as she sat at the table going over her household accounts, Abner came riding in with a battered letter in the side pocket of his brown coat. It had followed Norah to Camp Greenwood, and then on to Greenwood Junction, and had been in transit for weeks. Abner came into the house, banging the door behind him, and threw it on the table before her.

"Something for you," he said, watching her face. "All the way from Massachusetts."

Norah picked up the cream-colored envelope hastily, not meeting his eyes. She didn't want him to know what she was about, and tried to keep relief from showing on her features.

As she scanned the front of the envelope, a weight of despair settled inside her. It was the same letter she had sent to Belinda Gregory before her marriage, but across her careful copperplate a masculine hand had scrawled: "No such person at this address. No forwarding address." Dully, she noticed that someone had broken the seal. She was too stunned to care. Belinda had been her last and only hope. Then Abner threw down another letter. The one Norah had asked MacPherson to mail for her. It also had been opened.

"Well? What do you have to say for yourself?"

She looked up at him, her face drained of color. "You had no business opening my private correspondence!"

"I have every right to know my wife is thinking of leaving me!"

Norah rose to her feet. "I told you I can't continue to live with you, knowing what you've done."

He took her face between his palms. "We've been over this before. Women have odd humors when they're pregnant. You'll get over this."

"I will never get over the fact that I married a murderer!" Her eyes seemed darker blue against the whiteness of her skin.

"You have no choice. I will not be cheated of my son." He dropped his hands to her shoulders. "And there is no way you can leave the ranch, even if you weren't pregnant: you don't ride, you can't hitch a team or handle the carriage, and we are miles from the nearest town."

Listening to his hateful smugness, Norah felt trapped and breathless. The very walls that sheltered her from the heat became a prison. "I'll find a way, if I have to crawl on my knees!"

Abner laughed. "You won't get very far. I've already given Kincaid instructions that you are not to leave the ranch. After all, everyone knows that women are subject to strange fancies when they're breeding." He looked at her strangely. "I heard your old friend Sergeant LeBeau has been seen hereabouts lately. I've given orders to have him shot on sight if he shows up."

When he left, Norah sat down again and wept hopelessly. For the first time she saw how truly isolated she was: no family, no money, no friends except Abigail and the Captain, and Father Ildephonso. Another face flashed before her tear-filled eyes. Oh, if only LeBeau would come back again! He would rescue her, take her to Camp Greenwood, where she would be safe from Abner.

She dried her tears. There was no profit in them. Instead she would just wait and bide her time. Abner couldn't keep her on the ranch forever, nor could he prevent visitors from coming. She wrote another letter, this time to Abigail. Without going into details, she begged her friend to come and take her away to the Army post. Addressing the letter before she lost courage, Norah took it outside.

Harry Roberts, one of the men who rode with the supply train, was approaching the house. He was new to the ranch, a young man with guileless eyes and a kindly but nervous smile. Norah intercepted him.

"Mr. Roberts, if you will be going into town in the next day or so, would you kindly post this letter for me at Henderson's General Store? Mr. Slade will not be riding out until next week, and I am most anxious to have my letter sent off speedily."

Roberts went red above his checked shirt, and he shuffled his boots. His eyes shifted to some distant point on the horizon. "I'm sorry, ma'am, but I can't rightly do that. Mr. Slade's orders."

"I see. Thank you." Norah whirled around and walked away. When she got to the door she shifted her direction. She didn't want to go inside the house that had become her cage. Setting out aimlessly, she walked and walked, just as she had in Boston when pondering some problem.

She examined her predicament from every angle, making plans for any likely contingency. Going wherever her feet carried her, she was oblivious to the heat of the afternoon sun, until a growing thirst demanded her attention. Suddenly her lips felt dry and in danger of cracking, and her tongue had turned to a flap of felt. Norah looked around for the way back. Nothing looked familiar. She was lost.

Was the ranch house that way? Or this way? She went back and forth, hoping to catch a glimpse of one of the buildings, or to spot someone on horseback. No matter where she turned there was a sameness to the land. There was nothing but tan rock, burnt sand, mesquite, and prickly pear, with saguaro cactus here and there, standing against the sky like many-armed sentinels.

She was unable to follow her own footprints over the stony soil, and the valley was so vast it might be days before she was found. Norah was not one to sit helplessly by while Fate made decisions for her. Choosing a likely direction, she started off. Her legs were weary, and thirst was driving her half mad with thoughts of cool draughts of water. Her footsteps began to flag, and she searched desperately for a landmark.

"Surely I have passed this spot before," she said aloud in a hoarse croak. "And more than once!"

She picked up a sharp-edged rock and scratched a mark on a spineless succulent, then began in a new direction. A few minutes later she saw it again, dripping milky tears from its wound. She had, indeed, been walking in circles. Which plants were poisonous, and which were safe? Touching her finger to the substance oozing from the plant, she brought it to her tongue.

It was sticky and extremely bitter. Norah scrubbed her mouth on her sleeve, and started off in still another direction. At last she stopped. She was going nowhere, and might well be wandering farther away each time. She hadn't seen that oozing cactus in some time. *I will sit here and rest, and surely someone will find me soon.*

Something caught the sun with the warm gleam of old ivory. Norah reached out and picked it up, then dropped it immediately when she saw what it was: the skull of a small animal. She looked up, shading her eyes, and saw a bird slowly spiraling over her, coming lower with each curving flight. A bird of prey.

She put her head down on her knees, groggy with heat, sunburn, and dehydration. Her ears buzzed, and she didn't hear the hoofbeats until Abner was almost beside her. Eagerly she reached for the water he offered, afraid he was a mirage and would disappear.

"Stupid little fool! Did you plan to walk back to Boston?" He held a canteen out to her. "Just a little bit, or you'll be sick."

It was warm but tasted like nectar from Olympus to her. Norah drank gratefully, feeling her tongue come unglued from the insides of her cheeks. She gulped again, and Abner pulled the canteen away. "Easy. Put some on your face and neck, it will cool you off."

He poured some in her palm, and Norah splashed it over her face, letting it dribble down her neck and between her breasts. She made no remark when he placed her on his horse before him, but clung to the saddlehorn with both hands. It didn't take long for them to reach the ranch, and soon she saw the green clump of sycamores and the pale adobe of their house and outbuildings.

"So close! So close all the time…"

Abner swung down from the horse and reached up to catch Norah as she slid down from her perch. If not for his arms, she would have fallen. "You see," Abner told her. "There is no escape for you. You are mine, and what is mine, I keep!"

Although weak, Norah still had spirit. She stepped away from Abner, and her eyes burned with determination. "You can't keep watch over me every minute of the day. Somehow, someday, I will find a way. *I will!*"

Abner's smile mocked her. "And how do you expect to do that?"

Norah didn't answer, but in her heart she clung to a single thought: surely LeBeau would ride up to the ranch one day, just as he had before. And this time she would ask him to take her away. Yes, when LeBeau came, everything would be all right.

11

The weather changed overnight as cool winds blew down from the far mountains, bringing with them a restlessness, a sense of things about to happen. Abner stormed into the house, where Norah was sorting through a chest of linens.

"I have to go down to Mexico. There's trouble: Apaches raiding across the border, and Rodriguez has sent for help. By God, I'm not going to let those damned renegades destroy everything I've built up! I'll leave a few men behind to look after things here while I'm gone."

She didn't acknowledge his presence, keeping her eyes cast down so he wouldn't see the sudden light that came into them. This might be the chance she'd been praying for! The spotting had stopped and she felt strong again.

Abner came over and grabbed her by the arm. "Don't try anything foolish while I'm away. You'd never make it on foot, so don't even think about it."

He tilted her chin up. "Did I ever tell you about the hand I fired last year? He tried to walk cross country and intercept the stage. A roustabout found his body a few weeks later, dried up like a mummy. I'd hate to have that happen to you."

Her blue eyes met his levelly. She'd learned that he was aroused by any show of fear or weakness, and had no intention of playing into his hands. His face became red and blotchy, engorged with rage. She hoped he'd have an apoplectic fit.

"When our son is born you'll change your mind about everything, Norah. You won't want to see the father of your son hang! And after this next shipment, life is going to be much better. Maybe I'll take you to San Francisco with me in the spring. I'll outfit you in velvet and silks, and we'll stay at the best hotel and eat at the finest restaurants.''

His rage turned to anticipation. ''You'll love San Francisco, and you'll do me proud, Norah. Every man will look at me with envy. Maybe I'll bring you back some aquamarines to match your eyes.''

So, he thought he could bribe her to condone his murderous deeds! She looked through Abner as if he didn't exist. She hadn't spoken to him since that terrible day of discovery.

Abner watched her in bafflement. He would have handled wrath or defiance with violence, and tears with laughter and humiliation; but he had no idea of how to treat such stony indifference. *Damn her!* After a moment he let her go, and Norah returned to her task.

He went over to the cupboard, where his whiskey was stored. Filled with excitement and new hope, she kept about her task with smooth, deliberate movements. Inside, her mind was racing like her pounding heart. She would find some way to leave the ranch while Abner was gone. Sergeant LeBeau would return. She would be safe then. Before leaving the room, Abner stopped and looked over his shoulder. ''Just a reminder for your half-breed friend: I've given Jase and Aaron orders to shoot any trespassers on sight.''

He left, and her breath eased out in a long sigh of relief. If only she could get word to LeBeau. Regardless of Abner's precautions, he could find some way to rescue her one more time. Outside the wind laughed through the eaves.

Three days later, the man who had once called himself LeBeau sat his mount on a low hill and waited. The turquoise fetish and the copper disc around Storm Caller's neck rose and fell against his naked breast with every breath. The disc still bore the dent of the would-be assassin's bullet. That attack alone would have been reason enough for vengeance, but there were greater crimes Abner Slade would answer for, and soon. The smoke from the burning supply wagons billowed and curled up to haze the morning sky, and orange flames licked at the hated puma emblem emblazoned on their sides. Several braves rummaged through the goods of the last wagon before setting it in flames. Limping Bear and Soft Talking Man, a saturnine Kiowa, rode up the hill to join Storm Caller and spat on the ground. "He is not there among the others. Limping Bear says perhaps he has turned himself into the mountain lion, and slipped away in the darkness."

Storm Caller's eyes looked black as he watched the smoke. "He has no magic. Abner Slade is merely an evil man. And so cowardly he crept away at the first sign of trouble. The next time he will not be so fortunate."

The search for Dove-in-Flight had ended in White Horse Canyon the day before his enlistment in the Indian Scouts ended. Her remains had been newly interred in another place, where small blue flowers bloomed in the springtime. It was a makeshift grave, a shallow crevice in a canyon wall, mounded over with smooth round rocks from the dry creekbed. The ancient prayers had been said, the grave goods placed alongside her. But it was not over. Not yet.

"At least," Limping Bear said, "you have struck a powerful blow at your enemy. This will cause him much loss of face as well as his goods."

When Storm Caller looked up, the other men flinched before the blaze of naked hatred in his eyes. "This is nothing! A mere loss of goods. It does not touch either my enemy or his pride, and I will not be satisfied with less." He ran the ball of his thumb along the razor edge of his knife. "Slade escaped this time, but he will not live to do so again."

Soft Talking Man spoke again, in the low, diffident tones that had given him his name. "My father once told me there were many ways to torture a man...even an absent man."

The other two looked at him, and the Kiowa grinned. "It will take Slade many days to reach his home, for he will have to detour around us." He saw that he had their full attention. "Meanwhile, Slade's wife is alone...and at your mercy."

Storm Caller laughed grimly, and his horse shifted its feet in quick, nervous patterns. "You have spent too much time with the priest, Soft Talking Man! Mercy is a white man's concept." He looked out over the burning wagons. There was no such word in his philosophy.

The other braves fired the last wagon and rode swiftly up the hill. The band of men nudged their horses and headed north without further comment. As they rode, Storm Caller turned over the words of Soft Talking Man in his mind. He had always despised men who wreaked their vengeance on women or children. He knew men who had raped and avoided their company. It did not occur to him that the plan slowly forming in his mind was against his deepest ingrained feelings. The marks of mourning he had slashed on his arms were still red, like the blood that had run down upon the grave, symbol of his grief and pain, promise of his vengeance.

The sun was westering when he made his decision. "Continue on to join Horns-of-Buffalo," he told his comrades. "I will make my camp near Slade's ranch tonight." His gray eyes were dark and brooding. "Tomorrow I will act."

Norah woke as morning broke, red and angry, over the land. The sun bled along the horizon, filling the eastern sky with unholy light. She opened the shutters more fully, aware of the chilled tiles beneath her feet. To the north, heavy clouds were bunched in tight folds like rolls of soiled flannel. The world seemed to hold its breath, watching, waiting.

"It's going to storm," she said aloud, and shivered, but not with cold.

With a feeling of apprehension she realized there was no sound within the house, no odor of coffee boiling. She threw on her robe and went toward the kitchen, increasingly aware that everything was much too still.

"Elena?" Norah had not seen the woman since the night before.

There was no fire in the kitchen hearth, and the stone crock was empty of water. Perhaps she's gone outside to fetch some, Norah thought. And yet, the house seemed too empty. Almost as though she were the only human being in the world.

She stepped outside, conscious of the coolness in the air. In the high country to the north winter was poised, ready to sweep away the last remnants of the short autumn; but here in the south the orange sun blazed in defiance of the massing storm. There was a sense of waiting in the air, a hushed expectancy that communicated itself to Norah while she called in vain for the housekeeper.

"Elena? Elena!" The rising wind snatched her voice and carried it away like a wisp of smoke.

She hurried back inside and shut the door firmly. There was no sign of Elena in the small room off the kitchen where she slept, and it took Norah a moment to discern something else. Everything of Elena's was gone, even the soiled red ribbon. Comprehension dawned. The two hands had evidently sneaked off to town for the Saturday night doings, and Elena had gone with them, taking all her belongings. If she thought to do Norah a mischief this way, it had rebounded: this would be the perfect time for her to escape.

"Oh, if only I can harness the horses!" Hurriedly she dressed, putting on the dress of serviceable blue gingham and the calf-length boots Abner had given her. She had no money, and no real idea of what to do, except flee to Greenwood Junction. Once there she could surely find some way to get to the safety of the Army post. Abigail would take her in.

Stopping to supply herself with some sugar lumps, Norah ran all the way to the horse barn. Perhaps she could bribe one of the horses to stay still while she attempted to harness it, something she had never tried to do before. She was filled with adrenaline and a growing feeling of confidence. "I can do it! I know I can."

Inside the corral, four horses stood, tossing their heads and snorting. Something was making them jittery. She called to the gentlest one, a compactly built bay gelding with a white blaze down the center of his face.

"Here, Jupiter. Here, boy!" She held out her hand. The lumps of sugar glistened in the morning light. "Look what I have got for you."

Jupiter approached cautiously, weaving and bobbing as he sidled up to the fence. Norah clucked encouragingly, as she had heard the men do, and the gelding came closer. She reached up tentatively, and the bay bared his teeth. They were huge. She tried to ignore them.

"Here, boy! Here's some nice sugar for you."

A stiff breeze blew up from the north, bringing with it an unfamiliar scent. Jupiter whickered, then rose on his hind legs, whirled, and pounded away. The other horses had picked up both the alien smell and the bay's fear, and trotted aimlessly back and forth, sharp hooves churning the hard-packed soil. Their speed increased, and the horses ran the perimeter of the corral, rolling their eyes until they shone white.

Norah was badly shaken. If Jupiter was so skittish when she only tried to pat him, what would he do if she tried to bridle and saddle him? There was no way she would be able to do it. Perhaps there was another animal in the barn. She entered the barn but found only one horse in the stalls. A piebald mare lay on its side with pain-glazed eyes. A bran poultice had been applied to the open sore on its left foreleg, but the beast had worked it off.

"Poor Freckles!" Norah sighed. The horse lifted its head and eyed her listlessly. "You are not able to bear your own weight, much less mine."

She had to acknowledge defeat, at least temporarily. Returning to the house, she prayed that someone would ride out to the ranch. It was unlikely, but she clung to that idea. It was her only hope. A stray memory brushed her mind, like a cobweb. It was an old Spanish proverb: *Be careful what you ask for—you might get it.* She pushed the thought away.

The day wore on and nobody came. Norah was filled with a growing unease. A feeling of being watched had been growing stronger by the hour, and the hairs on the back of her neck prickled. She began to close the inside shutters, and when she reached the north side of the house something startled her. In the distance against the background of the coming storm, a shape was outlined. The shape of a man and a horse, unmoving. A flare of lightning illuminated the scene. *An Indian, watching the house!*

She slammed the shutter and dropped the bar into place, then ran for the rifle over the mantel. She didn't even know if it was loaded, and cursed her ignorance of firearms. Earlier the house had seemed like shelter: now it might be a trap, she thought. When she peeked again through the rifle hole in the shutter, there was no horse, no rider, just the empty land stretching out to the horizon. An hour passed with no incident as Norah paced restlessly from shutter to shutter, peering out.

It was just a figment of my imagination. Or just a lone Indian passing by. Still she kept the rifle handy and didn't change into her nightclothes, although the hour grew late. She brought out a quilt she had sewn, and began hemming it while the wind sang mournful tunes outside the windows. There was a cannon boom of thunder, a white flare of light that sent the shadows dancing eerily, and then a loud bang from near at hand.

"That was close! It must have hit one of the outbuildings." The sound of her own voice was startling in the quiet. She jumped up, and unbarred the door, opening it warily. She would have even been glad of Elena's company at this moment. Nothing moved in her line of vision.

Suddenly the door was flung back on its hinges with a protesting groan, and a man's form filled the doorway. She shrank back and looked around for the rifle as he pushed her into the house and slammed the door. His shadow flickered around the room, looming over Norah.

"What do you think you are doing?" She could hardly speak for the lump of fear in her throat. The man advanced on her, and Norah retreated strategically across the room.

She experienced a series of jumbled impressions, like the tiny pieces of a kaleidoscope tumbling into place. The Indian was tall, and the bronzed muscles of his naked chest and arms rippled in the lamplight. A copper disc hung from his neck by a leather thong, catching the gleam of the lamp's flame as he came toward her.

Norah barely took in the tight-fitting buckskin breeches that molded powerful thighs, the thick black hair plaited into two braids and wrapped with red cloth and bands of otter fur. Her eyes were drawn instead to the high-cheekboned face daubed with wide streaks of red and white paint, its expression stern and forbidding as the intruder advanced. The shadows distorted his features. His eyes were a dark smoky gray and rimmed with charcoal, making them seem huge and fearsome. In the dimness of the room they appeared black.

"What do you want?" she demanded, trying to appear calm and in command.

Every story of atrocity she had ever heard roared through

her brain. The Indian only came closer, the whites of his eyes glittering in the amber light. There was something of unstoppable force, of implacable purpose in his lithe movements. *This is how an animal feels when it is stalked!* Norah thought in a frightening flash of insight. She knew, too, why the victim sometimes ran toward its killer: her terror was so great that she was almost ready to rush forward and meet her death—anything to have this moment end and be free of the nightmare.

"My husband is asleep in the next room! You had better leave at once, or I'll rouse him!" Her empty threat went unanswered.

Then the instinct for survival overtook her fears, and rage burned through her veins. She would not be taken so easily. No, she would fight with the last breath in her, and perhaps, by the Grace of God, she would emerge the victor. All this took place in a split second, and Norah railed at the Fate that had put her too far away from the cleaver or butcher knife that might have felled her foe. As he stalked her with savage grace, the only sounds in the room were his almost soundless footfalls and her own rapid breathing. She stepped back and grabbed for the only weapon at hand, a cast-iron frying pan, wielding it like a battle-ax as her adversary came silently closer.

"Do not come a step further!"

The man who had been called LeBeau closed in. His lips stretched back from his teeth in a wide grimace, until his face was a grinning devil's mask. At that moment he had no object except to avenge himself on the wife of his enemy. He had fasted and chanted until all memory of anything else was blotted out, and he was as deadly, as single-minded, as a panther hunting a fawn. In one swift movement he caught her wrist, crushing it in his strong fingers until her hand went numb and the pan clanged to the floor at their feet.

He grabbed her other wrist and held them both with one hand, then took Norah by the waist and pulled her to him. She was soft and warm and womanly, and fragrant with the scents of lavender and rose petals. Suddenly his urge for vengeance became mixed with another, more primitive one, and taking the woman superseded Storm Caller's plans of revenge. His hand went to the bodice of her gingham dress.

Norah resorted to less civilized tactics. Her teeth sank into his bare arm above the elbow. The metallic-salt taste of blood tingled against her tongue, and she heard him grunt with surprise and pain. The next thing she knew, she was sailing backward through the air. Her fall was broken by a chair, and she grasped it as she went, pulling it down on top of herself.

Sprawled on the floor, shaking with fear, she was all the while looking around desperately for some lethal object to use in defending herself. She sprang to her feet, holding the chair for a clumsy shield. He wrenched it away as if it were a jackstraw. She saw that his arm was bleeding and felt a brief satisfaction. She would tear his eyes out with her bare fingers if he came any closer. Then he spoke.

"Take off your clothes. All of them." His voice was harsh and unrecognizable.

His faultless English was as much a shock as his words were to Norah. She stared at him, then drew herself up defiantly.

"How dare you!" Her outraged dignity ill became the circumstances, but she saw no reason for his mocking smile. "It was bad enough when I thought you some ignorant savage, but I see you have had the benefit of acquaintance with civilization."

He only repeated his words. "Take off your clothes—or I will take them off for you."

"No!"

Before Norah could think, she was pinned against the wall, and he was systematically ripping her shirtwaist and skirt away, until she stood in her underthings. His arm was across her throat, and she stood helpless while he slit the laces on her corset with the tip of his knife. This was it. He was going to kill her.

Then the garment fell away, exposing her white breasts, baring her to the waist. His face altered subtly, and even in the dim light she could see a flush of desire darken his skin. His hand closed on one breast while he pulled her hard against him. Norah felt the hardness in his loins, saw the hot light of arousal in his eyes, and felt physically ill. She turned her head and looked away.

Storm Caller's blood was singing in his veins. This was his first moment of triumph over his enemy, his first blow to Abner Slade's manhood. But as he felt her skin, so warm and silken beneath his rough palm, something changed. He realized the unwelcome and overwhelming truth then. He had never meant to force this woman against her will. He slid his hand down along her ribs, then up to capture her other breast, feeling his passion grow, and wanting to create a response in her.

Skilled in the ways of pleasing a woman, he suddenly wanted to see *this* woman's mouth soften, see her features blur with an answering desire. He would show her the difference between her husband and a real man. Every time Abner Slade would lie with his wife in the very short life he would be granted after his return, he would think of this night.

Storm Caller inhaled the fragrance from the woman's hair, and nothing else mattered except to make her want him, as he wanted her now. He would make her body arch toward his in need, make her cry out when his mouth sought her breasts, and only when she shuddered and clung to him would he take her. And he would take her in Slade's own bed. At least there was some justice there.

He wanted to see her face, and his fingers stopped their stroking inventory of her body long enough to force her head up. Her lips were soft and full and trembling. He wanted to taste them in the way of the white man that he had learned. She licked her lips nervously, the little pink tongue darting out quickly. Then both his hands were at the waistband of her pantalets, dragging them to the rounded curve of her hips.

Norah closed her eyes, and her flesh shrank from his touch. She would have preferred death, but not having that option, instead retreated into her mind as she had so many times when Abner had touched her, willing herself not to feel, not to flinch. Her rigid muscles went slack with conditioned response. She would no longer resist. She would not move. She would merely endure.

Nothing happened. The hot hands stopped pulling at her clothes, and she heard him curse beneath his breath. Slowly she opened her eyes to find him watching her face, his own features still and unreadable. She could still feel the imprint of his fingers on her skin, but stood proudly, meeting his gaze with quiet courage. He could touch her, rape her, kill her; but he could not extinguish her spirit.

Storm Caller stepped back, still holding her. Except for her dark hair and the rosettes on the tips of her breasts, she looked like a statue in marble. The strange look in her eyes held him, challenged him, and finally defeated him. He made a quick change in his strategy, and flung her away, then picked up the quilt she had been hemming earlier and threw it at her.

"Wrap yourself well in this blanket. It will be cold in the mountains tonight."

12

Despite the cotton pantalets she wore, Norah's legs were sore from chafing against the horse's sides, and the rawhide thong that went under the animal's belly, tying her ankles together, bit into her flesh. At first the tether had stung her skin, then burned. Now the pain in her ankles was just another dull ache that kept her conscious as they rode endlessly through the night.

She had no choice, as they flew through the darkness at a steady speed, but to keep her arms about her captor's waist to avoid falling beneath the churning hooves. Earlier she had thought she would rather be dead than raped and carried off, and perhaps later she would be of the same mind; meanwhile, she had no desire to be dragged beneath the body of the straining beast, nor to have her brains dashed out in such a manner.

Her feet were cold, her hands were frozen and only the warmth radiating from Storm Caller's naked back kept her face from going numb. Norah had long since ceased asking where they were going, and now was so chilled and weary that she hardly cared. After a time they left the arid plain and began climbing to a higher altitude. Massive shelves of tilted rock defied gravity, looming gray and black against the night. The wind became a razor, cutting so deeply it seemed to scrape along her bones. Still the horse plunged on, slackening only when the going was especially tricky. Then they came out on a high ledge, and a trick of perspective made it appear they were almost level with the icy moon, peering from its sodden cloud blankets.

"We will stop here," her abductor said, sliding off the horse.

While she slumped forward, feeling the cold even more without the windbreak of his body, he raised his hands to the sky. Storm Caller began to chant, a low, eerie sound in counterpoint to the rising wind that made the hairs stir on the back of Norah's neck. She watched him dully. He took something from the pouch at his waist and gestured to the heavens, then dipped in the leather bag again, repeating his action three times.

His tone was monotonous, the same notes over and over, until they pierced Norah's indifference, and she wanted to scream with frustration. He kept the chanting up until the moon was covered, and she saw spots before her eyes. No, she saw with a start, not spots. Snow. Well, she would freeze to death, and that would be the end of her ordeal. Already the blood in her veins felt sluggish, as if it were turning to frigid slush. She saw the flakes come faster and faster, clumping together until they were the size of moths, then huge butterflies in the dimness. They settled on her hair and lashes, and she welcomed them, praying the snow would fall fast and deep, until she was turned to a pillar of ice.

"Lot's wife," she murmured, then realized she was being carried somewhere. Her lids fluttered up. "How can he stand it?" she said thickly, her face against the warmth of his bare chest. Then she was on the ground, and her hands were being briskly rubbed until circulation came back. With it came painful stabbing sensations in her extremities, as if her blood cells had been transformed to jagged icicles, shearing their way through her veins and arteries.

"Leave me alone," she slurred impatiently. She was trying to sleep.

Someone shook her by the shoulders, and she became irritated, but it was too much trouble to say anything. Didn't he know it was rude to disturb someone who was dying? She drifted into enveloping blackness and dreamed she was back home, curled up in her mother's big feather bed.

"When is Daddy coming back?" she asked, and was only held more tightly in the comforting embrace. Then the warmth began to seep into her bones, and she felt cozy and safe and loved again.

Slowly wakefulness came and the cold returned with it. Light shifted and darted around her, orange and yellow and leaping red. She thought she was in her house, the one the Indian had set fire to, then remembered he had taken her out and tied her onto his horse first. The answer came to her from far away.

I'm in hell. I've gone to hell for hating Abner. She wondered why the flames gave no heat. Perhaps this was the true essence of Hell, a cold place filled with shadows and loneliness. A place where she would never be warm again.

Full awareness came gradually. After a while she knew her face was cradled against a bare arm, her naked breasts against an equally naked chest. Her lids flew open. The fire was to her back, and cast enough light on the high-cheekboned face that was inches from hers. The paint had worn from his features, but the charcoal about the dark gray eyes only served to make them more recognizable.

"Sergeant LeBeau!" Norah's countenance lit with joy and relief. She was saved. LeBeau had come to rescue her, as she had dreamed he would. He would protect her, as he had in the past.

The man holding her loosened his embrace, and he pulled his face back from hers, watching her warily. Norah's brain cleared away the last of its hypothermic fog, and she knew where she was and how she had gotten there. She sat up, realizing she was almost nude as the blankets slipped. She covered herself quickly, folding her hands across her breasts. Yes, it was LeBeau, there was no mistaking it; but why was he daubed with streaks of paint and dressed in the buckskin breeches and soft boots of an Indian?

And why had he kidnapped her? They stared at each other, and for a moment she thought he looked quite as startled as she felt.

Storm Caller felt an unexpected stab of guilt, like a lance beneath his ribs. The trust in the woman's features shamed him. Then he lowered his thick short lashes, veiling his eyes. He must not think of her as a woman he once knew, he must think of her only as his enemy's wife. The past was wiped away as cleanly as a child's slate.

When he glanced back at her, his face was aloof and blank, robbed of the human quality that had softened its lines a moment earlier. "LeBeau is dead," he said bluntly. "I am Storm Caller."

"No," Norah whispered softly as her eyes scrutinized every line of his face. "You are Sergeant LeBeau."

She reached for the edge of the blanket and pulled it up to her chin, her mind reeling with confusion. "I don't understand. I thought you were an Indian. I thought you were going to rape me."

"I am," he said. "I was."

At his words anger, indignation and disbelief had all been apparent in her eyes, along with something very like hurt. They are like blue mirrors, Storm Caller thought, showing all her emotions. He felt his stomach tighten as if he had received a blow.

"Why?"

Somehow he couldn't go into his bereavement. It would have been like digging up a corpse. His face was stark in the shifting firelight, deep lines carved from nose to mouth, deep hollows beneath his gray eyes and high cheekbones.

"You are a white woman, one of the Enemy. I have seen children starved to death, women raped and tortured and slaughtered by your people in their greed for our land. The Indian Agents have given out poisoned flour and blankets taken from smallpox victims, killing even more of our numbers. I could give you a thousand reasons more!"

"But that doesn't make sense! These things you tell me are terrible, yet *I* never did you any harm. Why should you want to hurt me?"

"Your husband ambushed me, left me for dead. And that is only one of the scores I have to settle with him. He managed to slip away from us in Mexico, but I will find him one day soon. Meanwhile," he quoted Soft Talking Man, "'There are many ways to torture a man...even an absent man.'"

Norah closed her eyes a moment, then opened them and met his probing gaze. "Why didn't you rape me then? Why did you abduct me instead?"

There was a loud popping and siss from the fire, where a piece of wood snapped and sap sizzled. He leaned up on one elbow and looked at her for a long time, while her eyes searched his face. The words seemed to be dragged from him, reluctantly.

"I don't know."

There was something about this woman that made him act differently than he'd planned, something about her vulnerability that made him vulnerable in turn. He didn't like it. He must not think of her as a person, as a woman. He must remember only that she was Abner Slade's wife.

Silence held sway while minutes ticked away, and still they faced each other without speaking. A sudden intuition sent a wave of ice up and down Norah's spine. It was Fate that had brought her together with LeBeau, here in the shadows of this small cave. For good or ill, the strands of her life had been woven into the fabric of his. There was a definite design, but she couldn't discern its pattern from a few threads of coincidence and deliberate actions. She shivered.

Abner had abused her, mentally and physically, treated her as if she were a mindless possession; and now this man she had trusted—this man that she had once thought she loved—had betrayed her trust. Suddenly she was weary.

"What will you do with me now? Where are you taking me, Sergeant LeBeau?"

He looked up sharply. "I told you before: Sergeant LeBeau no longer exists. I am Storm Caller. And we go to my people."

"Why?"

"You ask too many questions." He got up and paced around the perimeter of the fire, then went to the back wall of the small enclosure and lifted several flat slabs of rock. He unwrapped something from beneath one and took out an oilskin packet. He unfolded a faded blue shirt and a leather vest decorated with deep fringes, then brought the other contents over to Norah. "Put these on. They'll be too large, but you can roll them up."

Her eyes were wide and dark as violets in the firelight. She took the buckskin shirt and leggings from him but didn't move. "I said put them on, now!"

"Turn around." Her chin tilted up.

"Don't be stupid. I have already seen your body." He

leaned against the rough limestone wall and kept his eyes on her insolently.

Norah's back stiffened. She could have huddled under the blanket and tried to dress that way, but a stubborn Irish streak underlay her personality. She stood up, turned her back, and dropped the blanket, stepping into the leggings. They were much too long, and too narrow in the hips, but since the top was composed of flaps that tied at each side of the waist, she was able to secure them, leaving an expanse of smooth white flesh uncovered on either side. She slipped the shirt over her head. It came down well past her knees, hiding the gravid shape of her abdomen. Norah turned back the sleeves, then rolled the pants into wide cuffs at the bottom, never once glancing his way.

Storm Caller gave a short nod of satisfaction. He hadn't felt the effects of the weather himself or realized how ill-suited she was for such rugged travel and exposure to the elements. He tried to feel contempt for her softness and failed: the woman had fought and been defeated but had not groveled. She had never once complained of the cold, never once wept or sobbed or begged to be set free. Even now she eyed him defiantly.

"You would have silently frozen to death, rather than let me know you were cold, wouldn't you?"

"Of course."

Norah sat with her hands held out to the fire. Now she turned her back on him with calm deliberation, determined to show him her disdain. Her Irish blood was indeed stirring: she was a daughter of a race kept subject against its will; and like her ancestors, she would fight when she could, endure when she could not fight, and always, always, be waiting to snatch the freedom that was just out of reach.

He hunkered down beside Norah and forced her to look at him. "Don't you realize that you are my captive? That you are helpless?"

A wild fury shook her, making her limbs weak. "Let us understand one thing, Sergeant LeBeau...or Storm Caller or whatever name you choose to call yourself! You can hold me captive. You can try to force your will on me; perhaps you will even succeed. But turn your back on me or close your eyes, be careless for just one moment, and you will see how helpless I am!''

Already her eyes were assessing her surroundings, her mind plotting possibilities. Whether her plan would merely be escape, or vengeance and escape, would depend on the circumstances; but when the moment came, she would be prepared. She turned her shoulder to him and stared into the flames as if he were not present, as if he did not exist, and her attitude communicated itself to him. It was as if she were alone in the cave.

Storm Caller stood. ''Look at me,'' he said softly. She ignored him.

''Look at me!'' He pulled her to her feet and spun her around to face him. This time it was her face that was distant and aloof, his that twisted with emotion. Her eyes looked right through him, filling Storm Caller with a baffled anger. Whatever it was he wanted from her, this wasn't it. He slid one hand alongside her head, tangling his long fingers in her black hair and forcing her chin up with his thumb.

''Damn you, look at me!''

It was a contest of strengths and wills, one he finally thought he had won when anger flashed in her eyes and she began to tremble in his hands. His thrill of triumph was short-lived. He saw her anger was directed not so much at him, but at her own self because she couldn't overcome her body's weakness. Damn her!

He let her go abruptly. ''Roll up in the blanket. We'll stay here until the storm slackens.'' She wouldn't be foolish enough to try to run away from him into the face of a blizzard. He added more dried branches to the fire, put on the blue cotton shirt and the leather vest, then dropped down on the gritty cave floor with the oilskin over him.

Norah was hungry and exhausted, but willed herself to stay awake. She had warm clothes now, and with the blanket and the stallion tethered inside the mouth of the cave she had the means to flee. Although she knew little of horses, she had been on this animal's back for hours without mishap. She would have to trust the beast a while longer. Her best chance was to wait until her abductor was deep in slumber, slip the horse free, and ride...where? It didn't matter. In time she would come across a dwelling. The important thing was to get away. Even her fear of horses was subjugated in her need to escape, her need to act.

If only she could stay awake until he slept! Closing her eyes would be disastrous, and so Norah watched the dancing flames until it seemed they were hypnotizing her. She looked over at her companion and studied the face of the man who was LeBeau and Storm Caller both. With his eyes closed he seemed younger, and the stern lines were softened. He looked like the man who had aided her on arrival in Greenwood Junction, not a man who would kidnap a woman in revenge. Norah had no clues to his plans for her and, remembering his face when he had burst into the house, hoped she would never have to find out.

Well, she had a few plans of her own. Could she lift one of those flat stones where he'd removed the cache of clothing? She doubted it. She had even stronger doubts of being able to drop it on his head while he slept. It was one thing to fight an enemy face to face, another to smash the skull of a sleeping man. After all, he hadn't hurt her in any way. Yet. And if he heard her or if she fumbled, it would all be for nothing. No, she had to wait until he slept soundly.

When his breathing seemed deep and regular Norah began to inch away from the fire, keeping the blanket around her. She rolled over and away, watched for the slightest movement from him and seeing none, repeated her action. Her heart thumped against her ribs so forcefully that she felt the very sound might awaken him. She waited, then rolled away again.

When she felt at a safe distance, she rose to a crouching position and tiptoed awkwardly toward the mouth of the cave. As she drew near, the stallion stepped sideways, looking at her over his shoulder and whisking his tail from side to side. Fear trickled down Norah's spine, but she steeled herself. This was it, this was her chance. She reached out her hand tentatively, as she had seen Storm Caller do, and patted the animal on its withers. Instantly the stallion whickered and shied, then rose up, pawing the air with its forelegs. Norah backed away from the sharp hooves flailing so near her head, saw Storm Caller leap to his feet in one smooth movement, and she bolted from the cave, running blindly into the wind.

"Norah!" The rest of his cry was whipped away by the wind. Storm Caller was hard on her heels, following the sounds she made that carried faintly over the wind. The little fool! He knew this place well, but even he would not have run off into the face of the blizzard. And there were too many places where the path narrowed to mere footholds, where the rock suddenly dropped away to sheer canyons and deep gorges. He might never find her. Then he felt the direction of the wind seem to change, knew he was near the sharp bend by Window-in-the-Rock, and heard Norah just ahead.

The sky had opened like a torn quilt, dumping clumps of snow feathers into the surging air currents. The wind tore at her with icy grappling hooks, almost knocking her off balance, and Norah could scarcely see where she was going. Still she ran in a state of panic, only hoping that the poor visibility would make it as difficult for her pursuer to see her as it was for her to see the terrain. The snow was thick and soft and came past the top of her boots. Trying to run through it was like trying to run through frozen cream.

Just when all the world seemed blotted out by the blizzard, she came to a limestone wall that reared up out of nowhere, and followed it to the left. Where there was one cave, there were liable to be others, she knew. She stumbled and fell three times with the added impetus of the wind at her back. If only she could find someplace to hide, she could make it. Suddenly there was an opening in the solid stone.

"Oh, thank God!" A miracle. A cave!

Then she was falling through the air, falling through the whirlpool of cold white flakes, and there was no time to think of anything, except dying. She didn't even have time to scream.

Skeleton fingers caught at Norah, tearing her clothes, scratching her face and hands with their bony fingers. She reached out desperate hands and felt twigs bending, cracking, breaking with dull snapping sounds. She hit something with terrible force, landing on her back with a stunning jolt. The wind was knocked from her, and when she could move and breathe again Norah was surprised to find herself still alive. Nothing seemed broken, although she felt a good deal battered. She had landed on a small ledge, saved from anything worse than scratches and contusions by a foot of snow and the stunted trees and bushes that clung tenaciously to the cliffside.

Suddenly the wind sank and the flurries diminished. The moon broke through its cover, reflecting brightly from an earth cloaked in sparkling white. Norah saw that she had only worsened her condition by her efforts to escape. The ledge was twenty feet above a sheer ravine, wooded at the bottom, and the rock above her was a smooth sheet also. There was no way up, and no way down.

"Well, at least I'll die of cold before I starve," she said bitterly. If only she'd waited! She buried her face in her hands and turned her back on the long drop. She would dream of Christmas Eve in Boston, back in the good times, and wrap herself in the warm memories while she waited for the end. There were worse ways of dying.

"Are you injured? Can you move?" The voice came from above. Storm Caller's head and shoulders protruded over the edge of the path from which she'd fallen.

"Stay still," he commanded. "I'm coming down for you." When he'd peered over the edge to see her body lying so still below, it seemed as if his breath had been trapped inside his lungs permanently. He couldn't breathe. Then he went into action. There was time now for neither anger nor guilt. Once he was sure she wouldn't move, he went back to the cave and got what he needed.

He returned, passing the braided leather thong around his waist and looping one end through a natural hole in the rock. Coiling the rope from his pack around his waist, he rappelled down to the ledge where Norah lay. Storm Caller didn't think the rope would hold their combined weight. He made his decision.

"Stand up." Again she obeyed him without hesitating, and he quickly rigged up a harness of criss-crossed rope around her. "When I tug on the rope, the horse will know to move away. I will also pull on this end to keep you as clear of the rock face as possible, and you will be hoisted to the top. When you reach safety, remove this harness and throw it down to me."

Norah looked him straight in the eye. "And if I don't?"

Storm Caller met her glance with a steady one of his own. "Then I will die."

His calm acceptance shamed Norah. Her resolution wavered, and she looked away. He had kidnapped her, but he had still risked his life to save hers. Honor alone said that she owed him something for that.

"All right."

He smiled at her suddenly, a flash of white, a flash of warmth. "You would not be able to find your way in these mountains, in any event; I know them well. Now, go."

He tugged on the rope and up she went, with a jerk of the line that she felt in every muscle and bone in her body. She inched along the jagged cliff facing, grasping at any crack that might give the slightest handhold but found none. Five feet, ten, fifteen, and she began to think she would succeed when she suddenly slid back down two feet. Her skin was only saved by the buckskin covering it, as she dangled helplessly at the end of the rope like a fly in a spider's webbing. Then she felt it, the tiny vibration and an infinitesimal drop, followed in quicker succession by others. Her lifeline, caught on some sharp edge, was fraying and parting in ever-increasing degrees.

"I'm going to fall. The rope is breaking."

Storm Caller heard her words, wondering at the quiet resignation of her tone, even as he leaped to action. He tried to catch her legs, but she was out of his reach. She fell six more inches, and he saw her face, white as the snow that now lay around them in smooth billows and folds. He reached out his arms. "I'll catch you."

It all happened in a blur of motion that paradoxically seemed to spin out with excruciating slowness. Time fragmented into a thousand discrete pieces: Norah was hurtling toward the ledge, and yet she had time to see every cranny and shape and color of the stone before her eyes; Storm Caller rushed to intercept her, and yet he could see that she would just miss the edge of the natural platform where he stood and smash into the bottom of the canyon. He tried to balance himself securely to catch her as she went past, and the next second they were falling free in their strange embrace, clutching each other like frantic lovers.

Luck, having betrayed them earlier, changed its whim and

favored them now. Had they landed anywhere else in the rocky bottom they would have been killed instantly, but a stand of scrubby trees and spreading shrubs cushioned them. Norah, landing across his chest, was stunned. She'd felt and heard something crack. Gingerly she poked at her ribs, but there was no pain. She gasped in breaths of icy air and looked straight up. There was a patch of sky visible in an irregular V-shape, and she sat up and looked around.

Curtains of rock towered above them, cutting them off completely. They were in a deep box canyon, and there appeared to be no way out but the way they had come in. Something moved on the rim of the canyon.

"Look! What's that?"

There was no answer, and she turned to Storm Caller. His eyes were closed, his face as pale as hers in the moonlight reflecting off the limestone walls of their prison. She shook his arm, but there was no response.

"Sergeant LeBeau!"

Norah put her ear to his chest and heard the steady though rapid beat of his heart with relief. There was a slight crepitation along his side, and she realized that the crack she'd felt earlier had been Storm Caller's ribs. She lifted her head and looked down at him with growing unease. Did people die from broken ribs? She didn't know. She hoped not.

"LeBeau? Sergeant LeBeau?" She leaned over and shook him again, her face almost touching his, and her long hair swinging down on either side of his face.

"Storm Caller?" She touched his cheek with her fingertips, and slowly his eyes opened. He moaned softly, and she was dizzy and faint with relief. Norah let out the breath she was holding and smiled in reaction.

Storm Caller's gaze seemed unfocused at first, but when his vision cleared he saw a woman looking down at him with concern. He felt her hand brush at his cheek, soft and warm. As he watched, trying to remember how to put words into sentences, the woman smiled at him. It was a look that illuminated her face, flooding it with an unearthly light. She was very beautiful. He smiled at her and found the words he wanted.

"Have I died then?" he said clearly.

The words hung on the cold night air like notes of music.

The woman didn't answer. Then his sight glazed over. It took too much effort to fight against the darkness that pulled at his consciousness. He was with the Spirit Woman. What could possibly harm him now? Storm Caller slipped contentedly into the deep warm void that opened beneath him.

"Storm Caller!"

Norah shook him gently, but his eyes closed again, and she was unable to rouse him. She lifted his lids. His eyes were not rolled up to show the whites, but stared blankly at her, the pupil of the left one slightly larger than the right. She placed her hand over his left breast and felt the drumbeat of his heart, the rise and fall of his breathing.

She realized he must have hit his head, and her gentle fingers soon found the knot along his temple. The important thing was to keep him warm until he regained consciousness; she refused to consider the alternative, for he was her one hope of getting out of the canyon alive. She made a sign of the cross and said a fervent prayer, then checked her patient again.

His breathing was deep and regular, and although he didn't respond to his name, he did frown when she touched his ribs. Norah tried to make him comfortable and lay down alongside him to share her warmth, as he had done for her earlier. Again she saw movement from the corner of her eye, this time halfway up the canyon wall. Norah strained her eyes but couldn't see clearly. Were those shadows? Animals? While she watched they shifted their positions again.

A soul-shattering wail split the silence into a dozen echoes, and Norah started nervously. *Wolves?* She glanced quickly at her companion. *In a little while he'll wake up, and then he'll know what to do. He'll find a way to save us.*

Her sudden faith in the man who had brought her to this time and place didn't seem at all incongruous to Norah as she curled up by his side. Too much had happened in the past few hours to keep her thinking clear, and she was operating on instinct alone. She put one arm across his waist, the other behind his neck and placed her head on his chest on the side where his ribs were intact. Lulled by the strong rhythm of his heart and the strange comfort of his nearness, she fell asleep embracing him, with teardrops still beading her lashes.

Sometime later she awakened to a touch on her shoulder.

Her eyes flew open, but the face she saw was not the one she was expecting. A scream was stifled by the icicle of steel pressed against her throat. A long-faced Indian with one eyelid stitched shut over a scarred and empty eye socket leered down at her from his remaining orb. He grasped Norah by the hair and pulled her to her feet. Her scalp stung and burned and she yelped and kicked out at him with her remaining strength.

She connected with his groin. Grunting in surprised pain, the brave's grip on her relaxed, and Norah slipped out of his hold. Spinning around, she checked abruptly. Everywhere she looked an Indian crouched, grinning. Moonlight gleamed on the whites of their eyes, their teeth and the blades of the knives they held. She was encircled.

And there was no sign of LeBeau.

13

Earlier Norah thought she faced death, but it had never worn so cold and certain a face as it did now. She inched away from one brave, twisted in the other direction, but there was no escape from the ring of savage faces. As she whirled around she noticed a doe carcass thrown over the rump of one horse, and several rabbitlike creatures with death-dulled eyes dangling from a rope tied around their long ears. *A hunting party!* she thought in relief. They could have easily been a war party in such unsettled times, and she began to feel the situation might not be as desperate as it seemed.

One of the hunters pointed to Norah's buckskins and said something to his companions. Although their faces showed no change of expression, she knew they were laughing at her odd appearance in LeBeau's clothes. The incongruity of her position came over her, and she smiled grimly: all those years in Boston, dressed with the utmost propriety and surrounded by bright-faced girls and sad-eyed women, and now she was somewhere in the heart of the Arizona Territory, dressed in a man's clothing, and surrounded instead by horses and half-clad Indians! *Well, I wanted adventure,* she thought with a grimace, *and by God, I have gotten it!*

Her sense of irony vanished as the man with a scarred face and one eye sewn shut came closer, speaking in a guttural tone to his companions. She held her ground this time, trying to evince courage while her heart froze to an immobile lump beneath her breast. Shoulders square, chin up, she waited, praying her trembling was not noticeable. The brave approached and studied her in silence. His scrutiny went on so long that Norah repressed the urge to scream and shatter the tension.

He sprang forward suddenly, moonlight glittering coldly in his one eye, and touched Norah's face. Unable to control the involuntary movement, she recoiled. He drew back, uttered a short harsh phrase, and his comrades grinned. Once again her tormentor came closer, reaching to grasp her hair and twist her face upward for his inspection. His breath was fetid, his fingers rough, and he smelled of stale urine. Norah tried to break away, but he clasped her about the waist and pressed her body tightly against his. There was no doubt of his meaning, and she panicked, kicking and scratching at his hands.

"Help me! LeBeau! Storm Caller!" It did not seem strange to cry out for him in her distress. Her shriek of alarm was torn away by the wind that gusted along the canyon floor, hurling twigs and stones and small branches before its chilling breath. They stung her legs, but she was unaware of anything but her immediate danger and the ominous absence of LeBeau.

Then she saw him, flung sideways across the back of a restless horse the color of night. "Oh! What have you done to him? His ribs are broken!"

She ran toward his motionless figure, stumbling in her haste. She skinned the palms of her hands but rose unheeding and started to run again. A tall man in buckskins and a plaid shirt of brown wool intercepted her, catching her in his outstretched arms and holding her firmly as she tried to free herself.

"Let me go! Is he dead? Is he...?" Her voice trailed off as the man shook her roughly.

Eyes as black as carbon scanned Norah's face. When he spoke in heavily accented English his voice was soft, his tone diffident as he indicated LeBeau's unconscious form. "Storm Caller friend. You his? You Storm Caller's woman?"

Norah didn't know what to say, but reason warned that her safety might depend on the answer. She tilted her chin up boldly.

"Yes."

Still the dark eyes searched her face, and Norah stared back defiantly. Then, as if satisfied, the soft-voiced man released her.

He mounted his horse and took hold of the reins to the animal that held LeBeau, then gave some order, and the others went to their mounts. The leader nudged his horse's sides, and the animal started forward. The others moved to follow him. Again, panic clutched at Norah.

"Wait! You can't leave me here alone.... Lebeau...*Storm Caller!*..."

The words were cut off as she was grabbed by the waist and flung over a bony shoulder. The impact to her midriff stunned Norah, and with the wind knocked out of her she could do nothing. The Indian carried her to where another steed waited impatiently. He threw her up on the horse and leaped on behind, and within seconds the beast sprang away, the ground blurring beneath long strides of its legs. Her captor kept his arm tightly about Norah's ribs so that it was an effort to draw breath.

By the unpleasantly familiar odors emanating from his body she deduced it was the one-eyed brave who rode behind her, and she tried to turn her head to confirm it. She shifted her weight, and he tightened his hold painfully, pinning her arms at her sides. She tried to think, but extreme fatigue and the effects of the grueling events combined with the jouncing of the horse to make it impossible. With the remnants of her strength, Norah twined her fingers in the horse's tangled mane and held on tightly.

The small band filed slowly along the rock face, silent as ghosts in the silvered light, and as Norah watched, the lead horse disappeared. While she stared, two more horses and their riders vanished. Then she found the explanation: there was a way out of the canyon, after all. Hidden along the dark shadows at the base of one sheer wall, a deep and narrow cleft gaped behind its screen of camouflaging brush like the passage to some netherworld. The band moved single file into the rift and into a darkness that seemed blacker than anything Norah had known before. It was more than an absence of light, rather a palpable presence of something brooding, waiting, and old as the earth itself. Atavistic fears danced up and down her spine as her imagination ran rampant, and she held her breath until she saw a triangular opening loom ahead.

When they came out a few minutes later into the clear frosty moonlight, her eyes were dazzled. The pace quickened, and they rode on until she was benumbed with fatigue and shock and the deadly cold. Dawn came with no warning. One moment the sky was a pool of ink, the next a clear gray pond, and within seconds rose and gold and amber light spilled over the high rim to the north, flooding the lower ground with welcome warmth and color.

When the first faint smell of coffee came on the freshening breeze she thought it was a hallucination, born from her longing for the strong hot drink. Suddenly Norah realized how bone-weary she was. And how hungry. Her stomach growled to announce its interest as the aroma of coffee grew stronger. She began to hope it was real, and moments later they stood on the lip of a low valley that sheltered an Indian camp.

It wasn't much of a camp. Below were a hodgepodge of shabby tepees, a few winter lodges of bramble and mud, and a small and battered Army tent taken on some long-ago raid. Women moved about the campfires, old men and a few youths stood warily watching their approach and dogs snuffled for scraps in the cold gray dirt. Although some of the women appeared to be of childbearing age, there were no children visible anywhere.

As the party of braves rode into camp the men and women gathered around, talking and gesticulating. Seeing LeBeau slung over the back of one mount and Norah riding before the one-eyed brave, a squaw broke away and ran to one of the lodges. A young woman came up to Norah and prodded her leg as if she were a piece of meat, then made an aside to the crowd that brought a few titters of laughter. The brave dismounted, and the moment Norah was free she slid down the side of the horse and ran to LeBeau. He hung limply, like a sack of soiled laundry. His eyes were shut, and his lips blue despite the fevered flush of his cheeks.

"LeBeau!" No answer. "Storm Caller?" She touched his cheek. It was warm. Too warm. And his breathing was loud and stertorous. She turned to the men.

"You fools! I tried to tell you he has broken ribs!" She gestured to her sides and back to him. "Get him down from there!"

An old woman with a face the texture of tree bark came

GET 2

HOW TO GET YOUR
2 FREE BOOKS AND FREE GIFT!

1. Peel off the MIRA sticker on the front cover. Place it in the space provided at right. This automatically entitles you to receive two free books and an exciting mystery gift.

2. Send back this card and you'll get 2 "The Best of the Best™" novels. These books have a combined cover price of $11.00 or more in the U.S. and $13.00 or more in Canada, but they are yours to keep absolutely FREE!

3. There's <u>no</u> catch. You're under <u>no</u> obligation to buy anything. We charge nothing – ZERO – for your first shipment. And you don't have to make any minimum number of purchases – not even one!

4. We call this line "The Best of the Best" because each month you'll receive the best books by the world's hottest authors. These authors show up time and time again on all the major bestseller lists and their books sell out as soon as they hit the stores. You'll like the convenience of getting them delivered to your home at our special discount prices . . . and you'll love your subscriber newsletter featuring author news, horoscopes, recipes, book reviews and much more!

5. We hope that after receiving your free books you'll want to remain a subscriber. But the choice is yours – to continue or cancel, anytime at all! So why not take us up on our invitation, with no risk of any kind. You'll be glad you did!

6. And remember...we'll send you a mystery gift ABSOLUTELY FREE just for giving "The Best of the Best" a try.

SPECIAL FREE GIFT!

We'll send you a fabulous surprise gift, absolutely FREE, simply for accepting our no-risk offer!

Visit us at
www.mirabooks.com

® and TM are trademarks of Harlequin Enterprises Limited.

BOOKS FREE!

Hurry!

Return this card promptly to GET 2 FREE BOOKS & A FREE GIFT!

The Best of the Best™

Affix peel-off MIRA sticker here

YES! Please send me the 2 FREE "The Best of the Best" novels and FREE gift for which I qualify. I understand that I am under no obligation to purchase anything further, as explained on the opposite page.

(BB3-00)

385 MDL CY22   **185 MDL CY23**

NAME   (PLEASE PRINT CLEARLY)

ADDRESS

APT.#   CITY

STATE/PROV.   ZIP/POSTAL CODE

Offer limited to one per household and not valid to current subscribers of "The Best of the Best." All orders subject to approval. Books received may vary.

The Best of the Best™ — Here's How it Works:

Accepting your 2 free books and gift places you under no obligation to buy anything. You may keep the books and gift and return the shipping statement marked "cancel." If you do not cancel, about a month later we will send you 4 additional novels and bill you just $4.24 each in the U.S., or $4.74 each in Canada, plus 25¢ delivery per book and applicable taxes if any.* That's the complete price and — compared to cover prices of $5.50 or more each in the U.S. and $6.50 or more each in Canada — it's quite a bargain! You may cancel at any time, but if you choose to continue, every month we'll send you 4 more books, which you may either purchase at the discount price or return to us and cancel your subscription.

BUSINESS REPLY MAIL
FIRST-CLASS MAIL   PERMIT NO. 717   BUFFALO, NY

POSTAGE WILL BE PAID BY ADDRESSEE

THE BEST OF THE BEST
3010 WALDEN AVE
PO BOX 1867
BUFFALO NY 14240-9952

NO POSTAGE
NECESSARY
IF MAILED
IN THE
UNITED STATES

forward. Years of knowledge and authority looked out from her eyes. She said something that Norah was unable to interpret, but it didn't matter. She understood.

"His ribs," she said again, repeating her gesture. "He fell." Her hand made a long arcing movement, and again she clutched at her own side before pointing to him.

The old woman spoke, and the braves hurried to remove the injured man from the horse. They stretched him flat on his back while the woman bent down. She prodded his rib cage swiftly with knowing fingers, then nodded curtly at Norah. "Ribs, yes," she said. Overtones of Spanish were noticeable in her inflection. "Broken."

She motioned for the men to carry Storm Caller to her lodge, then indicated that Norah should follow. She did. There was something in the old woman's air of command that Norah recognized, and she ducked through the low opening and entered the lodge. By warm light of the fire blazing beneath the smoke hole, she examined the interior. Two pallets lay on either side of the central fire, and a few possessions—baskets, bowls, blankets—were placed here and there in orderly fashion, either hanging from poles or stacked on the floor.

Norah edged close to the fire to take the chill from her hands, all the while keeping an eye on the others. When two of the men had laid Storm Caller on one of the pallets, the Indian woman waved them out of the lodge. As the one-eyed warrior went past Norah, he grasped her arm possessively and pulled her along behind him.

"Take your hands off me! I am not going anywhere with you!" Norah dragged her feet and tried to catch at something to halt her forward progress.

The brave rounded on her, and impatience flashed in his remaining eye, turning the brown iris to a reddish hue in the flickering light. He yanked on her arm, and Norah sprawled at his feet, feeling as if her limb had been jerked from its socket. While she lay in pain, his fingers twined in her hair, and he began dragging her out. In desperation she clamped her hands around his ankles and tried to upset him. With a roar of rage he pulled her upright by her hair. Some pulled loose from her scalp and brought tears of pain and indignation to Norah's eyes. Without thinking she bit his arm with all her might, and received a cuff across the cheek for her action. She lashed out at him with her hands clenched into fists, and he caught them in a cruel grip.

The old woman spoke, once, sharply. Norah fell to the ground as the brave abruptly released her. He protested volubly, but the woman advanced on him, speaking rapidly and gesturing. A one-sided argument began, with the man complaining loudly, but the woman merely repeated the same stream of words, and he retreated, mumbling viciously beneath his breath. Norah realized he had considered her to be his booty, and she was grateful to be spared. Sitting up slowly, she pushed the hair from her face while the old woman observed her. Norah had the distinct impression that her fate was being weighed.

"Long time, no English..." the woman said shortly, intelligence and conjection in her obsidian eyes. She sucked her teeth a moment, rummaging through the vast storehouse of her memory for the words she needed. "Rides-the-Storm—you his woman? He brings you?"

For the second time Norah faced that question. "Yes." It was easier this time, and she met the shrewd black glance squarely.

"I am Elk Dancer. Rides-the-Storm, I am his mother's mother. While he lives, you stay...and if he die..." She shrugged. "I make medicine for him." She gestured for Norah to remove her clothing and lie beside the still-unconscious man. "You keep him warm."

Norah hesitated a moment, then shucked the buckskin garments and slipped beneath the buffalo robe in nothing but her pantalets; at the present moment she needed the warmth of his body as much as he needed hers. She lay with several inches separating them, but the chill of the night in the canyon and the frosty early morning ride was still in her veins. Cautiously, she placed her feet against the side of his legs. Beneath the surface coolness of his skin, she felt the heat radiate to her, and edged closer until her face was almost touching his shoulder and she could feel her own breath deflected back to warm her cheeks. Too cold and shaken to feel any modesty, she inched up against him until her breasts rested against the sinewy muscles of his arm.

Now that her immediate danger was relieved she was able to give thought to the future. Time passed while the firelight lost its battle to determined shadows that gradually filled the lodge, and Norah wondered sleepily what would happen next.

Disjointed and alarming dreams of riding with Death at his side tormented Storm Caller, alternating with periods of soothing nothingness. Eons seemed to pass before he floated to the upper levels of near consciousness, and he hovered there, unwilling or unable to return to the world of reality.

Hearing returned first: the sibilant sighs of the wind, the crackle of a wood fire, the gurgle of liquid being poured, intruded gradually into Storm Caller's blurred dreams. Next he became aware of odors: the peculiar pungency of willow bark and fever-bane steeping in hot water, the crisp smell of roasted meat, dripping with fat, and finally, the familiar and reassuring scent of a woman. He made a great effort to open his eyes, but couldn't.

"He is waking. I saw his eyelids move," a woman's voice murmured.

Another answered in swift-flowing Comanche interspersed with Spanish, and Storm Caller realized the first voice had spoken in Spanish also. He heard the rustle of soft leather, and the red glow visible through his closed lids darkened as a figure leaned over him. A hand touched his arm. He tried again to shake off the tendrils of lethargy that bound him, but they wound around and pulled him down once more into the deep and welcoming blackness.

When he woke it was much later. His brain was remarkably clear as the first thing he saw were the embers of a banked fire glowing fiercely red in the center of the lodge. There was another body lying soft and warm against his. He looked down. Slade's wife. *Norah.*

"Norah!" He didn't know he spoke aloud, and was startled to hear his own voice echo in the silence of the lodge.

She didn't stir. Lying on her side, one small hand cradled beneath her cheek, she slept as if drugged or exhausted. Her face was hollowed, and there was a bruised look to the translucent skin under her closed eyes. She wore nothing but his faded blue shirt, which was much too large for her tiny frame, and Storm Caller smiled without knowing it. He had no idea where they were or how she came to be with him. Perhaps this was only a dream.

He raised himself up on one elbow, and the movement cost him a moment of dizziness and a sharp blade of pain along his ribs, which were bound with strips of cloth. This was no dream: the pain was far too real. He lay back down, eyes closed against the giddy whirling of the walls, and pieced the puzzle together, until the only remaining questions in his mind were who had brought them back to the Indian camp and how…and when. Had hours passed or days? He coughed, grabbing his side against the sudden flame of agony.

"So, you wake at last, Came-with-Thunder!" a satisfied voice said softly from the shadows. At the sound of his child-hood name, Storm Caller's eyes flew open. "Ah," the voice continued, "I never knew you to be so fond of your bed before, but perhaps that is because you share it with a woman now." A hand, stiff and gnarled as a blackthorn branch but incredibly gentle, reached out to touch his fever-ridden flesh.

"Elk Dancer!" He relaxed as the old woman approached and memory rolled over him in a warm familiar wave. Elk Dancer, his own grandmother, who was also grandmother to Horns-of-Buffalo. Her last years should have been spent in comfort, not on the sharp edge of danger with a desperate band of freedom fighters. He struggled to sit up once more and white-hot wires burrowed under his ribs and pierced into his lungs. He coughed and gasped for air.

She eased him back down. "The fever has broken, but it is too early for you to move about. Tomorrow you may get up, but today you must rest." She put a wiry arm behind his neck and held a drinking gourd to his lips with her other hand. "Drink this. It is bitter, but it will ease the pain and make you sleep."

"Pah!" The brew was so vile he spat the first mouthful out reflexively. Elk Dancer tilted the gourd inexorably and poured a thin but steady trickle into his mouth until she judged he had swallowed enough.

"How many days…?"

"Three."

"And the woman? She is ill...or injured?"

"She is only weary. And afraid, although she tries not to show it. Sleep is the best cure for her, and she will be all right when she awakens."

Elk Dancer's voice went on, but her medicine was already taking effect on him, and after a while her voice was only sound without meaning, like the rustling of trees in the wind or water flowing over smooth stones.

The sleep was deep and refreshing, and the next time he opened his eyes he felt wide awake and fully alert. All his senses seemed sharpened, as if his visit with Death had given him a heightened awareness of everything: the darkness near the top of the lodge seemed richer, deeper, the colors of the banked fire, impossibly bright, impossibly brilliant.

His gaze went full circle and came to rest on the woman lying beside him. The fire had dwindled and the lodge was cold, but it was warm beneath the buffalo-skin robe with the heat of the woman's body augmenting his own. She was nestled against him, her dusky hair spilling across his shoulder like skeins of silk, her soft breasts touching his arms with the rise and fall of her breathing. For a few moments he merely watched her, then he sat up cautiously and placed his feet on the ground.

Norah awoke to find her patient standing near the brightly burning fire. She saw him sway, then jumped up and braced him with her hands for support. His face was sickly white and beaded with sweat.

"You are not to get up until Elk Dancer says you may," she told him sternly, steering him back to his pallet.

Storm Caller sank back down thankfully. "I am not as strong as I thought," he said with heavy disappointment.

"Of course not. You have been very ill for three days, and you have had only a few liquids. You need food and rest." She pulled the robe back over him. "It is not warm enough in here yet, anyway."

She circled the fire and reached for the woman's clothing Elk Dancer had given her from its hanging place. She kept her back to him as she stepped into the leggings and pulled the long dress of doeskin over her head. Storm Caller watched her as she took a porcupine-tail brush and pulled it through her long, thick hair. It was rich and glossy. He wanted to touch it, feel the strands slip through his fingers like flowing water.

When she'd finished her toilette, Norah brought him a carved wooden cup. "Some fresh broth. Elk Dancer says you must drink it all."

He looked at her suspiciously. "How do you know what Elk Dancer says? She speaks no English—and I doubt you know the Comanche tongue."

Norah's chin tilted up. "We understand each other well enough. Women always do." She tested the temperature of the broth. "Elk Dancer knows a few words of Spanish, and we use gestures to communicate. Now drink."

She held the cup, and he lifted his head, but became dizzy again. It seemed like a terrible effort just to support its throbbing weight upon his neck. Norah slipped her arm behind his shoulders to hold him forward, and between the two of them he managed to sip at the broth. Some dribbled around the lip of the cup, and he put one hand up to assist Norah. As his fingers closed over her wrist, she pulled back with a cry and the hot liquid spilled across the buffalo robe.

"Did you burn yourself?" He grabbed her hand, and just as quickly Norah snatched it back.

She looked at him with frightened eyes. "I will get you some more broth."

She started to rise, and Storm Caller put out a hand to stop her, then let it fall. He lay down, and a frown creased his brow. When she touched him, when she initiated the contact, there seemed to be no problem; yet when he did the same, she cringed or bolted. He could find no logic to explain her actions. When Norah came back he tested his observations and found them to be correct. Although she managed not to drop the cup this time, she stiffened imperceptibly when his hand closed over hers around the belly of the bowl.

"Why do you shrink from me? Norah...don't be afraid of me." Storm Caller felt the powerful current that flowed between them. Her lips were open; her breathing quickened. He knew she felt it too. "Don't be afraid. I won't hurt you."

She sat back on her heels while the broth sloshed against the sides of the vessel. "You already have."

Rising, she turned her back on him and hastened outside.

When she returned later her eyes were puffed and reddened. They did not speak, and the day passed awkwardly, each aware of the other's every move. Norah worked at punching holes in a piece of tanned hide, a task that Elk Dancer had set her to. She had a bone awl, the handle shaped like a horse's head and worn to satin smoothness over the years. Though the tool was unfamiliar to her, he saw that she handled it competently, if not quickly. He watched her with a strange contentment until his eyes grew tired, and he dropped his lids to rest them.

Mere seconds seemed to pass, but when he opened his eyes again the fire was low, and Elk Dancer's soft snore was the only sound. Norah lay beside him, deep in slumber. Storm Caller marveled and fretted that he, who had slept like the dead for three sunsets, had fallen asleep yet again in the middle of a thought, like a tired child. And now, when all the world was quiet his brain was wide awake and restless. He looked at Norah. Now her hair was black silk drifting across the white curves of her throat and shoulders. He reached out and wound a strand around his finger. It fascinated him, and he lifted a handful to his face. Finer and softer than his, it had a light fragrance he would have identified anywhere as hers.

On impulse he reached out to gently follow the line of her cheek with his fingers, feeling the fluttery moth-wing sensation of her breath against his skin. He let his fingertips glide along her throat and over the rounded shoulder, then down to her waist, inhaling the scent of her sleep-warmed body. She stirred and rolled on her back, and his hand slipped beneath the shirt, coming to rest on the soft valley between the curve of her hip bone and the feminine swell of abdomen. Suddenly, incredibly, he felt a surge of desire. He wanted her with such urgency that his hand trembled as it stroked the length of her thigh and then swept up to her breast.

She sighed in her sleep, and Storm Caller merely held her in his arms. At first that was enough, but soon his blood was coursing hot through every vein and artery. He'd always supposed that pain or illness would supersede a man's basic needs, but it was untrue, at least in the present case: he wanted to make love to her. Now. He shook her shoulder until she awoke, and was unprepared for the reaction he elicited.

Norah was in the grip of a nightmare, dreaming that Abner

had come to press his attentions on her. His hand was on her shoulder shaking her roughly, and she knew that pain and humiliation would follow in due time. Roused at last from her deep sleep, she was confused, disoriented, and filled with fear.

"Oh!" Her eyes opened wide, and she pulled away, seeing Abner's face dissolve and change into that of LeBeau. She had seen that same look in her husband's eyes enough times to understand its meaning. Her only knowledge of physical love between a man and woman was based on her relationship with Abner; to be brutalized by her husband was one thing, but to be treated the same way by LeBeau was more than she thought she could bear. Something inside her died a little, and she shrank from his touch with a despairing groan.

He stifled the sound with the palm of his hand, but he could not as easily blot the horror from her face. "Why do you look at me like that?" he demanded in a harsh whisper, stroking her hair as he would the coat of a frightened mare.

Tears of anger and betrayal flashed in Norah's eyes, and she hated herself for showing the signs of weakness. She thrust his hand from her mouth and sat up. "Leave me alone! Haven't you done enough? You abducted me, ruined my reputation, endangered my life and now...!"

Her voice caught in her throat, and she lashed out at him with her hands. Ragged nails scraped his cheek before Storm Caller caught her hands in his. He forced her back down, still trying to quiet her. Roused by their voices, Elk Dancer woke and saw what he was about instantly. She grinned, showing a missing incisor on the right.

"So, a little rest, and you think you have recovered *all* of your strengths, Rider-of-Storms." She chuckled dryly. "My grandson, you are a lusty man, but it is not good for you to take a woman yet, or the ghosts might steal your spirit away again. For now, go back to sleep, and let my medicine heal and protect you." She lay back down and rolled herself up in the soft hide once more.

Storm Caller turned back to Norah. She hadn't moved, but was watching him closely. Beneath his hand he felt her heart pounding in her breast until it seemed it would break through her ribs. He let his hand wander to her other breast, cupping its roundness, letting his fingers spread over it and close gently in restrained possessiveness. She shuddered and bit her lip while her eyes accused him of things he didn't understand.

With an oath he rolled away from her, facing the firelight. For a long time he watched the tiny flames leap and twist and change colors. Once again he was conscious of the ache at the back of his head, and the pain of his broken ribs as they see-sawed with his breathing. They were nothing to compare with the pain in his loins.

As the night waned, his need for her became an obsession, and he was sensitized to her nearness. He heard her every sigh and breath, knew when she fell asleep, knew when she woke. When he closed his eyes he relived their fall in the canyon, saw her again plummeting down the cliff face before his eyes. The need to touch her, to hold her and prove that she was safe, that she was real, blotted out everything else. Lowering his head to her hair, he cradled her face against his shoulder and pressed her body against his, feeling how small she was, how delicate her bones, how smooth her skin.

She sighed in her sleep and curled up against his side again, as if in sleep she sought the intimacy she shunned while awake. Perhaps, he thought, it was only the cold that made her turn instinctively to the warmth of his body. Whatever the reason, it did little to ease his state of mind. He ground his teeth and tried not to think of the half-naked woman sleeping near him. It didn't work. Sweat beaded his forehead and upper lip.

While his consciousness warred with his desire, morning came. The fire was almost out and Elk Dancer had gone from the lodge. Storm Caller steeled himself to rise from the pallet and try his legs again, hoping it would be easier to deal with his desire for her when a few feet separated them: the effort had already sapped him. Elk Dancer returned and saw the sheen of sweat on his face, and for the first time in her life made a mis-diagnosis.

"Your fever has returned, just as I warned you it would." She poured another draught of willow-bark infusion and forced it down his throat.

He swallowed it meekly, and without an explanation.

14

Breakfast in the Indian camp consisted of several cups of *too-pah*, coffee that was strong and dark and almost as thick as sulfur molasses. This morning when Norah woke there was no odor of boiling coffee to tempt her from sleep, although the enameled pot and coarse-ground grains stood waiting near the hearth. Wrapped in a buffalo robe, she got up and stirred the fire into new life as Elk Dancer entered the lodge.

The old woman picked up a dented tin pail and an oiled pouch of material Norah couldn't identify and handed them to her. Inside the pail was an oval stone, flaked and sharpened on one end, smooth to fit inside the palm of the hand on the other. "Dress and go with the women and fetch water for the coffee. They will show you what to do."

While Norah dressed she rummaged in a basket and pulled out a triangular section of matted wool blanket. It was boldly stamped U.S. ARMY in one corner.

"Here, this will keep you warm."

Norah took the blanket, wondering at its history and how it came to be Elk Dancer's. Ignoring the dark stain near one end, she wrapped the piece of old blanket around her head and shoulders to ward off the chill and escaped into the fresh air. Although the temperature had risen to just above the freeze level, the morning was crisp and bright, the sky a vivid blue.

Beneath the gnarled branches of a crippled pine several women chattered, casting quick glances her way as she approached. They made room for Norah amongst themselves and set out, keeping her always under surveillance although they never met her gaze directly.

Mea-dro! "Let's go!" someone said, and the group started off.

As she fell in with the women Norah wondered what they thought of her: she had been six days in their camp now, but had not had contact with many of its residents. The time had been mostly spent in nursing her restless patient back to health and recovering her own stamina. As for the babe she carried... Norah pushed the thought from her mind, but in her heart she knew the child was dead.

At least, she thought, *I've put the time to good use, learning some of Elk Dancer's herb lore and a fair smattering of the Comanche tongue.* Understanding some of the words and simple phrases made her less afraid, for initially she had suffered from the captive's delusion that every word spoken must concern her fate in some way. Now she'd discovered that most talk was about food, weather, horses and health, just as it had been on the ranch.

Keemah! "Come!" a voice called, and Norah realized she was straggling behind. She quickened her step and caught up with the others.

There was only a light dusting of snow in the valley, but farther down the trail a deep stream split the rocky soil, and this was their destination. A few of the women talked together, laughing and gossiping as they went, their breath changing into frosty puffs of crystallized vapor before their faces. A girl of perhaps fourteen walked close to Norah and eyed her with great curiosity, apparently fascinated by her pale skin and blue eyes. The girl's flat features were open and held none of the malice Norah had noticed in certain other faces, and she attempted to communicate with her.

"I am called Norah," she said in halting Comanche, carefully repeating the words Elk Dancer had taught her. "What are you called?"

The girl shied away from her in horror, and the others drew away, clucking and scolding shrilly. Another girl, slim and graceful, made a deprecating sound. Norah realized she'd made a grave error. Too late she remembered what Father Ildephonso had said in her first days at Santa Magdalena: the use of one's name was a gift to be given carefully, for it conferred power over the name's owner: to ask a person's name was a terrible gaffe. For the rest of the way she walked alone, inside a ring of disapproving faces.

The creek lay at the foot of a small incline, etched by eons of running water. At its margins the ice was thick, shining with a blue-green translucence. Farther out it took on a grayish hue, with irregular patches of near black in the new and dangerously thin areas. A short thin squaw, whose excess folds of skin revealed she had once been much heavier, set down her prized tin bucket and began to hack and chip at the ice. The others did the same, except for the flat-faced girl. She moved out on the frozen gray ripples and pounded a dark section at arm's length with the sharp heel of an old polishing stone. After a few minutes of fruitless effort, Norah followed her.

She knelt and began chipping at some near vertical ridges formed by an earlier ice jam. It was harder than it looked, and at first the only results of her labor were flying splinters that glittered in the sun. Cold seeped into her knees, and she changed to the squatting position the others used. As she hammered away, she felt a muted vibration and realized it was the flow of the dark waters trapped below the ice. Then, with a sharp cracking sound, a piece broke free. She placed it in the pail and attacked another glistening section.

She sensed someone behind her, and a moment later a shove sent her sprawling forward on her belly. Stifled laughter sounded behind her. She clutched at her abdomen, anticipating pain. There was none, had been none for over two weeks. Without a word she righted herself and went back to work. Pride kept her from looking at the others, and she set about hacking at the ice again, as if nothing had happened. She sensed the flat-faced girl was watching her, but gave no sign.

A moment later it happened again, this time a sharp blow between her shoulder blades that sent her sliding across the slick and bumpy surface toward a dark portion of ice. She felt it bend beneath her weight, heard the ominous creak and the low murmur of cold water flowing below the ice. For a few seconds she lay still, then began to scrabble backward toward safety. Before her she could see the flat-faced girl looking her way.

There was an odd popping sound, and the ice gave way, but not beneath Norah: instead it was the flat-faced girl who was pitched forward, sinking in the inky waters. There was only a small opening, and the girl did not appear again. Norah looked over her shoulder. The women had gathered on the bank in a silent knot.

"Help us! I can't see her! Help us, damn you!"

They stood like stones, except for one young girl who ran toward the camp. There was no time to waste. Norah crept across the thicker layers toward the gaping hole and then felt and heard something thumping beneath her. Through the whitish layers of ice she saw movement, and a lighter colored oval that might have been a face. The girl was trapped under the ice! Without thinking of her own peril, she inched forward again until her face was partly over the open water, rolled up her sleeve, and thrust her arm down into it. The burning pain of extreme cold throbbed through her limb, and she almost pulled it back. She persisted, and now it was rapidly numbing.

Then she felt it. Something feebly grasping at her fingers. With more willpower than strength, she reached down with her other hand and caught a thick braid of hair. Norah pulled up with all her might, unaware of the sounds of commotion from the streambank. A blanched face, flat-featured and terrified, broke the surface. The girl's hands were blue-gray and uselessly curled against their palms so that she was unable to assist her rescuer.

Again Norah shouted for help: the girl was beginning to slip back, dragging Norah helplessly along. There would soon come a time when she would have to let go of the girl to keep from slipping into the water herself. She grabbed for the other braid and prayed.

Someone grabbed Norah's heels and began pulling her back. Her hands felt frozen but still held fast to the thick plaits of hair. Another tug on her feet brought them both backward six inches, and the ice bowed beneath the girl's shoulders as they came out of the water. Behind them the others called out encouragement. Suddenly Norah's grip let go.

"No!" she gasped, but the girl was partially out of the water.

Norah was safe on the solid ice, and a small wiry youth named Two Horses Racing crept forward in her place.

A buffalo-hide robe was thrown around Norah, but she had eyes only for the drama being played out a few feet away. Two Horses Racing grasped the girl's wrists while a chain of men began to haul on the rope about his waist. He backed toward the shore as they heaved on the rope, and the girl broke free. She was held up and wrapped in another robe while one of the squaws pulled off the wet skirts and blouse that had weighed her down and were now freezing stiffly in the frigid air. Then Long Legs, a stalwart young brave, picked her up and carried her swiftly back toward the camp.

Norah was so weak with reaction that her knees jellied, and she tottered drunkenly. This time there were friendly hands to steady her, and the looks she received from the women were filled with admiration instead of malice. All, that is, except for the slim young girl, who scowled unconsciously at Norah all the way back to camp.

Their arrival was greeted with loud exclamations and many questions that Norah, despite her facility at languages, was unable to follow. Voices babbled out the story all around them. One word was repeated several times and caught her ear. When Elk Dancer joined them Norah turned.

"What are they saying? What does that mean?"

The old woman's eyes shifted away. "It means slave. The girl you pulled from the water is Old Gray Rocks' slave." Norah was appalled. A slave. Expendable. Was that why no one else had gone to the girl's assistance at first? Or had it only been fear that held them?

A rough hand grasped her arm, and she found Storm Caller's angry gray eyes boring into hers. His face was as pale as hers in the morning sunlight. "Stupid fool! How could you take such a chance? You might be lying dead beneath the ice at this moment!"

His fingers dug into her arm, and Norah pulled away, too upset to question the motive for his fury. "Yes, and then you might have lost *your* slave!"

"What...? A slave? You are not my slave!" He seemed stunned by her words.

"Then what am I?" Bitterness dripped from her tongue. "I

was a free woman with my own home and lands. Now I am your captive. I cannot come and go as I choose. I do your errands, fetch your water, cook your meals... My very life is in your hands! What else would you call me?''

She pushed away through the crowd, hurrying so Storm Caller would not see the tears that filled her eyes. He made no attempt to follow her. Norah suddenly heard someone coming up behind her. She stepped aside and turned, anticipating another shove.

"*Keemah*," Old Gray Rocks said imperatively. "Come with me."

Norah wanted nothing more than to collapse by her own fire, but she followed Old Gray Rocks into her tepee. The girl who had fallen through the ice lay on a pallet close to the fire, teeth clacking as she shivered beneath a pile of hides and well-worn blankets. A woman offered sips of hot liquid, concern in the lines of her face and body. The girl's lips were still slightly tinged with blue, but the blanching of her face was not as apparent now, and as Norah entered she lifted her head a bit.

"Come closer, Braves-the-Water," she said hoarsely, extending a thin hand.

Norah knelt by her side and took the cold brown hand in her own, feeling kinship with this girl who was as lost and alone as she. For a moment no one spoke, and the shadows moved along the hide walls, leaping and flickering as the flames danced below the smoke hole. The girl's eyes closed a moment, then opened wide.

"My name," she said, "is Snow-in-Summer."

Storm Caller was still angry when the sun began to set. He snapped at Norah the few times he could bring himself to speak to her, complained about the stew of venison and onions, refused Elk Dancer's brews and poultices, and cursed beneath his breath for no reason at all.

Norah watched him uneasily. His face was gaunt, his sinewy body thinner, and she did not think he should be up again, for fresh lines of strain marked his face and hollowed his cheeks. It was evident that the excitement of the morning's events had worsened his condition. She had learned much of healing from

Elk Dancer and knew that rest was often the best and only cure; at the same time she saw that his growing impatience prevented any true rest.

"How will we know when he may safely be up and about again?" she asked Elk Dancer in a low tone.

"When the time comes, you will see for yourself. It will be very soon, I think."

On the heels of her words Stone Caller suddenly rose from the pallet where he had been sitting and grabbed his garments from their hanging place.

"I will not lie swathed in blankets like some invalid!" he said defiantly. "I have been idle long enough."

Norah glanced from his face, set and pale, to Elk Dancer's impassive features and waited for her remonstrance. There was none. The Medicine Woman watched her grandson as he thrust his arms and legs into his buckskins, but said nothing at all.

Norah clasped her hands in concern, about to speak, but Elk Dancer made a small sign, and she held her peace. The old woman did nothing without purpose, and her instincts must be trusted. When Storm Caller stomped out of the lodge like a sulky bear Elk Dancer nodded with satisfaction.

"*That* is how you know your patient is well again. He will tell you."

The wind changed, and smoke swirled back into the tepee. Quickly Norah grasped the two long poles that regulated the direction and width of the smoke-hole "ears" and changed their orientation, unaware of the approval in Elk Dancer's eyes. Next she cleaned up the few utensils and made sure there was enough wood to keep the fire going through the night: with Elk Dancer's advanced age and Storm Caller's injuries, tending the hearth had become one of her tasks. Carefully she checked to see that all was as it should be, while Elk Dancer made ready for bed.

In the course of a few short weeks she had again adapted her life-style to her changed surroundings: in Boston she had brushed her teeth and hair and said her prayers before climbing in her narrow iron bed; on Abner's ranch she had checked the shutters and doors, put out the lanterns, and set a fresh candle on the nightstand beside the heavily carved double bed. Here, in the middle of a rocky and isolated canyon, she found herself settling once more into prudent housewifely habits, except this time her home was a hide tepee, her bed a hard pallet.

There was a discreet cough, the usual announcement of a visitor, from outside the lodge, and Blue Feather, wife of Horns-of-Buffalo, slipped through the entrance flap. She was slim and straight in contrast to the stockiness of most of the other women, and had a broad, rather flat face and softly bowed mouth.

"*Hi, Pohawe.*" She addressed Elk Dancer first, as was proper. "Horns-of-Buffalo sends greetings and to say that the sore on his foot is healing well with your salves." She faced Norah. "*Hi tai*, Braves-the-Water."

In her hands she carried a basket tightly woven of dried reeds and decorated with chevron patterns of silky wild grasses. It was finer than anything in the lodge. She held the basket out to Norah. "Accept this poor gift of my own hands, Braves-the-Water, as a measure of my gratitude."

Norah looked her bewilderment. This was a valuable gift. "Is this for me? I have done nothing to earn your thanks." Blue Feather erupted in a spout of earnest language, too rapid and oddly accented for Norah to follow. She looked from the visitor to the old woman.

Elk Dancer explained. "Blue Feather is sister to the one called Snow-in-Summer, whose life you saved yesterday. She gives you this basket to show her thanks. It is of her own weaving in the way of Blue Feather's people, and is very fine. You must accept it."

"But I have nothing to give in return as custom requires."

"There is no need in this case."

Norah took the basket in her own hands. Gravely, Blue Feather nodded and bowed her head. Norah blushed and smiled and did the same. With quiet dignity, Blue Feather turned and left them.

Examining her new—and only—personal possession with a puzzled frown, Norah settled herself next to the old woman. "I think I have not understood you well. How can it be that Blue Feather is the wife of a war chief, while Snow-in-Summer is the slave of Old Gray Rocks?"

"They are not *Nermenruh*, the People, but of another tribe far to the south. They were taken on a raid and sold to a trapper, who brought them to Horns-of-Buffalo in return for many goods and favors. Since he had no use for two wives, he traded the other girl to Old Gray Rocks for a string of fine horses. Ah, we were wealthy in horses and goods in those days!''

She shook her head in sorrow, lost in the more prosperous past, while Norah stared. It seemed incredible that one sister would gain high status and the other be doomed to slavery. ''But couldn't Blue Feather ask her husband to buy her sister's freedom? Surely she is not happy with things as they are!''

''Some do not treat horses or slaves well, and others treat them as if they were their own children. Old Gray Rocks has only a nephew and her slave to look to her comfort, and she treats Snow-in-Summer as if she were her daughter.''

This made no sense to Norah. She had learned that slavery was common among the tribes of the Territory; she also knew that children captured in raids were frequently adopted, with all the rights and privileges of tribal members. The factors that made one child a slave and another a cherished son or daughter eluded and angered her. The last embers of her view of Indians as ''Noble Savages'' abruptly extinguished themselves. They were like any other race, and vice existed side-by-side with virtue, wisdom and tenderness with stupidity and cruelty. It did nothing to lessen her sense of outrage over the owning of slaves, for she was not free herself.

Soon darkness fell, and the old woman's even breathing told she was asleep. Storm Caller had not returned, and Norah moved restlessly about the dwelling. It was too dark to sew, too cold to sit up, and too late to stay awake. She stripped off her clothes and slipped beneath the buffalo-hide robes. Her body grew warm and rosy, her limbs relaxed, but she did not sleep. Where was Storm Caller? What was he doing out alone in the frozen darkness? And when was he coming back?

While Norah waited and wondered, Storm Caller wandered aimlessly about the camp until he suddenly found himself at the edge of the frozen stream. The dark hole had already skimmed over with new ice in the silvery light, but the scene of the near tragedy was otherwise unchanged. The aura of Death hung in the air, as if it waited with cold patience for another victim.

Somewhere up the canyon a small animal cried out once, a

shrill desperate cry, then fell silent in the jaws of a hungry predator. Storm Caller listened, but did not hear. Shadows loomed up tall and purple along the face of the high ridges, and Storm Caller saw, but did not see. He stayed for a long time, and the longer he stayed the more his anger grew. His wrath was wild and unreasoning, aimed as much at himself as at Norah for risking her life, but that knowledge did nothing to assuage it. His life was out of control, and he was no longer master of his fate. Somewhere he had made a wrong turning, but he didn't know where or how, or even if he wanted to go back.

White streaks of cloud swirled against the black-glass sky when he finally headed back to Elk Dancer's lodge, and the wind hummed tunelessly through the shallow valley. Inside the tepee the fire was banked for the night, glowing orange and red beneath its gray coat of ashes. Norah lay curled up beneath the buffalo robe in a half sleep, drowsily listening for the sounds of Storm Caller's return. Reassured, she turned away from the mellow light and drifted deeper into slumber. It was not long before Storm Caller joined her.

He tried to close his eyes but saw only black-and-white images of the frozen stream that had almost claimed Norah and Snow-in-Summer. Suddenly he needed the reassurance of touch to know she was alive and safe. He rolled toward her and put his hand on her shoulder, letting it rest there a moment. That did not content him, and he moved closer, placing his hand over her heart, feeling its soft rhythm against his palm.

Norah's quick intake of breath told him she was awake, and he felt her heartbeat racing beneath his touch yet she neither moved nor spoke. It seemed as if her heart trembled within her. Desire for her washed over him, sweeping caution and restraint away. His hand slipped sideways to cover her breast and Norah tensed. Storm Caller brought his passion under control and waited unmoving, letting her become accustomed to this intimacy. After a time her rigidity eased, but he bided his time until her breathing slowed to a more normal rate.

Raising himself on one elbow he looked down at Norah. Her eyes were closed, her face emptied of emotion, and he had no clue to her thoughts. With slow deliberation he cupped her breast in his rough palm, closing his long fingers possessively over the softness of her flesh. Her eyes opened and, as he brought his face down to hers, she turned away. He pulled her around to face him, drawing her against him. Moments passed while he kept her captive in his embrace, feeling her breathing feather against his skin.

Slowly Storm Caller's thumb circled her nipple. Her lids fluttered down to hide her eyes while his fingers explored and kneaded and stroked. He brought his hand down to clasp her waist, then over her thigh. His mouth found the hollow of her collarbone, then traced a path between her breasts.

Though passive in his arms, Norah's thoughts were wheeling and circling in upon themselves. The very gentleness of Storm Caller's approach confused her, as did the curious sensations rippling hot and cold through her body. Abner had never touched her in this way. He had grabbed and pinched with cruel fingers and teeth, he had thrust his way through her protests or the angry tears that came unbidden to her eyes. In all the times Abner had taken her, he had never given her any pleasure, and at the height of his passion he had given only pain.

She had only her deepest instincts to counter the experiences of her marriage bed, and beneath Storm Caller's arousing and persistent touch they were brought to sudden life. When his fingers drifted over her skin Norah did not stop him, and when his hot breath whispered against her breast, a soft sound came from her lips. Then his mouth surrounded her nipple, and she felt a deep pulling sensation in her loins, new and extraordinarily exciting. A sweet lassitude spread through her limbs. Her hands crept up to touch Storm Caller's head, and her fingers laced through his thick hair, gently pressing the hard planes of his face into the softness of her breast.

Her first tentative response heated his blood, and Storm Caller was caught up in the urgency of his need for her. He had no thought but to claim her as his own and was unprepared for the change in her. As his hand swept down and over the mound of her abdomen, fearful remembrances grasped and held Norah's mind. She could not bear to have him do to her all the things that Abner had done, and when Storm Caller's hand slid between her legs she began to fight and push against him in blind panic.

The alteration in Norah startled him. He didn't want to stop, was almost to the point of not being able to stop: but if he didn't stop now it would be too late, and she would always hate him. He lifted his mouth from her breast, still tasting her, still feeling the textures of her on his tongue. He covered her mouth in time to stifle her small cry, and one look at her face was all it took to cool his heat: her features were twisted with emotion, set into hopeless, agonized lines. He didn't want her to look at him like that!

"What is it?" His hand lifted to cradle her cheek, and she flinched. Storm Caller frowned. "Have I hurt you?"

"No. No!" She shook her head, almost weeping now with sudden humiliation and the unrecognized cravings of her own deep sensuality. Burying her face in her hands, she wept without making a sound, although her body shook with the effort.

Elk Dancer rolled over in her sleep. Otherwise there was silence except for the soft crackle of the banked flames. Storm Caller looked down at Norah a long while. He made no attempt to touch her. After a while he turned away from her and tried to slow the tumult in his mind and loins. She was no virgin. And he was not cruel. Then why did she shrink from him now? Did she fear him so greatly? Or did she hate him? And yet, when she nursed him, her hands were gentle in their ministrations, and she never seemed hesitant to touch him. His thoughts chased around in circles, searching for some logic in her behavior.

Finally he thought he'd found the answer. Even now there were bruises on Norah's body, some old and yellowing among the blue and more recent ones. Slade had abused her until she retreated instinctively from a man's touch. The poisonous cup of Storm Caller's guilt ran over. Was he any different? He had wanted to take his vengeance on her, had abducted Norah, humiliated her, and placed her very life in danger. And then he expected her to turn to him, to give in to him willingly. He heard a small sob in the darkness, quickly covered and not repeated, and cursed himself for ten times a fool.

The two halves of his personality warred with each other anew: while the white man inside his head reviled the barbarism of his Indian ways, the Comanche warrior inside his soul scorned the soft sentimentality of his other self. Neither among *Nermenruh*, the People, nor among the pallid-skinned *tosi tivo* had he found the comfort of belonging that he had so urgently sought all his life. Suddenly he was weary. His head ached. A sense of loneliness, terrible in its intensity, bubbled up inside his chest until it seemed his lungs would burst. Would he never find peace?

The long night brought good counsel, and in the morning he was more objective. While Norah put the coffee on to brew, he considered their situation. He had no intention of letting her be free of him. He wanted her, as a man wants a woman, and had every intention of taking her. The only obstacle to achieving this was the strong notion that had rooted in his brain: when he took her, she must be willing.

No, she must be more than willing—she must want him, too. It would be difficult, but not impossible, and his blood warmed at the thought. He would woo her, lure her gently to him as if she were a wild mare. And then, when she finally came to him, she would be his.

"Good morning, Norah." He threw off the covers and rose.

"Good morning." Her voice was stilted and breathless, and an embarrassed flush colored her cheeks.

He did not look at her as he went about his dressing, acting as if nothing had occurred between them in the night. Norah poured out another cup of coffee into an enameled mug. Her hand trembled, and drops hissed and splattered in the flames. She handed him his mug of coffee steadily enough though, and she was glad that he looked into the hot liquid rather than her face.

He took a deep draught of coffee. "Ah, this is good!"

Norah made no reply, relieved that she need not confront him now. As the day progressed they fell into their familiar patterns of behavior, and neither by word nor gesture did he remind her of the way his hands and mouth had caressed her so intimately. Yet later when she bathed herself she could not keep from looking at her body and wondering what he had thought and felt as he touched her. His constraint made her wonder also, for Abner would have continued no matter what she said or did: why was Storm Caller different? Was he ashamed of his actions? Or had his desire for her been only a brief notion? Perhaps he didn't find her pleasing.

So went her thoughts as the day wore on and, as she pondered, her relief turned to a bewildered sort of gratitude. Storm Caller saw all this and smiled inwardly. His plan was already working.

15

The wind blew from the west all week, pushing a mass of
warm air before it. On the seventh day, bright hard sunshine
poured down on the frozen earth, luring small animals from
their holes and burrows in a fruitless search for spring. The
human inhabitants of the hidden camp came forth from their
lodges and turned their winter-scoured faces to the sky. They
were fugitives, exiled from their tribal lands and losing ground
swiftly in the battle against hunger, disease, and despair; still
they gathered in loose knots as they went about their daily
tasks, talking and laughing. Today the sun was warm, their
bellies full, and life was good. They enjoyed this respite, knowing it would be all too brief.

As the morning had brought unexpected sunshine, the afternoon brought unexpected visitors into the narrow valley. Norah
sat in the lodge of Old Gray Rocks, sewing as Snow-in-
Summer slept. A chill had settled in the girl's chest, and she
had drowsed off after a medicinal posset. The old woman
dozed near the fire, toothless mouth agape, but now her wheezy
respirations stopped. She blinked, and her eyelids uncreased
their owl-like folds and slid wide over white-filmed eyes.

"White man's horses! Someone comes," she announced and
began to rise. The process was slow and done with great difficulty, for her bones were soft and painful from her calcium-
poor diet.

Norah set aside the moccasins she was clumsily stitching and listened. At first she heard nothing, but after a bit she picked up distant sounds. Adrenaline poured through her body as hooves rang on the iron-hard ground, and wild speculations grew in her mind: perhaps Captain Gartner has sent a rescue party for her. A welcome image of a blue-clad Cavalry troop sprang up before her eyes. A less pleasant thought occurred— it might be Abner and his men, come to take her back. Whoever they were, she prayed they would not take vengeance on Elk Dancer or the others who had been kind to her. She had no illusions as to what they would do to Storm Caller when they knew the truth.

Half blind though she was, Old Gray Rocks sensed that rescue was in her mind. "Perhaps they are horse soldiers." She smiled slightly, and her mouth folded in upon itself.

Snow-in-Summer spoke then, her voice low and fierce despite its weakness. "If they are horse soldiers, you must run away and hide."

Norah rose to her feet eagerly. "I have no reason to fear the soldiers! What could they do, kidnap me and return me to my home?"

"They would do worse than kidnap you," the girl answered. "I know." She spoke so quietly that an icicle stabbed up Norah's spine. "Your hair," she went on, "is black, as is ours. Your clothes, they are the same. How will they know you are of the *tosi tivo*? You must run away, I tell you!"

Near the lodge entrance now, Norah hesitated and Snow-in-Summer continued urgently. "Do you know what the horse soldiers do to women? Not long ago a group of them came upon three women of the tribe who were out gathering roots: the horse soldiers, they shot them without warning, then dismounted and raped them while they died."

Old Gray Rocks nodded. "Do you *really* think a soldier would stop first to hear you speak or stay his hand to check the color of your eyes?"

Norah was stunned. Here was another fear, another horror to haunt her waking and sleeping. Since Storm Caller had abducted her, she had prayed for white men to find her and take her away. The destruction of her sudden new hope was a terrible thing, and she went more cautiously to lift the edge of the flap. Old Gray Rocks limped up to her and poked her small head out into the fresh air. Storm Caller and Two Horses Racing mounted their geldings and rode to intercept the newcomers, who approached from the arroyo below. Then Two Horses Racing suddenly wheeled his chestnut around and called back toward the camp. The tension left Old Gray Rocks, and she resumed her place by the fire.

"It is only Cut Face and Trah-vees." She made a sound of disgust and spat into the fire. "Almost as bad as horse soldiers, those two. They are not men of good heart."

Soon the four horsemen came in view, and Norah glimpsed the brave who had first brought her to the camp, the one with the scarred face and one eye sewn shut. A woman rode behind him, her hands clasped around his waist. The second rider came abreast, dressed in buckskins like the others, but a shirt of dark blue homespun was visible inside his open jacket. He pulled off his brown knit cap, and tufts of thick yellow hair glinted gold in the sunlight. Norah's pulse quickened. A stranger. A white man.

His features became clearer as he neared them, and she saw a puckered scar extending from the corner of his nose to within an inch of his mouth. There was an air of suppressed violence in his sudden jerky movements, and his horse rolled its eyes backward warily, as if in fear of its rider. Norah drew back inside. "Who is the man with Cut Face?"

Old Gray Rocks scratched her sides. "Him! He is no friend to us. Trah-vees gives with one hand and takes with the other. A wise man does not turn his back to that one. Why has Cut Face brought him to this place?" She nodded and rocked back and forth.

"But who is he, and why is he here?"

Old Gray Rocks washed her mouth out with a swallow of cold coffee and spat again, as if she had tasted something foul. "He is evil on two legs. Stay out of his shadow, I tell you. Now, go *namasi-kohtoo*, quick-quick, and tell Elk Dancer of his coming."

Snow-in-Summer had drifted off to sleep again, and Norah slipped out. She would find out more about the newcomer from Elk Dancer. As she stepped out into the sunshine, she noted that half the camp seemed to be gathered about Cut Face and his companions. The men seemed angry. Cut Face was speaking, but she could not hear him for distance. Whatever it was, it certainly held the attention of his audience, which stood motionless and silent.

She went into the lodge and found Elk Dancer preparing tea from an infusion of bark chips, roots, and dried berries. Norah knew that mixture, for the Medicine Woman had taught it to her: it was a potent painkiller. And there was no one in the camp receiving that treatment, as far as she knew. She glanced at Elk Dancer's face, and in the split second before it turned away, saw the underlying pallor and the gray-blue of the wrinkled lips. Her affection for Elk Dancer was deep and genuine, and she was filled with foreboding.

"What is it? What is wrong?" She hurried forward, but the Medicine Woman waved her away and drank the dark liquid.

"It is nothing!" Elk Dancer began, but changed her mind. She sighed. "You have sharp eyes. I will not lie to you. I am an old woman, Braves-the-Water, and am entitled to my pains. And I am entitled to ease them if I will, in my last days."

"You are ill! Why have you said nothing? You should have told me! We must tell Storm Caller. He does not know. I can see it in your face."

Elk Dancer drew herself up commandingly. "I myself will tell him when it is time; until then we will say no more of this."

"But what can I do to help you? There must be something...."

"All you can do to help me I have already said: you will tell no one, especially you will not tell Storm Caller. Now we will speak no more of this. *Suvate*, it is finished."

Norah nodded dumbly. She would have to honor Elk Dancer's decision, yet it was impossible to imagine the camp and its people without the guidance of this wise old woman. Elk Dancer was an important person, one whose advice and assistance were sought by all. She was the eldest of the band and their only link with the bountiful past when the buffalo herds had made the plains echo with their thunder. When she was gone, so would be their hope that those days would return. All this Norah saw, but it was for herself and for Storm Caller that she ached the most.

She pulled back a hide blanket. "At least you must rest now.

I will make a new salve and change the dressing on Horns-of-Buffalo's leg myself.''

"*Toquet*. It is good that you learn the old healing ways," Elk Dancer murmured. "Storm Caller has done well to bring you to his lodge." She lay on the pallet and closed her eyes, so did not see Norah's expression as she pulled the cover up over her.

It bothered Norah that Elk Dancer thought she was Storm Caller's woman. She wished with all her heart that she had never identified herself as such that first day in the camp. To be "Storm Caller's woman" implied a permanent—and voluntary—relationship between herself and Elk Dancer. One that was as nonexistent as such a relationship was with Storm Caller himself. And if his nightly actions and attentions meant anything, he was erroneously assuming even more than his grandmother was.

Selecting several fat roots from among their small store of vegetables, Norah sat on the edge of her pallet and began to slice them with a sharp knife. Her relationship with Storm Caller had taken on another phase, one that both terrified and fascinated her. Every night while they lay together beneath the warm robes, he touched and caressed and stroked her, yet demanded nothing. She no longer feared that he would cause her pain and humiliation as Abner had done, and indeed began to look forward each day to the setting of the sun.

Last night as his fingers had drifted along the insides of her thighs she had felt as if something were building inside her, as if some overwhelming experience lay just out of reach. Even now she felt a pull, deep in her body, and her breasts tingled thinking of him. She guessed Storm Caller's plan was to make her crave the pleasures of his touch, and she hated herself for falling into his trap, a not unwilling victim.

Angrily, she banished him from her thoughts and tried to concentrate on preparing the stew, but her mind roamed free of the repetitive task, and her thoughts looped back to Storm Caller. Norah did not understand how he could possibly be the same man she had known as LeBeau. She still looked for signs of the Army Scout she'd known at Camp Greenwood in the man whose pallet she shared, but there were none. She feared that he had been only a myth of her own making.

The knife thwacked rhythmically as she took her frustrations out on the hapless roots, and in her haste she nicked her left thumb. At first it didn't hurt, and the bright red crescent dripping along the thumb pad was her only indication. Then the injured thumb began to throb, and she sucked at the warm coppery-tasting fluid while tears pricked behind her eyelids.

Storm Caller entered the lodge and strode over to her. "There is a stranger in the camp. You will have nothing to do with him. You will stay within the tepee until he leaves."

Norah glared at him. "Yes, that would suit your purposes quite well! I've already seen him. The white man. Are you afraid he will take me back to—"

She had almost said "to Abner," and caught herself; wherever she wanted to go, it was *not* to Abner. "—to where I belong?" she corrected hastily.

He paled and grasped her upper arms and shook her, his mouth a grim line. "If you left with him you would never return. *Never!* He would take you no farther than the nearest bushes! Do I make myself clear enough?"

"You have a filthy mind, and I don't believe you. You are saying that to keep me from speaking to him!" Her voice was filled with disdain, yet her eyes showed the stirring doubts.

Storm Caller loomed over her, his gray eyes darkening to onyx. "Whether you believe me is not the issue. You *will* obey me."

His fingers were hurting her. Norah's bosom heaved with indignation, and she wrenched herself away. "Like *hell*, I will!"

Now it was Storm Caller who reacted heatedly. He caught her around the waist and, when she struggled, pushed her down on the sleeping pallet and pinned her helplessly beneath his weight. She clawed at his face but he held her wrists easily and laughed angrily down at her while she fumed.

"If necessary, I will bind and gag you for your own good. You have led a sheltered life. You have no knowledge of men such as this one. He hates women. After Travis had you, he would kill you—or give you to Cut Face, which would be worse than death. Is that what you want?"

As he held her, so soft and alluring beneath him, his wrath grew. The thought of Travis pawing at her white body made him feel sick; the thought of Cut Face raping and torturing her was beyond contemplation. The rise and fall of her breasts, the brightness of her blue eyes, the rosy flush of her cheeks worked like alchemy on his emotions, and he was swiftly and thoroughly aroused. While desire surged through him, lighting his eyes and darkening his skin, he held her motionless and let her feel the impact of his superior strength and his physical power over her.

Norah bucked and kicked, but her movements were effectively stifled. She turned her face away from him and went slack, in the reaction that had defeated him so many times before. But this time Storm Caller was distracted, and her tactic did not work.

He saw the smear of blood along the side of her mouth, but not its source. "You've hurt yourself! You have bitten your lip."

Before she could speak his mouth lowered to hers, softly brushing over the sensitive skin. Her lips burned where his had touched. Gently he tasted the corner of her mouth with his tongue, licking away the thin red line. She was undone by the gesture, all the restrained-virgin years and weeks of married bondage wiped clean. Now Storm Caller reaped the fruits of his patience in Norah's sudden sexual arousal. Bewildering heat coursed through her, and her mouth sought his, opening, ripening with the sweet sudden longing that swept through her. Her legs shifted apart, cradling him, while her breathing accelerated to match his.

She didn't know when or how her shirt was removed, but felt the nakedness of his chest against her own and felt the smooth hard touch of his body bringing her nipples erect. He was caught up in the same all-consuming flame of need then, and she welcomed his mouth and hands upon her flesh. With her own hands, she pressed his face to her breasts, twining her fingers in his hair. It was only when the rest of their clothing was gone that she became shy.

In the darkness of the night fires she had thought him strong and handsome, but now with the sunlight patterning through the translucent walls of the tepee she found him beautiful beyond comprehension. Her eyes as well as fingertips feasted on the supple muscles of his body, the sinewy strength of his arms and shoulders, the flat planes of his abdomen, the bunching muscles of his calves and thighs and buttocks. She wanted to be possessed by him, to be entered and filled with him, to be swept away by his skillful lovemaking and her own mounting passion.

Storm Caller sensed the change in her, and triumph flared hotly in his blood. His fingers explored between her legs, and found her moist and ready. This was as far as he had gone before, caressing and urging, but never invading. But this time he slipped them inside her, seeking the velvety warmth. Her body shook, one swift sudden tremor, and she clutched at him, burying her face against his breast. Her heart was thudding so hard he could feel it, too. For a moment he was completely still, holding himself in check and waiting for Norah to make the next step of her own volition.

She relaxed but kept him locked in the embrace. Slowly he began to move his hand again, looking down at her, exulting in her pleasure. Norah had left all her inhibitions behind. She thrust herself against his fingers and arched up, gripping his arm with her thighs. She came up to meet his rhythm and then her head fell back, and her eyes opened wide in surprise. Something was happening to her, something exquisitely pleasurable and deliriously intoxicating; something unknown and overwhelming and almost frightening. A second later she gasped and cried out again and again.

Storm Caller held her as she shuddered in ecstasy. When he released her she clutched at him, clung to him. This was what he had waited for, tortured himself for all those many long nights. Deftly, he entered her, feeling her flesh close about him, and he groaned in satisfaction and pleasure. He kept himself still at first, prolonging the dizzying anticipation until he could bear it no longer, and then thrust deeply into her. Norah's body stiffened beneath him, and her palms came up against his chest as if she would have pushed him away, and even in his passion he felt a stab of disappointment. He had wanted her to want him, utterly and completely. Well, it was too late for regrets and too late to hold back. He thrust again, filled with the rapture of possessing her at last.

He was extraordinarily aware of every sensation, from the satin texture of her inner thighs brushing along his, to the cushioning of his chest against her full breasts, the erotic touch of her hardened nipples as he moved over her and claimed her. Then he was spiraling skyward like the eagle in its flight, borne up by the rising winds of passion. His thrusts were faster now, but he was unaware of anything until he shivered and cried out her name, then crashed to earth again, spent and sweat-slicked in her arms.

Norah felt dazed. Dazed and wondering. At that moment when he had called her name, she had felt an impossible closeness with him, of both body and soul. For the first time in her life she had not felt alone. Now as he gasped for breath she held his head between her breasts and stroked his hair over and over. She was calm and for the moment, at peace.

They both slept, and when they wakened Storm Caller made love to her again, bringing Norah once more in thrall to his sensual skills. If he had not been the first to take her, he had been the first to awaken her womanhood; and if each time she held something of herself back from him when they finally joined, she was no longer an unwilling partner.

It was almost enough.

The meal was late that afternoon, and while Norah prepared it, her glance flew to Storm Caller a hundred times. He hunkered before the fire, hardening the tips of his arrows in the flame, and it was as if she could not keep her eyes from him. Her mood swung from elation to despair. She realized that in Storm Caller's arms she had finally learned to be a woman, for her body craved his with a wild desperation far beyond her ken. And she feared that this knowledge had taught her one more definition of the word *slave*.

The men sat in a circle within the lodge of Horns-of-Buffalo, the younger and less important ones sitting behind the others. The war chief was a stocky man with a massive head and intelligent eyes. Although he was older than Storm Caller by ten years, they shared equal status as war chiefs and were more like brothers than cousins. He lit the ritual pipe and passed it to Travis, who sat to his right. The fire's glow fell on the scarred face, and the puckered scar tissue seemed to writhe in the flickering light. The trapper inhaled, held the smoke, and passed the sacred pipe to Storm Caller. No one spoke until each man had had his turn.

Etiquette demanded that Horns-of-Buffalo, as host, lead the conversation, and Storm Caller, who sat beside him, grew irritated by the slowness of the conventional exchanges. He eyed the Kiowa with dislike. If Cut Face had a good reason for bringing a white man to their hidden camp, he wanted to hear it. Now. And it had better be a damned good one.

Horns-of-Buffalo nudged him indulgently and addressed the company. "My fellow war chief grows impatient. He has lived too long among the white men and walked too long on their path." He nodded to Storm Caller. "Ask what would you know of our visitor, Rides-the-Storm."

Storm Caller eyed Travis somberly. "You have been lately among our brothers of the *Quohadi*. What news of them and of Iron Knife do you bring?"

Travis spit into the fire. "Bad news." He shot a malevolent look at Storm Caller and answered in English. "Real bad news. Some of your friends...on both sides...have gone and killed each other, *Sergeant LeBeau*. You was smart to light out fer the high country when you did."

In the flash of an eye Storm Caller reached out and grabbed the trapper by the throat. A knife gleamed in one of his hands. "I don't take insolence from any man, Travis," he said from between his teeth. "And certainly not from a poor specimen like you."

No one moved to separate the two, but Horns-of-Buffalo, who knew a good deal of English himself, spoke mildly and in that language. "My brother, you are too hasty in your actions. Let us first hear what tales Trah-vees bring us."

Two Horses Racing grinned, and the other men nodded. They might not have understood the words, but they knew Horns-of-Buffalo's sense of humor, and the growing fear in the trapper's eyes was plain to all. He looked to Cut Face for succor, but the Apache was busily paring his nails with the tip of a steel blade, studiously ignoring the byplay.

Storm Caller released Travis, but the white marks of his long fingers turned to bright red welts along the other's throat. "Tell us of Iron Knife...and choose your words carefully, lest I take offense and decide to cut them off. Permanently.'' He swung back on his heels and waited impassively.

Travis cleared his throat once or twice, and his watery blue eyes avoided meeting the ring of dark ones that watched him now with interest. He pulled a flask from his pocket and took a quick pull.

"Iron Knife and his braves was heading up along the rim when they run inter a small party bound for Camp Verde. They was only gonna take them some fresh mounts an' ammunition and everthing woulda been peaceful-like, but one of the whites, name of Henderson, took exception.'' He cleared his throat nervously and rubbed his Adam's apple.

"This Henderson, he had his women with him and got all excited an' pulled a pistol on Legs Too Fat. Caught 'im in the shoulder. Only a scratch though, hardly bled a'tall. Iron Knife, he give his braves the word, and them whites was wiped out right then and there, everyone of 'em. Gen'l Crook is mad as hell and swearing to track Iron Knife down if it takes a hunert years.''

Storm Caller was silent. He felt as if a fist had smashed into his midsection. He knew Caleb Henderson and his wife and four daughters well. Henderson was a peaceable man, and not one to lose his head. The story was all wrong. He narrowed his eyes.

"How do you know this?''

Travis seemed to shrink into himself. "I hear a lot a' things.'' His hand edged surreptitiously to his collar and something gleamed coldly in the firelight. "A lot of things.''

Storm Caller grabbed at the neck of the man's shirt, then leaped up and hauled him to his feet. "You sonofabitch! *You lying sonofabitch!*''

He tugged sharply at Travis's neck. The man cried out in pain as the sound of a breaking thong echoed in the lodge, and Storm Caller's hand came away with a dried and shrunken scalp. Dirty and stained, the hair that dangled from it was still an unmistakable silvery-blond. Nausea and rage swept through Storm Caller. He recognized that hair, fine and moonlight-pale.

"No one in the Territory but the Henderson girls had hair that color!'' He grasped Travis around the throat by one hand

and raised him right off his feet while the man coughed and choked on his own spittle.

"Iron Knife doesn't make war on his friends, and Caleb Henderson was his friend! You were there, weren't you? At least you were there when the Hendersons were slaughtered. *But I doubt if Iron Knife was!*"

He cast the trapper away from him as he would a piece of filth, and Travis went sprawling. Quickly Storm Caller repeated his suspicions in Comanche. "This man has killed the Henderson family and blamed it on Iron Knife. Look at this scalp!"

The circle grew smaller as the braves moved in to examine the scalp. It glittered in the dim light, mutely accusing. Someone cursed, and Two Horses Racing moved forward, but Soft Talking Man was there first. Horns-of-Buffalo stood and raised his arms.

"This man has caused our friends to die and our brothers to be hunted down by horse soldiers. Perhaps we should kill him now. Perhaps we should give him up to the soldiers. Tie him near the fire outside, and we will discuss this among ourselves."

They bound Travis quickly with twists of hide thongs while Storm Caller and Horns-of-Buffalo watched in ominous silence. Cut Face made no moves to interfere. When the trapper was taken from the lodge they sat down in solemn council.

Twilight was drifting over the camp like a blue haze when Norah ducked out of the lodge to answer a call of nature. No one was about when she returned, so she knew the men were still in the lodge of Horns-of-Buffalo. She sprinted across the clearing to Old Gray Rocks' tepee to check on her patient. Snow-in-Summer was recovering, but tired easily, so Norah's visit was brief. It was on the way back that a voice called out as she skirted the main cookfire.

"*Kee-mah*, come here!" a hoarse voice whispered.

She stepped closer. Someone was lying on the ground just beyond the bright circle of firelight. Perhaps Old Wind Singer had fallen and injured himself. She hurried to his side, then stopped short when she saw it was the white visitor, bound hand and foot. His face was gray with fear and sweat beaded his upper lip.

"My God! What have they done to you?" she exclaimed.

"Sweet Jesus! A white woman!" His startlement was, for a moment, as great as hers. "What the hell are you doin' here, girlie? You a prisoner?"

"Yes."

"Untie me, girlie. For God's sake, untie me or them savages will kill me. Help me, and I'll get us both out of here alive!"

Norah knelt at his side and fumbled with the knots. It was dark, and she was not carrying a knife. "I can't get the knots. I'll be right back!"

She rose and dashed off toward the lodge, then stopped outside to slow her breathing. Elk Dancer must not notice anything unusual. She entered quietly, relieved that the old woman was still asleep. Snatching up a skinning knife, she hurried out again. It took longer to cut him free than she would have believed. With persistent sawing motions she finally worked her way through the twisted thongs. Travis limped a few steps from the awkward positioning, then grasped Norah by the arm and pulled her away into the gloom.

"But..." She wasn't sure of what she meant to do, yet found her feet following Travis as he yanked on her arm.

"Come on, dammit! We gotta get outta here, fast!"

Storm Caller came out of the lodge at that instant. He saw the prisoner was gone and raised the alarm. The sky was partially overcast, and the moon not yet up, but the horses whickered and stamped nervously, so he knew Travis was making his way toward them. He sprinted, covering the ground quickly. As his eyes adjusted to the gloom he saw the escapee, and that he was not alone.

"Oh, God! Norah!" He ran as if the Great Owl Monster was after him, ran despite the pain of his healing ribs. Nothing deterred him: not Travis's threats, nor Norah's shout of warning, nor the gleam of a rifle barrel in the faint starshine. He could not let Travis take her away.

She flung out her arms as a rose of flame burst from the rifle barrel, followed by the whistling zing of a close shot. It ruffled the hair of Storm Caller's temple as it whizzed past, but left him untouched. Travis fell flat on his stomach from Norah's push. Soft Talking Man grabbed the trapper's arms viciously and tied them behind his back. Two Horses Racing had a knife at the white man's throat when Horns-of-Buffalo stopped him.

"No! First I want to hear all Trah-vees has to tell. It might be valuable to Iron Knife and his men. Truss him and bring him to my lodge."

After a few punches, kicks, and buffets at the fallen man, his orders were obeyed; Travis, somewhat battered and bruised, was restrained and taken to the tepee, and the others went along. All except Storm Caller.

He walked to where Norah waited, sobbing and shivering. She didn't believe what he had told her about Travis earlier. She really thought he would take her away to the safety of her own kind. And she had given it all up to save his life. He went to her and caught her up in his arms.

"Why? Why did you do it?" he asked over and over, crushing her against him, but he could get no sense from her.

"He was going to kill you! He was going to kill you!" was all she could say, over and over and over.

"*Ka taikay, ka taikay!* Don't cry, little one!" Storm Caller lifted her in his arms and carried her across the clearing to his lodge.

A man came out of another tepee and stepped in front of them. It was Cut Face. He let his gaze roam hotly over Norah's body, then licked the corner of his mouth and leaned forward. "I envy you in my heart. A man would get a fine night's ride from that mare. Let me buy her from you. I will pay whatever you ask."

Storm Caller set Norah on her feet. "Get inside." He gave her a shove in the small of her back. His eyes were gray ice, deep and cold as the frozen river. She started forward.

"What will you take for her? I have fine horses, gold coins... I like the pale-skinned women, although they do not last as long as the others. But I would keep one like that for many days before tiring," Cut Face said. His smile was ugly.

From the corner of her vision Norah saw a blur of movement, heard the unmistakable sound of bare knuckles on bone and turned around. Storm Caller was on his feet, every muscle taut as he stood over a prone figure. It was Cut Face. He was out cold with his feet touching the flames, his bloodied mouth

slack. His moccasins were singed and smoking before someone
dragged him away from the fire.

Storm Caller pulled Norah into the lodge with him, without
looking back.

16

Storm Caller was still tangled in sleep when Two Horses Racing came to wake him before the sun was up. "Trah-vees has escaped!"

"What? How!" He flung back the heavy robes and began to throw on his clothes.

"The woman that Cut Face brought with him. She drugged Horns-of-Buffalo and his wife last night. She is gone too, and Cut Face with her."

Storm Caller swore as he pushed his feet into his high winter moccasins. He glanced at Norah, but she lay dreaming, her mouth soft and pink as a flower. He hated to leave the warmth of her side for the cold gray dawn. Especially after the events of the previous night. He needed to talk to her, to find out what she was thinking...feeling. A separate part of his mind was listening to the other man's tale.

"Horns-of-Buffalo...he is well? And all in his tent?"

"Yes. Perhaps Trah-vees thought we would not follow them if they did no harm. Horns-of-Buffalo is humiliated and wants them hunted down. He asks you to lead."

"I will take only you, Horns-of-Buffalo, Soft Talking Man and Runt with me. Set a guard around the camp. I will be with you in a moment."

When the brave left, Storm Caller leaned over and touched Norah's cheek. Her eyes opened wide, and she smiled at him. That smile lit his heart like the morning sun. He wished he could pull her into his arms and make love to her again, but that would have to wait now. "Norah, I must go after Travis. He has gone with Cut Face."

She sat up and stretched, no longer shy of her nakedness. He lifted a lock of her hair in his hand and rubbed it with his fingers. So soft. He touched her lips with his fingertip, outlining the curves. So soft and warm.

"I wish I didn't have to leave you now. I'll be back as soon as I can; meanwhile, do not leave the camp. Promise me."

"I promise. Be careful...." She caressed the curve of his cheek.

He leaned down and touched her mouth with his. "I will." With a regretful sigh he got to his feet and picked up his weapons. He looked back over his shoulder before ducking under the flap. She was still smiling.

Norah was in no hurry to leave her bed. It was warm beneath the hide covers, and the mingled scents of their lovemaking lingered. She rolled on her side and let her hand sweep across the place where Storm Caller had slept beside her through the night hours.

Her breasts were still tender from his kisses, her limbs languid and sweetly heavy in the aftermath of passion's storm. How different he was from Abner...from any other man she had ever known. Happiness welled within her, and she knew it was time to be honest with herself: there was nowhere on earth she would rather be than with him.

The reason for her precipitate actions of the previous evening were clear now. She had not been running toward freedom, she had been running from her growing attraction and dependence on Storm Caller, afraid to face what it might mean. Even now she was not quite ready to pursue this thought to its logical conclusion. Stretching lazily, she sat up, still smiling to herself without realizing it, and she hummed as she dressed.

Elk Dancer came into the lodge. "You are happy today! What is that you are singing?"

"Oh, a song my father taught me. 'Barbry Allen.' It is about a young man who dies because a girl named Barbry Allen can't return his love."

Elk Dancer sat down heavily. "Well, there is no fear of that happening to my grandson, after all I heard last night!" She put herbs into a bowl and began grinding them with the heel of a smooth grinding stone.

Norah blushed and lowered her head, measuring out the morning coffee. She was just setting the pot over the fire when it came without warning. A sudden pain ripped through her abdomen, and she dropped the utensil into the flames, burning her wrist. She fell onto her side, gritting her teeth and rolling in agony.

"What is it!"

Elk Dancer was bending over her, pulling her away from the fire. Norah tried to answer, but it came again, taking her breath away. There was a gush of warm liquid between her legs, and she was faint and too weak to move. Everything seemed dim, as if blanketed with dark fog. Cold sweat drenched her face and upper torso. Nausea advanced and receded like a relentless tide, and bile rose in her mouth. She was slipping off the world and tried to hold on, digging her fingers futilely in the hard-packed dirt of the floor.

Sounds came and went like buzzing hordes of bees. Sometimes they seemed to be voices, other times just the noisy pumping of her heart and the wheezy bellows of her lungs. She was burning up yet chilled at the same time, and wondered if she'd fallen in the river. Yes, that must be it, for now she was borne along on a current into the bright sunlight, and then carried beneath the black ice, into a darkness like nothing she had ever known.

She heard Snow-in-Summer cry out: "The blood! Oh, the blood!" and wondered what that could mean. Had the girl cut herself? No, there was no blood here beneath the ice, only blackness and painful cold that was turning her numb. And then the pain came again, pushing her upward. Her hands were caught in something, buffeted back and forth. She thought she yanked them away but nothing happened. Concentrating all her efforts, Norah opened her eyes. Blue Feather's face hovered over hers. What was Blue Feather doing in the river?

Norah's hands were slapped, again and again. "Stop!" She wanted to shout, but her voice came out like a kitten's soft mewling. "Where is he? Where is he? I need him. I need to tell him something...."

"He will be back soon," Elk Dancer soothed, holding a cup

to Norah's lips and forcing her to sip from it. It tasted of burnt leaves and mold.

There was a chorus of relieved sighs as Norah finished the draught. "Now she will not fight us, and we will be able to help her," someone whispered. Snow-in-Summer moved in from the shadows. Her eyes were reddened and puffy, and she snuffled against her sleeve. "Will she live?"

What were they talking about? The agony was easing now, but the shadows grew tall and overpowered the firelight, looming over Norah and pressing her down, down, down. She had neither will nor strength to resist their onslaught, but as they covered her, muffling the sounds in the tepee, Norah listened for Elk Dancer's reply. It was very important that she hear the answer, that she know what to do next. It was so good to let go, to give up the struggle. To slide down that long black tunnel opening up before her and leave the pain behind. The old woman's voice echoed hollowly after her as she rushed through the black tunnel toward the waiting spot of light.

"She must live. She must!"

They had been tracking for three hours and Horns-of-Buffalo was in a thunderous rage. "When I find them," he muttered, "I will rip out their living hearts. I will cut out their eyes and make moccasins from their skin."

Storm Caller rounded on him grimly. "I will not have your anger undo everything. Calm yourself or go back to camp."

With an effort, Horns-of-Buffalo clenched his jaw and clamped down on his temper. "I hear you. *Suvate.*"

"Good. Let us continue."

They found many tracks of elk and rabbit and once those of a wolf, aged and alone. It had tried for several small animals without success. Cut Face was good at hiding tracks, but Storm Caller was an expert at uncovering them. Signs were everywhere to his knowing eyes, and they had hopes of catching up with their quarry before noon.

Soft Talking Man slowed his horse suddenly. "One of the horses is lame now. Do you think they will separate?"

Storm Caller shook his head and rode on. Near a wash covered with scrub cedar and round balls of juniper bush, he dismounted without speaking. Leaving the bay gelding, he followed the wash for twenty feet, then hunkered down and examined the ground.

"What are you seeking?" Horns-of-Buffalo said impatiently. "Their tracks go straight ahead."

Storm Caller lifted a branch of cedar, filling the air with its clear piney tang, and pointed. Against the covering of dried needles and branches the mottled deerskin tunic and leggings were almost invisible, and the woman's black hair blended into the darker patches of ground. It was the squaw who had accompanied Cut Face and helped him free Travis. She had saved Travis's life, and they had used her and discarded her. Unnecessary baggage. Expendable. He wondered who she was, where she was from, and if anyone would grieve for her.

Soft Talking Man made a sign to avert evil. "So that is how Cut-Face and Trah-vees reward their friends." He spat into the dirt.

"Evidently they thought she would slow them down too much now with one horse lamed. She has not been dead long. We will catch up with them soon." Storm Caller wiped his sticky hands in the dust, then stood up and brushed them off. The sun flamed over the distant buttes but the air seemed colder, darker suddenly. He had been so happy with Norah in his arms all night and nestled close to him this morning; and now this ugliness had intruded. And if Norah had gone with Travis last night, it might be her body lying under a bush, her gaping throat bathed in blood. Storm Caller had killed in his lifetime, but had never understood the cold rage that drove men to murder. Now he did. If Cut Face and Travis were in his hands he would have torn them apart limb by limb, shred by bloody shred.

They went down and away from the high country, into side canyons and arroyos that were nothing but frustrating mazes to the *tosi tivo*. The horses were used to the rugged land. In less time than seemed humanly possible they were below the Mogollon Rim and closing fast with Travis and his Apache benefactor. And then they found another sign.

"Horse soldiers!" Storm Caller reined in.

Soft Talking Man agreed. "We must bide here, or else cut around Eagle Rock and through Singing Canyon." He sounded discouraged. Travis and Cut Face could be far away before their pursuers could gain any ground now.

"I could approach them," Storm Caller said quietly. "I might know these horse soldiers." He wanted very much to get his hands on the two men. His fingers curved against his palms.

Horns-of-Buffalo shook his massive head. "No. They might shoot before you had the chance to get close enough to speak." He brooded a few minutes in silence. "I can wait for my revenge. I know the places where Cut Face hides, and I know the places where Trah-vees goes. Let us return to our camp and see that all is well there. When this trouble they have stirred up dies down, then we will seek them out. *Suvate.*"

They turned their horses back toward the north and west, and vanished like mist into the wrinkled folds of the land. The return journey was slower, for time and again they had to detour around troopers swarming like angry blue ants along the ridges and valleys. The evening star was the only point of light in a sky softening to violet and gray as they drew near the hidden camp. Smoke from cook-fires blended into the shades of advancing night.

Storm Caller felt his heart lighten. For the first time as a grown man, he felt that he was coming back to his home. Norah would be waiting for him, perhaps sewing while the fire struck red highlights from her dark shimmering hair. The venison from yesterday's hunt would be simmering in the kettle or the paunch, and there would be coffee, rich and black. He could almost smell it. He dressed down his mount and hobbled it, then headed for his lodge with a light step.

Before he was ten yards away he knew something was wrong, and as he drew closer dread closed around his heart. He lifted the flap to find the lodge in darkness. There was no savory dinner simmering, no fire on the hearth. And no Norah. Had she run away then, after all that had been between them in the past days? Or had Cut Face and Travis come back for her? He turned and ran out, calling her name.

From the far end of the clearing he heard someone shout to him. Elk Dancer stood near the women's tepee, reserved for their use during their monthly times. What a fool he was, to forget about such things! He stopped in his tracks, laughing at himself in relief. Elk Dancer waved him on, and Storm Caller joined her, unhurriedly. It was only as he neared that he saw the lines of strain and worry on her face.

"What is it? What's wrong?"

The old woman pursed her lips and blew softly. "She is losing the child. It does not go well with her, but do not worry. I will bring her through this, and she will give you strong sons yet."

It took a moment for Elk Dancer's words to sink in. "The child…"

She placed a hand on his arm. "She called for you, but now she is sleeping. Go now, there is nothing you can do here."

She started to go back into the lodge, but Storm Caller brushed past despite her objections. Norah lay beside the fire, and her face was like tallow, waxy and drained of color. Even her lips were bleached. She was naked beneath the covering with her hair unbound and eyes closed in exhaustion. He knelt down beside her, unable to believe he had been so blind; yet he had never seen her undressed in strong light and even now she did not show. She had been carrying another man's child, and he had not known. Or had not wanted to know.

She had called for him, and he had not been there. And now she could be dying. He remembered the night of Abigail Gartner's birthday, when he had still had the wisdom to leave Norah to her own kind. How long ago that seemed now. He moved to touch her but pulled his hand back as Norah twisted sideways and groaned. She panted like an animal in pain, and when she reached out to grasp the blanket, he slipped his fingers through hers.

Norah did not notice. She was alone in a world of darkness and fear, where nothing was real but the agonizing efforts of her body to rid itself of its burden. She neither knew nor cared that the hands that supported her or brought the wet cloth to her lips belonged to Storm Caller, and he watched helplessly. Elk Dancer kneaded Norah's abdomen and burned herbs in the fire, chanting under her breath. Snow-in-Summer did what she could, and from time to time Blue Feather came to help. It seemed so useless. Nothing eased Norah's fevered thrashing.

Storm Caller bathed her temples with cool water. No one had spoken in a long time, and the silence weighed heavily upon him. It seemed that he was born under an evil star. Suddenly Norah gasped, tensed, and went limp. He sat back and rubbed his forehead wearily. So. It was over.

Elk Dancer lifted Norah's lids, then felt the pulse at her neck. It was steady and stronger now. She lifted the covering to check her patient, then sat back on her heels. "*Toquet.* It is good. She can rest now." She brought a cup with a small amount of dark liquid. "Raise her up and see if she will drink this."

Unbelieving, Storm Caller leaned forward. He could barely feel her breath on his cheek, fluttering lightly against his skin. Gently he cradled Norah in his arms and lifted her shoulders. Her eyes opened slowly, and the blue of her irises was echoed in the blue hollows beneath her eyes.

"I couldn't leave," she said in a hoarse whisper. "I couldn't leave…because I had to tell you…to tell you…" Her brow crinkled in puzzlement. She couldn't remember what it was she had to tell him. It didn't matter. She was content to be held in his arms while the potion took effect, and this time when she slept there were no tunnels, no blinding lights to lure her on; only welcome rest.

"She will sleep now," Elk Dancer urged. "You must go. It is not right for a man to be here at such a time."

"I do not care how many customs I break or how many offenses I commit. I will not leave her until I know she will live."

"Pooh! I tell you she will live now. It is over. She has lost much meat and will need time to recover. She will need fresh blood and raw livers. Go and get some rest yourself so you can bring down many animals in the days ahead. It is almost morning."

Storm Caller was amazed at how much time has passed, yet would not leave Norah's side until her breathing slowed and became more regular. While he kept his vigil he pondered on the changes she had brought to his life: he had learned the extraordinary delight and joy that one particular woman could bring; and he had learned the terrible fear of loss that walked hand in hand with it, like a dark shadow cast upon the sunlit earth. Altogether, he thought, it was safer not to care too much for anyone.

But it seemed it was too late.

* * *

Norah sat on a blanket in the warm spring sunshine, beading a pouch for Elk Dancer. Across the way Old Gray Rocks nodded and dozed while Snow-in-Summer scraped a small hide clear of clinging bits of meat and sinew, and all around the camp there was activity. Norah was only allowed light duties although she felt strong again, and twice a day she ate the revolting jelly that Elk Dancer prepared to restore her blood. It seemed to help, and if she closed her eyes and held her nose she could manage to keep it down.

Although her physical recovery had been swift, Norah's spirits remained low in the weeks that followed her miscarriage and her mind was in confusion. She had not wanted Abner's child, and yet she had wanted her baby. *Her* baby. She had known for a long time the child was dead, and yet once it was definite she felt the shock of loss and mourned for it. Not even Elk Dancer's pronouncement that the miscarriage was inevitable eased the sadness. She felt hollow inside, and her arms longed for the child that would never be.

There were other things she mourned as well. The actual loss of the baby made her realize the loss of all the bright dreams she had brought from Boston to the Arizona Territory. There was no respectable husband, no companionable marriage, and no child to ease her sense of failure. Although treated kindly, she was a captive among strangers and the uncertain future stretched ahead like a long gray road. It did not help that Storm Caller spent so little time within the lodge, and that he avoided her company. He had not touched her once in all these weeks.

Perhaps he was tired of her, or perhaps he did not want her now that she had shown herself unable to carry a child to term. Whatever the reason, he was remote and cool toward her, and there was only indifference in his eyes when he looked at her.

There was a sudden commotion, and she looked up from her work to see a strange parade approaching. Two Horses Racing, dressed in his finest gear, rode his spirited sorrel and behind him came a string of horses loaded with goods. The small cavalcade stopped before Old Gray Rock's lodge, and the youth leaped down from his horse and stood before the old woman. Everyone was watching now, but it was Snow-in-Summer who caught Norah's attention. The girl was beaming and blushing, while pretending not to notice anything unusual.

Norah got up and poked her head into the lodge. "*Kaku, Keema!* Grandmother, come here! What is happening?"

The Medicine Woman came out. "Hah! So, that is how the story ends," she said with deep satisfaction. "Two Horses, he seeks himself a wife in the lodge of Old Gray Rocks. And he never looked at Snow-in-Summer until he pulled her from the water!"

By now Old Gray Rocks and Two Horses were deep in talk, the young man waving his hands toward his animals. After many minutes and much discussion, the young man went back to his horse with a disgusted expression, and Old Gray Rocks looked smug. Snow-in-Summer, still diligently scraping the hide, appeared ready to burst into tears. There were a few snickers and rude shouts from some of the other braves.

"What is going on?" Norah demanded.

"Two Horses has offered for the old one's slave. He gives all these goods and animals, and he will provide for Old Gray Rocks all her days. If she lets him have Snow-in-Summer, the old one may live in his lodge or maintain her own; he will hunt and care for her as long as she lives, but Old Gray Rocks says the offer is too low. We will see."

An hour later, Two Horses came back, this time with more animals and goods. He left them before the lodge, never looking at Snow-in-Summer, who was watching him with quiet desperation. Old Gray Rocks waited till he was gone, then opened her eyes. She hobbled to her feet and examined the new offer, then called to her slave. Snow-in-Summer leaped up, took the lead horse by the single string rein, and led it behind the lodge.

A few minutes later Two Horses came striding along. He reminded Norah of a strutting peacock. He stood before the lodge and Snow-in-Summer came out with her belongings wrapped in a blanket. Bowing her head, she followed Two Horses to his tepee while he strolled along as if oblivious to the fact that she was there at all. The two disappeared into his lodge, leaving the women to nod and smile and the men to make ribald comments. Norah turned to Elk Dancer.

"That is all? One minute she is Old Gray Rocks' slave, and

the next minute she belongs to Two Horses? Doesn't she have any say in the matter?''

Elk Dancer narrowed her eyes shrewdly. "I think that Snow-in-Summer is very pleased with everything. It is good for a young girl to have a brave husband. Now she is no longer a slave. Her status in the camp is raised, and she has her own lodge. Two Horses will make her a fine husband. *Toquet.*''

Norah threw up her hands. Yes, this arrangement would be good for the girl, but she could just as easily have been traded as a slave to someone else, someone who would beat her or even kill her, and no one would have intervened. The situation only pointed up her own predicament. What would happen to her now that Storm Caller no longer wanted her? Would she, like Snow-in-Summer, be traded blithely away for goods or horses? After all, what did she really know of the man who was Storm Caller? She had been so very wrong about him before.

He entered the lodge on the heels of her thoughts, and dull color flushed her cheeks. Storm Caller checked when he saw Norah, and his glance slid away from hers. He hoped he had the guts to do what he meant to do. There was no other way. Ignoring Norah, he addressed his grandmother.

"We are breaking camp. The horse soldiers know we are here. And they know we have a white woman. Horns-of-Buffalo intends to go into the mountains and then join Quanah in the spring. You must go with him."

"What will you do?"

"I will go south, into the canyons. They cannot find me there."

"And your woman?"

He shrugged and turned away. He couldn't look at Norah, couldn't meet that open blue gaze. She had almost died. The guilt of that would be with him a long time. He couldn't take her where he was going. There was only one thing to do.

Elk Dancer stared at him. "I will bring in my herbs and then prepare my things," she said slowly. She went from the lodge, leaving Storm Caller and Norah alone.

The fire hissed and crackled, and outside the wind blew softly. Storm Caller began shoving his belongings into a leather bag while Norah stood dumbfounded. What was going to happen to her now? Would they leave her behind for the Cavalry, or would she be traded away if Storm Caller left the band? And why didn't he look at her? Was he too embarrassed to tell her?

Storm Caller turned as if to leave, but Norah went to him and placed her hand on his arm. She was trembling, and her mouth was dry. "What...what will you do with... Where will I go if you no longer want me in your lodge?"

He was completely still. His eyes were smoky crystal in the dim light. Except for the long nights when he lay rigid on the pallet, pretending she was not inches away from his hungering flesh, he had not been so close to her in weeks. Her nearness blotted out everything, and he stared at her as if he had never seen her before.

"Will...will you trade me to someone else...?" Her trembling had increased, and now she was shaking violently.

"What nonsense is this! Trade you? What are you talking about?" He lifted her face and looked down at her gravely.

Her heart stopped, skipped a beat, and then went on erratically. Her fate depended on his next words, and she was afraid to hear them. He had taken her away from everything she knew, surely he would not abandon her now! She licked her lips.

His hands were on her shoulders, feeling the warmth of her body through the cotton overblouse she wore. She was so beautiful! He remembered the silken texture of her skin, the rounded weight of her breasts in his hands, the soft yielding of her body beneath his own. He pulled her against his chest, winding his arms around her, holding her closely until the shaking ceased. She had lost weight and felt so vulnerable, so small. Norah's cheek lay just over his heart, over the image of her that was lodged there. He couldn't do it. Knowing he was wrong, cursing himself for his weakness, he knew then he could never let her go.

"I will never give you up, Norah. Not while I have life and breath. *I will never give you up!*"

His mouth claimed hers. He picked her up in his arms and carried her to the pallet. Slowly he lowered her down, then covered her with his length while his tongue outlined her lips and slid within the softness of her mouth. A wild possessiveness came over him, until he wanted to erase the memory of the other man who had known her body intimately. His hands began to sweep up and down her sides, her legs, the curve of her hips and thighs.

Norah was weak with relief and her need for him. Her hands stroked beneath his shirt, over the hard planes of his chest. She tugged at his clothing, wanting to feel the smoothness of his body against hers. He knelt over her, stripping his shirt off, then tore open the trade-good blouse she wore, not caring as the tiny buttons went bouncing into the shadows of the tepee. Norah pulled him down, guiding his face to her breasts. They ached for him, and the first touch of his mouth, hot and moist, sent jagged bolts of sensation through her. She needed the affirmation of his touch and his joining with her. She wanted to be absorbed by him, melting into him until they were one flesh, one soul, one thought held captive in time.

Storm Caller pressed her down against the pallet, savoring every fragrant inch of her skin. His lips skimmed her breasts, hovered over the swollen nipples, fanning them with his breath. How could he have ever thought of sending her away!

He entered her then, thrusting deep, losing himself completely in her. Suddenly she tensed beneath him and then cried out, reaching for him, her nails biting into his skin. His release came quickly, violently, and afterward he lay still, murmuring against her throat and into the black cloud of her hair.

"I will never give you up, Norah. Never!"

17

Norah carried her few possessions and a metal canteen of water up the almost invisible path along the cliff, while Storm Caller came behind with other supplies. He looked at her. Her cheeks were too rosy. They would have to stop soon. It was cool now in the early light of morning, but before long the solid rock face would reflect the sun with fierce blinding brightness.

He was stripped to the waist above buckskin breeches and knee-high moccasins of soft leather. His hair hung down his back in two plaits banded with otter fur and blue cloth, and he looked as wild as the landscape. Norah, dressed in a wool skirt and deerskin tunic, envied him, for she was dressed much too warmly for such exertion. Although determined to show him she was as strong as any Indian woman, she didn't know how much longer she could keep up her imposture. Already her face was hot with effort and her hair was coming loose from its single braid. Her legs moved steadily, automatically, as they climbed higher, and she ignored the burning sensation in her calves.

She was sure her soles were blistering, and wished belatedly that she had taken more care in turning the seams of her moccasins flat. At least, she thought, I no longer huff and wheeze like a winded horse! Head lowered, she plodded along doggedly.

He looked again at her flushed face, then took the canteen

and packet from her hands, setting them on the stony ledge. "We will rest here."

She had held them so tightly, so long, that her fingers remained clenched. Tucking them out of sight, she looked out over the canyon, where indigo shadows were lightening to purple and blue and rose.

Pride made her lie. "I can go on. I am not tired."

"Not yet. But eventually you will tire, and I will have to carry you the rest of the way!" Unconsciously his hand went to his healing ribs.

"I am perfectly able to continue!" Without waiting she snatched up the articles she'd surrendered to him and tried to move past Storm Caller. He blocked her way.

"I said we will rest here." He took her chin in his hand and forced her head up until she had to look at him. "Are you trying to prove your courage, Norah? You have no need of that with me."

She studied his face in exasperation, searching for meaning in the lines of his mouth, the expression in his eyes. Laughter and something else lurked there behind the shadow-gray irises, and she thought he mocked her lack of endurance. Pushing him angrily away, she stumbled and tripped on the hem of her skirt. Before her startled eyes there was nothing but air, and then far below she saw the thin gleam of water that was the river, tossed like a silver ribbon at the foot of the talus slopes. She pitched forward, grasping at emptiness.

Instantly she was caught up and whirled backward and around in Storm Caller's arms. His face was pale and harsh, a granite sculpture as he pushed her against the safety of the cliff. His body covered hers, as if for protection, and there was no sound except his heavy breathing and the sharp gasps that escaped from her. For a moment he held her in a painful grip. Then he stepped back and placed his hands on her shoulders and pushed down until her knees buckled and she sat on the ground, hard.

"*You will sit here and we...will...rest!*" The words came out forcefully, through clenched teeth.

She sat. The world was going around so giddily she had no other choice. Norah closed her eyes tightly and put her head against her raised knees, but still she saw the river spinning below, shining like bits of broken mirror.

"Dizzy?" His voice was rough in her ear.

She nodded, and Storm Caller put his arm around her shoulders, drawing her close to the safety of his body, sheltering her with his strength. She felt his skin, warm and damp with sweat, beneath her cheek, and heard the steady pounding of his heart. His familiar touch and scent were the anchor pins that kept her mind from reeling as she realized how close she had been to sudden and frightening death. For a moment she placed her hand against his breast, as if drawing comfort from the rhythm of his heart. Then she took a deep breath, cleared her throat, and sat up straight, brushing the pieces of grit from her skirt.

"I am quite all right now. Thank you," she said in a stiff formal tone.

There was no answer, but Storm Caller moved away, aware that the strangeness was between them again. When would she stop pulling away from him, when would she stop pretending? They had lived together, lain together. Even laughed together. And still she retreated from him, hiding behind her white woman's facade of etiquette. One moment they would share a closeness, and then she would withdraw, become as cool and distant as the moon. Well, here in the canyon she would learn. There was no place for her to run, no one else to lean on, and in time she would turn to him willingly enough.

"It is not much farther."

He rose to his feet, and Norah did the same. They climbed the last two hundred feet to the overhanging ledge, lost in their own thoughts but tethered by silence to one another. Soon Norah perceived that they followed an ancient path etched in the smooth rock face beside a natural fault, moving upward on a diagonal line until the way was blocked by a massive escarpment.

Norah searched for an opening. The path seemed to vanish in the air. "What do we do now?"

"We go up!"

Storm Caller stepped into a patch of deep shade, where a buttress of stone on the right hid a crude ladder. It was made of poles with widely spaced cross-bars attached by tightly woven splits of reeds and grasses and reinforced with crumbling leather strips. To her way of thinking, it looked unsafe.

"Wait. I will check it first." Storm Caller put his moccasined foot on the lowest cross-bar and tested the joinings. Although it creaked and groaned, the wood was as hard as the surrounding canyon walls, and the skillfully woven lashings held beneath his weight. He went up a few more, then dismounted and motioned for Norah to precede him.

She balked like a mule. She had been given no choice of where she was taken or where she lived, but here at least was something she could protest. "Up that decrepit contraption? Don't be ridiculous!"

He only looked at her with the expression of indomitable stubbornness that she was coming to know too well. Norah didn't care: she had her own brand of hard-headedness, transmitted through generations of Dooleys and O'Sheas. She stood her ground and stared back at him, undaunted. If he insisted she go up that makeshift ladder he could carry her for all she cared; but she was damned if she'd do it on her own.

"I will not climb that rickety ladder. I will not set one foot on it!" Without further remark she plopped down in the shelter of the overhang and folded her hands primly in her lap, as if perfectly ready to wait out an eternity.

He shrugged, then grasped the sides of the ladder and swung up in a few lithe movements. A loose pebble was dislodged from his foot, bouncing and ricocheting down. As it bumped and tumbled a scattering of fellows joined it, breaking off bits of loose rock in a suicide race to the canyon floor. Norah was appalled: it seemed to take the stones a very long time to reach the bottom, and it brought back the remembrance of her close call earlier. She settled back and waited for Storm Caller to return.

It was impossible without a timepiece to gauge exactly how long she sat there, but the sun's progress told her that hours had passed. It was almost overhead now, and the banded rocks lost their astounding colors until they were a uniform golden buff. She wriggled back beneath the scant protection of the overhang, but her nose was already burned and peeling. Thirst became her main concern. *Oh, for a sip of cool water!* And still there no sign of Storm Caller.

Her stomach rumbled complaint against its lack of food. She thought longingly of the food she had prepared and packed, and especially of the tasty dried berries Old Gray Rocks had given her at their final parting. She could almost taste them. After another estimated hour her lips were dried and cracked, her tongue furred and her temper as hot as the rock she sat upon. Finally she had to face facts: it was evident that he had no intention of coming back down for her.

As she had no confidence in her ability to go back down the cliff and she was afraid to spend the night on the ledge, there was only one thing she *could* do, and that was follow Storm Caller up the ladder. With no good grace, she called out for him. He would have to hold the ladder for her. There was no answer.

"Storm Caller!" Only a thin echo of her own voice answered. Temper gave way to fright: what if something had happened to him? He might have gone higher and fallen. No, she would surely have heard the sounds of a fall. But what if he had been bitten by a snake? What if he didn't return and she was left to fend for herself...or worse, to slowly starve to death on the ledge?

The same determination that had helped her through her other trials now came to the fore, and Norah placed her foot on the lowest rung of the ladder. It creaked but held her weight. She lifted her other foot high to catch the next rung, and the ladder swayed away from the wall. Her heart pulsed in her throat, trapping her breath, but she leaned forward, and the ladder thudded against the rock. Each step was an agony of fright, and by the time Norah reached the top she was shaking. She scrambled to her feet and looked up and into the strangest world she had ever seen.

She was in a ghostly city, silent and long dead. Three tiers of mud-brick and adobe buildings rose over her head beneath the protective arch of an immense but shallow cavern. The dark interiors of the rooms were visible through doorways reinforced by wooden supports, some shaped like capital Ts. Here and there blank-eyed window holes stared back at her, and ladders of the type she had just used leaned against the walls. Nothing moved. Invisible mouse feet tiptoed up Norah's back, and she felt the hair stir at her nape. Where were the people? What had happened to them all? And where was Storm Caller? She did not like to be alone in this place of dust and death. It made too clear the fact of her own mortality.

"Storm Caller?"

She was hesitant to go forward toward the houses and walked instead along the front of the ledge, footsteps soft as if not to wake those who had slept for centuries. A stick of wood or perhaps bone cracked beneath her foot, and she hurried on, afraid to look down. In the angle formed by the last building and the cavern wall she finally found Storm Caller. Eyes closed, he sat propped against the sun-baked wall, his face turned up to the afternoon warmth. Scattered at his side were the remains of a tasty luncheon. Norah marched toward him indignantly, sarcastic words and phrases forming in her mind.

I am glad to know my absence caused you no concern! For all you knew, I could have been lying dead on the rocks below. How fortunate that such thoughts did not disturb your appetite!

As she approached she saw him glance her way before he quickly lowered his lashes. It was only a fleeting glimpse, but beneath his hard-planed warrior's face she suddenly sensed a small, mischievous boy. They had both been acting like children. Her wrath melted away like butter in the sun, leaving only a warm puddle of laughter behind.

She spread her skirts and sat next to him as if nothing had occurred between them. "Did you happen to leave any food for me?"

Storm Caller grinned and pulled a packet from behind his back. "Not much."

Norah took it, and found only two small pieces of cold rabbit and a flat piece of Indian bread. She picked up a piece of meat and examined it. "After I dressed the rabbit and baked the bread, this is all you saved for me!"

"I was hungry. It was heavy work shepherding you through the canyon and then herding you up the cliff."

She polished off a rabbit haunch and, as she licked her fingers greedily, noticed Storm Caller watching her. "How you have changed in your eating habits," he teased. The easy relationship was back between them. "What would your friends in Boston say if they could see you now?"

"This is not Boston, and your habits have undergone the

same change: I do not remember Sergeant LeBeau eating with his fingers in front of a lady, either.''

He didn't like to be reminded of his other self. He leaned so close that his lips brushed her hair. "Look! Look out there. When you lived in Boston—even when you first came to Camp Greenwood and knew me only as LeBeau—did you ever think to see such a sight? Isn't this finer than anything you knew back in the East? Nothing but the sky between you and your God. No churches or prayer meetings, no collection baskets or cathedrals, no gold and silver candlesticks.''

She had been too hungry to admire the view. Now she looked out over the vast landscape of rock temples and palaces carved by wind and water and time. Everywhere she turned there was some fantastic sculpture, some unbelievable height or depth. It was awesome and frightening and eerily beautiful, touching some deep inner chord in her soul. Suddenly she felt close to the beginnings of time, when the world had just come into existence. She understood then something of Storm Caller's soul, and the land that had made him what he was. She did not want him to see how it had affected her and tried to pass it off lightly.

"Never in my life did I expect to be sitting on a dirt floor at the top of the world while eating dry bread and cold rabbit with my bare hands." She sent him a wry glance. "And Sergeant LeBeau would not have eaten all the berries. He would have saved me half!''

Storm Caller drew away from her, and the special moment was past. He rose. "Sergeant LeBeau would have never brought you here." He looked at her coldly. "This is where we will make our lodging. Choose a suitable dwelling while I go to bring the rest of our things.''

After he left, Norah stubbornly ate the rest of her meal and then sat idle, watching the colors of the canyon shift back toward rose and orange as the sun began its slow descent. Let him choose a dwelling when he returned: she would not sleep penned-up inside the haunted walls.

Time passed with nothing but her own thoughts for company, and as she waited her curiosity grew. She decided to investigate the lower level, at least from the outside. The first room was a crumbled ruin with two walls intact and the roof open to the air. She went in a few feet, and stopped dead at a dry rustling sound. Then a dun-colored creature, like a large-eared mouse, ran across the patch of sunlight cast by the open doorway. Norah laughed out loud. Almost frightened to death by such a tiny creature!

Peering into the doorway of the second room, something half hidden in the corner beneath a piece of woven rush mat caught her eye. Again, curiosity was all the spur she needed. She entered and kicked the matting aside to disclose a few pieces of broken pottery, rusty-red with a pattern of cream and black. She knelt and picked up a jagged shard, amazed at the quality of the fired clay and the intricacy of design.

Running her fingers over the smooth piece, she wondered if she could have made such a fine article from the earth itself, and ruefully decided such talents were not among her small repertoire. She had not expected such sophisticated technique from a group of primitive cliff dwellers. No wonder he had laughed so long ago at her pride in Geometry and Deportment and Use of the Globes. The memory made her smile.

"Well, since I have no skill to make such items, perhaps I can find some unbroken pottery," she said aloud. Surely there might be some usable bowls or containers among the household goods abandoned by those who had once lived here. With new purpose she began a systematic search of the nearby houses, sorting through small heaps of discards, undeterred by the tiny animals and armored insects that scuttled away from the light.

In the fourth walled cell she found a treasure: a piece of heavy cotton fabric in a black and gray chevron design. It was tightly woven without slubs or misweave and, except for a thin coat of dust and one ragged edge, as perfect as the day it was made. Norah was delighted. It was like a gift, and she imagined some prehistoric woman working on her crude loom, little dreaming that one day far in the future a strange woman from a strange time would make use of it. After this find she was eager for more, and when the lower tier had nothing left to reveal, she went up the ladder to the second story without a moment's hesitation.

As she set foot on the mud roofs that floored this level, Norah smiled at her earlier refusal to climb up to the ruins. She began her search thinking that drastic circumstances could have a more profound effect on immediate behavior than anything else she had ever known. In the second house she found a small flat dish and a basket of curved grasses lined with unfired clay. She placed the dish carefully inside the basket and went on with her investigation, and it was in the last dwelling that she made her great discovery.

"Oh! What is this?" She pulled away two heavy grass mats that almost disintegrated in her hands. Underneath was a collection of nested bowls of the cream-on-red variety she had found earlier, and in the corner behind them stood two huge clay storage jars, at least three feet in height. They greatly resembled Roman *amphorae* used to store wine and grain, except these lacked the Roman ware's characteristic handles.

Norah's excitement grew: this was far better than a museum where one could only look at the artifacts through a pane of glass or from a roped-off distance. She touched the nearer one. It was lighter than she expected, and empty. Moving it aside, she reached for the second. A long crack, hidden by the swirl design, widened as she groped for the neck. Without warning it fell away from the main body of the vessel and broke into a dozen pieces with the dull ringing sound of cracked bells.

In dismay, she grabbed the neck of the storage jar to keep it from falling also, and the contents were flung out against her skirt. It was an irregularly shaped bundle, wrapped in a splendid piece of gray and red fabric and tied with strips of black cord. She worked to free one end of the cloth but could not, for the knots in the cords had shrunken impossibly. She tried to guess what might be inside. It felt like cloth and sticks. The pieces of a loom, perhaps, and more of the fine fabric?

Beneath the first layer there was another, coarsely woven and of a plain, unbleached ivory shade. She pulled at it, and suddenly the cords parted into dried strands, and the bundle fell open. It appeared to be nothing but dried leaves and rags wrapped around a core of large sticks. A stringy copper mass, matted and twined with red cloth was at one end. For a moment she didn't know what it was. She nudged it over with her toe, and it rolled over with a dry crackling and a puff of ocher smoke.

A wizened face grinned at Norah, its eyelids sunken and sewn shut over empty sockets, the skeletal cheeks speckled with the remains of ocher paint. She had stumbled on an urn burial. For a heartbeat she stood frozen, staring uncomprehendingly at the withered bundle that had once been human flesh and bone. The arms were not crossed flat upon the chest as was usual, and the long slim bones protected a little skull and fragile bones, too tiny to be that of a child at term. This was the relic of a pregnant woman who had died, and her child with her. As Norah could have died when she miscarried. Horror and revulsion overcame her, and she ran from the room, shrieking.

From his place on the cliff path Storm Caller heard Norah cry out. He dropped his burden on the ledge and swarmed up the ladder to the ruins imagining terrible things. There were scorpions, snakes, and poisoned lizards in the canyon. He raced across the flat area and up the ladder toward her. She ran blindly, stumbling and weeping, and flew to meet him, calling his name over and over again.

He swept her into his arms. "What is it, Norah, what has frightened you, little one?"

She only clutched at his shirt, weeping incoherently. He tried to put her away from him so he could see her face, but her arms wound more tightly around him.

"Don't leave me, don't leave me!"

He held her until the storm of weeping passed, soothing her and smoothing her hair beneath his wide palm. "*Ka taikay, ka taikay.* Don't weep. Tell me what has frightened you so?" Tenderly he touched her face, a frown between his eyes as he pieced out the story.

"You must not be afraid, Norah. Some of the old ones buried their dead in that manner. There are many such in these canyons." She was trembling less now. "Wait here, and I will go see this thing you found."

He located the room that contained the burial. The mummy rested against the nested baskets, its dried yellow face grinning at him with leaf-thin lips shrunken away from the ivoried teeth. He squatted down before it. Most Indians feared the places of the dead and their remains, but Storm Caller prided himself on his lack of superstition. After all, this was only the shell of someone long dead.

He hunkered down and examined the body, mummified from centuries of dry heat. The lids, sewn shut over empty sockets, still had a thin fringe of red-brown lash that matched the copper mat of hair. A necklace of shell beads hung around the withered throat, with a carved soapstone pectoral. He touched the carving, and the dried flesh beneath turned to powder and fell inside the chest cavity. He checked no further.

"Forgive us, Old One, for disturbing your sleep and that of your child. Leave us in peace, and we will leave you the same. May you rest well in the next world."

He started to leave, then turned back and removed a thin silver bracelet from his wrist. "Sleep in Peace, Old One." He slipped the offering under the mats and left, finding nothing strange in this sudden shift in his philosophy.

Norah was waiting for him, her body rigid. He doubted she had moved since he left her side. Her skin was cold as he gathered her into his arms. Her eyes were wide and darkly blue, her lips slightly parted. Without thinking he leaned down and touched his mouth to hers in the way he had learned. She quieted in his arms. When he would have released her, Norah prolonged the kiss, and he pulled her tightly against his chest. This time she did not try to move away as she had in the past. Instead her arms crept round his neck, and she pressed against him as she had never done before.

Her mouth was hungry on his, and her fingertips began questing over the muscles of his shoulders and arms and chest, as if she sought to prove that he was real. Holding her against him, Storm Caller brought them both gently to the ground. Still she did not turn her head or push him away. Her body arched beneath his, her lips explored the curve of his jaw and her hands tugged at his shirt. Slowly, as in a dream, he removed their clothing and made love to her, and this time it was as he had always known it could be. She clung to him, whispering his name over and over, welcoming him as she had never done before.

Later they kissed, and he held her and stroked her until she fell asleep with her face cradled against his breast. He had waited so long for this, and at last she had come to him. At last she had joined with him of her own free will. He should have been happy and satisfied, and yet the triumph he had expected was not there. Instead there was a hollowness inside him, a cold ache encasing his heart.

Norah was dreaming. He could tell by the faint smile that curved her lips. He watched her a moment, then wandered to the mouth of the cavern and saw the sunset paint the spires and turrets of the canyon with gilt-edged carmine shading to violet. The discontent was still upon him, weighing his spirit down. Why was he oppressed when he should be glad? He had wanted Norah from the first moment he'd seen her in Greenwood Junction back when he was still masquerading in the white man's world as the Indian Scout, LeBeau.

A memory rattled loose in his brain, cascading through his thoughts like a fallen pebble, bringing other thoughts and memories hurtling down around him. He knew the reason for his dissatisfaction now, knew it with cold and bitter certainty. Darkness fell around him with terrible swiftness as the sun sank below the rim and the air grew chill.

When Norah had called out in her fright, she had not called out for him. She had called for a shadow-man, for someone who did not exist and never had. She had cried out in her distress, not for Storm Caller, but for *LeBeau*.

18

*"**D**on't move!"*

Norah did not question Storm Caller's command. She froze in midstep, bare toes hovering over the rust-colored dust. The dust moved. At least a part of it did. Her eyes focused on the strange creature. Beneath transparent armor, organs pumped and surged, and the segmented tail with the wicked stinger curved over the scorpion's back as it prepared to strike. It never had the chance. Storm Caller's knife flashed down like a stray sunbeam, and impaled it.

There was a liquid crunching sound, and Norah spun away from the sight of the ugly legs twisting and writhing out of synchrony. Unbalanced, she would have fallen if not for the iron arms that caught and held her fast. She leaned gratefully against Storm Caller's broad chest, unheeding of the way his turquoise talisman dug into her breast. His skin was warm against her cheek, and she sheltered against the hard strength of his body, prolonging his unintentional embrace: except for the afternoon they arrived in the cavern, it was the first time he had touched her in three weeks.

His arms tightened about her as protection changed to possession, and she felt his breath on her hair in ever-quickening gasps. He stroked her back and buried his face against her hair. Relief and fierce joy filled her chest until she felt her lungs would burst. He still wanted her. He had not tired of her after all. She looked up to read the expression in his eyes and saw, behind the hunger, an agony of doubt and loneliness. A glimpse of his soul. It was a bleak landscape, dark and littered with the bones of remembered pain.

As her face lifted to his, for a fleeting second it seemed that Storm Caller's mouth softened. Abruptly he thrust her away. "Where are your boots? Put them on at once."

She smiled inwardly at the anger in his voice, sensing that she had become more important to him than he knew himself. Storm Caller sounded exactly like Captain Gartner did when he scolded Abigail because he was anxious or worried about her. Norah hugged this revelation to herself. In the past days and the long, lonely nights lying awake at his side, she had begun to wonder if he meant to take her back to the ranch.

And she did not want to go.

Obediently she crossed to her pallet. Dusting her feet, she slipped them into the calf-high moccasins of soft leather that served for boots, grinning all the while. When she came back he looked abashed. Norah kept her eyes lowered, feigning a meekness she did not feel. Happiness welled within her, but she was too preoccupied to seek its source. Storm Caller strode to her side, slowing his pace as he neared. He maintained a few feet of distance between them, but she felt the intentness of his gaze.

"What is wrong? Did the scorpion sting you before I saw it?"

"No." Norah looked up beneath her lashes. His face was tense, the gray eyes hard with concern. "I'm not injured. Thank you."

Hastily she averted her eyes, afraid he would see the light shining in hers. Storm Caller let her go, and she sat down near the ledge that overlooked the canyon. Beside her were the pieces of soft doeskin she was making into a shirt for him. She picked one up and placed it across her lap, piercing it at intervals with her bone awl. It was hard to pay attention to her task with laughter dancing inside her skin.

Storm Caller came to stand a few feet away. After a while he sat and stared out over the canyon. He had done this often in the past weeks, and at times Norah felt sure he was thinking about her; other times he was as far away as the moon.

He cleared his throat. "A scorpion can be dangerous. When

I was a boy my sister was struck by one. She was very ill. We feared for her.''

So, she thought, struggling to keep the corners of her mouth down, *this is his idea of an apology for speaking roughly.* Norah thought it was not too bad an attempt for a man not used to apologizing. She threaded her needle with sinew and drew it through the puncture holes she had made.

"I did not know that you have a sister."

He looked up, as if surprised. "There is much you do not know about me."

"Tell me of your sister. Why did I not meet her?"

There was a pause before his answer. "She is dead."

"Oh! I am sorry." *Why did I not keep my tongue still?*

"But you did meet my sister. And you were kind to her. For that I am in your debt."

Norah started and jabbed her finger, remembering the interest of an Indian Scout named LeBeau for a certain young girl at Santa Magdalena, remembering the girls's story of another scorpion. Her throat was dry. "Dove-in-Flight." It was not a question.

"Yes. I thought you knew."

She did not even need to hear his reply as the puzzle pieces fell into place in an unexpected pattern. She turned to him with tears stinging against her lashes. Shock and sorrow rendered her incoherent. "Dear God! I am so sorry! What happened?"

If desolation had shown in his eyes before, it was Hell that lived behind them now. In that instant Norah would have given her life to blot away whatever had put it there. Her skin was suddenly damp, as if she wept blood for him through every pore. She half rose to go to him, but he spoke again, as if to himself.

"I knew she was dead when I left Camp Greenwood for the last time, but I did not know the details until later. She was murdered by her lover. When he tired of her. When he took a wife...."

Certainty descended like a sword stroke, cleaving Norah's brain and burying itself in her heart. *Abner.* Horror grew inside her. She understood so much more about everything. It was no wonder that Storm Caller hated Abner so fiercely, so unrelentingly. *Abner and Dove-in-Flight.*

Without hesitation she slipped on the thorny crown of Abner's guilt. She wanted to know when the girl had died. And how. Then she could loathe herself as she loathed Abner. Her chest hurt from holding her breath. She felt as if she could never draw another one.

"That is why you abducted me. I understand."

"No. But I tried to tell myself that was the reason."

She was afraid to meet his eyes, but forced herself to look at him. Storm Caller was staring out over the canyon, his face in three-quarter profile and empty of the hatred she had expected to find there. His face was pensive as he wandered back in time. "As a small child she used to follow me like a puppy around the camp. And she would wail and kick her feet whenever I rode off without her. Life was hard," he said softly. "But it was good."

His voice trailed off. There was no movement, no sound but their breathing. A tiny rodent with a long curved tail popped out from its hiding place, sniffed the air, and retreated. Silence spun out like a web, holding Norah and Storm Caller in its center.

Minutes passed before he spoke again. "When my father took me away I cursed him. Although I was only a boy, I would have killed him, but my mother and Elk Dancer begged me to try the white man's ways. It seemed a good idea to learn the enemy ways, so we would know his weaknesses."

The harsh lines at the sides of his mouth relaxed and his brow smoothed. His face was softer, younger, and Norah could see the proud eagerness of the boy he had been. Her hands stilled, and the needle slipped between her fingers unnoticed. Storm Caller had stepped into the safety of the past, and she did not want to recall him to the anguish of the present.

"My father was a Frenchman, but of a different faith than yours. He took me far away from the tribe, to a school where I would learn to be like him."

This is my son. He has been raised as a savage. Take him and make him a man. A white man.

I will never be like you. I would sooner be dead!

"I would not do their bidding and vowed to run away. For this, they put me in a hole in the ground and placed boards on top with stones over them, to keep me inside."

I know that his fingers are bleeding, Martha, but he did that himself. Darkness and a few days alone will cause him to repent his sins. He must learn respect and obedience, for the road to Salvation is not an easy one. You may give him bread and water once a day. And you may dress his hands if you like.

Gradually Storm Caller's face took on the lean and forbidding lines of his adulthood. "For three days and nights I stayed inside that dark shaft, refusing to 'repent.' The preacher told me to spend the hours learning humility. Instead I learned to hate. And that is all I ever learned from him."

Twilight sifted across the rocky walls and spires as Norah followed him on his long-ago journey from the familiar routine of the Comanche camp to a mission school on the plains. His words were few and halting, but slowly a picture formed in her mind of a bewildered young warrior thrust into an alien life. A life ruled by a strapping parson, smug in the superiority of his inherited religion. A man who believed salvation was administered with the end of a hickory rod. A man who bred hatred while preaching the love of God.

"There were ten other children there, three from among my people. We had no warm tepee fire at night and only a thin blanket against the cold. Our stomachs grumbled with the lack of meat, and we grew soft without riding or running. We could not understand the white man's ways, and we could not understand the white man's God. Each night we spoke of escaping, but when the time came I went alone. The others were too fearful of the preacher's medicine.

"I walked for days until I stole a trader's horse. And when I returned, my mother was dead, killed by smallpox from infected blankets purposely handed out by the government. And I discovered that the preacher had had his revenge after all. Six months among the blue-eyes had changed me. Since then I have walked in both worlds, and belonged to neither."

As he spilled out his story Norah read between the lines, feeling all the pain and grief and bitterness that lay beneath his words. She wanted to reach out to him, touch him, but sat back on her heels instead: he would not take kindly to her pity. She fought back her sorrow for the boy he had been, and for the man he had become, lost and searching all his life. If there was some way at that moment that Norah could have taken his burden upon herself she would have done so without the slightest hesitation. And then the knowledge burst into her mind like an exploding sun, blinding her to everything else. *I love him.*

The realization was shattering.

This, then, was love. Not the spark of attraction, nor the brief red flare of desire nor the white blaze of passion. Love was all of them, compounded with this gentle healing, this all-consuming peace that settled in her heart. *I love him. More than my life.* She picked up a piece of the doeskin and held it up as if examining it, screening her face and tears that could not be denied. She wiped them away with the back of her hand. When she set it down her face was still and blank with the effort of composure, and her eyes had the dazed look of one who had just received an unexpected blow.

Storm Caller shook off his reverie and turned to face her. She was drawing the sinew through the holes as if fascinated by the rhythm of the ivory-colored needle. He noticed the stunned look in her eyes and misinterpreted it as boredom. *Why am I baring my heart to her? What can she know of my life and my people? And my loss. She does not care. She is not even listening.*

He rose and left the cavern, and Norah sighed and put her mind to her work. He was gone a long time, much longer than it took to check on their horses, hidden in the safety of a sheer-sided gorge. Norah was restless, and although she kept busy with all the necessary little tasks, her mind ran in ever-smaller circles. Dusk settled over the high plateau, turning the canyons to bottomless black rivers before Storm Caller returned. He went to his sleeping pallet, stripped off his clothes and lay down without speaking.

Norah did the same. They lay side by side in aching loneliness, but neither spoke. Slowly her hand crept from beneath the cover to touch his shoulder and linger there. He jumped as if burned and then lay still. Her fingertips moved lightly over his skin, softly insistent, tracing questions and demanding answers. She leaned up on one elbow, letting her hair drift over his naked chest as she stroked his side and down along his thigh. With a muffled groan, Storm Caller rolled over and gathered her into his arms.

And when they made love each thought: *At least I have this much.*

Light flared, orange to blinding white, from an outcrop of rock in the purple distance. Norah waited, and it happened again. She blinked her eyes against its painful intensity. Balls of color, red and green and black danced before her, regardless of whether her lids were open or closed.

"What is it?"

At her side on the trail, Storm Caller gestured for silence, muscles bunched in sudden tension. They stood unmoving for five minutes on the winding path high above the canyon floor, and below them the river snaked silver and green between the umber talus slopes.

Norah had learned to mimic Storm Caller's quiet concentration, and waited without moving or questioning again. The light came lancing down again, piercing her eyes, and she had to look away as the pattern repeated. *A mirror*, she thought. *A message sent with mirrors.* The outside world was intruding itself on their fragile happiness. She was cold, and shivered, although the sun was hot. Something was going to happen. Something bad. Fear slithered up the bones of her spine and wrapped itself around her throat. She could not have spoken if she tried.

Storm Caller frowned and started up the narrow ledge that served as their trail, so abstracted Norah wondered if he had forgotten her presence. He hadn't. She was the center of his thoughts. He had been expecting this summons, but now found himself strangely reluctant. He did not want to leave Norah. And he could not take her with him. When they reached the cavern he extracted a square of some shiny metal from one of his packs and chose a spot near the lip of the twenty-foot drop. He made an arcing motion with the metal, paused, and repeated it. From the distance came one burst of light. Acknowledgment of return message received.

As he replaced the piece of metal, Norah joined him. "What is it? Is something wrong?"

His eyes were candid, but shadows lurked in their gray depths. "I don't know yet. Two Horses Racing promised to send for me if I was needed." He took her hand in his, feeling the calluses along her palm, then held the soft back of it against his cheek.

"I must leave you for a few days. I will take the roan. The other horses have enough forage and water in the gorge. They will be safe, and you will be safe here in the cavern, Norah. But you must remember all that I have taught you. And in seven days I will be back."

She clutched his arm. "Let me go with you. Don't leave me here alone."

He shook his head slowly, but with finality. "I cannot take you. Much as I would."

There was regret in his eyes. Since they had made love again two weeks ago, their relationship had resumed as if that brief period of physical alienation had never occurred. There was something new between them, deep and restful as a wooded glade, powerful and as unstoppable as a river in flood. His eyes sought Norah's a hundred times a day, only to find her doing the same. He could not be near her without touching her: her hair, her skin, the graceful curve of her neck, the soft swell of her breasts that fit his palms so perfectly. His loins ached just looking at her now, and his heart ached at the hurt in her eyes. No, he did not want to leave her.

"Horse soldiers are everywhere, and I do not know why. Perhaps there have been raids, or they may be searching for you. I will not risk losing you, Norah."

Her eyes met his, vividly blue around the dilated pupils. "I cannot stay here alone. I am afraid."

He smiled and touched her face. "What, do you still fear the ghosts of the Ancient Ones? Here! I will leave you this Piece of Sky. It will keep you safe."

He lifted the thong that held a small fetish around his neck. It was crudely carved in the shape of a bear and blue as a morning glory. Blue as her eyes. He dropped the thong over her head and the roughly fashioned lump of semiprecious stone rested in the hollow between her breasts. Norah touched it, turning it over in her hand. It was warm from Storm Caller's skin, and brought her a sense of comfort and protection. She did not want the Cavalry troops to find her and take her back, either.

"This talisman," he said, "is very old. It has been handed down in Elk Dancer's line for many generations."

"What did you call it before?"

"Elk Dancer has a story that is older than our people, handed down with this amulet. Turquoise nuggets are Pieces of the Sky. When man came forth into this world he was greedy and wicked, offending the gods. The Sky wept at his folly, and the tears fell from the heavens and hardened into turquoise. These stones, these Pieces of Sky, Elk Dancer says, are potent medicine. They protect us from evil. You need not fear the ghosts of the old ones, Norah, for they will not approach you while you wear this. Not even the ghost of a little rabbit!"

He was laughing now, teasing away her apprehension. And yet a part of him still believed in the power of magic and the protection of talismans. So did Norah, but of a different sort. She felt calm. Strong. As if the piece of turquoise radiated a powerful force along with Storm Caller's absorbed body heat. Civilization, she thought, had lost something of value when it summarily discarded the old beliefs and practices. That silver medal of Our Lady that Father Ildephonso had given her on her Confirmation Day—she had believed that it brought her luck and preserved her health, and had been quite upset when she lost it. Until it had been replaced, she had been filled with anxiety. Was that so different? She thought not.

Seven days. Seven nights alone. Norah had sufficient supplies: acorns, roasted piñon nuts, dried corn and jerky and precious coffee. Even a bag of barley candy. She could easily survive for so short a time without Storm Caller. But she would not like it. "When will you leave?"

"As soon as possible."

She started away without looking at him. Seven days. "I will pack you some food for your journey."

"That can wait." Locking her inside his arms, he bent his head to touch his mouth at the nape of her neck, tasting her skin. When he lowered her to the ground everything but his nearness was banished from her mind.

But later, when he had gone, fear settled in her bones like an ague. Norah was terribly afraid, and she did not know why.

She sat on the ledge, rubbing the talisman between her fingers, and wept.

With every step his roan took away from the canyon, Storm Caller wanted to turn back. He was pledged to Iron Knife, and feared what the future would bring. It was not war or Death that weighed upon him, but his feelings for Norah. There was a time when he did not care if he lived or died, as long as he lived or died bravely. But now, if he died, what would happen to Norah? Where would she go, who would take her in? He was torn inside by the inevitability of war, the necessity of his participation, and the futility of its outcome.

He rode through the rocky defiles and along the rugged escarpments in a state of deep perturbation. When he had taken her away he had not wanted to look ahead to whatever the future might bring, and now Norah would suffer for his lack of foresight. Certainly he could not bring her with him when he rode with Iron Knife to join Quanah Parker. That circumstances might put her once again in reach of Abner Slade was unthinkable. No matter how he examined the problem he came up with the same answer: Norah would be forced to reap the harvest of his ill-planned sowing. He wished he had his grandmother's wisdom to guide him. Perhaps he would seek Elk Dancer out before returning to the cavern in Endless Canyon.

At least Norah was safe for now. He dismissed the scorpion incident from his mind: she made mistakes from time to time, but she never repeated her errors. What harm could come to her in a few short days? He nudged his horse into a canter on the level ground, impatient to discover the reason for his summons. And while he covered the miles northward, two horsemen journeyed back along the way he had come, seeking sanctuary in the hidden places of the canyon country.

When darkness fell he made camp for the night, but sleep did not come easily. In the morning he quickened his pace, and by afternoon was close to the previously arranged meeting place. Hobbling the roan where it was unlikely to be seen, Storm Caller went on foot through the cedar and scrub that edged either side of the narrow creek for a hundred yards. It did not take him long to find his friend's painted horse, well hidden behind an el of rock.

The ground was soft and sandy for the most part, but littered with rock and scree to the west. Storm Caller took to the rocks, examining the ground closely before he found a sign. It led through some pine needles and on to a stretch of sand. Yes, Two Horses had come this way, and not long before. And he was in a hurry, as the length between strides proved. Two Horses must feel secure from ambush here. Silently he followed the almost invisible traces: a broken twig, a bent blade, a pebble newly turned over.

The sign indicated a descent into a dry arroyo, but he headed noiselessly up the rise, which was capped by a massive block of limestone. He slipped into its shadow and saw that the gray-gold stone was split almost in two from top to bottom, leaving a vertical crack only a few feet across. Peering around the slab, Storm Caller had a clear view of the surroundings, and of Two Horses a short distance away, relieving his bladder.

A gleam of devilry lit Storm Caller's eyes, and he stepped into the cleft in the rock. Pressing his back against the rough surface and pushing off from the opposite side with his feet, he began to ascend the narrow fissure. In seconds he reached the top, and crawled up and out on the hot stone. Two Horses stood a few feet off, straightening the breechcloth he wore over his leggings. Without a second, Storm Caller launched himself off the rock toward his friend's unsuspecting back.

As the large shadow passed over him Two Horses reached for his knife and tried to whip around, but it was too late. Recognition showed briefly in his eyes just before Storm Caller's feet caught him between the shoulder blades, and the two hit the ground, rolling down the gentle incline. They pummeled each other with balled fists, mock-fighting like carefree boys, until Two Horses was bested, and lay panting on his back with a wide grin on his square face.

Storm Caller released his friend and sprang to his feet, laughing. "You grow careless."

Two Horses picked himself up. "And you grow reckless! It is lucky that I recognized you, or you would lie dead at my feet now."

Storm Caller gave him a pitying smile. "I could have cut

your liver out before you knew it was gone. You are getting soft now that you have taken a wife."

Two Horses grinned and punched him in the arm. "You, of all others, should know what a woman can do to a man! It is too bad, my friend, when Horns-of-Buffalo must send me to tear you away from your woman's bed."

The laughter died. The remark had hit too near the bone. "Why has he sent for me?"

"To meet with Iron Knife and set our plans. There is much unrest."

"Then let us lose no time."

They climbed the rise and were soon picking their way along the dry bed of an ancient river, Two Horses on his speckled mount, Storm Caller on his powerful roan. They skirted the open areas they would normally have taken, and twice spied columns of troopers in the distance. They cut across an area of open semidesert land, then back on a northwest diagonal until the ground began to rise in sudden folds that left deep valleys and gorges between the high ridges. The roundabout way lengthened their journey, but they still reached their goal an hour before sunset. Only a few stunted trees and scraggly creosote bushes awaited them in the narrow gorge.

"They have moved on," Two Horses said in surprise. "Something has happened."

They dismounted and began a systematic examination of the area, but there was no sign of an ambush or fight. And there was no sign that anyone had ever been there before them. As they searched there was a snapping of dried brush from the far end of the gorge. Limping Bear showed himself from behind a screen of rocks. He came forward, rapidly closing the short distance between them despite his uneven stride. In the waning light he looked his age, but it was more than the passing years that drew such dreadful lines upon his features. Storm Caller hurried to meet his comrade.

"Greetings, Limping Bear. Where is Iron Knife? And where are the others?"

The old man stopped a few paces away. "Iron Knife has gone on to meet his men. He asks that you join him at Willow Creek before the new moon."

"And Horns-of-Buffalo? Where is he?"

Limping Bear's face twisted awry. "Gone to join his ancestors. I found him this morning."

The new arrivals were stunned. When Storm Caller spoke
he hardly knew his own voice. "That is evil news, indeed
How did it happen?"

"In his sleep. From a slit throat."

Angry disbelief met his words, yet the truth was mirrored
bleakly in the old man's eyes. Two Horses threw back his head
and made a low keening sound, like a wounded wolf. An instant later he whipped out his knife and made a diagonal cut
deep in the skin of his forearm as a sign of his grief and rage.
Storm Caller caught the young brave's wrist and forced him to
drop the weapon.

"Save your blood and your strength. You will need it to
help me hunt down his murderer." He clasped Limping Bear
on the shoulder. "Who has done this, and which way have
they gone?"

"No one was seen. But if we follow their tracks I think we
will find the one-eyed Apache and the fire-haired trapper. They
are headed south. Toward Endless Canyon. Cut Face knows i
well."

Iron fingers closed over Storm Caller's heart, squeezing the
life from his chest, and the light drained away until he saw his
friends as pale ghosts against a landscape leached of color. He
fought the sensation, dragging a ragged breath deep inside his
lungs. Toward Endless Canyon, where Norah waited, alone.
Leaping on his horse, he wheeled around and headed back the
way he had come, leaving the others behind.

19

By her third morning alone, Norah had settled into the quiet rhythm of life in the ancient cavern. She became acquainted with the kangaroo rats that hopped across the dusty floor and the lizards, brown and yellow, that sunned themselves on the heated rocks. Today her fears seemed as foolish as a child's dread of the bogeyman. Touching the turquoise fetish, she thought of Storm Caller and smiled.

She fried some corn cakes in oil, ate a handful of roasted nuts, and sipped black coffee with her feet dangling over the lip of the cavern. Above was a lemon sky, fading to blue over the tops of the distant pinnacles and mesas. The river sparkled below, green as bottle-glass in the deep shadows, winking now and then to catch her eye. Norah looked at it longingly. She was hot and dusty. She needed a bath.

There was enough water stored in the cavern to sponge off with, but that never seemed to quite do the job. She wanted to cool her skin in fresh running water and wash her hair free of the fine-sifted red dust that clung to everything. Storm Caller had given her a dozen warnings before he left, but he had not said a word about going down to the river. She knew, of course, had never occurred to him that she might make her way down without his assistance. The sun-warmed canyon walls were the color of marmalade, and the sheen of water below was as inviting as the first notes of music to a dance. Norah surrendered to the temptation.

Taking a piece of woven cloth to use for a towel, she started down the narrow path, planting each footstep firmly as she went. Norah had climbed this path many times with Storm Caller, and had no doubt she could do it alone. She knew the trail well: where to step, where not to step. Old Woman Rock, Balancing Rock, the steep pitch downward where an earthquake had lifted up a slab of different material, and silver ore streaked a low, jagged wall, branching out in two blue-gray veins. There one of the Ancient Ones had carved a many-horned beast and left a handprint behind in dark red paint. And here. Here was the place where they had rested and Storm Caller had made love to her in the early morning light. Soon she would know the canyon as well as he did.

She reached the bottom and looked up in grinning triumph at the red and gold-banded ramparts. She had done it. It had taken, she guessed, over half of an hour and a few heart-pounding scares along the way to her goal, and would probably take twice as long to return. But in the meantime, she would indulge herself in a long, refreshing bath. And *that* was certainly worth the effort.

The river, so emerald green from above, was pale tourmaline in the deepest waters, lightening to topaz along the shoals. Stepping out of her clothing, she folded it neatly and splashed into a shallow pool formed by a half-circle of water-smoothed boulders. It was cool and flowed over her body in silken ripples, bathing her parched skin like Balm of Gilead. Her muscles relaxed, massaged by the steady current. Slowly the knots of tension melted, dissolved, and were washed away.

The air rumbled with the rush of water over submerged rock, punctuated by the short shrill notes of the large white and brown birds overhead. They nested in holes and crevices high above the river, and lived on fish and water-loving lizards. A man lost and in need of water could find it if he spotted one of these birds and followed it. Storm Caller had taught her that. She had learned many things from Storm Caller. But his habit of silence in the open was not one of them.

The birds called and sang, and without thinking, she sang back at them. "Black is the color of my true love's hair, his lips are ruby red... " The canyon caught up her words and

ent them ringing back from the steep walls. "Black is the
olor...is the color...is the color..."

The feathered creatures screeched in alarm and flapped up-
ard toward their nests. From time to time she could hear them
colding and complaining about the noisy intruder below. Sud-
enly Norah realized how alone she was, more alone than she
ad ever been in her life. She missed the sound of another
uman voice: Storm Caller had been gone for three days. Next
he tried a line of poetry. Anything to shatter the stillness that
egan to weigh down upon her. The words echoed and were
wallowed whole by the vastness of the canyon, too flowery,
o dainty to survive their setting. Norah decided that nothing
ss than Homer or Shakespeare would do in this splendid scen-
ry.

Lying on her back with her head in the water, her hair
treaming out behind her like Ophelia's, she quoted aloud from
amlet to a robins's-egg sky. "...Blasted with ecstasy: O, woe
s me! To have seen what I have seen, see what I see!"

Suddenly her voice faltered and stilled. She floundered up-
ght and listened. There was nothing to strike her ear except
e river's deep-throated song, not even the distant cry of a
ird. The back of her neck prickled as if she were being
atched. A rapid scan of the riverbank revealed no visible pres-
nce; but along the wind-carved cliffs and in the miles of crev-
es and twisting canyons that curved and doubled back again
nd again along this stretch, there could be an army of observ-
rs hidden and she would not spot them.

She splashed out and onto the loose chert that bordered the
ver. A year earlier she would have caught up her clothes and
ruggled into them to preserve her modesty. Now she stood
aked, sun-spangled rivulets running down her body, and
ook her moccasins out to rid them of any lurking insects.
hey were the first item she put on. Her mouth turned up
ryly. *"A lesson learned is a lesson remembered."* Maxim
umber 22 from Miss Emerson's Academy—which had ex-
ted once upon a time in another universe, one that had ab-
lutely no bearing upon this one.

Her skirts caught against the wetness of her limbs as she
limbed back toward the cavern with more haste than she had
lanned. She was only slightly out of breath by the midpoint

up the cliff, and thanked the hardy life of recent months fo
her improved stamina. Once she would have rested in th
shadow of a tall spire, but even as she considered doing so,
strange noise echoed somewhere below, resonating back an
forth between the perpendicular walls. A familiar voice. *
man's voice. And it was not Storm Caller's.

Danger! Danger! Hurry, hurry! The barely discernible trac
forked ahead, and Norah made a split-second decision, pickin
a quicker but less secure route to the cavern. She had neve
gone this way before, although Storm Caller always used i
whenever he went alone. Half-climbing, half-scrabbling, sh
made her way up the perilous approach. Her nails, short a
they were, splintered and broke as she grasped for any hand
hold she could find. Reaching a vertical stretch, she realize
too late, that she was not tall enough to reach the triangle o
red rock that protruded from the next natural ledge. She woul
have to jump and grab on to the outcrop of stone.

Norah never doubted she could do it, and jumped upwar
with a strong spring of her legs. Her fingers closed over th
tip of the outcrop, giving her little purchase to lever herself u
Dangling over the slope for endless seconds, her sweaty hand
slipped on the rock. She fell to the ledge below, landing heavil
on her right hip. Her arms felt pulled from the sockets, he
bones were jarred and she had bitten her tongue. The near mis
only strengthened her determination. Swearing like a mule
skinner without knowing a word she said, she wiped her blood
ied palms on her skirt, then rubbed dirt into them to absorb th
perspiration as she had seen Storm Caller do. The sharp par
ticles ground into her lacerated flesh until her eyes smarted wit
tears of pain and anger. With a desperate lunge she launche
herself upward, and met with success.

For a dizzying moment she dangled, then gathered her en
ergies for the next step. Wrapping her arms around the roug
outcropping like a woman embracing a lover, she worked he
way until she straddled it. With her face hanging over the edg
she finally glimpsed her pursuer, and understood her first blin
instinct to run for safety. Down in the crotch of the canyo
wall, an Indian peered up at her with his one remaining orb
Below and beyond him, a man with red-gold hair made hi
way along the fallen sandstone slabs. Cut-Face and Travis.

Norah jumped to her feet and raced up the forty-five degree slope before her, sending pebbles and shards falling like hailstones with every step. Ahead she could see the narrow ledge and the ancient ladder resting against the lip of the cavern. She sprinted the final distance and swarmed up the ladder with the ease of a sailor on a ships's rigging, the same ladder that she had feared to climb a few weeks earlier. Now she didn't bother to give it a thought. As soon as she reached the cavern, she pulled the ladder up behind her so there was no access to where she stood. And then her boneless legs gave out, and she sank to the ground. Safe. She was safe.

From her vantage point she could see movement on the trail below as two heads appeared, one black, one red. She had beaten them to the cavern by seconds: had she taken the other route... Norah had no time to consider further. The Indian and his companion arrived on the ledge where the ladder had rested only moments before. The Apache had lost one of his front teeth.

Travis cupped his hands. "Halloo up there! Can we come up?" When there was no answer he called out again. "We don't mean you no harm. We was up there in your cave earlier, jist to git some water, and we didn't take nothing. Look around and you'll see I'm telling the truth."

Norah looked around. It was true. Someone had been here while she was gone. The covers on her pallet were thrown back and someone had rifled through the small store of supplies. There was a gout of tobacco juice in the dirt, and the gourd dipper, which usually lay beside the water storage vessel, had fallen inside. She took it out. Already it was becoming pulpy and water-logged.

"Whatsa matter, you scared of us? All alone, are you? I'll bet you could use some company. Put that there ladder back, and we'll come up and chat awhile. Must be lonely for a white woman all by herself up there."

Norah's stomach turned over. She wore Comanche dress, and her face and arms were tanned from exposure to the sun. With her long black hair, she should have been taken for an Indian woman from a distance. But Travis knew she was a white woman. They had watched her bathing, had seen her body naked, seen the pale untanned flesh that had betrayed her to them. Her skin crawled at the thought.

"C'mon, let us up, Miz Slade. That's who you are, ain't it? Miz Slade what run off with a Comanche? You ain't scared of me, and I know you ain't scared of Cut Face. You cain't be scared of Indians. Not when you been living with them. Not when you let that half-breed LeBeau climb between your legs." He went on and on, alternating oily pleasantries with vulgar suggestions.

"I know what it is," he said. "You heard 'bout that settler's woman we had with us. Everything would have been all right if she done what we wanted. We wouldn't of hurt her none. And she wasn't near as pretty as you. We're gonna treat you nice, Miz Slade. Real nice. Unless you like it rough. I know that's how your husband gives it to you, don't he?"

Knowing silence was her best response, Norah bit her lips against the scream rising in her throat and sat motionless like an animal trapped in a blind hole. When they could not reach her they would tire and go away. If they remained, she would outwait them until Storm Caller returned, rationing her food and water in case he were delayed. *Like the siege of the Moors at Grenada*, she thought, taking heart from history and conveniently forgetting that Grenada had eventually fallen to the Spaniards.

Suddenly she heard a slithering, followed by soft grainy sounds. Sand and stones falling. Edging forward and to one side, she looked down. The trapper stood alone on the ledge, watching something halfway up the limestone face, something hidden from her view by the overhang of the cave lip. The Indian was nowhere in sight, but as she looked for him, a scattering of pebbles came from below and to the right of her vantage point. She stuck her head out a little more. There was a crosswise bulge in the rock, halfway up to the cavern. Cut Face would be beneath that bulge now, trying to find some place to get another foothold. Her heart banged against her ribs as if trying to pound its way out through her chest wall.

She was dizzy and nauseated with fear, but willpower sustained her. *I will not faint! I will not faint.* She forced herself to think clearly. Perhaps Cut Face and Travis would overcome her, but she would make them pay dearly. Her knife was long and sharp, and she knew the cavern and its secret places. But it would be best if she could prevent their entry. If this were a medieval keep and she its chatelaine, how would she repel attackers? What would Eleanor of Aquitaine have done?

The answers came quickly, and she thought to herself: *I will tell Storm Caller that my lessons in history were not so useless after all, when I see him again. If I see him again.*

"Miz Slade? C'mon and let that ladder down and we can parlay. That other woman?—I never meant to mess her up like that. God's truth. But you see, she kept crying and trying to run away and it made me mad. Now I don't mind if a woman cries. In fact, I kinda like it. Shows she's womanly. But it don't pay to get me mad. Now if you'll just be nice and friendly-like, there's no reason we can't just enjoy ourselves awhile. Ol' Cut Face, he ain't so bad when you get used to him. And you'll get used to him, real quick."

Norah tried to block out his words, listening instead for signs of the Apache's progress as she worked. She didn't know if it was possible to scale the rock face, but she was taking no chances. There was a time when the Indian would have to come over the top of that bulge, and when he did, she'd be ready. Her fingers were clumsy at first, but as she reached a state of odd calmness they became steady. She had passed beyond the boundaries of her fear, into that land of doing-what-must-be-done. She would die, or she wouldn't. But in the meantime, she was going to give them one hell of a fight.

Finishing her task, she went to the edge of the cavern again and peered over. Cut Face was past the bulge, his foot secure in a wide fissure as he pulled himself upward. He saw her and grinned like a skull, all teeth and gaping mouth. Norah stepped back and picked up a heavy pot of fired clay that she had stuffed with rocks and potsherds, then rolled it over the edge. It was off target, crashing against the rock to one side of Cut Face's right hand. He spat out a curse and made another hand-hold higher up, scraping along the escarpment. Travis grabbed for his rifle, but it was just out of reach, and Norah sent another missile crashing down.

The barrel shape was perfect for her purpose, falling true this time. It hit the Indian on the left face and shoulder, and he went spinning down to the ledge along with the shattered shards. He hit the ground, bounced, and did not move again. A jagged piece caught Travis, cutting his forehead to the bone. Blood welled up and fell over his face like a crimson scarf, and he clapped a hand to try to staunch the flow.

"Goddamn you, woman! You goddam Indian's whore!" Travis cursed long and loud, describing in obscene detail what he would do to Norah when he got hold of her.

She waited till he stopped for breath. "Mr. Travis, that is not the only surprise I have up my sleeve. You would be wise to leave without forcing me to defend myself again. In any case, my friends are due to arrive momentarily. You had best be off at once."

"You ain't got no friends, you Indian bitch. And if you're talking about LeBeau, we heard he was seen going north. He won't be back. Not in time, he won't. And I'll tell you, what I did to that little woman from over to Eagle Pass ain't nothin' to what I have in mind for you. You're going to beg to die before I'm finished."

Cut Face stirred, groaned, and vomited as he tried to rise to his knees. Travis ignored him, and instead bound his own head with a bandana. He removed a flask from the pack at his feet and took a long pull, then another, and Norah stepped back, out of his line of sight. After a while she could hear them murmuring, but when she peeked they were gone. They had taken refuge in one of the crevices below the ledge. Darkness fell, and silence with it. She tried to eat; her stomach balked, but she managed to keep some water down.

She spent the night awake and was heavy-eyed by morning, but they made no appearance. At dusk Travis showed up on the ledge, threatening and cursing, his face caked and black with dried blood beneath the makeshift bandage. Cut Face joined him, carrying a leather pouch in one hand, and seemed no worse for his fall except for an area on his chest where the skin was scraped off. They took turns drinking between catcalls, and Norah knew what they were doing: trying to get her to throw down whatever else she might have ready, so that when they made their next assault she would be out of missiles. After a while their voices became hoarse, the words slurred. Soon it was quiet. She thought it was another trick, then spotted on the ledge, two bodies, limply sprawled. It took her a moment to figure it out.

"Drunk! They're drunk. Thank God!"

Her stomach complained of meals not eaten, and she forced down some dried corn cakes, washed down amply with water. It was only after her third dipper that prudence took over: it was less than half full now, and Norah wondered how long her supply would hold out if they dug in for a siege. There was a natural cistern on a high pinnacle above the cave, but the way up to it was from the ledge below, where the two lay sprawled.

She doubted she could sleep, but anxiety and her rapid climb to safety extracted overdue payment for her carelessness. Fatigue gathered around her like a fog until there was no fighting it. Her eyes burned until it was an agony to keep them open, and her head bobbed on her neck like an apple on a string. Norah decided she would have greater need to be wakeful when the sun rose. Better to rest now, while they were passed out, and be alert for danger when they woke.

Taking refuge on the upper level, she pulled up the ladder to the second tier of houses, and made her bed in the corner of two ruined walls. If they managed to get inside the cavern she would at least have warning and a bit more time before they found her. She curled up with her head on her arms, wondering where Storm Caller was and what he was doing. And if he would arrive in time to save her. For the first time in many months, she prayed with the desperate faith of a child. She slept until dawn, when sounds from the cavern entrance signaled that her enemy had wakened.

Norah tried to rise, and the ruined walls spun around with the blur of a colored top. Her tongue was thick and furred, and her throat felt like raw meat. She tried to take a deep breath and instantly regretted it. Her lungs burned like coals, and she stopped, gasped, and stopped again.

Oh, God, I can't be ill now! She got on all fours and clawed at the dried mud floor to stop from falling off the world. Something clattered below, and there was a sound of breaking pottery. She didn't have to look to know Travis and Cut Face were in the cavern. Dragging herself to an upright position, she stuck her head cautiously around the wooden frame of the open doorway. A spear of sunlight struck her eyes and sent her staggering back, clutching her head. She leaned against the wall and let herself slide noiselessly down until she was sitting.

When the throbbing stopped she put her thoughts in order. *Influenza.* Once before she had been stricken with it. But not like this. Not this badly. What time was it? The butterscotch sun already hung low over the twin spires. That meant it was afternoon. Late afternoon. She had slept the night and more than half the day away. Neither time nor energy were available to waste on self-recriminations. But how had they gotten in? A dragging sound roused her to action. She crawled back to the doorway, her breathing light and shallow. God, it hurt to swallow! Norah shielded her eyes against the glare, wincing at the brightness. Cut Face was dragging the ladder from where she had put it, back toward the lip of the cave, back toward where a voice called from outside. Then Travis was still below, and Cut Face had found another way in.

As she watched, the Indian staggered and dropped the ladder. One of the poles splintered near the top, but it was still usable. Cut Face wiped his forehead with the back of his hand, then pressed it there a moment as if in pain. His skin was shiny with sweat, and Norah realized that he was stricken also. Now she remembered that they had drunk from her water supply. Was it possible that she had been infected that way? What did it matter? The important thing now was to find a place to hide where they would not find her easily. A place where she might surprise at least one of them with six inches of steel. Then Storm Caller would know that she had not died like a sheep to the slaughter. Her heart twisted in her breast. She did not want him to find her broken body, to remember her that way.

"Remember me in sunlight," she whispered. "Oh, I wish I had told you that I love you."

Cut Face had the ladder over the edge, holding it in place, and she could hear Travis shouting instructions. This was her best chance. She moved too quickly, and was almost overcome by dizziness. Her hand was on the hilt of her knife. Perhaps she would have to turn it on herself, instead. Her breath hissed in and out between her teeth. "No, by God! Not yet. Not while there's a chance to take one of them with me!"

Her fingers caught at the bit of roughly fashioned turquoise, her "Piece of Sky," and suddenly everything seemed clear. This level was nothing more than a trap, but she knew where she wanted to go. To the *kiva*, a deep pit dug below the cavern floor. Storm Caller had showed it to her over in the angle where the cavern roof arched down to meet the floor. It was used by the men of the Ancient Ones, he had told her, for meetings and ritual purification and their secret religious ceremonies. And the entrance was screened by a tumble of fallen rock and organic debris. They might not discover it. But if they did, God willing, she would be ready for them.

Steadying herself, Norah slid around the corner and into the open of the second level. She had brought the ladder up with her, and had neither the strength nor the time to replace it. Several yards to the left a row of mud-brick cells had collapsed in upon themselves, and the rubble sloped to the cavern floor. If she could clamber down it without attracting their attention—or fainting—she could make it to the kiva.

She passed the dwelling that contained the urn burial. *Help me*, she thought. *Help me, or I will be dead like you*. Time seemed suspended as she made her way toward the fallen buildings. The dizziness and pain had given way to a sense of weightlessness, and Norah floated to her destination on wings of delirium. She worked her way down through the crumbled mud brick and barely noticed when she turned her ankle savagely. She looked down. It was wedged at an impossible angle, and she thought it might be broken. There was no pain. Only the fire in her lungs, which had banked down to a steady and comforting warmth. The rest of her was cold. So cold.

In the distance she could hear Travis and Cut Face yelling back and forth, but their words ran together and made no sense. They were both in the cavern when she stumbled behind the rock and found the kiva. The entrance was a small hole that led into blackness. She didn't bother to look for a ladder. She could float down, effortlessly, like a feather on the breeze. Norah no longer existed. The feather stepped off the brink and fell to earth, changing to a chunk of lead that landed with the sound of dried twigs snapping. In the utter darkness a light bloomed. She had seen it once before, although she did not recall that now. It grew and grew until it engulfed Norah. Her last conscious emotion was one of great surprise.

"You stupid sonofabitch." Travis looked down at the Apache, sprawled facedown on the ground while his sides heaved like those of a winded horse. "Get up, damn you!"

Cut Face moaned something. His companion nudged him onto his back with one foot. The Indian's face was flushed with fever, his eyes glassy and unseeing. Travis swore. "I told you there was fever in the camp. I told you not to go down there. You poor, stupid sonofabitch!"

He took a swig from the flask inside his buckskin shirt. Whiskey killed most diseases. Anyone could tell you that. He tilted his head back and took another, for good measure. "Well, you'll just miss out on all the fun if you don't shake that fever off, fast." And if the Apache was still sick later, he'd have to be left behind when Travis was done.

There was a sound from behind, and the trapper spun around. Nothing. "Where are you, Miz Slade? I got something for you. C'mon out, and I won't hurt you. Not too much. But you done made me mad now, and I warned you 'bout that. I'll bet you bruise easy, too."

There was a trickle of falling stones, over in the dark corner where the cavern roof arched down to meet the ground. "Over there, are you?" Travis went forward on the balls of his feet, his blood running hot with anticipation. Oh, it had been a long time since he'd had him a white woman. That settler's wife didn't count. She'd been too scared to struggle, just laid there like a frightened rabbit. She was a skinny little thing, and had passed out the first time he hit her, her eyes rolling right up inside her head. That took a lot of the pleasure out of it. He liked to watch their eyes.

Movement blurred ahead. He rubbed the front of his pants with the heel of his hand and licked the corner of his mouth. "You got nice breasts," he said hoarsely. "Nice 'n' round. I'm gonna..." The words dried like spittle on his lips as a figure loomed out of the shadows. He reached for his gun, but Storm Caller was faster.

A knife spun outward like a lightning bolt, catching Travis

through the midsection. It hit edge on, slicing through skin and soft tissue, burying itself deep within his spine. The trapper fell backward, and lay in urine while his nerveless legs twitched and were still.

"Goddamn it, you killed me!" he said. It ended on a sob.

"Not yet. My aim is too good for that." Storm Caller came to stand over him, relentless as the Death he had brought with him. "There are a hundred ways to die, Travis. And if you live long enough, you will know them all."

20

She followed the light, casting off the body that had betrayed her with its leaden weight. Faster and faster she went, until she seemed to be flying toward that brilliant source. Voices encouraged her, calling her on. Faces appeared before her of people she had never seen, yet she thought she knew them. She sensed cool water and green trees ahead in meadows dappled with quiet shade. A woman spoke to her in loving tones. It was hard to see with that light in her eyes, a light like the glow of a hundred suns. *Mother? Is that you?*

And then another voice called, not from the shining place but from the dark place that she had left behind. She turned and listened. It came again, and she was slowly drifting back toward it, pulled by an invisible cord. She knew she must follow that voice, yet regret filled her. Why did she have to leave this warm and beautiful light and its promise of safety and rest? She fought her way toward the light and again that deep voice called, filled with a desperate fear that belonged to that dim and shadowed world. A name came to her, and then a dearly beloved face, contorted now with wild grief. *Storm Caller.* And she remembered. She had to go to him. Eagerly turning her back to the light, she rushed toward him and was caught and held fast by a net of agony.

Her eyes flickered open. She could not see. *Am I blind, then?* She digested this development. *Let me see his face once more.* Light flared. Not the all-encompassing brightness that had pulled her along the black tunnel, but the yellow-orange glow of a man-made flame. Storm Caller's face floated into view, as stern and beautiful as she remembered it. A fleck of red paint showed near his temple, and a drop of clear rain glistened along his cheek.

"*I knew you'd come....*" Norah couldn't tell if she had spoken the words aloud. It didn't matter. He was here. She smiled and surrendered to an eternity of nothingness.

Storm Caller sponged Norah's face and throat again. He had not slept in three days and was half mad with fatigue and the effects of the stimulant plant he chewed to keep awake. He had the terrible fear Norah would die if he fell asleep before her illness reached its crisis stage. Her cheeks were hollow, her collarbone and ribs sticking out beneath the parched skin. The flesh between those ribs was sucked in with every irregular gasp of breath, and he knew her lungs were full of fluid. She had no reserves to fight off the pneumonia, for her body was being consumed by the fever that raged unchecked.

He had tried every available herb whose effects he knew, every remedy in his power, with no results. He might have carried her down to the river somehow, if not for her broken leg in its rude splint. The ankle was broken too. Unless the bones knit properly, she might not walk again, but that was the least of his worries now. Now he only cared that she still lived.

Two Horses came up the ladder bearing skins of water. The cistern high above the cavern was dry from lack of a rainfall, and he had made three trips down to the river in rapid succession. Short and bandy-legged, he was extremely agile and very powerful for his size. The exertion was nothing to him. He set the skins down, averting his eyes in politeness from Norah's half-naked form. They rested instead on Storm Caller, taking in the gaunt features and guilt-clouded eyes. *If he does not take care he will fall prey to the same angry spirits that have possessed the woman.* He touched the medicine pouch hanging from his belt, and made a quick and covert gesture to ward off evil.

Without speaking he took up a wet cloth, dipped it in the cold water, and handed it to Storm Caller, who bathed Norah's chest and arms with the cold liquid. Two Horses crossed to their supplies and took out some choice morsels of dried meat to tempt Storm Caller. "Come, you must eat something."

Storm Caller accepted the meat, chewing abstractedly and swallowing without tasting. Sometimes Two Horses hated the woman because of what his friend was going through; other times, thinking of Snow-in-Summer and how she had nestled into his own heart, he understood. Then he would remind himself if not for this woman's bravery Snow-in-Summer would have been lost beneath the ice. *Aiee,* he thought sadly, *a woman can destroy a man surer than an enemy lance.*

"Soon," he said, offering another piece of meat, "Limping Bear will return here with my woman. She will know better what to do than a warrior can."

Storm Caller nodded, but he feared it might already be too late. He wiped Norah's legs down with the fresh cool cloth and suddenly she stirred. Relief poured through him. It was the first spontaneous movement she had made since daylight. Surely that was a good sign. Her lips moved. Was she trying to speak? He leaned down, and her breath was hot as a desert breeze against his ear.

"Norah? Norah, can you hear me?"

Her lids fluttered but did not open. Fighting to breathe through the layers of hot gauze that choked her, she was only dimly aware of a murmuring voice, of being touched, and then of nothing at all. She had gone away to where she did not hurt and every intake of air was not a trial by fire. The next awareness was a tangled skein of dreams that wove themselves into nightmare tapestries. A skeleton with copper hair danced and grinned and danced again, and then Norah was holding Travis at bay with her knife. No, not Travis, but her husband. Still holding the knife she spoke sternly to Abner: "You should not have brought me here."

Storm Caller cringed from her whispered words, the first she had spoken since he'd found her. In the long hours of waiting he had been putting himself on trial, acting as judge and jury to his past actions. The evidence was irrefutable. Norah had been innocent of her husband's crimes, yet he had made her pay for them. He had not meant to hurt her, yet had harmed her almost beyond redemption. Certainly beyond his own forgiveness. If she lived he must make amends. That was his sentence.

No, Norah. I should not have brought you here.

"I can sit up." Norah squirmed back against the piled blankets until she was semiupright.

Snow-in-Summer frowned and clasped her hands over her swelling abdomen. She was three months pregnant, and her usual state of gentle contentment was disturbed by concern for her friend. It was only a week since Norah had passed the fever's crisis, and she continually overestimated her physical abilities. "You will do better, Braves-the-Water, if you go more slowly. It is not wise to push yourself so hard after having the lung fever."

"I want to brush my hair."

"I will do it for you. After you drink the broth."

Norah wrinkled her nose in disgust. Beside her was a tin cup filled with a thick dark fluid that was hot water and fresh horse blood mixed with herbs and medicinal plants. "It would be much easier to do so, if I did not know the ingredients."

Snow-in-Summer chuckled. "Then you should not have asked! I would not have told you, had I known you to be so squeamish. Now drink. It will give you heart."

The sight of her bony fingers, wrapped around the dented handle, induced her to swallow it. Gritting her teeth, Norah picked up the cup and tested it with the tip of her tongue. It was rather nasty but not as bad as she had expected, for the pungent taste of the dried leaves masked the metallic tang of the main ingredient. By the time she'd finished she was exhausted and more than ready to lay back and let her friend minister to her.

Although freshly bathed, and dressed in a straight-sided gown of blue and white calico, her hair was loose and snarled. She wanted to look nice when Storm Caller came back from his day-long hunting foray. He had not spent much time with her since she had shaken off the fever, and Norah hoped he would tonight. She missed being near him, sharing his thoughts during the day; and she missed the familiar hardness of his back against hers, the sound of his even breathing in the night.

"I must look frightful!"

Snow-in-Summer did not answer. Picking up the porcupine quill brush, she began to curry in long, smooth strokes. Norah closed her eyes, enjoying the soothing rhythm of the brush until it abruptly ceased. Her lids flew up, and she saw the other woman staring blankly at the brush and its loose clump of dull black hair caught on the bristles.

Her hand went up to her temple and found an area of exposed scalp, covered thinly with sparse downy hairs. She grasped the back of her head, and a handful of hair came away in her fingers. "Oh! My hair! My hair is falling out!"

"It is from the fever."

Norah had heard of such an occurrence following illness, but had never witnessed it herself; and she couldn't believe it was happening to her. Another exploratory gesture brought a cascade of loose strands scattering like black threads across the bodice of the calico gown. Nothing else had devastated her so: not the broken bones or the obvious weight loss or the utter weakness of her body; but as her fingertips touched the bare spots something snapped inside. It was the final, ugly indignity. She began to weep, softly and hopelessly.

Hovering anxiously, Snow-in-Summer comforted her. "It will grow back, Braves-the-Water. Do not upset yourself so."

Suddenly Norah quieted, scrubbing the tears from her eyes with the back of her hand. "I need a mirror. I want to see what I look like."

Snow-in-Summer pretended not to understand. "I do not know for what you ask."

"A looking glass, a..." She did not have the Comanche word for it. Perhaps there was none. "Something so I can see myself...like Elk Dancer's oval of polished copper. I have to know what I look like."

"I still do not understand. It is not important. Rest now, and I will be back after I prepare the meal." She hurried off. While pretending to be about her chores, Snow-in-Summer checked about for anything that might be used as a looking glass. Only when satisfied that there was no such thing, she began adding dried roots to the stock simmering over the open fire and wondered what to do.

Norah tried to sleep, but could not. Her mind was restless.

In the past days she had been too ill to wonder or question the very things that tormented her now. She was aware that Storm Caller had cared for her through the early days of the fever, never leaving her side for more than a moment. Snow-in-Summer provided most of her care now, and the men were gone from the cavern for most of the daylight hours. Surely that was the reason she saw so little of Storm Caller. Yet on the rare occasions when they were alone together, he avoided looking at her, and his eyes did not meet hers. When he lifted her or tended to her his hands were extraordinarily gentle; but they were the hands of a stranger, not a lover.

She looked down at her arms. Who could blame him? Thin as a stick with hair coming out in handfuls! She must look a fright. And for that reason, she was determined to discover how changed her appearance was. The afternoon hours whiled slowly away, and then Norah conceived an idea. Inventing a headache, she asked Snow-in-Summer for a shallow bowl, so she might dip a cloth into it from time to time and cool her brow. A perfectly ordinary request, and one which was promptly granted.

Norah waited until the girl went back to her chores, then leaned over the edge of her raised pallet. At first, all she could see was the watery image of a pale blue sky against the tan pottery of the basin. Leaning farther, she edged the vessel closer, and gasped as a nightmare visage floated before her eyes: a skeleton's face with deep shadows beneath the sockets and sharply protruding cheekbones looked back from the bowl. Dark hair stood in short tufts upon the skull, taut skin stretched across the bones and blue eyes flickered in the eye holes. A dead woman, yet alive.

For an instant she thought the delirium had returned, then saw the reflection of blue and white calico and knew the distorted figure to be herself. She lay back down, too shocked for tears, too stunned to do anything but lie there in misery. The small cloth had dried in the warm air, and Norah placed it over her ruined hair, tying the ends in back at the nape of her neck.

The men returned to the ruins, and Snow-in-Summer hurried to intercept them. Norah could not overhear their conversation, though some sixth sense told her that she was the topic of discussion. Storm Caller seemed angry, but nodded his head impatiently, conceding some point. They noticed her staring then, and broke apart.

Snow-in-Summer approached her. "Would you like to sit up for a while?"

"Yes. What I would really like is a change of scene. If you could help me over to the edge of the cavern, I could look over the rocks and watch the sunset. I would like that very much."

The other woman looked doubtful. "Do you think you can go that far?"

Storm Caller had been hesitating a few yards away, but now came forward and addressed Snow-in-Summer. "Take these blankets and arrange them against the big rock. I will carry her."

He scooped her into his arms, carrying her without effort toward the entrance to the cavern. Propping Norah against a buttress of limestone, he sat down a few feet away. Snow-in-Summer brought savory portions of stew and flat bread and set them down, but did not linger. The meal sat untouched while Storm Caller sharpened his knife against a stone, and Norah looked out over the magnificent vista.

"It is good to see the outside world for a change. It keeps me from feeling like I'm imprisoned."

He frowned, but she was watching the shadows eat their way up the canyon walls and did not notice. She plucked at the calico covering her lap. "I want to…to thank you. You saved my life, and…"

"Eat while it is hot." He kept honing his knife against the hard surface until blue sparks flew.

The sight of the moving knife turned Norah's thoughts to something else. "We have never talked about it, but I have wondered. What happened after I fell? What did you do to Travis and Cut Face?"

He let the knife slip through his fingers and examined his hands, turning them over and back again as if checking for invisible bloodstains. "It is better that you not know."

Silence. Nervously Norah toyed with the makeshift kerchief covering her head. "My hair will grow back soon, and I am drinking every horrid concoction Snow-in-Summer brews, so that I will put on more flesh. Look how baggy this gown is!"

She was chattering like a jay, and knew it, but was powerless to stop.

Now the canyon was gone, and nothing remained but the two of them, alone beneath the purple silk banners of the twilight sky. It was glorious to be sitting here companionably with him once more. Norah turned toward Storm Caller and smiled shyly. *This is how it used to be. How it will be again! As soon as I regain my strength.*

"As soon as you regain your strength," Storm Caller began suddenly, as if echoing her thoughts. He stopped, looked away, and began anew. "My way of life is not easy, but I grew up in it. I am used to its hardships. You are not. You were raised to a softer life, and you must return to it.

"As soon as you regain your strength, you must go back to your people."

21

Norah's leg ached with every jolt as her dappled gray mare picked its way along the rocky defile. The yellow sun melted across the noon sky like butter in a hot skillet. She could almost hear it sizzle. Sweat trickled down the back of her neck, turning her short-cropped hair into a cap of inky curls. Snow-in-Summer rode a few yards behind on a sure-footed brindle pony, while up ahead Storm Caller set the pace on his tireless bay.

They had been riding for hours, and no one spoke. Norah noticed how their clothing and the horses' coats blended into the land around them, as if they had sprung from the earth itself, all buff and gray and golden brown. They came out into a small clearing protected by a rampart of tumbled rock from the open country below, and Storm Caller stopped. "We will make camp now. Two Horses will join us here at nightfall."

Under normal circumstances it would be much too early to stop for the day, and Norah knew this early break on their long ride, as on the other days, was because of her. The aftereffects of influenza and pneumonia, compounded by the leg fractures, still drained her store of energies with a frightening suddenness. A relapse of her illness would disrupt the journey and make them vulnerable to attack from a host of possible enemies. Storm Caller always called a halt when she began to tire, but whether out of solicitude or sound survival tactics, she did not know. Either way, it was salt in her wounds.

Storm Caller swung down from his horse and came to assist

her. Norah gritted her teeth. She'd be damned if she'd take his pity! Before he had gone two steps she slid down the side of her mare. She miscalculated the distance and landed on both feet. All her fine Irish pride could not shield her from the sharp pain that took her breath away and left her knees shakier than before. Stars burst before her eyes, and she caught at her high-prowed woman's saddle for support.

Storm Caller reached Norah, catching her about the waist and taking her weight against his side. "I told you to wait for me to help you down!"

He spoke in English, which made her feel strangely forlorn. She pushed at his chest until he released her, then limped away on the leg that would never be quite right again. Storm Caller swore softly as she stumbled and almost fell, then continued with that head-held-high posture that commanded his admiration even while it fueled his anger. His body was so rigid with wrath that white lines etched his nostrils and the corners of his mouth. He felt the mixture of rage and helplessness threaten to overwhelm him. Storm Caller had never known such turmoil as he had since this woman had come into his life. The last time was when Norah lay ill, and he feared she was slipping away into the shadow-world. She had come back, but soon she would be gone forever, although in an entirely different way.

From her vantage point, Snow-in-Summer observed them both with caution. She swung herself down easily but awkwardly. Now in the fifth month of pregnancy, she was increasingly clumsy in her movements, but strong and healthy. The focus of her life had shifted, like her altered center of gravity, and now her first goal was to give her dearly loved husband a fine, lusty son. Her goal was to see Norah's physical strength and health restored. Her years with Old Gray Rocks had given much skill with herbs and healing, and to that end she applied the sum of her knowledge; there was nothing she could do for a grieving heart.

She looked forward to the evening when her man would join them. Then there would be someone else to shoulder the burden of playing peacemaker between Norah and Storm Caller. This journey was not an easy one, and the tension between her two friends was draining them all. Camp Greenwood lay another day ahead of them. How long one day could seem!

For Norah, that one day seemed too short. She stood at the rocky parapet fighting for calm. She had failed at everything she had attempted since coming west. Her marriage had been a disaster, her pregnancy by Abner had ended in loss, and she had not proved fruitful again. Now she was being returned to Camp Greenwood like damaged goods. A sickly woman or a crippled woman had no place around a warrior's campfire. She was both.

The impatient shuffling of hooves broke through her thoughts, and she turned back. She must see to her horse first and set up camp, two priorities she had quickly learned. Whistling softly, she brought Wind Dancer prancing over to her, and rubbed the mare's muzzle affectionately. The beast blew softly, toffee eyes filled with mild reproach.

"Poor old girl, did you think I had forgotten you?" Wind Dancer made a soft whicker of pleasure and nuzzled her mistress's neck.

Norah led the mare to a shady spot with good forage and tended to her. She gave her mount water and removed the bedroll and pack and the old Comanche saddle used by women, modeled in times past on those of the Spaniards. It seemed incredible to think that she had once been so fearful of horses. Wind Dancer was indispensable to her, especially now that her mobility on foot was limited. In the past days they had grown to trust and to rely on each other implicitly.

Only when Wind Dancer was settled did she stop to refresh herself with a drink from her two-handled canteen of unglazed pottery. Although not as durable as a leather bottle, the porous material kept the spring water icy cold. A drop trembled on the lip, catching the light like cut glass. In this arid stretch of country, water was too precious to waste. Norah touched a finger to it and dabbed her forehead with its coolness. She glanced up and saw Storm Caller watching her narrowly.

"I am not about to faint, if that is what you are thinking."

She closed the canteen with its oiled leather stopper and stared at him defiantly. His mouth thinned to a taut line, but he bent his head back to the task of checking his horse's hooves, as if she had not spoken.

At nightfall the soft clopping of an unshod horse came to them on the steady breeze. Storm Caller lifted his head and listened, then nodded, apparently satisfied. A short time later Two Horses rode in, and Norah could discern anger in his eyes and clenched jaw. He was off his horse before it came to a full stop. Storm Caller rose.

"What has happened?"

The young brave chewed his lip, then exploded in a staccato of Comanche, so rapid that Norah had difficulty following it. She caught the name of Iron Knife and something about the fort at Camp Greenwood. Dear God, had there been an attack? Her thoughts flew to Abigail and the gallant Captain, as they had so often in the past months. She limped over to where Snow-in-Summer sat patiently dishing up thin pieces of fowl stewed with meal and dried fruit.

"What is he saying?" Norah demanded harshly, irritated by the other woman's complacent attitude. "Has there been fighting?"

"No. He is only angry."

"Why?"

"It is talk for warriors, not for women."

"Nonsense!"

Her attempt to stalk off with dignity was ruined by the brave vulnerability of her halting stride. Two Horses was a few yards away, rubbing down his horse with a handful of grass. Norah swallowed her pride and accosted Storm Caller. She had followed an unspoken policy of avoiding unnecessary contact with him, but she had to discover what was going on.

"I heard Camp Greenwood mentioned. Has there been trouble? I think I have a right to know, since you are taking me there."

Spine straight, he surveyed the air about two inches over her head. "There has been no trouble at the Camp. Two Horses will not be continuing on with me. He is going to Camp Greenwood instead. Sergeant Woods is recruiting scouts."

"You mean...to spy?"

"I did not say that."

"There is no need. I am not quite the fool you think me."

He stabbed her with a cold gray stare. "Think what you like. Report your suspicions to Captain Gartner, if it gives you ease of mind. However, there is little fear that he will entrust the Army's military secrets to an Indian."

Storm Caller walked away, leaving Norah with mixed feelings. For the first time she understood how easy it was to have
divided loyalties, and how hard to know what to do about them.
She was still puzzling over the ethics involved as she prepared
her place for the night. For a few hours she would pretend that
tomorrow would not come. But when it did, she would have
to face questions and curious stares. And Abner. But that was
something she need not think of yet. Stretching out on the
blanket, she wrapped herself up in it like a cocoon, wishing it
could keep out loneliness as well as the night chill. She had
slept alone for eight weeks now, and should have been used to
it, but was not.

On the other side of the fire, Storm Caller stood staring
through the brightness at the small dark spot that was Norah
wrapped in her blanket. This was the last night they would
spend together. When morning came they would ride to the
camp and go their separate ways. Before he knew it, he was
moving around the fire toward her. When he reached her, he
stopped, uncertain, then arranged his own blanket beside her
and lay down upon it. Turning the other way he tried to ignore
her nearness. The sound of her breathing, her scent, her warmth
beckoned him. Rolling over, he saw that her back was to him
now and he got up on one elbow. Her lashes made a deep
shadow along the curve of her cheek and without conscious
thought, his hand went out, his fingers stroking lightly along
it.

The few inches separating them might as well have been the
distance from Boston to the Arizona Territory. Norah lay still
as a stone, and equally responsive to the touch of his fingers
on her cheek. Eyes closed, she feigned sleep while fighting the
urge to turn to him and be held by him. She would never let
him know how he had wounded her. Or know how much she
had grown to love him.

Storm Caller watched the play of firelight on her face and
hair. Her short curls gleamed with chestnut tones in the flame's
glow. This new growth of hair was lighter in color and soft as
down. He clenched his fingers to keep them from moving out
and touching it. Her shoulders quivered once, again. She was
awake and weeping. Her open wrath he could take, and even

he occasional outbursts of angry tears; but after all she had
borne so bravely, this silent weeping shamed him to his soul.

"Norah...?"

She went rigid, not even breathing, and he let his hand drop
from her shoulder. She did not understand the ghosts that drove
him, and he could not explain to her. It was better that way.

He looked up at the silver-edged clouds snagged on the thin
slice of moon. He might not have many more such nights to
lie awake and contemplate his fate. A storm was sweeping
down from the mountains, he could smell it on the air, just as
a storm of change was sweeping away the life he had known.
The old ways were going, and the old gods with them. Certainly they had deserted his people. Or it might be that the pale
god of the missionaries had conquered them and driven them
away. The white man's God, as rendered to him by Parson
Enders, was stern and demanded sacrifice. He had offended that
God by taking Norah, and therefore he must give her up.

He slept, and woke to the night chill. Norah was asleep,
cuddled against his chest for warmth. Instinctively he put his
arm around her, a gesture of protection. This was the last time
they would sleep so. Without thinking, he stroked her hair. So
soft. She always smelled good to him, fresh and womanly. He
pressed his face against her neck, inhaling the fragrance that
was Norah's own, and felt his blood catch fire.

Dreaming, she moved restlessly against his arm. She was
hiding from Travis, and it was cold in the kiva. Terribly cold.
His footsteps sounded close at hand, coming nearer and nearer.
But when she tried to scream only a thin cry came out. His
finger touched her neck, and she jerked awake, disoriented and
with pounding heart. The face near hers was not that of the
drunken trapper, and relief filled her. She wrapped her arms
around Storm Caller's neck. *Safe! She was safe.*

"I knew you would find me," she murmured, but the words
were lost as his mouth covered hers. She warmed to his embrace, still half awake as his hand moved over her body, cupping her breasts, then gliding down past her waist and over her
hips and thighs. Before the kiss ended she was fully awake,
fully aware of her loneliness for him, and of their mutual need.
She blocked out her anger of the past weeks and the cognizance
that tomorrow would inevitably come, melting into the heat of

his passion, welcoming the weight of his body upon hers. Ther
was no tragic past, no empty future. Only the moment, rar
and beautiful.

High above, the clouds trailed thin gauze streamers over th
spangled indigo sky. But far to the north masses of cool ai
collided with the warmer currents, declaring war on the passin
summer. Thick gray clouds overcame the pale starshine. Ar
rows of lightning flew across the sky from horizon to horizor
and distantly, a fanfare of thunder heralded the season c
storms.

"Lieutenant! Come have a look at this."

Newcomb's long legs took the steps to the wooden rampart
of Camp Greenwood two at a time. Sergeant Miles's voice and
posture did not indicate danger, but in times like these anythin
could happen. He reached the top and did a swift reconnoite
of the western approach, shading his eyes from the glare. Th
flat plain erupted in feathers of dust just below the horizon. /
small mounted party, three, maybe four riders at most.

The distance was too great for him to make out detail, bu
Sergeant Miles was the most long-sighted man in the Territory
He couldn't see to write his own name up close, but coul
count the hairs on a flea at a hundred paces.

"Who are they? Can you tell yet?"

Miles scratched his head, squinting into the sun. "Injuns
Not 'Paches. Comanche, looks like."

Newcomb's stomach muscles tightened. Comanche? What i
God's name were they doing out here in Arizona? He remem
bered that a small band had been spotted in the north. Refugee
from the Staked Plains, most likely. Possibilities ran throug
his mind: they might want to trade, or be in need of medica
assistance. Or it might be a trick to get him to open the gate:
By God, he hoped it was the latter. Then he'd have a chanc
to prove his mettle. He could distinguish four horses now, le
by a deep-chested bay, but he couldn't tell much about thei
riders. "Well, Sergeant?"

"Sir! The one on the dapple gray...hard to tell from her
and as brown as she is and dressed in them squaw clothes. Bu
I'd bet my next month's pay she's a white woman!"

Knowing they were under observation, the four riders came on. Norah watched the stockade fencing of Camp Greenwood shimmer in the afternoon heat. Journey's end. How ugly the camp looked, squatting in the sun. And how puny. Once she had thought of those high walls as a protective barrier, preserving the inhabitants from the wildness of the life outside. It looked like a prison to her now. In a few very short minutes they would arrive at the gates; and she still did not want to return. She had resigned herself to the inevitability, knowing she would be both a hindrance and a danger to Storm Caller and the others if she stayed. Her eyes strayed to him. She wished she could hate him for rejecting her, had almost convinced herself that she had succeeded. Lying in his arms last night she had realized that she had even failed in this.

They had hardly spoken a word today, and when they reached the gates he would turn around and ride out of her life. Suddenly the roan stopped. Storm Caller turned to Two Horses Racing. "Ride on. I will wait here."

Norah stopped alongside and started to speak, but he slapped her mare sharply on the rump, and it trotted off. She was startled, then hurt and furious. Her chin went up, and she kicked her horse into a gallop. *He would not even ride with me as far as the gates. He cannot wait to see the last of me!*

Storm Caller watched Norah ride off toward the camp. Although he waited until the gates swung shut, swallowing her, she did not look back. Not even once.

From his lookout, Sergeant Miles viewed the roan drop back and the other three come on, slowing their approach as a white cloth unfurled from the end of a lance. Now even Lieutenant Newcomb could make out their shapes: a wiry brave and two women, one in Indian garb, the other wearing a blue and white print dress. She was thin and poorly dressed, but her head, covered with close-cropped dark curls, was held up with the pride of a princess. And that was very familiar.

"Jeez-sus Godamighty!" Sergeant Miles exclaimed, pointing. "Begging your pardon, sir, but ain't that Miz Slade? That friend of Miz Gartner's what was took off by the Injuns?"

Newcomb swallowed, hard. The tender and elegant Norah of his dreams, entering his life once again? He had given up hope of ever seeing her alive. Over the months the real woman had blended with his imagination, and it was that false idol he worshiped in his heart. A faint flush spread over his face, almost camouflaging the scattered freckles. "Wave them in, Sergeant."

Troopers moved to the barked command. The gates swung wide, admitting three riders. Lieutenant Newcomb was halfway down the stairs when he halted and looked back. "Sergeant! What about the other brave? Did you recognize him?"

Miles shoved his hat back a few inches on his grizzled head. "I wouldn't want to take an oath on it, sir. But that tall brave on the bay surely had the look of Sergeant LeBeau of the Indian Scouts."

Newcomb froze for a moment. LeBeau. LeBeau and Norah Slade? No, that was too incredible. LeBeau had been gone for almost a year on private business. And why would Norah have been with him in the first place? He continued down the steps eagerly.

For months Newcomb had dreamed of finding Norah, of rescuing her. How often he'd lain awake in his bunk at night, envisioning that scene: a thousand times he had seen her eyes light up at the sight of him, felt her throw her white arms about his neck in gratitude; and a thousand times he had kissed her and whispered words of love as he pulled loose the pins that held her black hair captive. And then…

He was brought up short. Reality was vastly different from his romantic dreams. Who was this wan brown woman with the boyish cap of curls and eyes that slid past him without recognition? His relief at finding her alive and unharmed was tinged with unreasoning resentment. This wasn't the way it was supposed to happen. He made his way toward the newcomers.

Snow-in-Summer sat on her pony wearing the blank impassive face she had learned to adopt among white men. Two Horses Racing jumped down and questioned a young trooper in a crazy quilt of mangled English, Spanish, and sign language. Norah was oblivious to everything. There was only one thought in her mind and that was to reach Abigail, her refuge, her friend. Abigail would help her. Abigail would understand.

A private helped Norah dismount, and she eagerly turned to Newcomb. There were no signs of the young lieutenant who had once followed her with such puppylike devotion in this bitter-looking, hard-faced man. She presumed him to be a stranger. "My name is Norah Slade, and I have come to see Mrs. Gartner. Will you take me to her, please?"

His jaw tightened. She *didn't* recognize him. "I'm afraid I can't do that...ma'am."

"You do not understand. I am a friend of hers. However, if you will not escort me, I shall go myself. I know the way."

His fingers caught her arm as she turned away, and Newcomb was shocked at how thin she was beneath the cloth. Shame at his base reactions softened his tone, but did nothing to soften the blow. "It's you who doesn't understand, ma'am. Mrs. Gartner is in no condition to be receiving visitors. Mrs. Gartner is dying."

22

Norah smiled politely at her guest as she presided at table in the gold and brown dining room of the Gartners' home. The only other person present, he was a thin man, nervous and balding, with the face of a kindly rabbit. His biscuit-colored suit and blue and brown striped waistcoat were expensive and well tailored, but appeared to have been made for a much larger frame. He eyed the coffee cup mournfully, hoping a stronger potation would be offered instead. A young trooper with a well-scrubbed face hovered at the man's elbow with a silver coffeepot and was continually ignored for all his efforts.

Norah smiled inwardly. She knew what he was waiting for, but couldn't resist letting him stew a bit. "Would you care for more coffee, Dr. Swansea?"

"No, no thank you. But it is delicious coffee. Quite delicious. Yes, indeed."

Upstairs a chair scraped across the uncarpeted bedroom floor where Abigail lay in a drugged sleep, while Captain Gartner kept his weary vigil. Norah listened for a moment, but there was only silence from above. Reassured, she resumed her hostess duties with well-bred ease of the born lady, as if her sojourn among the Comanche had been nothing more than an odd and unsettling dream. She inclined her head slightly, and the striker removed the dessert plates, then placed a cut-glass decanter of amber liquid on the table. At her next discreet signal he withdrew.

"Perhaps you might care for some stronger refreshment, then."

The sparsely lashed and pink-rimmed eyes brightened perceptibly. "Oh, ah. Yes, yes. I do indulge from time to time. Thirsty country out here. Yes, indeed."

She poured a glass of whiskey and didn't blink an eye when the surgeon drank it neat. She refilled his glass. The second shot went down as quickly as the first. The past week had acquainted her with his habits, and after last night, he had certainly earned it. She filled his glass a third time without any change of expression, but the lung specialist from St. Louis shook his head.

"Two drams of whiskey wake a man up: three put him back to sleep. And Mrs. Gartner may have need of me again this morning."

"You do not expect another crisis so soon!"

"No, no, but then one can never be quite sure. No, indeed. And, from what you say, the episode Mrs. Gartner had three months ago was severe, possibly worse. Yes, indeed, possibly worse."

Stirring her glass of cold tea, she nodded politely and tried not to grit her teeth. Dr. Swansea was an eminent practitioner and a humane man; but his habit of constantly repeating himself like an echo in a roundhouse was rapidly driving her to distraction. *"Yes, indeed,"* indeed! Someone entered the room, and she looked up expectantly, but it was only the striker, making sure he hadn't forgotten anything.

"Anything else, ma'am?"

"No, Corporal, that will be all. Thank you." She smiled at the trooper, and when she glanced back at the physician, his shot glass was empty again. Courtesy prompted that she should offer him a fourth dram: prudence dictated otherwise. Dr. Morton Swansea had an excellent reputation and evidently an enormous capacity for holding his liquor, but Norah was taking no chances. If Abigail needed medical attention, she wanted him available and certainly sober enough to treat her properly. That was the reason Captain Gartner had paid the specialist's way to Camp Greenwood and offered him a very handsome retainer for his services.

Swansea looked mournfully down at his empty glass. "Pulmonary hemorrhage is a terrible thing, Mrs. Slade. A terrible thing. It is my opinion, my considered opinion, that the Captain's lady has survived the severity of her condition thus far due to your tireless devotion and nursing skills. Ah, yes, devotion and nursing skills. Often of more use than all the medicaments in the pharmacopaeia. Mrs. Gartner is fortunate to have such a friend in you, very fortunate. Yes, indeed.''

"Sir," she said with quiet conviction. "I am the fortunate one."

Setting down her tea, Norah folded the white linen napkin and replaced it beside her flowered china plate. Swansea recognized the sign that the meal was officially over, and stifled a sigh. Well, he'd look up the Post surgeon. Perhaps the man would bring out a bottle while they discussed the ramifications of rampant consumption. Damned thirsty country hereabouts. Yes, indeed.

When he had taken his leave Norah mounted the stairs to the upper floor, leading on each step with her good leg, swinging the other up after. By now it was second nature, and she gave it no thought. In her absence the house had been completed, and there were now four rooms where there had only been one. It was ten degrees hotter up here under the eaves and the black shingle roof, but after living in the canyon country she was inured to it. As she reached the landing Norah gave no heed to her heavy petticoats, although she wished she hadn't laced her corset so tightly. It really nipped in uncomfortably at her waist. In the past twelve weeks at Camp Greenwood she had regained all the weight she had lost while ill and, ironically, a few pounds more.

Tapping gently on the polished mahogany door panel, she entered the pink and white room where Abigail slept propped against the massive carved headboard. Gartner sat upright in an upholstered armchair of rose-watered silk, dwarfing it with his large frame. Norah hurried to his side, and he took her hand, squeezing it gratefully.

"I don't know what we would do without you, Norah. We would be lost."

She covered his hand with her other one. "My dear Charles, I am the one who would be lost." *More surely than you know.*

If not for Abigail and Charles's acceptance of her—and her

somewhat revised history of the past several months—Norah would have been shunned like a cholera carrier. To her face, for the most part, people were polite enough; but they could not hide the curiosity, the speculation, the frank disdain in their eyes. Even so, there were bold glances, and occasional whispers, even snickers when she was nearby, though no one dared cut her society in the face of the Gartners' steadfast backing.

She had lived among the Comanche for almost a year, and everyone knew "what Indians do to white women": she had overheard that refrain more than once. And she knew what some said of her, what some called her: "white squaw" and "filthy Indian-lover" and "Indian's whore." That wasn't how it had been, something dirty and shameful and debased; but some of the thrown mud clung to her lacerated emotions, soiling the brighter memories of her time with Storm Caller. Yet they were partly right. She had been prepared to give him anything.

Everything.

Gartner closed his eyes briefly, and for a moment he looked older and incredibly weary. "You must rest a while, Charles. You have not slept at all."

Gartner's lids snapped open. He shook his head, and the thin slit of sunlight from the crack between the curtains turned the silver at his temples to gold. "I'll grab a few winks later if I can, but there are matters I must attend to now. And I can do that with ease of mind, knowing Abigail is in your good hands." He stood up, squared his shoulders and went out, slipping on again, like a cloak, the air of military authority which he always left at the threshold of this room.

Every time Gartner left his wife's room, he wondered if she would still be there when he returned. Camp Greenwood was always there, waiting for him with a list of problems and crises, from mold in the flour sacks and brawling among the enlisted men all the way to the other end of the spectrum: outbreaks of dysentery or attacks of typhus or renegade Indians. Today was no different. He could not walk a hundred yards without being stopped three times on his way.

"Captain, six of the men from C Company are down with the flu."

"Captain, Supply Depot reports two more cases of cartridges missing."

"Captain, cook says that shipment of rutabagas is all rotten an' the turnips, too."

"Captain?" This from a burly muleteer. "Something's wrong with my team. Don't think it's distemper." He scratched his ear. "Act like they've eaten crazy weed. Every beast is gone clean berserk."

"Did you happen to feed them any of the turnips and rutabagas that were thrown out today?"

"Yes, sir, I did. Seemed like a waste not to."

Gartner sighed and smiled crookedly. "There's nothing wrong with your team that a good night's sleep won't cure, but they'll be damned ornery in the morning after getting drunk on fermented vegetables. Keep them secured so they don't kick the stalls and one another to flinders. And tell the men to keep out of their way until those mules sober up."

"Yes, sir!"

The muleteer saluted and went away, not at all astonished that the Captain had a ready answer for him. That was why he was Captain: he had all the answers for everything. Gartner continued across the grounds, wishing all his problems could be diagnosed as simply, knowing he had no real answers for any of the most important questions. No sooner had he reached his desk when another messenger came in.

"Captain, sorry to report that Private Meechum fell from the barracks roof and broke his arm in two places."

"How did he fall off the roof, Sergeant?"

"Don't know, sir. No one knows what the hell he was doing up there in the first place."

The round of petty and not-so-petty details that came with a camp command demanded Gartner's attention, but today there were twice as many as usual. Finally he realized what was happening. Women were rare at Camp Greenwood, and ladies, even more so. There was not a man in his command who had not given at least a small piece of his heart to Abigail, and now they sought reassurance at seeing him about his daily routine.

A few minutes later he heard carriage wheels go past, followed by a party of mounted men. Young Jones's voice carried on the still air: "Warn the Chief that the old banty-rooster's hen jist rode in with a shitload of baggage. Looks like she's diggin' in for a bloody siege, by the size of it."

There was a murmur of voices, the sound of stamping hooves, and a firm feminine voice issuing instructions. The striker hurried in, translating the message to a more formal mode: "Captain, Colonel Boyle's wife just rode over from Camp Verde with an escort and a wagonful of trunks. She's going directly over to the house to see Mrs. Gartner, sir."

"Thank you, Corporal. Please deliver her my warm regards and say that I'll be there as soon as I possibly can."

"Yes, sir! Mrs. Boyle sent you word, too, sir." He blushed and looked as if his kerchief were knotted too tightly. "She ordered me to say it exactly like she did, sir."

"Well?"

Jones cleared his throat nervously and spewed out the quotation at top speed: "'Tell Captain Gartner that I'm an old soldier's wife and I know he has better things to do in the middle of the afternoon than waste his time exchanging pleasantries with an old biddy when his mind is elsewhere.'" The trooper loosened his neck scarf and continued. "'I'll see myself settled without his help. You tell him to stick to his knitting, and I'll stick to mine.' And those are *her* words, sir, not mine."

"Thank you, Corporal. That will be all."

Gartner kept a straight face until he was alone and then a faint smile lifted his mouth. Cora Boyle was as formidable in her own way as Henry Boyle was in his. The Colonel frequently commented with amused affection that, had Cora been born a man, she would have made General in five years. The Captain wondered why she had come though, especially unannounced.

He walked to the open doorway and looked up to the bedroom in his fine clapboard house across the way. The panes sparkled like frost over the heavy rose draperies that were drawn shut against the white heat of the sun. No flag hung between them and the glass. That meant everything was still under control. His shoulders relaxed, and then he became aware of a presence behind him.

The Captain spun around as an apparition from the past walked in. A Comanche, tall and lean, with gray eyes and a hard jaw. They faced each other across the room without speaking.

"Here," a voice shouted. "You can't just go walking on in there." Lieutenant Newcomb and the striker entered with two more well-muscled troopers at their heels. "He slipped past before we could stop him, Captain."

Gartner looked across sharply. "We'll discuss that later, Lieutenant. At length."

Newcomb stepped toward the buckskin-clad newcomer and was forestalled by his senior officer. "Leave be! I know this man—and so do you. Don't you recognize the best Scout this camp ever had?"

The Lieutenant stared at the man dressed in buckskins and moccasins, and a dull red wave crept up his face. His hands curled into fists against his thighs. "LeBeau!" He spat the name out like a curse.

"Yes, it's LeBeau. And when you're done gaping, you can go out and shut the door behind you."

Gartner watched the two men exit, then turned to Storm Caller and put him under careful scrutiny. He looked different, and it was more than the deeper hollows beneath the high cheekbones or the lines of fatigue around the eyes. It was the eyes themselves. They had the distant and empty look, as if they had sought the future and discovered there was none.

"By all that's holy! Is that really you?"

Storm Caller's lips quirked up in a tight little spasm that might have passed for a smile. "I am not a ghost. Yet."

"Someone told me you were in Texas," the Captain said with quiet deliberation. The challenge went unanswered. Pulling open a drawer, he removed a full bottle from behind a stack of papers. He took two glasses from the same drawer, but Storm Caller shook his head. Gartner poured out one shot and left the bottle uncorked. "Seems to be a lot of folks heading for Texas these days. I heard that Iron Knife and his braves were down there raising hell."

Storm Caller eyed him levelly. "I heard that, too."

"I heard Quanah Parker and his band will be rounded up and taken to the reservation before the year is out."

"I heard *that*, too." A slow smile crossed Storm Caller's face. "A man shouldn't believe everything he hears."

Gartner laughed, and the tension leaked out of the room like air from a pricked balloon. He sat down, and Storm Caller took the chair beside the desk. "I'll take that drink now, if the offer's still open."

"The offer's always open." He trickled a golden stream into the shot glasses, almost to the rim. "To old comrades—may they never stand on opposite sides of the river."

Storm Caller stopped the glass a half inch from his lips and amended the salute. "To old comrades." He tipped his glass and solemnly completed the ritual. There were so many things he wanted to say, so many questions he wanted to ask, but there was only one that seemed safe. "How is Mrs. Gartner?"

The Captain took a deep breath. "She's dying."

For the first time Storm Caller glimpsed the controlled despair beneath Gartner's brave facade, and he was filled with pity for them both. "I am very sorry." Inadequate words for an inadequate emotion.

"Yes, well…some things are too good to be true—I've known from the start that Abigail was one of them." His fingers drummed on the desktop. It was a habit so ingrained and unconscious it had worn the varnish through in that one spot.

"Thank God that Norah Slade is staying with us. I'm sure you heard she was carried off last year. No one knew what had become of her until she rode into camp three months ago, accompanied by a Comanche and his squaw. She's refused to go back to her husband. But he wants her back." He glanced up swiftly, but the other's face was unchanged. Perhaps his surmise was wrong, after all.

"She says she was carried off by an Apache named Cut Face, but that Two Horses Racing and a hunting party came across them and rescued her. Supposedly she's been with them ever since. They would have brought her back sooner, only she broke her leg badly and couldn't travel." He looked up, fingers stilled.

Storm Caller had not moved at all. "That is unfortunate. I hope she is recovered from her accident." No one could guess what it cost him to look politely disinterested when he so desperately wanted news of her.

"Oh, the leg is healed, although the break didn't mend well. Physically she seems to be in excellent health, but...she changed. I can't put my finger on it exactly, but she's changed. Something happened out there."

A horse and rider went by the open window at smart trot, harness and spurs jingling. Storm Caller reached into the pocket of his buckskin shirt and took out a small oilskin packet. "I brought you something."

Carefully unwrapping it, he uncovered the object within: a tiny piece of dried greenish-yellow clay with a small imprint on it, and covered with clinging bits of golden sand.

Gartner looked closer. He knew that imprint. "That mountain lion is Abner Slade's symbol. That looks like the clay seal from a jug. Where did you get it, and what does it mean?"

Storm Caller's hands clenched and unclenched. "Under the body of a couple of Mexicans who were seen passing through near Greenwood Junction a few days ago. They bought some firewater from a trader to take back with them. They told a few people they bought it for another man who was going to sell it for a big profit and cut them in on it. They got greedy and sold some themselves, to some Jicarilla Apaches."

"And?"

"And when the Jicarillas passed the jugs around they started dying, and their friends set out after the Mexicans. And the Mexicans set out after the man who sold them a wagonload of the poisoned swill. Evidently they found him. But Slade and his foreman were a little too fast for them. A little too careless, too."

Gartner leaned back in his chair. "What makes you think it's Slade who's to blame? That bobcat mark isn't enough evidence."

Storm Caller's eyes met the Captain's levelly. "The bodies of the Mexicans were found halfway to Tucson in that same sandy gully where Iron Knife was captured. You know the place I mean, where all those giant saguaro grow." He hunched forward. "And you know there's no clay down there like this— or of any other color. There's only one place in the Territory where that type of clay is found. On Abner Slade's ranch."

"That's not enough to hang a man."

Storm Caller jumped up. "Goddamn it, how long are you

going to let Slade go on murdering?" He strode to the window and back. "Or are a few dead Indians and a couple of dead Mexicans not worth bothering about?"

Gartner's chair landed on all four legs with a thump. He rose, face crimson with the effort of restraining his temper. "You damn well know better than that, LeBeau! But we need a solid case against him."

"Then what is it, what do you want?"

"You say it's Abner Slade who's behind all this. I'm not convinced, but I'd sure as hell like to be! I want enough evidence for a trial, because when the noose tightens about Slade's neck, I want it so damned tight he can't slip out of it! But it will take time."

Storm Caller leaned across the desk, his neck corded with anger. "We don't *have* time. Nothing is done, and every day more die...very conveniently for the Government's policies."

"Are you accusing me of purposely dragging my feet?" Gartner's voice cracked like a whip in the otherwise quiet room. "Or are you after Slade for reasons of your own... reasons that have nothing to do with poisoned whiskey or flour, and everything to do with Slade's wife?"

"Say what you mean!"

The sounds of their breathing filled the room, which had grown too small to hold them both safely. All the restrained energy in Storm Caller's body seemed centered in his eyes, cold and dark as glacier melt. It was Gartner who looked away first.

"Damn it, LeBeau, I'm not blind. I saw how you looked at Norah. I knew what you felt, and I saw what you were going through when she married Slade. At the time I thought you made the wise decision when you kept your distance. Now I don't know...."

He rubbed a hand along the back of his neck. "When Norah and the two Comanche returned to the camp there was a second man with them. He stayed out on the plain, but Sergeant Miles was up on the lookout that day. You know Miles—he can see an ant piss at twenty leagues—and he swears that other man was you."

Gartner saw he held the other's full attention now, and pressed the issue. "All the camp gossip gets back to me eventually. Some people think Norah was with you the entire time. That the two of you ran off together. That's what her own husband thinks.''

Gray eyes met blue and held. ''And what does…she say to that?''

''Nothing. Just holds her head high and says nothing. But there's more to the story than what she's telling. We both know that.''

Storm Caller's lips compressed to a tight, painful line. ''For her sake I will tell you this much: I took Norah. But she did not come willingly.''

Gartner fought to master his surprise. He had not expected this, yet he had no reason to doubt it. He thought that he knew LeBeau. Knew him well. Now he was looking at a stranger. A dangerous one, at that. While he stared the former Scout moved toward the door.

''For the love of God, LeBeau, don't do anything rash! Let's try it my way a little longer.''

''Your way doesn't work.''

Gartner's jaw squared. ''You've been my Scout. You've even been my friend. But if you break the law I'll have to take you in like any other man.''

''You'd have to find me first. And then you'd have to catch me.'' Storm Caller stepped out into the harsh sunlight and was gone.

Norah slumped in the armchair, exhausted. It was stifling in the sickroom, even with the door open, and impossible to keep the dust and sunlight from penetrating the thin window draperies. There were no inside shutters. Motes like glittering gold dust floated lazily in a wide ray. She could almost feel them settling on her skin, clogging her pores. God, she wanted a bath, and it had only been a few hours since she'd sponged off in the basin. It was the clothes, she decided, these tight and confining ''civilized'' fashions that restricted movement and held in her body's heat. Well, uncomfortable as they were, at least they served her purpose now.

The heat did not seem to bother the invalid. Abigail smiled through her drugged dreams, and Norah wondered at it, remembering when she herself lay almost dying in the kiva. Was Abigail seeing that wonderful, healing light? Or was she in the safety of an imaginary world with Charles and a little rosy-cheeked, russet-haired boy who had been born healthy and whole instead of gray and stillborn?

A soft tread on the landing brought her upright. Dr. Swansea looked in, wrinkling his rabbit nose. An aura of whiskey and carbolic entered the room with him. "She will be sleeping yet awhile, Mrs. Slade. I do not anticipate any danger while the coughing is under control. No, indeed. If you like, I will sit by her, and you may rest."

"Thank you."

She rose, smiling warmly and regretting her earlier lack of charity toward him. He drank too much and could be a repetitious bore, but he was a kindly man and had brought Abigail through two near-fatal hemorrhages. Crossing the hall, she opened the door at the very end. Cool creams and pale yellows predominated, giving the bedroom a deceptively airy look, but it was at least a hundred and ten degrees inside. Norah heard, without taking note, the sounds of the Camp traffic outside her shuttered window: rolling wheels, stamping hooves, the creak of wagonwood.

Thankfully she pulled off her dress, chemise, stockings, and petticoats damp with perspiration, and then the hated corset. It was stuck to her skin like plaster of paris. She peeled it away, and her breasts were firm and painful without its support. Pouring water from the yellow and white china pitcher into the matching basin, she sponged off, letting the droplets fall from her arms to spatter on her feet, pretending it was summer rain.

Without warning the door opened, and she grabbed for the embroidered linen towel. A small, well-corsetted figure stood there, shrewd brown eyes taking in everything. Colonel Boyle's wife entered and shut the door behind her.

"Mrs. Boyle! What are...? I did not expect you." Norah reached for her cotton wrapper lying across the bed and slipped into it.

"There was no time to waste in writing back and forth. Not when I am needed here."

The little woman pursed her lips, gathering the loose ends of her thoughts up like a ball of twine. "I do not mean to intrude on your privacy, Norah, but there is little likelihood we will have much opportunity to talk alone any other time. I think you know why I am here, and will curse me for an old busybody, but it is yourself and the Captain I am thinking of. There's little enough I can do for poor Abigail.''

Norah stared at her blankly. "I am afraid I do not understand.''

Mrs. Boyle scrutinized her long and hard. "No, you couldn't look that innocent if you weren't. Not that I gave any credit to the gossip, now, but human nature being what it is... I've lived long enough to know life can play strange tricks on us.''

"I still do not...''

"This is very awkward! Sit down, my dear.'' It was not like Mrs. Boyle to beat around the bush, but Norah had no idea of what she was trying to say. Perching on the edge of the bed, she waited. The Colonel's wife came to stand over her, taking Norah's hands in her own rough and reddened ones. "My dear, with a good heart and the very best of intentions, you have created a difficult situation for yourself. And for Charles Gartner.

"For three months you have been living in the same house with a handsome and virile man. A man whose wife is dying and who has not been a wife to him in many months. Child, you are still a beautiful woman, healthy and nearer his age than Abigail. There are those who say you have already taken her place in his bed.''

"No!'' The cry was wrung from Norah. "How dare they! Oh, the filthy, lying, cowardly...! Who is saying such terrible things?''

Cora Boyle's face melted into a mass of sympathetic wrinkles. "No one *dared* say them to me. But the rumor is widespread enough. As soon as it came to the Colonel's ears he told me about it. We decided I must come to you, stay with you as long as...as is necessary.''

"But it's so cruel! So untrue! Charles loves Abigail dearly. He would never turn to another woman. And I will—'' *Always love Storm Caller*. She bit the words off just in time. *Storm Caller, why did you ever bring me back to this? How could you ever leave me to face this alone?* Her arms curved protectively around her abdomen, unconsciously cradling it.

"Child, between the two of us we will put a stop to the gossip, never fear. But after seeing you I am glad I did not waste a day in coming."

She sat down on the mattress and put her arms around Norah's shoulders. "You will not be able to keep it secret much longer. When is your baby due?"

23

Norah finished a note to Father Ildephonso and handed it to the striker for delivery, then went up the stairs to check on Abigail. There was no need to keep the hem of her yellow and white sprigged dress out of the way: she had gained a few more pounds and the skirt was now an inch shorter from the added weight.

The door to the sickroom stood open. The voice of Mrs. Boyle floated on the still air as she read aloud from a well-thumbed copy of Miss Austen's *Pride and Prejudice*. The scene, Mr. Darcy's badly bungled proposal to Elizabeth Bennet, was a particular favorite of Norah's, and she smiled: how comforting the familiar was in trying times!

Cora looked up as Norah crossed the threshold, then exchanged a glance with Abigail, who sat propped up in the armchair near the window, where she could watch the activities of the garrison. Her long hair was unbound, her thin cheeks flushed with hectic color, but she was feeling strong enough to have put off her nightgown for a loose dress of light blue lawn trimmed with rows of lace. Norah's heart lifted at the sight. "Abigail, what a charming picture you make! Soon you will be able to take your meals downstairs with us."

A smile illuminated the invalid's face. "Yes, that is what Dr. Swansea told me, so I took his nasty tonic without even making a face."

Mrs. Boyle rose and put the book aside. "My throat is dry

from reading. I believe I will make us a pot of tea, and perhaps you would care to take my place, Norah.''

Norah took the seat she vacated and picked up the morocco-bound novel, running a finger over the satiny gilt edges. ''I was sixteen when I first read *Pride and Prejudice*. Initially, I thought Mr. Darcy a proud and insufferable boor, but by the end of the book I had fallen quite madly in love with him.''

''Yes, I felt the same. How close the characters came to losing each other because of pride. That is why I had none when it came to letting Charles know that I cared for him, long before he had spoken of his own feelings.'' Abigail smiled, remembering. ''I had been quite the belle in St. Louis, you know, and was not used to being ignored by a handsome and eligible man. That is when I knew I loved him—when my love for him became greater than my foolish pride. And if I had not, I would never have known such happiness.''

Suddenly her smile went awry. ''Or Charles such pain. And I am such a weak and selfish creature that, could I do it all over again, I would do the same!''

Norah took Abigail's frail hand in her own strong one and spoke in low fierce tones. ''Don't regret it. Don't ever regret it! The joy outweighs the pain. I know.''

The soft brown eyes searched Norah's face. ''What will you do now?''

''I am not sure.'' She could not forget the evil rumors Mrs. Boyle had warned about. Sometime soon she had to make a decision. But not until Abigail's condition improved.

''If you do not wish to remain at Camp Greenwood, I have both family and friends in St. Louis. They would welcome you. My cousin Ethyl is widowed and lives alone. You could stay with her. I...I know about the baby.''

Norah was dismayed, having hoped that her full-skirted dresses and new corset would hide her secret for another month or two. ''Forgive me for not telling you, my dearest of friends. But I did not want to distress you.''

''I understand.''

''How did you guess?''

''Your sudden dislike of coffee or fried meat. The way you stand. The way your eyes take on that dreamy inward look at times, as if you're listening to music that no one else can hear.

Once a woman has carried a child of her own, she learns to recognize that look in another.''

''Are you sure it was not because I am about to burst out of my new corset? I hoped people would just assume I was getting fat!'' Norah's face became serious. ''Others will be noticing, too. I had better come to a decision soon.''

Abigail looked away. ''There is something I wish to say to you, but I do not know quite how to begin. Earlier I asked Cora to leave us alone for a while when the opportunity arose.'' She caught Norah's hand between her own. ''I am dying.''

Norah made a sound of protest, but Abigail's fingers tightened on hers. ''No, please don't speak yet. I am dying, and I cannot leave with an easy mind the way things stand. The worst part is knowing that I will leave Charles alone. He has been my life, and I cannot bear to know he will be unhappy.'' Her eyes were brown as pansies, and dewed with tears. ''Outside of Charles, Norah, there is no one else I love so well as you. You are so beautiful and so brave. And you are strong and healthy. You could give Charles the sons...''

''Abigail! No!'' Horrified, Norah put her fingers over Abigail's mouth. ''You must not say such things! Every day you are stronger with Dr. Swansea's care. You must not think of dying.... You must not speak of it! You must get well. You *will* get well.''

The brown eyes were wide and gentle in the pallid face. ''No. Do not try to spare me, Norah. I have come to terms with myself about it. But I do not mean to overset you. Just think of what I have said.''

Abigail leaned her head back against the chair, closing her eyes. After a moment Norah picked up the novel and began to read in an unsteady voice. There must be no talk of death or dying. As soon as Abigail became stronger, she must leave the shelter of the Gartner's hospitality, and start a new life somewhere else.

During the noonday meal, her thoughts were occupied with deciding where she would go when she left Camp Greenwood. Norah arranged and rearranged plans in her mind while Mrs. Boyle chatted with Captain Gartner, paying little heed to the conversation. She barely noticed when the striker brought an envelope of heavy white paper and laid it beside Captain Gartner's dessert plate.

"Just brought in from Camp Verde for you, sir."

Gartner slit the envelope and removed a folded sheet of heavy white paper, covered with several lines in a delicate feminine hand. "It seems we might be entertaining guests, ladies. One of Abigail's friends from St. Louis is passing through the area with her husband, and they expect to spend a few days here at the Camp if he completes his business soon enough."

Norah finished pouring out a cup of tea for Mrs. Boyle. "Oh, dear. They will be much distressed to arrive when Abigail is so ill. Is there no way of reaching them?"

"No. This came in with the supply wagon. It doesn't say where they are now or when they will be arriving. Or mention where they are putting up along the way."

Cora pursed her lips. "We will have to put them up for a few nights; however, I am sure they will not linger under the circumstances."

Norah put down her empty cup and rose. "I will see that the guest house is in readiness."

Although the cleaning of the guest quarters was assigned to Private Harris, the spindle-shanked private still waiting for his first beard growth, Norah set herself the task of providing the little touches of comfort that a woman knows best. When the beds were aired and the floor swept of the ever-present dust, she scented the stale interior with herbs steeped in bowls of water and brought armfuls of freshly ironed linens for the beds. A small vase on a lacy dresser scarf here, a pink and blue floral carpet taken from the house there, a cake of lavender French-milled soap on the washstand and the sparsely furnished room took on a new aspect. At her instructions the private brought over two upright chairs and a small deal table previously stored under the gables of the house.

"Where'd you like 'em, ma'am?"

"Over by the window where the chest used to be." She looked at his red and sweaty face and took pity on him. He looked so young. Had she ever been that young herself? "That will be all I need you for, Private Harris. I can finish up in here. Thank you very much."

For one of the smiles such as Norah bestowed on him, the

boy would have cheerfully carried a piano upstairs and then back down again, without a word of reproach. "Yes, ma'am. Thank you, ma'am."

Spreading the fresh linen on the hard pallets that served as mattresses, Norah let her mind go free of her routine tasks to remember the past and dream of the future. Under her heart she carried Storm Caller's child, a part of her as that first still-born babe had never truly been. She wrapped her arms around her abdomen in a protective caress. The day she arrived back at Camp Greenwood she had thought she had no future. And now her future lived and grew inside her womb. Son or daughter, she welcomed it and prayed that it be healthy. She thought it was a boy. It *felt* like a boy, a tiny insistently male presence growing within her. Either way, she hoped it would look like Storm Caller: this was all she would ever have of him. Perhaps, in time, it would be enough.

Unfolding the down comforter, she placed it at the foot of the bed. Nights were growing colder. She would have to make some warm clothes for the baby. Sacques and jackets and tiny gowns with tucking and ribbons to cover a rosily squirming body. Booties and stockings for pink little toes. She was so wrapped up in her visions that the sound of the door swinging open was masked by the lullaby in her mind.

A boot stubbed on a knot in the uneven floor, and she whirled around, expecting that the private had come back for some forgotten item. But the bulk that blocked the light from the open door in the instant before it slammed shut was that of an older man, heavier and hunched over to spring. She could not scream, for a hard hand covered her mouth as she was borne backward onto the bed. She knew him: the cruel hands, the rapacious mouth, belonged to the man she had once promised, in all innocence, to love and obey. *Abner!*

He crushed her into the mattress, knocking the breath out of her. His knee was between hers, pressing her thighs apart while his fingers scrabbled against her, pulling dress and petticoats up, ripping at her underclothing. His wet mouth tugged at her bodice, searching for the soft breast beneath the cloth. Taking the fabric in his teeth, he tore the top of her gown down the front seam bruising her flesh. And all that time the heel of his other hand ground her lips against her teeth until she tasted blood.

He worked in deadly silence until she lay beneath him half-stripped, lower body bare, and her breasts spilling out of her torn corset. His face was distorted with triumph and a hatred so intense that she wondered if she would leave the room alive. No one could hear this noiseless struggle, and few would intervene between a man and his wife if they did. Mrs. Boyle would be with Abigail, Charles at his post, the Doctor still at the Infirmary. They would not miss her until it was too late. There was no one to help her but herself.

Abner's alcohol-tinged breath filled her nostrils, as his ugly whispers filled her ear. "Indian bitch! Whore! Do you think I don't know who you were with all those months? I've been talking to Newcomb. You were with that stinking half-breed LeBeau, weren't you? I should have known from the beginning! Everybody's been laughing at me behind my back, while the two of you were rolling around naked together, rutting like dogs!" His fingers dug into her groin. "Was he good? Was he?"

Unable to speak, one hand jammed behind her back until she thought it would break, Norah still bloodied his nose and gouged at his eyes until a clout to her jaw made the world blur and darken. Shaking her head, she tried to clear it of the buzzing sounds and whirling lights.

"Did he do this to you? And this?" His hands invaded her painfully. "Did he, Norah? Did you ever wish he was me? Or when I was in you, was it LeBeau you were itching for all the time?"

His hand caught at the thong around her neck, the one that held the carved bit of turquoise, smoothed by time and a hundred hands. "Now, isn't this a handy little thing." He twisted the thong around his hand once, twice, until it cut deeply into her throat. He twisted again, and her breath whistled in and out. "Tell me that you want it, Norah. Tell me, and I'll stop."

It was a lie, she could see it in his eyes. He had killed before, and he had enjoyed it. He would take even more pleasure in killing her, for she had humiliated him before the world. Panic lit her eyes, and Abner smiled, pulling the thong upward until her head was lifted off the bed. She felt as if the leather cord would bust through the skin of her neck, severing bones and arteries. He pulled at his pants and, as she felt his readiness to take her, all of Norah's energies concentrated on one fact: she would have to kill him to stop him. At that moment, Norah would have traded her soul for her skinning knife, tucked safely away in her bureau drawer. Surprise was the only weapon she had at hand, and she wielded it well.

Her body went limp, and she opened her legs as if to welcome him, raising her arms languidly above her head. He pulled back a bit, and that was all she needed. With a quick twisting motion, she reached for the glass vase she had placed on the bedside chest earlier and swung it at his temple with all her might. Abner parried the blow, catching her wrist in his hand and compressing it until her arm dropped back. The vase, still clenched between her rapidly numbing fingers, smashed against the metal hinges of the chest.

He shifted his weight, and that was all the opening Norah needed. Thrusting her knee up sharply, she caught him between the legs. As he doubled forward, the broken neck of the vase lashed out at his jugular vein. He reared up, dodging the mortal blow in time but a jagged line scraped along his jaw and across his Adam's apple. The movement threw him off balance, and he fell backward to the floor. As he leaped to his feet, she snatched the heavy pottery ewer from its basin and threw it with all her might. It hit Abner squarely on the forehead, and he fell like a pole-axed mule.

Snatching up one of the sheets before her, she edged to the door, still grasping her makeshift cut-glass dagger. A second later the door flew open. Norah ran out into the arms of the startled Captain, unaware that she was half-naked and her face drained of all color except for scarlet smears of blood. Gartner swore, then gently he put her aside and into the care of the Sergeant at his heels. The Colt .44 was out of its holster and in his hand, cocked and ready as he went in.

Norah waited rigidly while the trooper tried to wrap the sheet around her and keep it in place. From inside the guest quarters came the dull cracks of bone on bone. Silence. Then Gartner came out, his face like flint, dragging a dazed Abner by the scruff of his collar.

"Bailey! Jones!"

"Yes, sir!"

"Yes, sir!

He threw Abner down in the dirt. "Escort this man to the gates immediately. If he tries to turn back, shoot him."

The grizzled Sergeant thought he hadn't understood the order correctly. "Sir?"

"Are you deaf, Sergeant?"

"No, *sir*!"

Grabbing Abner up by the elbows, they hauled him to his feet. In addition to the scratches on his face and the oozing cut along his neck and jaw, there was a bruise puffing up along one side of his face, and his right eye was swollen shut. Norah knew she hadn't done that much damage herself. He tried to straighten and stood swaying between the soldiers, lank hair falling over his eyes. His head had cleared, and his face was red with rage.

"Butt out of this, Gartner! This is no business of yours. I got every right to…"

Gartner towered over him. "You've got no rights here, *mister*! Count yourself lucky that I'm letting you go. And don't come back, because I meant what I said: I'm issuing orders to shoot you on sight."

"You can't do that, it's illegal! I'll go over your head to the Colonel. I'll see you court-martialed."

"You're a fine one to take shelter behind the law, Slade. But I'm not worried: a complaint from a dead man doesn't hold much importance out here. Now pick up your hat and get out of my sight."

The troopers took him by either arm, and half-dragged Abner off. Gartner turned and saw Norah still standing there, death-pale and wrapped like a corpse in a winding sheet. Cora Boyle stood a few feet away, watching. Although a crowd of men gathered about them, the Colonel's wife made no effort to assist Norah inside. He wondered at that briefly, but there was no time for more.

"One of you men go rout out the visiting surgeon. You'll find him at the Infirmary. The rest of you clear off!" He turned to Cora, who stood still as a scarecrow on a windless day. "Mrs. Boyle, I would be grateful if you would assist Mrs. Slade inside. She's suffered a severe shock."

Slowly Cora came forward and put her arm around Norah, guiding her up the boardwalk and into the firebox heat of the frame house. They went up the stairs, slowly because of Norah's limping gait, and into her bedroom. Mrs. Boyle sat her on the bed, helped her into a clean lawn shift, dosed her liberally with an herbal draught, and made her lie down. Fetching a clean cloth, she dabbed gently at Norah's face and the dried brown crust at the corner of her mouth.

"Did he…? Are you hurt, child?"

"No. But I wish *he* was! I wish I'd killed him!" Of all the emotions roiling through her now, regret was uppermost in her mind. "I should have! I should have killed him. That bastard!"

The Colonel's wife had lived on an Army post thirty-two years and didn't blink as she pulled the pins from Norah's hair. "At least be thankful for one thing. After what happened here today, no one will have reason to call your child that epithet."

"What?" The potion was working already, and Norah's thoughts were growing fuzzy around the edges.

Mrs. Boyle brushed Norah's hair softly, soothingly. "I mean, some good can come out of all this. A lot of people know you have not been living with your husband. But word will get around, people will hear about today and guess at what might have happened. After a while they will forget *when* it happened, or think they counted wrong. And when your baby is born, no one will dare call it a bastard."

Norah sat upright, fighting to keep the world in focus. "I would rather acknowledge my baby a bastard than that monster's child!"

"Now that is enough of that! You will think differently when the time comes. Go to sleep now, and dream of holding that baby in your arms. That is the best cure I can prescribe for you."

Drowsily, Norah smiled. "It will be a boy," she murmured, just on the edge of sleep. "With gray eyes. Like his father."

The buggy, driven by Lieutenant Newcomb, swayed and bumped toward the Santa Magdalena Mission. Although Norah held an opened parasol it rested across her lap, while the honeyed sunlight caressed her face. Eyes closed, she pretended she was riding Wind Dancer along the rocky passes that led to Endless Canyon. Her daydreams were interrupted, as they had been regularly, by her companion's attempt to make conversation.

"I hope the long ride in this oppressive heat is not tiring you, ma'am. It's unseasonably warm for this time of year."

"No, I have become quite accustomed to it." *And I have ridden far less comfortably than this—one time in nothing but my drawers and an old woolen blanket.* Norah wondered how he would react if she had said those words aloud. Picturing how astonished his face would look, she laughed softly.

His weathered skin darkened with a flush of color. "It's good to hear you laugh again. I have been wanting to say something to you for a long time now...Norah."

Without warning he shifted the reins to one hand and reached out to cover hers with his other one. Quickly she withdrew her hand from beneath his, aware of the admiration in the blue eyes that glanced her way. Newcomb had changed while she was with Storm Caller. The eager boy had been replaced by a man; but where the youthful puppy love had been endearing, if at times irritating, the frank devotion of the grown man made Norah acutely uneasy. The rumors had not shaken his idealized vision of her as a woman victimized first by one villain, and then another.

He brought the buggy to a stop in the middle of the plain. "Norah—I cannot address you as Mrs. Slade, the words stick in my craw—you must know by now how I feel about you! When you married I swore I would never do so myself, and resigned myself to a bachelor existence; but you have not returned to your husband, and that has given me reason to hope."

"Lieutenant..." Before she had time to speak his arms went around her so tightly the buttons of his uniform pressed into her. She felt them denting her skin. His mouth touched hers, not with the hunger of a man for a woman, but with the reverence of a pilgrim worshiping a saintly relic. Her first reaction of surprise was elbowed out by anger.

She was tired of being a symbol to the men around her, when all she wanted to be was a woman: to Abner she had been a sign of financial success, to Storm Caller a tangible blow to his enemy's pride; and now, to Newcomb, a wronged Guinevere to play opposite his noble Lancelot, and the truth be damned.

"How dare you! Let me go at once!" Tears sparkled in her eyes as she pushed him away.

Newcomb was aghast at his behavior and her tears, misconstruing their origin. "Forgive me! I've acted the complete cad, taking advantage of your vulnerable position and our being alone together...." He took her hand and pressed his lips to the back of it before she snatched it away. "Norah...Mrs. Slade... I am so sorry. Please accept my profoundest—"

"Please, Lieutenant, drive on!" She sat upright, spine straight, and swung the parasol so that it was between them, hiding her face. The irony of the situation was not lost on her. In the lonely frontier of the Territory, a woman of her age and education could pick and choose from among many eligible suitors. And the only man she wanted, the only man she ever loved, had sent her back like a piece of unnecessary baggage.

The ride was completed in awkward silence, and Norah was relieved when Newcomb left her at the convent gate. Sister Thomasina, the Infirmarian, greeted her with great warmth and went in search of refreshments, leaving her a few moments to reflect alone. For the first time Norah understood the lure of the religious life, the urge to turn one's back on the world, trusting everything into God's hands. At the Mission, life centered around the pattern of work and prayer repeating over and over again, while time slipped through the fingers like Ave Marias on a rosary's polished beads. How peaceful this place was, how healing with its comforting sameness. And yet, how enclosed and confining, surrounded by high adobe walls that cut off the view of the open landscape, the towering mesas and the distant gray-blue mountains.

From the side door, Sister Thomasina sailed out in her over-large habit. Since the death of Mother Immaculata in the spring she had taken over shepherding the convent's inhabitants. A born follower, rather than a leader, she found the responsibility a great ordeal, and had worried herself into a lean bundle of skin and bones wired together by nervous energy. If only she could hold out until the Mother House sent out a replacement for poor Sister Immaculata, God rest her soul! And meanwhile, here was dear Norah, come for a most welcome visit. She set the tray down on the table and smiled warmly. "It is good to see you again, and looking so well. You are blooming like a flower in this desertland!" Pouring out two cups of weak tea, she offered sweet butter and rolls fresh from the oven. "Maria, our new student, has gone to gather more herbs for Abigail's tonic."

Exchanging news and recalling Norah's teaching at the Mission filled a pleasant half hour. Norah had just finished her second cup of tea when a door opened, and a graceful girl slipped into the arcade. For a moment Norah stared, and then the newcomer danced out into the sunlight. Not Dove-in-Flight, as she had first thought, but a young girl with much the same build and mannerisms. And the same too-old eyes. This must be the girl who had run away from Mercy Michael's brothel during the winter to seek refuge at the convent school. And she was just a child! Norah's heart went out to her.

Sister Thomasina clucked her tongue. "Ah, Maria. Have you found the leaves I require?"

"I am not sure. They look so much alike to me." She pulled two small green stems from her pocket, each bearing four oval leaves. "Is it this one? Or this?"

The old woman inspected them closely. One set of leaves was covered with fine hairs, the other wrinkled and tough-looking. She put her hands on her knees and rolled her eyes skyward. "Neither."

Maria hung her head. "I am no good at plants and herbs. You would do better to put me back in the kitchen."

"No. I must have someone to learn these things, for if I fall ill, who will assist the others? And you have the best memory for telling one plant from another. You will go back again. Lung-heal is very like these, but the leaves are both wrinkled and covered with fine silver down. Now hurry, for Mrs. Slade must be back to the Post before sundown."

Norah stood up, smoothing her skirt, anxious to escape from the convent walls, which had once seemed a place of refuge to her. For the past five minutes they had been closing in on her. "I know the herb. I will go along with Maria."

Maria ran inside, returning quickly with a small basket. There was no sign of Lieutenant Newcomb in the main court-yard. A young monk sat on a stone bench at the far end of the complex, a prayerbook open on his lap, while he idly contemplated his fingernails and dreamed of home. The area had been quiet in the past weeks, and the massive iron-barred gates stood open for the approaching supply wagon from Greenwood Junction.

Norah hesitated. They were only going along the edge of the arroyo and would be within hailing distance of the walls. She saw no reason to drag her lovesick escort out with them. It was irksome to have Newcomb nipping at her heels like a Shetland collie dogging a wayward lamb—and would be more so today, after his actions on the ride in. The urge to kick off the restraints of past weeks would no longer be denied: with Maria following, Norah crossed to the far side of the square, and they slipped outside as the supply wagon rolled past.

The vast semi-arid plain spread out in front of them, and to the left the arroyo cut deeply through the ancient stone, revealing the brown and gold strata like the layers of a chocolate torte. Generations ago a rock slide in the far mountains had altered the terrain. The run-off from the spring melt that had cascaded down through it for centuries now found another outlet, and the wash had become the home of flourishing opportunistic flora. Prickly pear, creosote bushes, and roly-poly juniper dotted the upper slopes, while plants of a more tender sort had rooted along the lower margins. Underground water still seeped beneath the wide flat bottom, nourishing groves of oak saplings and stands of cedar.

They covered the short distance from the gate quickly and began their descent. Maria led the way. The tallest cedars were only ten to fifteen feet high, but each parent tree had younger ones clustered densely about it, where its seedlings had sprouted. It was good to be out in the open again, after so much time spent within four walls. Taking a deep breath, Norah filled her lungs with the clean scent of evergreen. The pungent perfume was everywhere, and reminded her of the mountain camp and of the wooded areas fringing the canyon rim. It brought back strong memories of Storm Caller that filled her with mingled pleasure and pain.

"Over here, *señora*." Maria knelt at the foot of a scraggly shrub. "Is this not the plant you seek?"

Norah peered down and shook her head. "However, it looks

very similar. Once we find the lung-heal I will show you the difference.'' For the next few minutes they searched in silence, and when she looked up at first she did not see the girl.

''Maria?''

A brown face popped out of the foliage. *''Señora?''*

''Stay where we can see one another.''

Hunting in the shade of the larger rocks, Norah found a plant resembling the fever-balm Snow-in-Summer had often used to make a medicinal tea. She would take it along to Sister Thomasina: the Infirmarian would likely know if this herb had the same soothing properties. Widening her search to include more specimens, she soon had her basket half full. She looked up to see how her companion was faring, and discovered the girl had vanished once more. Suddenly the back of her neck prickled. It was eerily quiet with all sound from above blocked off by the side of the arroyo and the foliage screen. Nearby, a horse whickered softly, and the cold wind of presentiment blew over Norah.

She turned quickly, lost her balance because of the weakness in her leg, and went sprawling in the carpet of dried red-brown needles. Abner was ten feet away and closing on her. ''I came in with the supply wagon, and heard you were here. I hope the presence of your lawful husband doesn't throw a kink into your plans. Who are you meeting here, *whore*? One of the pony soldiers? Or your half-breed lover? Is that why he's been hanging around hereabouts?''

Storm Caller near Camp Greenwood? She doubted it. This was one more example of Abner's insane notions. She pushed herself to her hands and knees, then rose. As she backed away, her fingers slipped inside the deep skirt pocket, feeling for the small knife she kept there. ''Leave me alone, Abner. Do not come one step closer.''

He came on, drawing his revolver as he neared, but grasping it by the barrel like bludgeon. ''I would have given you everything, Norah. The finest home in the Territory. Gowns of silk and velvet, jewels, anything you wanted. Every man would have looked at you and envied me. And see how you've repaid me!''

His face was contorted, lips pulled back over his teeth in a parody of a smile. From behind her Norah heard a rustling in the bushes. Maria would hear and go for help. If only she could stall for time. "I never asked for silk gowns and jewels. All I wanted was an honest husband, a man I could respect, and a decent way of life."

"*Decent!* You don't know the meaning of the word. You've made me the laughing stock of the Territory. The man whose wife ran off with a dirty half-breed! And when you returned and I offered to take you back, you spurned me. Everyone knows, too. They laugh at me behind my back. Do you know what that does to a man, Norah? *Do you?*"

She flinched from the hate in his eyes. There was no lust in them now as there had been in the guest bungalow at the camp, only a killing anger. The truth rang in her head like a knell: one of them would not leave the arroyo alive. She would do her best to see that it was not her. The knife was out of her pocket, catching the light as she moved. He lunged at her and, as she took a step away, her injured leg betrayed her again. White-hot augers bored upward through her bones. Pitching backward, she fell down the slope, crying out with pain.

His horse whinnied above, and Abner paused to listen, just long enough for her to get upright again. Biting her lip against the throbbing in her leg, she limped down in a broken run toward the bottom of the wash. She would have a better chance there: the growth was thicker, the ground more level. If she might put enough distance between them, she might make a break up the steep incline to the top. A sharp rock zinged by her cheek, and there was a puff of tan dust and splintered rock three feet ahead. And then she heard the report, deafening as a cannon roar. Not a rock but a bullet!

Desperately searching for cover, she raced beneath some low-hanging boughs and almost blundered straight into Maria. The girl blocked the way, frozen with terror. Her face, framed by coils of shining black hair, was as white as her convent-school dress. They were on a collision course. Norah slid awkwardly, trying to change her trajectory, and fell a third time. She heard rather than saw what happened next. There was a queer muffled sound followed by the echoing roar of gunfire, and then a high-pitched scream. As Norah lifted herself, she saw Maria fold at the waist and knees, crumpling to the ground like a discarded marionette.

Maria lay on her side, staring at Abner with horror. A splash of red stained her bodice, unfurling like the petals of a terrible scarlet rose. Expecting to feel the impact of a bullet in her own body at any second, Norah twisted around as a thundering shot filled the air. A nightmare thing stood before them, wavering from side to side. It wore Abner's clothes and blood pulsed and spurted from the shattered head. Then the thing that was no longer human tipped forward and fell like a diseased tree.

Maria groaned. "*Madre de Dios*... He has no face! No face!"

Abner lay on the ground, his limbs bent beneath him at odd angles. Dried pine needles floated on the crimson flow that soaked the thirsty ground. The man Norah had come west to marry, the man who had tormented and abused her, was dead. She was numb. There was no feeling inside her, except the relief one might expect at seeing a venomous insect crushed beneath a boot heel.

Soft footfalls neared as she rose to go to Maria. They seemed to come from two sides, and at first she couldn't tell their direction. The overhanging cedar branches parted just behind the wounded girl. If Abner's face had been a nightmare, this one was from Norah's dreams.

"Storm Caller!"

"Norah..." He stopped, cradling his rifle. What was there to say? When he'd tracked Slade to this place, he had no idea that she would be here, too. But it had been her voice, her danger that had sent his hand to the trigger without thought of the consequence.

She stretched out her hands to him, and he stepped forward eagerly. Just as he did so, the click of a gun being cocked came from somewhere behind Norah. Storm Caller's eyes flicked from her face to a spot on the slope level with where he stood.

"Don't move, LeBeau! You're under arrest for the cold-blooded murder of Abner Slade. I saw the whole thing." It was Newcomb's voice, and he followed it out of the shadows of the trees.

"No!" Norah knelt by Maria, trying to staunch the blood with her bare hand while she looked over her shoulder at the Cavalry officer. "Abner shot Maria, and he would have killed me, too!"

"Why would he try to kill you? I tell you I saw the whole thing. LeBeau, throw down your rifle. I'm taking you in."

"What nonsense are you talking? I was right here! Storm... Sergeant LeBeau saved my life." All the while she talked, Norah's hands were stripping lengths of her petticoat to use as makeshift bandages for Maria. She wasted no time on Abner. He was gone beyond the reach of anyone but God.

It was Storm Caller who interrupted. Because he had taken Norah, anything she said would be discredited. Especially since it was her husband he had just shot. It seemed the white God had a sense of irony in the payment he extracted. "Save your breath, Norah. No one will believe a word you say. Not if it's your word against his."

Norah was sick at heart, knowing what he said was true. Too many people wondered if there had been a liaison between them, and that would render her word suspect if Newcomb told a conflicting story. And he would: one look at the Lieutenant's face was enough to confirm that, even before he spoke.

"Slade had no reason to shoot a convent girl, much less his own wife!" Newcomb saw the events, not as they happened, but as he wanted them to be. Fate had intervened to rid him of two rivals with one stroke. And only himself left to comfort the widow. "All right, LeBeau. Throw down your rifle."

Storm Caller still cradled the barrel across his arm. "I'm not going anywhere with you, Lieutenant." The officer's Army revolver lifted a fraction. Newcomb could shoot him where he stood, claiming he had resisted arrest. Again, anything Norah said would be dismissed. Well, he would not go meekly to his own hanging. Of course, he could shoot the Lieutenant: but the man was only a soldier doing his duty, however misdirected.

Newcomb tensed, gun ready. Storm Caller kept alert for the smallest diminishment in the officer's concentration. Then he could make his escape. Norah's nerves were drawn as taut as bowstrings as she knelt at Maria's side. She was going to snap inside unless something happened soon. When Newcomb moved upslope of her she acted. Grasping the end of a gnarled stick, she thrust it into his path, sending him end over end t the bottom of the arroyo. His gun discharged, and the bullet thunked harmlessly into the trunk of a cedar.

She looked up at Storm Caller, but he had vanished. There was nothing but the faint trembling of the branch ends to show he had ever been there at all.

24

Norah paced up and down the length of the tiny room, listening to the homely sound of a sharpened saw on wood. Out in the sunshine of the main courtyard they were building Abner's coffin. Time and again she heard the chuff of the saw biting into the planks, then the rasping of the metal teeth. Even here, in the little quiet room that had belonged to the late Mother Superior, she could not escape the remembrance of violent death. *"He has no face!"*

The spartan nun's cell reminded Norah of her bedroom under the eaves at Miss Emerson's Academy. A narrow, virginal bed, covered in white, the small table of scoured wood holding the heavy china pitcher and basin, and a dark crucifix upon the wall were the only relief from its whitewashed simplicity. Somewhere a bell rang and feminine voices spoke softly, and she could almost imagine that her afternoon class of uniformed pupils waited below to conjugate Latin verbs and read on Gallic wars. But that was in another lifetime. There were no stately maples and elms outside the Mission walls, no ice wagons or fruit vendors hawking their goods while children spun their hoops and lazy cats dozed on doorsteps. Instead there were miles of heat and emptiness, filled with things that scurried and scuttled and burrowed and basked. And somewhere out there beyond the Mission walls, Storm Caller fled for his life.

A wild fury filled her, a hatred for the desert and the mountains and the high country that had brought her to such grief

Oh, to be back in Boston, away from this terrible place. And then she remembered the happy golden days, the black and starry nights of Endless Canyon and could not hate after all. She knew her pain was because she was alive and able to feel: she had never been alive in Boston, just drifting in a dull and dreamlike haze. It had taken Storm Caller to awaken her from that trance. She regretted many things, but never that.

A bell jangled distantly, and a heavy door opened and shut. Soon she heard a familiar footstep in the corridor and threw the door open wide. A small figure stood there, hand poised to knock, and Norah flung her arms around the woman.

"Cora. Oh, thank God!"

The Colonel's wife embraced the new widow. "Why, child, you are shivering! You need a glass of wine and some good, hot soup." She stepped inside, neat and precise in a green and white pin-striped dress. She looked older today, and the white streaks in her brown hair were more noticeable. "I came as soon as I could." Opening the basket, she took out a parcel. "Abigail sends her love. I have brought you a black dress and stockings that she wore when she was considerably plumper. The dress should fit if I let the hem down."

Norah could hardly speak around the wooden block that lodged in her throat. "I am so glad you are here. You cannot know what a comfort your presence is to me: you are so re-assuringly efficient and sensible, and just now everything seems totally insane!"

"Well, I will say it this once, and not again, for I do not hold with speaking ill of the dead: but you are well rid of your husband, though I would not have wished him to meet his maker in such a manner. But you are free of him now."

To hear her own feelings put into words by Mrs. Boyle healed some of Norah's guilt. "I have felt such a terrible hyp-ocrite, meekly accepting condolences all afternoon! And I will feel despicably false, dressed in mourning with everyone think-ing me a grieving widow! I do not know how I can carry through."

"My dear, you are not the first dry-eyed widow I have seen in my time, and I sincerely doubt you will be the last! But it is important that appearances are kept up." Norah made a dis-ressed sound, but the Colonel's wife went on. "For the most part, people are fairly indifferent to their fellows' sufferings—they will not give a good solid *damn* about whether you grieve or not—as long as you do not offend them by ignoring the proprieties.''

The fact that the little woman had cursed had an even more powerful effect on Norah than her words did. ''You are right, of course. I have no wish to cause any more problems for Abigail and Captain Gartner at such a time.''

''They are not the only ones I am thinking of now. There is yourself and the child to worry about, too.'' She paused. ''And Sergeant LeBeau. I always had a soft spot in my heart for him. For his sake you must stick to your story, and you must not give anyone reason to doubt your word. That is his only chance to escape a charge of killing your husband in cold blood.''

Norah wheeled around, ferocious in her intensity. ''It is the truth! God strike me dead if I lie! Abner shot Maria and tried to kill me, and Storm Cal— LeBeau shot him to save me. Newcomb wasn't even there when it happened!''

Mrs. Boyle chewed her lower lip absently: it was better if she told Norah now. ''They have ridden out after him—Captain Gartner and a column of soldiers and a couple of new Apache scouts from Camp Verde. They will bring him back to stand his trial. Then it will be your word and his against Newcomb's. If this Mission girl lives—and tells the same story—he has a chance to be acquitted. If not, they will hang him.''

''Maria will tell the same story, because it is exactly what happened!''

''Then you had best pray that she recovers.''

Norah changed into the black dress. Cora had already ripped the hem out, and now she pinned it carefully in place. ''There. I can sew it for you later, but at least you will not offend anyone. I have brought a bit of crepe to put around your bonnet for the ride back.''

Norah smoothed her hair in place. Suddenly she was exhausted. ''I would like to see Maria again before we leave.''

''Of course. Oh, dear, I need more pins. I will go fetch some.''

She left the room, and Norah paced aimlessly again, now hearing the squeak of nails being driven into the plain board of Abner's coffin. There was a small arched niche in the room holding a painted and gilded Madonna and Holy Child. Norah was drawn to it, magnetized by sudden memories of her wedding day at Santa Magdalena. She remembered the agony of mind she had felt that day, torn between her formal betrothal to Abner and her growing feelings for the man she had called LeBeau. And she recalled the peace that had descended upon her, contemplating another Madonna as she waited for the ceremony to begin. How hopeful she had been then that she and Abner could, between them, make a successful marriage, filled with mutual respect, if not love.

She had hated him and was, even now, glad to be released from her marriage vows; now that he was dead she could be generous. The hatred drained away as she knelt on the wood prie-dieu and offered up a prayer for his soul in the way she had learned at her mother's knee. He had been warped with jealousies and the need for power and revenge. But what had he been like before that? Had there ever been a time, at least in childhood, when he had been loving and innocent? Or had he been born with a canker in his soul? Looking at the gentle carved faces, she prayed to those they represented, pouring her heart out in all its doubts and fears.

Holy Mary, Mother of God, pray for me. Ask your son to forgive me my weaknesses and to give me the strength to overcome them. I beg you as one woman to another, one mother to another, intercede for me. Guide me, for I am so lost and alone. Holy Infant, watch over my baby. Keep it safe from harm. And bless Storm Caller and keep him safe until Maria can clear his name and he can return. Adding prayers for Maria, for Abigail and Charles, she prayed that the benediction of peace she remembered from her wedding day would descend upon her again. When Mrs. Boyle returned, some time later, Norah was still on her knees.

Lieutenant Newcomb and the Indian Scout from Camp Verde rode around the waist-high stretch of impenetrable green and headed toward Gartner and his small group. The Captain reined in, annoyed. He had purposely sent Newcomb off in another direction, but the ruse hadn't worked. For some reason he couldn't quite fathom, he did not want the junior officer with him when they caught up with LeBeau. His instincts had never proved wrong in the past.

Newcomb saluted. "No sign of him to the east, Captain."

"All right. Spread out, and we'll circle around this manzanita. There's no way his horse could have picked its way through it."

Gartner nudged the mouse-colored gelding into a trot with a touch of his rowels, and Chollo, the Yuma scout, followed suit. While the animal covered the ground the Captain's eyes searched for a sign, knowing already that there would be nothing to find on the hardpan. No, they'd have to look along that creekbed or where the grass began a goodly distance ahead. Slowing his horse to a walk, he dismounted as soon as he reached the softer ground. In his heart, duty and friendship grated against each other like millstones.

He hated to leave Abigail, even for a day or two, but she was doing much better. Then, too, she understood that he wanted to bring his friend in himself. No, not wanted, *needed*. He only hoped they would catch up with LeBeau by nightfall or, traveling alone and lightly, he would outdistance them. Not that he thought him guilty; but if LeBeau wasn't brought in to face his trial, there would be a price on his head. Gartner didn't want to learn somewhere down the road, that LeBeau had been ambushed and shot down by some man-killer with a quick trigger and an empty purse. If only that Mexican girl snapped out of it! Under the nun's tender nursing, she was recovering nicely; but she hadn't spoken a single word since regaining consciousness.

"Captain! We've got him now." Newcomb dismounted as the scout pointed out a few blades of bent grass. "He went across that streambed over here."

Gartner knew better: that was just what LeBeau wanted them to think. Instead, he'd probably crossed back and forth several times between the hardpan and the rocks beside the stream. By now he was probably somewhere along the clifftops on the far side, or in the maze of rocks that began half a mile ahead.

"You and your scout continue along that way. Take McKenzie and Hardin." He nodded to Chollo. "We'll go on toward the Giant's Maze." Yes, that's where LeBeau would be

Somewhere in the Maze. He wiped his face with his bandana, wishing he were back on the Post with Abigail.

The sun was westering by the time they reached the mile-wide escarpment of twisted rock that was the Maze. From a distance the naturally formed landmark looked like the ruins of an ancient city. Shadows, like irregular stripes of indigo paint, streaked the red walls and the towerlike projections that caught fire in the dying light. Behind those massive walls were huge solid blocks and airy honeycombed layers, wide corridors and dim alleys, sunny open squares and deep-shaded galleries carved by eons of wind and water. An army could hide there with enough provisions. It would be impossible to get LeBeau out unless he could be convinced to surrender of his own will. Gartner hoped to God he could do it!

They found LeBeau's horse in a ravine, its neck broken from a bad fall. Nearby they found a moccasin print, and farther along another. The scout dropped to his knees and touched the earth. His fingertip picked up a few grains of gritty orange soil, and something damp and red.

"He is hurt," Chollo said in careful Spanish. "He is favoring his leg and must go slowly." The scout was both glad and sorry. He did not know LeBeau, but had heard much about him. Still, this was none of his affair. He was paid by the Army to scout, and it kept him off the reservation.

They followed the erratic trail between two sentinel rocks and behind the stony wall. They found a lot of signs here, indicating their quarry had come this way, and not too long before. "I don't like this. It's too easy," Gartner said. "Might be a trap. Or another false trail."

"A wounded man cannot take the effort or the time to cover his tracks."

"LeBeau would find a way." The light was failing when they reached a dead end. The Captain examined the sheer wall and the stark pinnacle that topped it. "If he's hurt he couldn't have climbed that. He must have doubled back."

Chollo shook his head. "He is up there, Cap-i-tan. But, *Madre de Dios!* what it must have cost him. He is hurting bad, now. I do not think he can go any more."

They scanned the rugged barrier. There was only one likely place the fugitive could be, the narrow ledge that stretched

below the limestone cap fifty feet above. Trapped like a
wounded bear in a blind cave. Gartner pushed away the pang
of pity that caught at him, and cupped his hands to his mouth.
"LeBeau? It's Captain Gartner. I want to come up and talk to
you."

There was no answer. Chollo stepped forward. "You want
that I should climb up, Cap-i-tan?"

"No." There were some things a man must do himself. This
was one of them. He stripped off his gunbelt. "I'm coming up,
LeBeau. I'm unarmed."

There was little purchase on the rock face, but if LeBeau
had climbed it, Gartner could find the way up, too. Placing the
toe of his boot in a crevice, he pushed up and got a fingerhold
in a long crack. He was a large man, but agile, and his age
was no handicap to one of his experience. And knowing his
friend as he did, there was no fear of a bullet or even a carefully
aimed rock crashing down on his head. Only once did he have
any qualms: his foothold crumbled while he was spread-eagled
on the hot sandstone face, and he thought of Abigail and cursed
himself for a fool who might die to prove a point.

There was a long fold of rock near the top, forming a protected ledge several feet deep. It looked like a likely place for
LeBeau to hole up for a siege. Catching an outcropping, the
Captain worked his way up to it. Rolling in, he went under the
slight overhang and got into a crouch. When his eyes became
accustomed to the light he shook his head in wonder. LeBeau
was not there.

Well, there was only one other place to go, and that was
straight up, toward the pinnacle. His navy fireman's shirt was
damp and sticking to his skin. Wiping his sweaty face on his
bandana, he leaned precariously backward and searched for a
route. A smear of blood on the tan rock exposed a shallow
cleft, hidden from below. Gartner wedged himself into it and
made the arduous climb, wondering how a wounded man could
have done it. By the time he wormed his way up, his back and
hands were scraped raw. Chollo could have made the climb in
half the time; but the hardest part was not reaching LeBeau, it
would be convincing him to surrender. Hauling himself up and
over, Gartner crouched against the stone to get his bearings.

He was on a bony ridge no more than three feet across.

sheering off steeply on either side to the canyon floor below. There was a click from just above. He looked up and into the face of the man he'd been tracking. As he brushed the sweat from his eyes with a shirtsleeve, Gartner was fully aware of the Army revolver aimed at his heart.

Storm Caller straddled a blunt projection ten feet higher. He leaned back against a rocky pillow, holding the gun across his other wrist. "I wasn't sure you had it in you."

Gartner smiled wryly. "I wasn't so sure myself." He nodded at his former Scout, noting the dried blood that soaked one leg of the buckskin breeches and the dirty cloth bound round it. "Chollo said you were hurt bad."

"I'll live." Despite the words, Storm Caller's face was haggard and drawn.

"Not out here without treatment, you won't. I've come to take you in, LeBeau. I'll see you get a fair trial. You know that."

"Not with my word against Newcomb's. I might not even make it back to camp: I know how the Army works."

"Damn it, and you know how I work! I'll guarantee your safety."

A hawk circled above them in the darkening sky, riding the updrafts as the earth cooled. The two men sat in silence, watching the blackness creep through the canyons, devouring first their colors, and then their forms.

Storm Caller shifted his weight. There were pain lines etched at the corners of his eyes and mouth. "If I go back, I ride in as a free man. I won't go back in manacles."

Gartner squinted at him, unhappily. "You've made a few enemies in your time, plus there's the word of Lieutenant Newcomb that you shot Slade down in cold blood. If you make one false move on the way back, some trooper with more hair than wit will think you're trying to get away and shoot you down. You'll have to go back as my prisoner. That's the only way I can guarantee your safety."

The pain lines were briefly vanquished by the ghost of a grin. "You speak very surely, for a man on the wrong end of a Colt."

"Goddamn it, man! It's your only chance. I know you too well to think you'd shoot me in cold blood."

There was no answer from Storm Caller, who had turned his head to look out over the landscape. At last he faced the other. Switching his grip on the Army revolver, he held it out to the Captain, butt end first. "End it now."

"Don't be a damned fool. You know I can't shoot you in cold blood, either."

Storm Caller's eyes were hooded, the irises dark as peat, and still he held the revolver out. Gartner rose. "We'll wait you out then. When you've lost enough blood and the heat and thirst get to you, I'll be back."

He started down, knowing that he made a clear target. Halfway to the canyon floor he heard the pounding of hooves, and stopped to catch his breath. Newcomb and the rest of the tracking party came around the sheer cliff in a pall of dust. Gartner was on solid ground again when they reined in.

"He's up there, and he's hurt, but we'll have to wait him out. From where he's sitting, he can pick climbers off one by one, like a frog catching flies."

"Cap-i-tan! Cap-i-tan!" Chollo pointed up toward the pinnacle. A man was silhouetted against the orange sky. Newcomb pulled his new Springfield rifle from his saddle scabbard and raised it.

"Hold your fire," Gartner roared, but his words were lost in the thunder of shots and their magnified echoes. "I said hold your fire!" He slammed Newcomb's rifle up and away, and turned his eyes to the pinnacle.

The man was still there, gilded by the light like a saint atop a church spire. But as they watched he staggered, then fell sideways over the edge of the precipice, into the waiting blackness of the canyon.

25

Cora Boyle picked at the braid on her navy cord skirt. It was an uncharacteristic gesture in someone usually so decisive. "Norah, I know it is difficult, but you must believe them."

"No!" Storm Caller dead? Norah whirled away from Captain Gartner and the hateful words, stumbling over a ripple in the carpet. "I would know it. I would feel it. He's not dead. He's not!"

Gartner and Mrs. Boyle looked at one another helplessly. "Norah..."

"If he's dead, where is his body? Can you tell me that?"

The Captain made a sound, part sympathy, part exasperation. "We tried, but you know what that country's like: a labyrinth of rock. A hundred men could search the area for a hundred days and not find anything."

"He's not dead, I tell you!" Her voice rose. "No, no, *no*!"

Cora urged the glass of brandy on her again. "Drink this. If not for your sake, for the child you carry. It isn't good to work yourself up like this. Now drink."

"I don't want it." Norah pushed the glass away without being aware of it and headed for the sanctuary of her own room, fleeing not only their sympathy and dreadful tidings, but also the terrifying pictures in her mind's eye. Storm Caller, tall and slim, poised upon the rocky peak, his body arcing downward from the sky, like a fallen angel. Storm Caller's body, broken and bleeding, fed upon by black-winged vultures and things that bit and tore and scurried away from the light. Moments of time frozen forever like the scenes captured on stereopticon slides. Norah pressed her hands to her face, trying to blot out the visions. No, it couldn't be true, or else her own heart would cease to beat, her own blood congeal in her veins.

In the days that followed, her belief that Storm Caller had escaped death began to alternate with periods of profound despair. He was always in her thoughts and in her dreams. She could not imagine his strength and grace and dark beauty wiped away as if it had never been, leaving nothing behind. And then her hand would come to rest just below her heart where she carried his child. At least, if what they said was true, she had this much of him, and her hopes and plans began to center around the precious life within her womb.

It seemed just and fitting that all Abner's scheming and greed and deadly deeds would provide the means to support Storm Caller's heir. She would remove to the ranch as soon as Abigail's health improved. Then she would learn to manage the ranch, to keep it profitable so she might one day hand it on to her child.

After Abner's hasty funeral and the inquiry, Norah divided her time between Abigail at the Camp and Maria at the Mission; and with every day that passed Maria grew stronger, although she never spoke. Not once. And when Norah came, the girl would cling to her hand in mute appeal, weeping silently when she left.

Norah would talk to her, brush her hair, bathe her temples. And before she took her leave she always said the same words: "You must tell them what you saw, Maria. You must clear his name." And the girl would stare blankly at her and then turn her face away to the wall.

It was after such a morning visit to Santa Magdalena, some three weeks later, that Norah sat alone in the drawing room, embroidering blue and yellow knots and flowers on an infant sacque of white cotton flannel. She was in one of her optimistic moods, sure that Storm Caller was alive. Sure that one day he would come back for her. Her imagination always balked at the point, afraid to go further. The striker's footsteps startled her out of her reverie.

"Miz Slade? There's, ah, someone to see you. Out on the

porch.'' The striker hovered in the doorway of the sitting room, red-faced and ill at ease.

Norah set aside her mending. "Please show him in, Private Harris.''

"Uh, ma'am, he's not exactly the kind of visitor that you show in.''

She rose with a puzzled frown, then brightened: perhaps it was Two Horses Racing, come with news. Snow-in-Summer should have been delivered of her child by now. Her steps were light and eager as she hurried to the door, but it was not the young brave who had come calling. Instead she saw a tall, stocky man, wearing a leather vest and chaps over his trousers. At first, as she stepped out, Norah thought his face was in shade. He removed his gray slouch hat to show crisp black curls against a brown scalp. His skin was a dark walnut color.

"Good afternoon. I am Norah Slade.''

"Pleased to meet you, ma'am. My name is Levi Hale. I was hired on, temporary, by your husband, just before he was killed.'' He saw her face freeze and dipped his head. "My condolences, ma'am.'' His voice was soft and melodious, his eyes gentle and inexpressibly sad.

She recovered herself nicely. "Thank you, Mr. Hale. I hope you did not undertake the long ride out to Camp Greenwood solely on my account.''

"In a way I did, ma'am. The foreman and most of the hands run off right away. Things are getting poorly. It seems to me that you need someone to take charge, like, and look after the stock and the buildings. What I'm thinking, is that you'll be needing to hire some new men, and as I'm looking for more permanent work, I thought we might strike a deal of sorts.''

She looked him over quickly. His manners were gentlemanly, his clothes worn but mended, his boots polished and in excellent repair. With surprise, she realized his faded breeches had once been light blue with the yellow Cavalry seam stripe. An ex-soldier from one of the Negro Cavalry units, the "Buffalo Soldiers,'' as Norah had heard the Indians call them. A quick examination of his brindle horse, hitched to the low rail, showed it to be as healthy looking and well tended as its owner.

"Come in, Mr. Hale, and we will discuss this further.''

"Thank you, ma'am, but I believe I would like to remain outside."

She hesitated, not wanting to offend him, yet unwilling to forgo what she felt was proper. "Mr. Hale, as you have mentioned, I am in need of a good foreman for my ranch, and I am willing to pay top wages. The person I have in mind would be someone who knows cattle and men, and who can give, as well as take orders. Do you know anyone with those qualifications?"

White teeth flashed briefly against the dark skin. "I had two enlistments in the Ninth Cavalry ma'am, and what I don't know about horses ain't fit to know. The last ten years I been a top hand on a Texas spread until I took a notion to travel on. Seems like I might be just the person you had in mind."

It was impossible not to smile back. She saw a way around his hesitation over what he thought was fitting. "It seems that you might be right. There is only one obstacle: I will not hire a foreman who is too proud to sit down and discuss business with a woman."

Levi Hale stared at her. Again that quick smile flashed, without lingering. "Mrs. Slade, ma'am, I would be right pleased to sit down and discuss anything you want to discuss."

Norah led the way into the parlor, requested refreshments from the astonished striker, and seated herself on the settee. Hale followed and balanced precariously on the edge of one of the carved walnut side chairs.

"How long did you work for my...for Mr. Slade?" The words *my husband* stuck in her throat. She was glad she would not have to say them, ever again.

"'Bout three weeks, ma'am. Then I looked around for another place."

"Why was that?" she asked sharply.

His voice was still slow and sad, but had a harder edge to it. "Seems there were some things I saw, I didn't much like. And then there were others I just guessed at. A man has to take a stand or he's not a man, to my kind of thinking: I can't work where I don't respect."

Norah was curious. "Then why have you come to me, knowing what you obviously know about Mr. Slade's transactions?"

Hale met her eyes squarely. "I soldiered under Captain Gartner during the war, and I came to respect him right highly. I heard you been staying here with the Captain and his lady, and I figured from what I heard that you're cut from a different cloth than your late husband."

She relaxed. "Mr. Hale, there *is* one other difficulty, quite a serious one. But I hope that we can surmount it by working together."

He turned the brim of his hat uneasily in his big hands. "I understand ma'am. I've worked with men of all colors, and gotten along with most of them. But if things get out of hand, why I'll be on my way, and no more said...."

Norah leaned forward, her eyes filled with sincerity. "Oh, no, you don't understand at all! The problem I referred to is not your color, but *my* ignorance: I know nothing about horses, except how to ride them—and I know less about cattle. As soon as Mrs. Gartner is well, I will be moving back to the ranch. I want you to teach me everything from the ground up, and I want you to take charge of the ranch until I can return. Are you willing to take that on?"

"Just tell me what you want done, ma'am, and it's as good as done."

"Good. Hire whom you need to get things in proper. Mr. Slade always dealt with the Johnstons in ordering things. If you will come back in an hour, I will draw up a letter, placing you in charge and giving you the authority to make any purchases you deem necessary."

She stood, and her new foreman rose to shake the hand she extended. He turned to leave, but stopped just short of the door and looked back. "When I rode by the ranch, I happened to notice the fancywork over the entrance gate was banged up in that windstorm. The part with the name and that wild cat sign."

Norah spoke with crisp decision. "Tear it down, Mr. Hale. Tear it down!"

Norah went to bed that night with a new sense of purpose. It helped to make plans, to be active in directing the course of her own life once again. She trusted Levi Hale, instinctively knowing he was honest, hard-working, and loyal. She did wonder at the air of sadness that clung to him. He had suffered terribly over something, but he had survived. It gave her courage. She would survive also. And as soon as Abigail was restored to her former level of health, Norah would move to the ranch and learn the day-to-day running of it. At the rate of improvement Abigail had shown in the past month, that day would not be too far off. She fell asleep, dreaming of a busy and productive future, accompanied on her rounds by a gray-eyed son.

It was sometime before dawn that she awakened, her heart pounding like a water hammer. One moment she was asleep, the next fully alert and apprehensive. Something was wrong. Voices, low but urgent. In Abigail's room. Throwing on her wrapper, she opened her door and went down the hall, her feet moving swiftly over the cool wood floor and the prickly nap of the long runner. The door to Abigail's room was flung wide, casting a triangle of light on the wallpaper at the end of the landing. Norah hurried toward it. In the golden lamp glow she saw Captain Gartner kneeling at the bedside with Dr. Swansea and Mrs. Boyle hovering nearby.

"What is it? What has happened?"

She crossed the room, and as she neared she saw the bed linens were covered with blood. Abigail lay back on the pillows in her blood-stained night rail, so white and silent that Norah feared she was dead, but at the sound of her voice the invalid's eyelids opened. Her eyes seemed overly large in a face carved from gray alabaster.

"Norah..." She tried to sit up, and a spasm shook her thin frame. A bubbling cough wracked her, and red froth trickled from the corner of her mouth.

Norah dropped to her knees beside the Captain and took Abigail's thin hand in hers. It felt like a cloth filled with sticks, not quite human, not quite alive. Fear, like a cold block of ice, settled around Norah. *Please God, not this. Not now. She is so young! Please, let her live!* "Do not try to talk dearest. You are going to be all right, Abigail. Doctor Swansea will bring you through this."

"No." The word was faint but firm. Another spasm overcame her, and she coughed and choked, eyes wide and startled. Abigail's eyes were dark coals, burning with an inner knowledge. "I am dying. I am not afraid...for myself. But I do not want to leave Charles alone. Norah…take care of him. Take care of Charles. You and he…'' Again, that bubbling horror of a cough, that glistening scarlet thread.

Norah clasped the hand more tightly in hers, as if she could pull Abigail back from the edge of forever by sheer willpower. She smoothed Abigail's hair, pretending she didn't understand. "Rest, dearest, and you must not exert yourself."

"Promise…Norah. Promise!" Abigail's fingers entwined with hers, suddenly strong in the desperate effort to get her message across.

Cora stirred on the other side of the bed, and Norah glanced up and read the command in those brown eyes. *"Lie!"* they said. *"Lie, and let the poor child die in peace."*

Norah swallowed her tears. "I shall look after Charles for you. I promise."

A wan smile lit Abigail's face and spread until her features were illumined with an unearthly glow. "Charles!" she called weakly.

"Right here." He knelt down and took Abigail in his arms as she tried to struggle up. "Rest, darling. Lie down and rest."

Abigail's fingers caught at his dark blue flannel shirt, and she rested her face against his breast, rasping with every breath. Gartner tried to lower her against the pillows, but suddenly she sat bolt upright and stared over his shoulder. Joy transformed the pallid face.

"Oh, Charles! Look… There he is…so grown up, already. Oh, he looks just like you.…" Her hand lifted, extended, as if reaching out to someone. And then, with a tiny sigh, she went slack in his embrace.

"Abigail!"

Charles caught her to his chest, pressing his face against her hair and rocking her like a child. He stared straight ahead, as if he had received a mortal wound. Norah was rooted to the floor, unable to comprehend what had happened. Cora came to her.

"It's over, child."

"No!" She stumbled to her feet and whirled to the physician, who stood silently in the shadows, weary and saddened that Death had defeated him once more.

His hands hung at his sides. "There's nothing I can do."

Norah gasped, unbelieving, then fled into the hallway. In the space of ten days she had lost the two people most dear to her. She felt neither sorrow or grief. Numb and mindless, she felt nothing at all. The doctor followed her out, with Cora at his heels. Mrs. Boyle shut the door, and the three of them stood on the upper landing, leaving Gartner to make his farewell in solitude. There was no sound from within the room. It was so quiet the tick of the clock carried clearly from the mantelpiece downstairs. No one spoke.

There was nothing to say.

26

The clouds were plump and pearly gray in the northeast sky, but the late afternoon sun still poured down on the level plains and dry arroyos of the ranch. The cook clanged the triangle with his metal spoon, and the wranglers nearby headed for the cookhouse, but Levi Hale remained seated on a rough wooden bench.

Deward, the youngster who had just signed on as a ranch hand a few days before, put aside the harness he was mending, idly scratching at the open neck of his patched blue cambric shirt. He was red-haired and fair, and his fingers left weals across the vee of peeling, sunburned skin. "Ready for your rations, Mr. Hale?"

"I believe I'll set awhile yet." Norah was out for a ride with the wagon, and he would not budge until she was home safely.

He knew it was hard for her when she had to give up riding horseback as her pregnancy advanced. She had loved the freedom it gave her. Mounted on her dapple-gray or one of her other favorites, she was anyone's equal; but on foot she was slowed by the slight hitch in her gait. These days she took the buggy instead and didn't usually go too far afield, but she'd been gone for hours now. She'd taken to going out alone lately. Sometimes she was making rounds, checking on things; other times he didn't know where she went or what she did. Once or twice in past months he had come across her accidentally— sitting on her mare as unmoving as an Indian, just looking out across the land, like a woman in a dream. He wondered what she was thinking about.

The object of his pondering was not far from the ranch house, but sheltered from view by a rounded wrinkle in the land. Just before reaching the crest, Norah brought the buggy to a halt. This was the same rise where she had first viewed her new home as Abner's bride. So much had changed since then, herself most of all.

Her gaze wandered past the outbuildings and barns and the adobe house that had been enlarged recently, pausing at the splash of brilliant green radiating out from the huge sinkhole sheltered by the sycamores. Far to the south Norah saw the little bouncing specks that would be Jessop and Randolph riding back to report to her after moving the main herd to the lower valley for fresh grazing. The rest of the men would be with the cattle, and when darkness fell Jamie Fergus would sing Scots ballads to them in his soothing baritone. She knew all the men who worked for her, by sight, by abilities and by reputation. They respected her for it and were always proper and polite; she would have been disbelieving if she were told that more than one dreamed about her on long, lonely nights.

Resting her palm over her abdomen, distended now in her eighth month of pregnancy, she spoke in her mind, in her heart, to her unborn child. *All this is for you, my little one. All this work and learning and sitting in the office late into the evening going over the books. And one day it will be yours.* The baby kicked, as if in acknowledgment, and Norah smiled. Aloud she said to it, "So impatient? You cannot be in any more of a hurry than I am!"

She was eager for the birth. Once the baby came she would have little time to brood over the past or worry about the future. To stand at the window or pause on the top of a rise and scan the horizon, searching for a slim rider on a strapping bay. Giving herself a mental shake, she snapped the reins and started homeward.

Hale lifted his head and listened: hoofbeats and wagon wheels. She was all right then, and headed for home. His posture relaxed. Deward didn't hear anything: he was eighteen and lonely and too busy just now watching the flash of Maria's eyes. She had come up behind them silently and was standing a few feet away, intent at trying to see what Hale was making.

Deward tipped his hat. "Evenin', miss. Ah…sure is a purty sunset, ain't it?" Frightened, the girl spun around and ran toward the house.

He stared after her. "Don't she never speak a'tall?"

"Not since I known her. She used to." Hale resumed his whittling.

"Mighty pretty, ain't she?"

There was no answer, and after a while Deward shoved his hands in his pants pockets and walked away, leaving Hale to his pastime and his thoughts. As Levi worked, the bit of soft wood in his big hands took on a roughly human shape, then developed arms, legs, and a smiling face. He heard the door of the adobe house open, but no one came out, and he smiled to himself. Curious as a cat, that little Maria was!

A moment later a shadow fell across him, and then she materialized at his side. He kept whittling, whistling under his breath, and she sidled closer. The carving had taken on the aspect of a smiling doll, whimsically charming for all its lack of polish. Now Hale brought out a big red bandana from the pocket of his red flannel shirt and wrapped his creation in it. He stuffed it in his shirt pocket and waited. Soon he felt a tap on his shoulder and looked up in feigned astonishment.

"Why, Maria. So quiet as you are, a body'd never know you were about! You should call out and warn a fellow; I could've jumped and whacked my fingers off. Here I'd be, nothing but a few bloody stumps, and then what would Miz Slade say?"

Maria looked at him from the corner of her eye, shyly at first, then more boldly. She pointed to his shirt pocket. "Why," he said, "what's this in my shirt?" Pulling the cloth-covered doll out, he offered it to her. "I don't have no need for this! Here, if you want it, it's yours. All you got to do is ask for it."

Her face fell, and she looked down, scuffing the toes of her boots in the dust. He relented and unwrapped his carving. "All right then, if you won't talk, how about if you give me a smile instead." He waited, but no smile was forthcoming. "Okay then, you can have it. I don't need no doll." He held it out toward her.

Maria snatched it from his hand. Once she had it in her own she turned and hurried away, looking over her shoulder just once, as if to see if Hale followed. He was still sitting on the bench. She smiled at him, a brief, blinding flash of pure joy, and then disappeared once more into the house.

Norah turned the wagon and brought it to a halt. "What did you make for her this time, Levi? She was beaming like the morning sun!"

"Nothing much. Just a sort of doll."

She took a seat beside him and slipped her hat off, letting it fall back and hang by its cord around her neck. "Maria looked as if she had been given the most wonderful gift in the world." The answer came into her mind all at once. "Do you know, I believe she has never had a doll before."

"No, nor I don't think she ever had a chance to be a kid, like any other. Her Pa should be horsewhipped first, and then skinned alive for what he done to her."

Norah nodded soberly. "I didn't know that you knew about her life before she ran away to the Sisters at Santa Magdalena."

Hale scowled. "What I don't know, I guessed. And her just a baby. Any man would be proud to have a daughter like that."

The old sadness, which had diminished over the months on the ranch, was back in his tones in full force. He stared at the horizon, seeing nothing. Norah guessed he was back somewhere in the past. She couldn't fault him: she did a lot of that herself.

"You are so good with her, Levi. You would make a wonderful father. You should have children of your own. Not," she added hastily, "that I mean to tell you your business! But you have so much patience and understanding."

He was slow to answer. "I had three kids of my own once, and the best wife a man could ever have. Now they're all gone."

She would have bitten her tongue out before willingly causing him pain. "Oh, Levi, how terrible! How you have suffered!" She babbled on, aghast and not knowing how to turn their conversation away from reminding him of his great loss. "I am so deeply sorry. Was it the cholera epidemic?"

''Not the cholera, but you might call it an illness of sorts. A sickness of the soul. Seems there were some men who didn't hold with a white woman marrying someone like me. Their way of telling us was to burn our house down. With Mattie and the kids inside it.''

Norah was stunned and sickened. She put her hand on his arm, offering wordless comfort for a tragedy too terrible to contemplate. And she had felt so sorry for herself, had been so wrapped up in her own problems! More than ever she admired Levi's patient goodness, his dignified strength. How had he survived?

He patted her hand. ''Don't fret yourself about me. I been living with it day and night for a long time now, and I keep on going. I don't even hate no more.'' A pause. ''Not much, anyway.'' He got up. ''I'll put the buggy away now.'' Climbing up on the wagon seat, he clucked softly to the horse. The only sounds in the stillness were the creak of harness and the crunching of the wheels over the ground as he drove toward the stable.

Norah turned her head away and faced the sunset. Ruby light shimmered in wide streaks across the golden blaze of sky, blurred and magnified by her tears. She grieved for Levi, her trusted foreman and friend. *Maria must remind him of his daughters*, she thought. *That is why he is so good and patient with her. What strength Levi has, to have surmounted such horror!* The stars were out when she finally rose and went into the house.

Inside, a box lantern cast amber squares over the walls and ceiling, but Maria was already in bed. The living area had been completely changed about, with new furnishings and colorful rugs and pottery, until it was hard to recall the way the room had looked before. Lighting a candle, Norah extinguished the lamp and counted her blessings. She had a home that was more than a mere roof over her head, a thriving ranch, and a precious gift of life, growing within her.

She went into her room, newly built on, and readied herself for bed. Unable to forget Levi's revelations, she lay awake for a long time before sleep came. In the small hours of the night she awakened from the baby's kicking. Something lurked in the back of her mind, and gradually it came to her. She and

Levi Hale had both suffered, and that was part of their unspoken bond. But they had another thing in common: children of mixed blood. For the first time she saw the pitfalls that awaited her son or daughter.

Throwing back the covers, she got up and crossed the room. The tiles were chilly beneath her feet, but she didn't bother to put on slippers. The square of unshuttered window looked like a piece of velvet, quilted with stars. Norah went to it and leaned against the deep sill, resting her head on her arms. Although it grew cold, she did not return to bed, but stood at the window until dawn. She convinced herself she was looking at the stars; but deep in her heart, part of her was watching the horizon for the coming of a tall, slim rider on a deep-chested bay.

The following afternoon Maria ran into the study, where Norah lay on the couch with her feet propped up. Her ankles were swollen, and the sleepless night had taken its toll of her energies: there would be no driving out today.

"What is it?"

The girl grimaced and gestured, but she was too excited to be comprehensible. Norah's head ached, and suddenly her patience snapped. "Maria, I wish you would stop the charades and *tell* me what you want!"

Maria went white, as if she had been struck, and Norah was all contrition. She swung her legs around to the floor and sat up. "I'm sorry! I'm just so...so *damnably* miserable!" The girl knelt down at her side and patted Norah's hand sympathetically, thus heaping coals of fire on her head. "For God's sake, do not kneel to me! Here, sit down beside me and forgive me my moods."

The gestures were repeated, but the only part decipherable was the one of two fingers moving like scissors toward the door, as if showing a person walking rapidly. Norah still couldn't figure it out and threw up her hands, with a wry face. "You want me to go somewhere? Oh, dear, I do not think I can move a foot off this couch today."

Maria shook her head and thumped her own chest with her forefinger. Norah blinked at her. "Oh, *you* want to go somewhere?" Rapid nods of the head indicated she had guessed correctly. "To town?" This was followed by sideways shakes of the girl's head. "All right, show me again. Slowly."

There was a repetition of the charade: hands folded in prayer, something over the head, eyes cast down, and then the fingers "walking" again. "Something on your head? Hair? A hat?" More negative shakes. "Someone *else* with something on the head? A woman?" Norah rubbed her brow. "Maria, I cannot make any sense out of this."

A sob of frustration escaped Maria, startling them both. It was the first sound of any kind she had made since the shooting. Norah took her by the shoulders, feeling the small body tremble beneath her hands. A tear rolled down the girl's cheek, leaving a wet trail, but no other sounds came out of her mouth.

Norah put her arms around Maria. "Hush, now. It is all right. Hush, hush." For a moment the girl clung to her, then pulled away. Her eyes were tear-filled and desperate. She made the gesture that represented, as far as Norah could tell, a woman with a head covering, followed by the Sign of the Cross. Everything clicked at last.

"Maria, are you telling me you want to go to Santa Magdalena, to the Sisters?" *Yes, yes!* The glossy blue-black hair shook up and down. "But why? And why now? You know I cannot travel that far?"

A shadow fell through the open doorway. Levi Hale stood there, holding his hat between his hands. His knuckles were blanched from the tightness of his grip, and his sad eyes were black with a hint of gold inside, like the obsidian stones called "Apache tears."

"It's my fault, Miz Slade."

"Yours, Levi! Why, what did you do?" She glanced from him to Maria and back again. The girl was staring at the floor, twisting her fingers together in apparent distress. But she didn't seem afraid.

"I…" He cleared his throat. "I asked Maria if she…if she'd marry with me. She's young, but she's seen more in her years than many a person my age. I love her, and I'd be right kind to her. But if she don't want me, that's the end of it." He made a soft self-deprecating laugh. "I should of known better, I suppose. But like the saying goes, there's no fool like an old fool."

Norah was too flabbergasted to speak. Maria looked up at

Hale without moving, and he took a step away. "You don't have to run away, girl. I didn't mean to scare you off. I won't be bothering you about it again. And I hope I can still be your friend. Make you trifles now and then."

He pivoted slowly and went out. Neither Maria nor Norah moved until they heard the outer door slam shut. The baby kicked Norah painfully beneath the ribs. She leaned against the leather backrest to give it more room. Her back began to ache.

"Come here, Maria." Reluctantly the girl obeyed. Her face was still pale, her eyes filled with pain. She hunched over, her knees together, arms resting along her thin thighs, and refused to look up. Once again Norah was forced to resort to questions.

"You are not afraid of Levi?" A vigorous shake of the downcast head for answer.

"I have always thought that you were fond of him, indeed that you regarded him highly." An equally vigorous nod.

"But you do not wish to marry him." Three times Maria's head shook side to side, but when she turned to Norah, there was a strange look in her eyes. There was something, Norah thought, that she was missing, something she was not seeing. Resting a hand lightly on Maria's shoulder, she held the girl's dark gaze with her own.

"I see," she said slowly, watching for the slightest flicker of response. "You look on Levi as your friend but not as a man you would want to marry." There was no response. The brown eyes were opaque to any thoughts that lurked behind. She continued, probing gently. "Well, that is understandable, Levi being so much older than you and being a man of color. I suppose that must have something to do with it."

Maria clutched at Norah's arm, vehemently denying her reasoning. She tried to speak, and her lips twisted, but once again no sound came out. She pounded her brown fist upon her thigh in frustration.

"Then why?"

For answer, Maria threw herself into Norah's arms, and wept in terrible silence. Norah patted her head and crooned sympathetically, but had no idea of how to help. Inwardly she prayed that Maria would be able to find her voice and tell what had upset her and why she had refused Levi's offer. Dr. Porter had seen only one such case before, where a young boy had recovered speech after five mute years following a fall from a horse; but he had warned that others with similar affliction never regained this faculty again.

After several minutes Maria's shuddering slowed, then ceased. She stood up, wiping the tear traces away with her fingers like a child, but her face had changed. In place of the careless gaiety and alternating shyness, her features were sharper, her eyes sadly wise. It was the face of a grown woman. An older and most unhappy one, at that.

Norah still had no solutions, but one thing was clear to her now: for a short time Maria had been able to revert to a younger emotional state, taking refuge from the past by living out the childhood she had been denied. And now Levi's proposal had shattered that false protection as if it had been a pane of frosted glass, leaving her face to face with reality. From Maria's expression, it was quite a shock.

She sniffled and wiped her nose on the corner of her apron, then left with a quiet dignity that was new to her bearing. Norah was edgy and disturbed. Without warning, the close relationships of the past months had fallen into new and uncomfortable patterns. Propping her puffy ankles up once more, she rubbed an aching spot low on her back, wondering what would be the outcome of it all.

27

Norah's fingertips caressed the amethyst brooch at the neck of her flowing apricot gown. The pin had been a favorite of Abigail's, for it had adorned her own dresses often in the past. Norah knew she would feel close to her lost friend whenever she wore it, and remember her courage.

"It was most kind of you, Charles, to bring me these. I shall always treasure them." She smiled up at the painting of Abigail hanging over the mantel. "And I will keep her portrait for you until you are settled and can send for it."

He clasped Norah's hand in his as they stood by the oak table. "Thank you for taking over the care of it for me. I trust it won't be too long before I am in permanent quarters."

Morning sun streamed through the unshuttered windows, haloing his hair, which was now completely silvered. Trim and fit in his new uniform with the major's insignia on it, he was still a splendid figure of an officer and a gentleman. He had gotten his resiliency back, but was not the same man Norah had known before. There was a different light in his blue eyes, an inward look to them, as if months of sorrow had accumulated and crystallized behind his irises. She knew it well: it was the same look Levi wore.

"Goodbye, Norah, and thank you again for everything. Take care of yourself, and don't forget to send me word."

She squeezed his hand in return, then released it. "I promise I shall. Oh, I still cannot believe you are really leaving Camp

Greenwood! I have hoped all along, quite selfishly I must admit, that you would change your mind.''

"My transfer came through more quickly than I'd anticipated. I'll be heading north in three weeks' time.''

He drew on his gloves, examining her. How tired Norah looked. And how very pregnant! She had certainly changed, in more ways than were physically obvious, since the day he'd first seen her. Her face had the same delicate bone structure and refined features, but there was a new depth of character to them. He smiled: the old Norah had been afraid of horses, afraid of shadows, probably afraid of life; the new Norah rode like a man, shot at suspicious shadows without a second thought, and reached out to life with both hands.

He almost envied her enthusiasm for it. Gartner felt too old, too hurt, too tired to make the effort himself. He had come to terms with the fact that Abigail was gone beyond his loving reach; he could not adjust to her absence. For the past months he had forced himself to continue his routine of command, but it had not been easy. He hoped sincerely that transferring to another unit would help. Even though the soldier in him was beginning to respond to the excitement of the coming campaign, Charles Gartner, the private man, wished it were possible to resign life as easily as one could resign a commission.

"I'd better be getting back to Camp Greenwood. God bless you, Norah, and keep you safe.''

"Goodbye, and God speed, Charles. Or should I say, 'Major Gartner'?''

He smiled. "I hope I'll always be 'Charles' to you.'' A horse whinnied, and he moved toward the door. "Don't bother coming outside with me. There's a wind blowing up, and you need to be off your feet.'' He cleared his throat. "Captain Newcomb will be checking on you from time to time.''

Norah bridled. "There is absolutely no need for him to do so!''

"Then show him the door.'' He knew how she felt about Newcomb. And why. He felt the same. But it was Newcomb's duty, as new Captain of Camp Greenwood's Cavalry, to see that everything was quiet in his part of the Territory. All Norah could do was to ignore him if he showed up on her doorstep.

Gartner reached up to straighten his bandana, and his wrist brushed against the pocket of his navy fireman's shirt.

"I almost forgot. I want you to have this, too." He withdrew an oval gold locket on a fine gold chain. It was half the size of a silver dollar, the cover engraved and chased with silver around an ornate *A*. "It has our portraits inside."

He opened it with his thumbnail and presented it to her. In one half, Abigail's face, only younger and fairly plump, smiled adoringly at the picture on the other half. There, a dashing Charles Gartner, hair chestnut instead of silver, mirrored her love. Norah was so moved she could not speak, and the newly promoted Major placed it into her hand. "I gave it to her for Christmas last year. I think Abigail would have wanted you to have it."

"Oh, no! I could not take it from you, dear friend." She could barely see his face through the shimmer of tears. "You have given me the picture she had taken in Greenwood Junction when the traveling man came through. And you have given me her hymn book and this amethyst brooch. You must keep this locket with you. Perhaps it will see you safely through the coming campaign."

He had already fixed it strongly in his mind that Norah was to have the locket. It cost him a struggle to come over to her point of view, but she would not be swayed. "I would not feel right keeping it, Charles. Please understand."

Replacing it in his pocket, he shook his head at her. "You are a stubborn woman, Norah. And a dear one." He reached down and embraced her, as much as was possible with her swollen belly in the way. When he stood erect his face was set in earnest lines. "A good soldier settles his affairs before going off on campaign. If ever you receive this locket by another hand, you will know that I have joined Abigail."

There was nothing to reply to this, and she accompanied him to the door without speaking. He swung up on his big gray, waved a final goodbye to her, and rode off to join his party. Norah watched until he was out of sight behind the rise.

As soon as he left the ranch behind, Gartner's thoughts turned back to Abigail. He touched the oval piece of gold in his breast pocket: some day when it didn't hurt so much, he would open it and look at her picture and touch the lock of brown hair, remembering the happy times. He sorely missed her, and missed as well the softening influence a woman could bring to an Army post. He was looking forward to the promised dinner with his cousin Libby and her General at his new headquarters with the 7th Cavalry. Libby always followed her husband to his various posts. She had been after Charles to find a wife for years, and had sent Abigail a handsome silver dish as a bride gift. His last correspondence from her had been a message of sincere sympathy upon hearing of Abigail's death. He wished his cousin and his wife had been able to meet, for he was sure they would have become fast friends.

Abigail, why did you leave me! The thought of her brought a weight of sadness down upon him, and he tried to outrace it. "Let's go!" He kicked his gray into a sudden gallop, and the rest followed his lead, wondering what devil had gotten into the Major. As the horse thundered across the open rangeland, Gartner thought of the months ahead. There would be hard fighting. A man could forget a lot if he kept busy enough.

The wind was picking up, bearing fresh and interesting scents. The gray breathed them in, nostrils flaring. Man and beast rode on, sensing adventure ahead. They slowed only when they reached a dry wash. Gartner pressed a hand to his pocket again, to be sure the locket was safe. Now he was glad Norah had insisted he keep it: he would show Libby the portrait of Abigail, and she would let him ramble on about the happy times. Yes, Libby Custer would understand. The thought was comforting.

By late afternoon Norah was uncomfortable both sitting and standing. She went into the living area and wandered about, straightening a scarlet and cream rug here, a shiny black pottery vessel there. She fussed with the arrangement of dried flowers and weeds that decked the long polished table, and rearranged the items in the large breakfront, but the strange restlessness grew as the day advanced.

Her hair, plaited into an ebony coronet, felt too heavy for her neck to support. Carefully unweaving Maria's painstaking handiwork, she reduced her coiffure to a ripple of black hanging down past her shoulders. It had taken months for her hair to grow. The new hairdo was too hot, and she finally settled on two fat braids. She hadn't worn it that way since before she had fallen ill in Endless Canyon. How long ago and far away that time seemed now; yet she had the indisputable truth of her adventures, quite literally, in front of her. Only two weeks before the baby was due. She changed into another position. It seemed that nothing she did could ease her backache.

She wished that Dr. Porter would stop by, but he was not due to check with her until the next day. Levering herself up from the wing chair in the living area, she began to pace the floor. For some reason, she felt better in motion. It was almost suppertime when Levi came in with gloomy tidings.

"We got sick cattle in the South Valley, Miz Slade. Sounds bad. Stu Whitley says it looks like it could be Texas Fever, but he's not sure yet. Thought I'd ride out there and check on it. Might be they et some Jimson weed or such like."

"Yes, of course, Levi. You must examine the herd immediately. If it's Texas Tick Fever, we will have to quarantine them from the rest of the stock." *And probably have to destroy them.* She suppressed the thought.

Levi was torn both ways. He knew a lot of cattle doctoring, and if it was plant poisoning that had them so loco, he might know a way to purge them of it; on the other hand, Miz Slade looked so round in the belly she might be ready to pop. "I don't like leaving you alone like this, Miz Slade. Everyone else's out on the range. Maybe I should stay until Deward and Maria get back from Greenwood Junction. You can't tell when a baby's going to decide to be born, my wife always said. And sure enough, two of ours come early."

He'd not spoken of his family since that one evening when he had revealed his tragic past. Norah thought it was a hopeful sign, and wondered if his suit for Maria's hand had progressed any further. Neither one had given her any indication thus far. "I shall be quite all right. Dr. Porter does not expect anything to happen for at least two more weeks. It is more important that you discover if it is the Texas Fever afflicting the stock."

"If Maria and Deward were here I'd be more easy in my mind about it." He thought she looked more tired than usual. If only there was a woman to stay with her for a while, but

Maria was in town getting a few things from Johnston's General Store.

Smiling brightly, if falsely, Norah forced herself to appear unconcerned. "I expect Maria any minute. I promise to rest until she comes home, if that will reassure you. The other option is for me to accompany you out to the valley in the wagon. And that is exactly what I shall do, unless you go out there now."

Her bluff worked. "Well, ma'am, I guess you have me hobbled! I'll go, but you rest up till Maria gets back, and if you need anything send Deward out after me."

When he was gone, she made herself a cup of tea and sipped it, resuming her pacing while she drank. She felt her back might break if she stopped walking. *Surely they will be back from Greenwood Junction soon!* But the sun was low in the sky when she heard the sound of wheels outside. Her relief was so great it surprised her, and she hastened to unlatch the door. The buggy was nowhere in sight, but a spanking black carriage with a yellow fringed top and wheels picked out in the same color rolled to a stop before the house. She had never seen it, or its driver before.

He was a ruddy-faced man of some thirty-odd years, with bleary eyes, red palms, and a nose like a wrinkled mushroom. Norah had never seen such a strange appendage before and did not recognize it as a signal of advanced alcohol disease. Despite his unprepossessing features, his buff suit was fairly new and well cut, and his boots recently polished. He did not look to be a ruffian, but she was taking no chances. Since she had not been driving out this past month, Norah had increased her daily target practice: she was an excellent shot with both pistol and rifle. The lady's special she kept near at all times was in her capacious pocket. Its range was short, but it was deadly accurate at close quarters. Slipping her hand inside, she pointed the short barrel at his heart.

He did not even bother to doff his hat or offer the customary greeting. "Mrs. Norah Slade, wife of the late Abner H. Slade?"

"Yes, I am Norah Slade." Her finger tightened on the trigger.

He thrust an envelope into her hand, not meeting her eyes. "I hereby serve you notice to quit these premises within sixty days, leaving all structures, furnishings, appliances, equipment, and stock behind for the use of their proper owner. If you are not off said premises in sixty days, you will be forcibly evicted. Any attempt to damage the structures or to remove said furnishings, appliances, equipment, and stock will result in your arrest and prosecution.''

"Are you mad? This is my property. You have obviously made an error!''

"Sixty days. It's all in here.'' Without another word he stepped down and marched back to the carriage with pompous precision.

Before he even had the vehicle turned around, she slammed the door and slid the bolt home. Norah had the distinct impression that he had enjoyed the little scene. She'd never seen him before in her life, and was completely confused. Well, the mistake was clearly his and she would not open the door to him again. Suddenly there was a spurt of warm liquid between her legs, followed by a constant trickling. At first she didn't know what had happened, then realized that her water had broken. Excitement and dismay clashed together. The baby was coming at last. And she was alone.

"Surely Maria will be back soon!'' The girl knew much about childbirth, for her mother, from what Norah could make out, had been the village midwife. There was no need for alarm. It might be hours, or even days before Norah actually gave birth. Still, someone should be aware of it.

Opening the door, she clanged the iron bell, hoping that one of the hands had stayed behind: then she could send him for Dr. Porter. There was no one about, and the bunkhouse door was closed. Manny Enriquez, who cooked for the men, might be around somewhere, but he was deaf and would not hear her summons. Although she rang the bell again, no one came in response. Her underclothes and the back of her skirts were wet. She would have to change and then go in search of Manny. He was probably sleeping in one of the outbuildings, rolled up against a pile of sacks, while his kettles simmered in the lean-to kitchen he used on warm days.

Halfway to the bedroom the first pang hit Norah. Starting at the base of her spine, it curled around to the front until her abdomen was hard as stone. The contraction was long and forceful, without the cramping overtures of milder labor. She doubled over and gasped, astonished by the violence of the pain. When it began to let up she discovered she was on her knees, hanging onto a carved chest for support. She unfolded herself slowly, barely noticing the imprint of the carvings on her right hand and inner forearm where she had grasped it.

Perhaps she should go out and find Manny first. She could always change afterward. She had not even turned around when the second contraction came, stopping her dead in her tracks. Her forehead was damp, her skin clammy, and she feared that something was very wrong. This wasn't the ripping pain she had endured with her miscarriage, but it was almost as agonizing. Norah was not made for easy childbirth, and though she tried to bear the pain, by the time it ebbed she was limp and exhausted. Many women delivered alone and without complications, but instinct warned that she was not going to be so fortunate.

This pregnancy had gone almost to term. It *couldn't* end the way her first one had. *No! Not Storm Caller's child! Please let the baby be all right. Keep it safe. Please.* The hand raised to her throat touched something tangled with the silver medal and chain Sister Thomasina had given her: the ancient turquoise talisman on its soft leather thong. Norah clung to it as if it were Storm Caller's hand she held and became calmer. No time to hunt for Manny, who might be anywhere among the outbuildings. She must prepare for the birth, and hope that Maria would return from town soon.

Reaching the bed, she grasped one of the posts to keep upright. Her gown was already laid out across the pillow. Now, if she could only get out of her wet clothes before the next contraction overwhelmed her, she would be grateful. Before she could undress she was caught in an onslaught that came in waves of pain for half an hour, leaving her weak and drained. Then, to her astonishment, they abated completely. She took off her wet clothing and donned the clean gown, listening for the sounds of Maria's return, waiting for the agony to begin again. As she folded the soiled garments paper crackled, and she removed the envelope she had completely forgotten.

Norah slit the envelope open with her finger. Inside was a notice to vacate the ranch, much as the stranger had recited aloud. It stated that one Abner Slade, late of Greenwood Junction District, Arizona Territory, had drawn up a Last Will and Testament. It was dated prior to their marriage. While her eyes stared at those words, another contraction began, and she read on with difficulty. The notice further stated that the ranch, upon Abner's death would revert to his business partner—one Mercy Michaels, of Greenwood Junction.

"Mercy Michaels!" She knew the name: according to the notice, the new owner of Norah's ranch was the foxy-haired madame of the bordello in Greenwood Junction. Norah knew the woman's perfume, too: Abner had come home enough nights reeking of it. "I'll see her in hell first!" She wadded the paper up in her hand, unaware that she had spoken aloud. Then her lower torso was clamped in the cold and implacable vise of renewed labor, and the safe delivery of her baby became Norah's only concern. She would deal with the rest of the world later.

There was no time to look for Manny now, and if she left the house, Norah feared she might be forced to deliver outside the house, lying in the dirt. It might be hours before anyone found her. Better to be alone with all the necessary accoutrements available for when the baby came. Over the next half hour, between contractions, she fetched the clean soft cloths and linen cord already prepared for the birth. Boiling water for a knife or scissors to cut the cord was out of the question, for she was unsuccessful in re-starting the kitchen fire.

At last, bathed in perspiration, she retreated to her room with a cold basin of water to wash the baby, and curled up sideways on the bed. It seemed to help when her knees were drawn up, but, Oh! how she longed for someone to rub her back. It felt as if it would crack in two along her spine. And then she was overwhelmed by a constant barrage of pains that increased progressively in intensity and duration, until she could no longer think coherently. With conscious thought abandoned, all Norah's exertions went toward the task of expelling the child from her distended womb.

Her next awareness was of the room brightening, and eyes barely focused on Maria standing in the doorway in a red skirt and her best white blouse, a lamp held high in her brown hand. The assistance she had prayed for was at hand, but now Norah was past caring. Her lips were drawn back from her teeth. She was wrapped, enfolded, cocooned in an agony that had no respite. The baby was fighting desperately to be born and Norah to push it out into the world, but something was terribly wrong, and this was all that really penetrated to her mind.

Maria placed her palm over the rock-hard abdomen and waited for it to soften as the contraction eased. It did not do so. That was not right. Lifting the damp and bloodied nightgown, she made a rapid assessment. From the experience of assisting her mother's midwifing, she realized this was a breech delivery: the baby was wedged, shoulder first, and would have to be turned. But that alone did not account for such excessive bleeding. This was nothing she could handle alone.

She patted Norah's shoulder and ran from the room and out the front door. Deward had already unhitched the team, for he was nowhere in sight. Then she saw Levi, Stu Ashley, and the Evans brothers approaching the corral. In her relief she didn't take in the evident tiredness of the men, the flagging energies of their mounts. Levi was here. He would go for the doctor, and then everything would be all right.

She caught up with him near the corral as he stripped the gear from his horse. Beast and man were weary and dust-covered. He hadn't found Texas Fever, but it was still bad. The cattle had foraged on poisonous weeds, and forty head were dead or dying, bloated up like the hot-air balloons he'd seen once at the St. Louis Fair. He didn't know how many others would be dead by morning. They'd moved the rest of that herd out to the west pasture by the light of the moon, having no other choice, and one of the Evans brothers had taken a bad fall and broken his nose and probably some ribs. Maria tapped his shoulder. Levi turned around, but his eyes were preoccupied and his usual smile missing.

He barely glanced at her. "It's late. You ought ta be asleep in your bed. Scoot on in the house. I got work still to do." Much as he loved her, Levi was in no mood for her childlike games tonight.

"I'll see her back to the house," Stu Whitley volunteered, a little too quickly. His gave Maria a look from beneath half-lowered lids, and his mouth was hungry, his smile false. She'd seen that expression on a man's face before, often enough to know what it meant: he thought she was a whore, and available.

Levi saw the look, too, and scowled. "You ain't goin' nowhere, Whitley, except to rub down this horse of mine and Shorty's pinto." He turned to the other two men. The taller one supported his brother, whose face was green with pain. "Elmer, you get Shorty inside the bunkhouse so I can doctor him up. I'll get my things."

Maria was already forgotten. He turned back to what he was doing, and her face fell as he undid the girth strap and pulled his saddle off. He didn't understand! She was too agitated think for a moment, then put both hands around his arm and tugged with all her might.

Levi hoisted his saddle over the corral rail, looked down, frowning. "Does Miz Slade know you're out here? A young woman like yourself shouldn't be out alone at night with all these men. Get yourself inside now. Go on, shoo and leave me be."

Maria wrung her hands and stared at him helplessly, and he relented. "Lookit here, I didn't mean to be rough, but it's been a worrisome day. Tomorrow, after I check out the herd, I'll carve you some more doo-dads for your necklace."

This promised treat got no response. As he picked his saddle off the rail, his thoughts were already back to the problem. Heaving the saddle onto his shoulder, he started for the tack shed, hoping no more cattle would be dead by morning. Maria stood where he had left her, twisting her fingers in the fabric of her red cotton skirt. Then she ran after him, almost hysterical in her desperation. She must make him understand, she must! She caught up with him again at the shed door and grabbed at his arm, missing it. Lunging forward unchecked, she landed in the dust.

"Now, what in tarnation...!"

Levi pulled her to her feet, and this time saw her face in the full moonlight. "What is it? What's wrong?"

Her face was contorted, eyes tear-filled. "D...d...doctor!"

"What?" An astonished grin made his teeth flash in the moonlight. For a split second he was so delighted to hear her speak that he didn't take in the meaning.

"D...doctor! *Por favor!*"

"Maria, you're talking! Well, Glory be!"

Her tongue felt thick and awkward with disuse, her throat dry and scratchy. Yet once the dam of silence was breached, a torrent of mingled Spanish and English poured out. Levi put his hands on her shoulders and steadied her. She was trembling.

"Whoa! I can't make out a word of what you're saying! Now take a deep breath and start over."

Maria did as he said, gulped, and plunged in again. "The *señora!* The baby, it is coming, but it is not right. There is too much blood, and she will die without help. *Madre Dios!* but you must fetch Doctor Porter at once."

He started for the house, concerned for Norah, but Maria ran alongside, pulling at his shirt. "There is not time. Go for the doctor at once! I will do what can be done until your return. But hurry, *undelay!*"

"All right then. You get back inside with her. *Whitley! Get out here.*" He saw the man coming out of the tack room. "Miz Slade's in trouble with the baby. You fetch and carry for Maria. Follow her orders. I'm going for the doctor."

He grabbed his saddle and bridle and whistled a fresh horse to the side of the corral. With the moon so bright, he could make good time. The animal, sensing his urgency, skittered and tried to shy away, but quieted under the touch of Levi's gentle hand. "Good boy. Steady now."

"I'm on my way." He had his saddle on a fresh horse and was riding hard for the main gates before Maria had even reached the house.

28

A new inquiry into the circumstances surrounding Abner
Slade's shooting was in progress in the refurbished dining room
of Greenwood Junction's only hotel. Norah was not recovered
enough yet to tolerate the longer ride to the Army camp, and
the site had been moved to town to accommodate her. The
participants filled the air with the murmur of voices, the shuffle
of papers, the occasional jingle of spurs or rattle of coins.
Among them was Charles Gartner, who had delayed his departure in order to give his testimony.

Colonel Boyle cleared his throat, and the room went still.
The occupants of the room became frozen in time, like the
figures in a Dutch Interior painting. *A Vermeer*, Norah thought.
All blue and ivory and gold, from the French-blue wallpaper,
newly hung, to the navy and buff uniforms of the officers. Then
a fly droned, a chair scraped on the uneven floor and everyone
sprang to life again.

Despite the setting, the proceedings had all the air and authority of a courtroom trial, and the row of uniformed men
seated along the wall added to it. Upholstered chairs had been
provided for the ladies, and both Norah and Maria had accepted
them; Mrs. Boyle, who had come along to sustain them, had
taken an upright wooden chair, however, suspecting the arm-
chairs had been conscripted from the bawdy house across the
street.

The Colonel bowed his head toward Norah. She seemed

calm, although her face was pale, and the skin seemed drawn too tightly over her bones. "I realize this is painful for you, ma'am, but I have to ask you to relate again what happened the day your late husband, Abner Slade, was shot. Realizing you have not quite recovered your strength, I will try to keep matters as brief as possible."

His formal manner intimidated her, although she knew he was only following form. It was hard to reconcile this perfunctory judicial character with the kindly and jocular Colonel Boyle who had come to Abigail's birthday party so long ago. "Thank you." Her arms tightened around the blanketed bundle cuddled against her shoulder.

Boyle nodded to the Major, who would do the actual questioning. His name was Hayword. He had a puckered mouth and belligerent eyes, so pale they were almost colorless. He looked, she thought, like something cast up by the sea, with those dead fish eyes. She did not like him.

He smiled thinly, unpleasantly. "Mrs. Slade, if will you relate *your* version—"

"I have taken back my maiden name of O'Shea, Major Hayword, as I have already told you more than once." She had had enough of his insinuations.

"Yes, yes! Now relate in your own words the events as they happened the day Sergeant LeBeau shot and killed your husband."

He could not hide his animosity toward being corrected. Norah ignored it, as she had before. He was not important. After today he would not even exist as far as she was concerned; but she did wonder how such a man had ever been placed in a position of leadership. Once again she told the story of that fateful afternoon, just as she had at the first inquiry at Camp Greenwood.

This time the outcome would have a different ending. This time she had Maria for a witness, although the girl was so apprehensive she feared her voice would vanish once again. Norah reached over and patted her hand. When Maria gave her statement, it corroborated what she had said. Major Hayword tried to frighten her to shake her testimony, and Colonel Boyle had to intervene, calling the man aside for sharply whispered discussion. Maria held her ground, although the questions and answers seemed to go on forever. When they had both given their testimony, Norah discovered she could not recall a single thing either one of them had said.

Gartner was called to give his statement next. "Then Major Gartner," Hayword said, "the body of Sergeant LeBeau was never recovered?"

"That is correct, Major."

Colonel Boyle leaned forward. "Was, in fact, the body of Sergeant LeBeau ever sighted, after he fell from the pinnacle?"

Gartner understood what Boyle meant to convey, by what was said—and by what was not. He gave his superior officer a level look. "No, sir, it was not."

Boyle eyed him back for a long moment, and Newcomb stirred slightly in the chair. His turn was coming next, and he did not look forward to it.

Boyle sat back. "That will be all, Major."

The next witness was Newcomb, who had assumed Gartner's old command as Captain at Camp Greenwood. For a moment Norah's attention wandered back to the first time she had met him, so half gauche, half gallant. She could not have guessed that he would be the one to turn her world upside down. She could hardly bear to look at him, and missed the first exchange entirely. It was the alteration of tone, when the Colonel broke into the questioning, that brought her back to the present.

"And can you explain, Captain Newcomb, why you fired after your commanding officer gave an order to hold fire?"

"R-r-reflex, sir!" His freckled face went maroon with mortification.

Boyle did not let it slip by. "In that case, perhaps you should be stationed at a desk, rather than out in the field where men's lives depend on your...*reflexes*."

The rest of the afternoon went swiftly, and by three o'clock the inquiry was over. Verdict: Roger LeBeau, late a Sergeant of Indian Scouts attached to Camp Greenwood, exonerated of the charge of murder. Tears of triumph and vindication filled Norah's eyes as Charles Gartner came to her side.

"I hope this was not too much of an ordeal for you, Norah." When she looked up, he saw her tears were not from sorrow or distress.

"No, Charles, thank you. I must ask you something. When

Colonel Boyle questioned you about...about not seeing a...a body, there was the strangest expression on your face. I have to know what you thought, Charles, when you looked down from the rocks and could not find him. Did you truly think he was dead? Did you?''

Her hand clutched his, and her pupils grew until her blue irises were only a thin rim around the black centers. He could see his reflection in them. He did not answer for a moment, and the others in the room milled about them. He spoke after careful deliberation. ''I did not want to give you any false hopes then, my dear, nor do I now.''

''Then you did have doubts that Storm—LeBeau was dead?'' Her voice was low, urgent. ''You thought he survived?''

''I didn't know for sure. I still don't. We could find no sign of him anywhere, and any other man would have been killed beyond a doubt: but LeBeau was different. He knew me well, and was aware of Newcomb's rashness. At times I have wondered if he did not plot that fall, if it was not a ruse, albeit a calculated and dangerous one.'' Norah's face was shining. ''Remember, he was already injured,'' Gartner cautioned. ''He might have escaped from us, only to die alone somewhere out there. You must be realistic.''

''No, if he got away, then he is still alive. I never believed he was dead. Never!''

Gartner remembered his own lost love. ''Perhaps it is wrong of me to say this, but I cannot keep silent: LeBeau loved you. Otherwise he would not have sent you back.'' The radiance of her face told him he had been right to speak out.

''Dear Charles! You have given me the courage I need to do what I must do.'' She bade him a warm farewell and turned to Maria. As they left the room, Newcomb tried to intercept Norah. Pale and grim-faced, he was furious at his humiliation, baffled by her coolness, and wracked by his jealousy. She swept past as if he did not exist and joined the Boyles on the boardwalk. Cora embraced Norah and the Colonel handed her into the buggy beside Maria and Levi. ''I am sorry, my dear, that we had to put you and the girl through this.''

Norah settled herself gingerly on the well-padded seat and smiled down at him. ''You had no choice, Colonel. And now everyone will know the truth about what happened. I hope you both will visit me at the ranch before your return to Camp Verde.'' Suddenly the bundle she held so possessively squirmed and gurgled. The blanket fell off to reveal plump arms and legs, and a round and alert little face.

Boyle put out a sun-speckled finger and chucked the tiny cheek. ''Again, congratulations my dear. You have a fine son.''

He stood back, and Levi snapped the reins over the horses' backs. As they pulled away, Norah looked down at her baby and smiled. Yes, he was a fine son, healthy and sturdy of limb, with black hair as fine and silky as her own. And eyes as gray as his father's. His name was Storm.

Storm O'Shea.

Spring ripened to golden summer, and still Norah found herself scanning the horizon for a tall, slim man on a bay gelding. Five months had come and gone since Maria gave her evidence and cleared his name, but there had been no further word. She had been so certain that he would return once his innocence was proved! But as each lonely day passed it was harder to fend off her doubts. Storm Caller's wounds might have proved mortal. Perhaps Charles was right in trying to prevent false hopes. Perhaps she had been living in a fool's paradise. *No! I will not think it!* Hope still burned within her soul, but it was no longer as bright or shining as it had once been.

Broadsides had been printed and distributed at her order, declaring the innocence of Sergeant R. LeBeau, late of the Indian Scouts. She had also made sure that Two Horses Racing and Snow-in-Summer were aware of it, trusting them to spread the word among their people. Norah built a new life as the weeks passed, immersing herself in raising her son, and running the ranch, busying herself with a hundred tasks, a thousand details. But in the daylight hours she hungered for news of Storm Caller, and at night she hungered for his touch. And still she loved him.

Turning away from the window one mellow August morning, she sat down at the wide desk and began going over her accounts. Despite the loss of sixty head of cattle in the fall, business was good. If only she didn't have the threat of Mercy

Michaels hanging over her, she could almost be content. Her solicitor, Jonas Coates, was pleading her case for ownership before the magistrate right now, and the thought of losing everything she had worked for made Norah's stomach knot. If she lost the ranch, how could she provide for all those who were dependent on her? There was a sudden wail from the cradle beside her, and she picked the baby up before he even had time to cry.

"Such a little piggy you are, Storm."

She laughed as he stuck one chubby fist in his mouth and tried to fit the other in beside it. As always, with the laughter, came an ache deep within her chest. If only Storm Caller could be here to share this with her! There was never a moment of joy for her that was not bittersweet with longing and the knowledge of what might have been. She wondered how Charles Gartner had learned to stand it. And *if* he had.

The housekeeper came in with a glass of milk and set it on the small table next to her. A rangy, raw-boned woman with knotted fingers and reddened hands, Mrs. Treacher was rather formidable on first acquaintance. Norah had been put off by her harsh visage until she had noticed the kindness in the mild hazel eyes.

"A glass in for every glass out, that's what's good for a nursing mother."

"Thank you, Mrs. Treacher." She dutifully drank the milk, even though she didn't care much for the beverage; but she would do anything that was good for Storm. Even eat liver. She set the glass down. "Uh, we are not having liver again for lunch, are we?"

"Nope. Stewed chicken and dumplings."

"Oh, my favorite! That will be lovely."

Mrs. Treacher picked up the glass. "And dried apple pie," she went on. "Liver'll be for supper tonight."

Norah made a face of dismay as the housekeeper left the room. Four times a week was a bit much to indulge in liver, as far as she was concerned. The breeze blew in the window, moving the heavy brown draperies. For the first time she noticed they had a red-brown cast. Liver-colored, in fact. She took them in deep dislike from that moment on, and made a mental note to order some new fabric from Johnston's General Store. Blue or yellow or soft rose, perhaps.

Unbuttoning the bodice of her pink-sprigged muslin dress, she gave the baby her breast and curled up on the leather sofa. She had recovered from her ordeal, although the loss of blood had left her feeling weak. With Maria's tender care and Mrs. Treacher's coddling and nourishing food to tempt her appetite, she felt more vigorous than ever. In fact, Maria had let out the side seams of Norah's dresses two inches at the waist, and this one still seemed a little snug.

The baby fussed and ceased nursing. She sat him upright on her lap and leaned him over one arm, patting his back until he burped. Storm's little face puckered in a frown at the sound and the sensation and Norah smiled at him. "So, it was only a burp after all! I wondered that you could be hungry again so soon."

She lifted him up and kissed his neck until he chuckled. His fingers grasped at her, catching the leather thong that hung around her throat. He took the turquoise fetish and began to gnaw on it. "Oh, are you after my necklace, little one? Well, it is really yours. I am only keeping it for you."

She tried to pull it away gently but Storm's feet kicked out and his back arched in frustration. "You want it now? Well, why did you not say so?" She slipped it over her head, and handed it to him. The small fist closed around the thong as the baby gummed the cool chunk of turquoise. The fetish was too large for him to swallow, even if it came off the thong, so she relinquished it to its rightful owner.

"I suppose this has been used for a teething child more than once before." He was too engrossed in chewing and exploring his new toy to pay her any heed. "If only your father could see you. He does not even know he has such a fine, handsome son." *If he is even still alive to know anything,* a small traitorous voice in her head whispered.

The familiar blue mood settled around her, but before it had a chance to really engulf her, Maria stuck her head around the corner of the door frame. She was very agitated, and her face was as white as the old shirtwaist of Norah's she had cut down to fit her smaller frame.

"There is a fight by the corral. Levi and Mr. Whitley."

Norah put Storm back in his cradle and followed Maria outside. Although the ranch hands had their share of disagreements, it was not like Levi to brawl with the men. She could hear shouts of encouragement as she crossed the tiled floor, and when she came out on the porch she saw a knot of men tightening around the combatants. "What in God's good name are they fighting about?"

Maria looked away. "About me." She spoke so softly the words were barely audible. "Mr. Whitley said I was a whore… and…and his money was as good as anyone's. He wanted me to do bad things, like Mercy Michaels did, and I ran away. And then Levi came."

The news was not entirely unexpected. A young and beautiful girl without the protection of a husband or father was likely to be the object of some unpleasantness on a ranch full of men. And too many of them knew about her past. If only the girl would accept Levi's offer of marriage! From what Norah had seen, his feelings were unchanged; and watching Maria over the past months, she was inclined to think they were reciprocated.

"Well, I shall put a stop to it, right now!" Picking up her skirts, Norah ran toward the corral. She didn't wait to see if Maria followed. The men were so engrossed in the fight they didn't hear her coming, but they parted readily before her sharp elbows and the scowl on her face.

Reaching the center of the gathering, Norah was just in time to see Whitley throw a hard hit to Levi's left jaw. The sound of fist striking bone was sickening. Before she could intervene, the black man recovered and slipped a blow below the other's guard. It hit Whitley in the stomach, and he buckled and fell flat. Levi hovered over him, waiting. Whitley got to his hands and knees, shaking his shaggy blond head. He staggered to his feet and waded in again. They were both stripped to the waist and covered with blood and dust. The air reeked of sweat.

Something held Norah back. This was not a matter of employer and hired hands. This was a man's fight, a personal fight, and it had to be settled on that level. She could not intervene, at least not yet. They were both large men, and appeared evenly matched, for Levi's powerful muscles and experience were offset by the other man's youth and agility. She blinked, and Whitley went down under a lightning left jab. He struggled to his feet, sides heaving with effort, blood streaming from his flattened nose and the corner of his mouth. He rose once more, was hit with a combination punch, and went sprawling on his back. There was silence from the onlookers as Whitley rolled onto his left side and curled up in a ball.

Levi hung over his adversary, poised to strike again if the other rose. His own face was battered but to a lesser extent, although the skin over his left eye was bruised and puffing up rapidly. His dark skin was wet and shiny. "You got two choices, Whitley: get back on your feet and try to kill me, or get your gear and light out."

Whitley had had enough. The words coming from between his split lips were so muffled they were unintelligible. He put up one hand as if to fend his opponent away, but Levi let his arms drop to his sides. "Get up, Whitley."

It took a while, but the beaten man finally got to his feet. "Ma'am, it 'pears I was outta line. I'd 'preciate it if you let me stay on here. There won't be no repetition. I swear it."

Maria untied the strings of her apron, then ran to Levi and dabbed at his face with a clean corner. For the first time Levi became aware of Norah's presence. Turning toward her, he waited, as if for instructions. "Miz O'Shea?"

She turned the matter back to him in a way that kept face for them both. "When I hired you on, Levi, I said I would leave any disciplinary matters to you, as long as I felt you were both honest and fair. This appears to be a personal matter between the two of you, and I will not interfere. I shall abide by your decision."

The eyes of the crowd were on the big black man now. Levi wiped his dripping forehead with the back of his arm. "You're a top hand, Whitley, and I'd hate for Miz O'Shea to lose you. If you think you can keep your mouth shut and treat the ladies proper, you can stay." He turned on the others. "And the same thing goes for the rest of you."

There was a shuffling of boots and murmurs of agreement Whitley blew his nose in his blue bandana, and it came away with spots of a deep purplish hue. "I 'pologize to the young lady. No offense, ma'am. It 'pears I didn't rightly know th circumstances. And I 'pologize to Miz O'Shea, too, for creatin' a disturbance.''

Levi held out his hand, and Whitley shook it earnestly. His bloodied face held a sheepish smile. "And it 'pears I'd best be tending this nose afore it floods the yard."

The others dispersed quietly, leaving the women alone with the foreman. Maria stood with eyes cast down until Levi strode away. Then she began to walk back toward the house. Norah ran after the girl, stopping her. When she saw the stricken look on Maria's face she finally understood.

"Is this it? The reason you would not marry Levi, I mean, and that you wanted to go to Santa Magdalena before? Because you were one of Mercy's girls?"

Her voice was bleak. "Yes. They look at me and see a whore! At the Mission it would be different. I would shave my head and put on the robes of a religious and be one of them. Here I am just a whore."

Norah shook her gently. "You know that is not true. What happened to you was not your fault. I know that, and Mrs. Treacher knows that. And so does Levi." She felt the little body go rigid. "Is that the reason? Because you think the men will look down on him for marrying you?"

The only answer she received was a spate of tears and some incoherent Spanish. Embracing the girl, Norah soothed her until she quieted. She had not pressed Levi's suit, fearing that Maria's experiences in the bordello had created a fear of men or of any sexual intimacies. Now she knew that it wasn't so. It was Maria's love for Levi and her feelings of unworthiness that had made her flee his proposal.

"Maria, look at me." Norah lifted the girl's chin, forcing her to gaze upward. "Did Levi handle the situation?" The girl nodded. "Then what are you afraid of?"

"*Señora*, he cannot fight all the men in the Territory for me."

"He would, if necessary. But after today's work, I would be astounded if he had to fight even one!"

She hugged Maria and saw Levi standing a few feet away. He had washed the blood from his face and put on a clean shirt. Slowly he came toward them. "It don't matter to me, Maria. I'd fight the whole world if it would make you happy."

The girl bent her head. She was trembling so violently her teeth rattled. Giving Levi an encouraging nod, Norah waited until he stood beside them, then gave Maria up into his care. His arms wound around her small shoulders, and the girl sighed, losing the will to continue fighting against what she wanted more than anything on earth.

Norah left them like that and blinked away a sudden brightness. She would have to get together and arrange a wedding feast with Mrs. Treacher and Manny. Her head was filled with ideas. She would give Maria that new bolt of silk for a wedding dress. Father Ildephonso would do the honors, and they could have the wedding here at the ranch. Or perhaps Maria and Levi would like to be wed in the church at Santa Magdalena. The rest of the afternoon she made lists and rummaged through trunks and boxes for ribbons and trims and other furbelows.

It was good to know that some love stories worked out happily.

The air smelled of blood and leather, horse droppings and the sweat of men. This isolated band of warriors was one of the remnants of the combined Kiowa-Comanche camp in Palo Duro Canyon. Since the soldiers, under the command of Colonel Ranald Mackenzie, had slaughtered all their horses and mules—well over two thousand of them—in the raid upon the canyon in September, their organized resistance had crumbled. Without their horses, the "god dogs," their primary means of barter and profit, the old way of life was impossible. The present mounts of this group consisted of three stolen Cavalry horses and two much less impressive beasts confiscated from a sleeping farmer after last night's skirmish.

The raw remains of a small skinned animal clung to a few gnawed bones. They had built no fire for fear of drawing down the horse soldiers upon them. A young man with a scarred lip and hunted eyes rose and disposed of what was left in a shallow hole beneath a flat rock. When he returned one of the braves huddled over their wounded comrade. Without any hurry, he made for them and hunkered down.

"Will he live?" If he could not travel by morning they would have to leave him when they went to rejoin their scattered brothers at the appointed place: taking him along in his present condition would endanger everyone.

The other one glanced at the improvised bandages that covered the injured man's head and chest and shoulder, then reached down and lifted the closed lids. Eyes gray as the evening sky looked back at him without seeing.

"I do not know," the older brave said after a pause. "I think he will soon join his ancestors. But he is tough, this one, like buffalo hide. Perhaps he will surprise us. One thing is certain: whether he lives or dies, tomorrow we move on."

29

Jonas Coates sighed heavily. "I did the best I could, Miz O'Shea, but there was no getting around that will. Not with Mercy Michaels holding the deed. Her petition's been upheld by the court. She owns this place, lock, stock and barrel."

Norah sank back in her chair, too stunned for words. Against the stark navy of her dress, her skin was as delicately pale as the inside of a seashell. All the work she and Levi and the men had put into building the ranch was effort wasted. Except for her mare and few personal possessions, she would have nothing. Mercy owned it all.

The solicitor checked the time on his gold turnip watch. "There's still a chance. I've filed an appeal, and her hands are tied until we know the outcome," he said, shrugging on his blue coat. "But until we get the court to issue a temporary injunction against them, you won't be able to sell any stock. Or withdraw any cash assets from the bank."

Roused by anger from her torpor, Norah slammed her fist against the leather desktop. The china inkstand danced, spraying black dots across the green blotter and along one of her white cuffs. "How can I meet my payroll? I cannot expect the hands to stay on under those circumstances. And they are getting ready to drive the cattle north before the bad weather hits the plains. My God, this could ruin us!"

Coates cleared his throat. "Mrs. O'Shea, I'll be frank with you. I think that's just what Merc—er, Miss Michaels wants."

He frowned. "In fact, I doubt she gives a good goddamn about owning the ranch—pardon my French, ma'am. I think she's doing this to spite you."

Norah was incredulous. "Spite me? That's ridiculous. I've never even met the woman. What have I ever done to hurt her in any way?"

"Of course I can't speak for her, but…" His voice trailed off as discretion overcame him. "Just a feeling I have, but I still think she's doing it for spite."

As he took his leave, Norah's mind was in total confusion. Evidently he thought she knew whatever it was that he referred to, but she was completely in the dark. Perhaps she could question Maria, although she hated to remind her of the hateful time in her life when she had had been sold into the bordello. No, best to drop it.

But she found she couldn't. For Storm's sake.

As the day passed she kept returning to Jonas Coates's odd words. Soon a plan began to form in her mind. There were many preparations to make for the coming wedding, and Mrs. Treacher discovered worms in the cornmeal and the fact that she had forgotten to order molasses. Since Norah was driving into Greenwood Junction in the morning, she would make one more stop in addition to the general store.

Early the next morning Norah dressed in her best driving gown of pale blue twill with military frogging along the high collar, down the front and edging the sleeves. Adding a wide hat of bleached straw for protection from the sun, and Abigail's amethyst brooch for luck, she was soon ready. The natty effect of this outfit was somewhat altered by the cradleboard she slung over her back. Snow-in-Summer had given it to her, and she found it wonderfully convenient: because she was breast feeding Storm, she could not go far afield without bringing him along. The cradleboard was the perfect solution for long rides or even tasks demanding both hands. Storm loved it.

She would rather have done without a companion, but young Deward had a tooth that needed to be drawn, and he refused to let any of the ranch hands remove it since there was a surgeon in town to perform the service. *At least it's not Levi coming along,* she thought gratefully. *I doubt that he would approve of this expedition.* All was readied, and as Norah took the reins and started the team, she called back to Storm, who drowsed in in the cradleboard: "Hang on, little man!"

"Yes, ma'am!" Deward answered, and blushed till his face was the same reddish shade as his hair. Norah was still inwardly chuckling about this when they arrived in Greenwood Junction.

The town had grown since her last visit. Two of the stores sported brown paint over their splintered fronts, and a new building of bricks brought in by muletrain was going up at one end of the main street. It appeared to be a bank. The greatest change was at the opposite end, where a small white church waited for its unfinished steeple. The saloon had enlarged its quarters, the seedy hotel now boasted a new sign with gilt lettering, and an adobe addition next to the general store held a stark sign: JAILHOUSE. For good or ill, civilization was coming to Greenwood Junction.

Letting Deward off in front of the candy-striped pole, Norah continued toward the general store. When she dismounted from the wagon, however, she headed the opposite way down the warped boardwalk. Her heart beat time with her footsteps, and she wondered if she was being wise and humble, or proud and foolish. By the time she reached her destination the morning's coffee was burning a hole in her stomach, and there were two dark semicircles of dampness under her arms.

She stripped off her gloves, removed the cradleboard, and took the sleeping baby in her arms. His dark lashes cast shadows on his rosy cheeks, and his determined little chin rested on one fist. She pressed a kiss upon his forehead. How sweet he smelled. How infinitely precious he was! She could brave anything for his sake. With a deep breath and a silent prayer, she pushed the carved oak door open, and stepped inside Mercy Michaels's house of ill repute.

A miasma of bad perfume and cheap cigars almost sent her back out into the street, as did the darkness of the entry hall. A massive mirrored sideboard stood against the far wall next to the staircase and the crystals of an unlit chandelier glinted dimly overhead. To the right was an open room, brightly lighted, and filled with overstuffed chairs and sofas of amber velvet in carved frames. Shrieks of laughter sounded, but no one was visible from her vantage point. Norah stared with great curiosity at the gilded picture frames containing opulent women in various stages of partial and complete undress. If these were purported to be works of art, they were the worst examples she had ever seen. Velasquez's Venus had nothing to fear from them.

"You the new whorehouse inspector or something?" A saucy girl with straw for hair lounged against the banister, staring at Norah. The tops of her breasts were exposed by the neckline of the cheap wrapper she wore.

Norah's words got tangled on her vocal cords, and she had to cough to free them. "I beg your pardon. I did not mean to be rude, but I have never been in a bord—a place like this before."

The girl eyed her. "Didn't 'spect you had." She came down the stairs with a leisurely tread. "An' it's not a 'bord.' It's a whorehouse. In case ya didn't know."

"Oh! Yes, I did know." *Oh, God! What am I doing here?*

The girl reached the landing. "Lookin' fer work? Lot's of action around here lately, if you know what I mean. I could use a break now and then."

"Ah, no. I am looking for Miss Michaels."

The prostitute ignored her answer. "Whatcher got in that bundle?" She put out a none too clean finger, and Norah jumped back, clasping her precious burden more tightly.

"I believe I have changed my mind.... I shall..."

"You'll think what, Mrs. High-And-Mighty Slade!" The harsh whiskey voice came from behind, and Norah turned toward it. Mercy Michaels stood in a curtained archway, in a red negligee trimmed with an excess of feathers. Her bosom sagged without the benefit of her boned corsets, and her face was sallow and puffy. "You too good to talk to little Lucy here?"

As she stepped through the arch, light from the room behind spilled out. Mercy saw that Norah held a child. For a moment she froze. "In here." The voice was altered, but still defiant.

Holding her head high, Norah followed Mercy into the room, knowing she had to fight with the only weapon she had left. Although it was noon, the drapes of apple green were pulled across the windows, and the light was furnished by several painted globe lamps placed about the room. It took a moment to register that this was furnished quite differently from the entryway and the other room she had briefly glimpsed: straight-backed chairs, tables decorously swathed in a long cloth to conceal its "limbs"; two time-dulled portraits, a man and a woman in old-fashioned apparel; and a curio cabinet containing china cups, souvenir dishes and, strangely out of place, a child's wooden toy.

The furnishings and accessories looked like family heir-looms, perhaps not of the best quality, but well cared for over the years. There was even a crocheted tea cosy on the pot residing on a small cherrywood table and a Bible on the dark oak desk. The entire room seemed to have been lifted from an Ohio farmhouse or a cottage in some small town. It was com-pletely incongruous inside a bordello, and only ingrained po-liteness kept Norah from making some comment.

There was a door hidden behind the curtains, and Mercy shut it now. She examined Norah from head to toe, brown eyes like small glass beads in her doughy face. "Aren't we the fancy lady, though!" she said in exaggerated tones. "What brings such a fine lady to my *whorehouse*, eh?"

Norah relaxed her hold on the baby, and the light blanket fell away, revealing a chubby hand and arm. Mercy's face con-torted with hate. She shot Norah a look of cruel satisfaction. "I know why you're here. You've come to beg for your brat. I'm right, aren't I?"

Norah adopted the same posture an ancestress of hers had worn after the Battle of Boyne. Head proudly up, blue eyes open and clear, she faced her adversary. "Yes. He is too young, you see, to plead for himself, so I have come to talk to you instead. I do not know how you induced Abner to sign that deed, and I don't care to. But we do both know that the ranch and all the holdings rightfully belong to me, as Abner's wife."

"Did you really think I'd fall for your sentimental guff?" Mercy poured herself a shot of whiskey and downed it in one practiced motion. "I can't believe your gall!"

"And I cannot believe yours! I do not understand your rea-sons for wanting to punish me. I have never done anything to you, and neither has this innocent child."

Mercy took another drink. "Never done anything to me? When you're living in the house that was going to be mine? When you married the man I wanted to marry?" Norah shook her head in disbelief as Mercy came forward. "Abner never told you, did he? That bastard! Before you came out here he promised to marry me! He promised, and all the time he was writing you love letters and making arrangements to marry you instead. Because *you* were a *lady!*"

Norah was flabbergasted. She remembered those nights when Abner had returned home, his clothes carrying the scent of cheap perfume. The same distinctive perfume that wafted from Mercy Michaels's body. "You…you were in love with Abner?"

Mercy laughed, a harsh grating sound. "In love? Hell, no! I knew him too well. But I wanted to get out of this business. Make a new life. I'm thirty-five years old."

This revelation was almost as great a shock as the first one: Norah thought Mercy looked fifty. She watched the woman's face twist into ugly lines, then realized that Mercy was trying not to cry.

"I'm thirty-five years old," the thin lips whined. "And I've never been married. I'm tired. I want to be respectable. I want a nice house, and I want kids before it's too late. If you're successful enough out here, people forget where you started out. We could've done it, Abner and me. But the sonofabitch cheated me out of it all."

She wiped at her face. "I had a kid once, but he didn't live. But if you hadn't come along, that baby you're holding could have been mine! It would have been me that had Abner's child."

Revulsion and pity filled Norah. She couldn't let Mercy go on believing what was not true. "No, Storm is not Abner's child. Abner did not father my son." Norah knew she'd ruined any chance of keeping the ranch. She waited for Mercy to fling her patent infidelity into her face, to call her as much a whore as any woman under the bordello's roof.

"What? Not Abner's?" Mercy began to laugh again. "*Not Abner's brat?*"

Without replying, Norah tried to slip past her, but Mercy caught her arm and dragged her to the window. She was a large woman, and strong: Norah was impelled to go with her. Pulling back the drapery, Mercy let the sunlight stream across Storm's face. His hair was blue-black, straight as an Indian's, his eyes a clear gray in the instant before he shut them tightly and began to fuss.

Norah handed him the fetish to chew on. "Hush, my darling. It is all right." She faced Mercy. "Now that you have seen for yourself, I shall be on my way."

The other woman wasn't listening. "I know that bit of turquoise. I saw it on someone: *Sergeant LeBeau!*" She was filled with triumph. "And that black hair and gray eyes! This is LeBeau's kid, or I don't know my own name. Seems some of the stories I heard were true. What a joke on Abner! His sweet little wife, his proper Boston lady brought a cuckoo into the fine nest he built for her!" A wild burst of laughter trilled from her, frightening Storm. She laughed until her nose was red, and her tears formed dirty runnels through the rice powder layer that covered her raddled cheeks.

Norah held Storm close and stroked his back, trying to push past Mercy at the same time. Mercy blocked the way. "Don't look so scared, I'm not going to hurt the kid. In fact, I'm going to give him a present! Just wait one minute."

Mercy rummaged in a leather-bound box atop the desk and removed a folded sheet of paper. Picking up a fancy green-plumed pen, she dipped the nib in ink and wrote something. When she finished her face was beaming with secret satisfaction. "What's the kid's name?"

"Storm. Storm O'Shea." The abrupt alteration in the other completely bewildered her.

Mercy made another notation on the paper, then sprinkled sand over it and shook it off. She held it out to Norah. "For the kid," she said. "With my compliments."

Norah was amazed. It was the original deed, now signed over to Storm O'Shea. "I do not understand..."

"Don't you? Well, think on it, and it will come to you." She hurried to the door. "Have a seat while I get dressed. We'll just step across the way to Judge Morgan's and get the deed transfer registered, all right and tight."

Mercy exited, smirking to herself, and was back in record time. She ushered Norah out onto the boardwalk, and the strange procession made its way before the amazed eyes of Greenwood Junction. When the change was duly recorded, she escorted Norah back to the wagon. Deward was just coming out of the surgeon's, pressing a poultice to his jaw. His mouth dropped open as Norah took the madame's hand in hers.

"Thank you for your generosity. I do not know what caused you to change your mind, but I most sincerely thank you!"

Mercy gave her a keen look. "Don't you? Hell, I'm not being generous. I don't need the money, and I guess I'm too old to take up ranching! I'm just getting back at the bastard for all he did to me! He used to talk about building an empire for his son to inherit some day. *His* son." She cackled maliciously. "It's a pretty funny trick of Fate, don't you think. Abner's ranch, everything he was proudest of, going to some kid that's not even his!" She went away in wicked glee, leaving Norah to ponder the strange turn of events.

On the long drive home poor Deward was in no mood for conversation. Although she felt sorry for him, that was all well and good for Norah. Now that the future of the ranch had been settled for Storm, she could turn her thoughts to other matters. To Storm Caller.

That night she thought she saw him. Looking out her bedroom window, she spotted a horse and rider silhouetted against the twilight sky, just as she had the night he abducted her. How long ago that seemed now! Caution kept her joy in check: if she called out to him, someone might send up an alarm, thinking an Indian attack was imminent. Without even stopping to grab a shawl against the evening chill, she dashed outside, limping a little on her injured leg.

He was gone. The horizon was unbroken as far as she could see. No horse, no rider. No end to the terrible longing. A deep ache began in her breast, spreading outward to her limbs. Was her mind playing tricks on her? Did she love him so much she had conjured his image from nothing more than her own loneliness? No, she knew every line and angle of his body, the tilt of his head, the way he sat a horse. He had been there on the ridge watching, but had not approached the house. Why? Abner was dead. There was no reason for Storm Caller to avoid meeting with her.

Unless he didn't care. Unless it was nothing more than curiosity that had brought him to the ranch. Her stomach gave a lurch. There was only one way to find out. She thought she knew where Storm Caller would go, and made a firm decision.

She had waited long enough. Very well: if he would not come to her, then she would go to him.

"I know he will be there," Norah insisted. "I am certain of it."

"You can't go alone," Levi protested. "We'll get up a party and escort you there."

She shook her head. "No, you and Maria have been married only three days. You need to be with one another, and I need you here to run things. I do not know how long I will be gone. I have sent word to my friends, Two Horses Racing and Snow-in-Summer at Camp Greenwood. They know where the cavern is, and they will take me there."

For all her brave words, Norah had nearly as much trouble convincing them as she did Levi and Maria. Two Horses Racing and Snow-in-Summer tried to dissuade her, but eventually came around to her way of thinking: he because he had heard Storm Caller was in the area, although no one knew exactly where, and she because she knew of Norah's deep and abiding love. Happy with her own husband and son, Snow-in-Summer could not bear that Norah and Storm Caller were not yet united. Maria felt the same. Mrs. Treacher threw her hands up in horror and took to her bed with a severe bout of dyspepsia. Norah would not be gainsaid.

On the appointed day Norah met them, dressed in buckskins and moccasins, with her hair in braids and Storm tucked safely in his cradleboard. She had brought the light supplies they instructed her to take on the journey neatly packed on Wind Dancer, and Two Horses nodded his approval. "You will make a good squaw yet."

It was the first time he had directed any personal remark toward her, and Norah was pleased at his acceptance. By nightfall they had covered considerable ground. Storm took the journey in stride, as did Face-of-Old-Man, the son of Norah's companions. At first she disliked the poor child's name, milk name though it was: but when he screwed up his face and peered at her like a wizened old man, she saw the aptness of his title. Perhaps he would outgrow it soon and gain a better one.

At the end of the second day Norah thought some of the

terrain looked familiar, but she could not have found her way unescorted. Once they neared Endless Canyon she recognized each landmark, every rock and tree. She was as brown as one of the People, and in her doeskin garments, could be taken for an Indian. Hours of riding the ranch had toughened her, increased her endurance. Snow-in-Summer was pleased. Braves-the-Water would adapt well to this life, she thought, forgetting the ranch and house and the herds of cattle her friend had left behind.

They made camp at the same spot where they had rested the first day on the way from Endless Canyon to Camp Greenwood. How long ago that seemed to Norah as she wrapped herself and the baby in her blanket for the night. She was healthily tired from the day's riding, but could not sleep as unwanted doubts crept into her mind and nibbled at her assurance. What if Storm Caller had taken another woman? What if he didn't want to see her? What if this, and that? But surely he would want to see her. Surely he would want to see his son. Wouldn't he? Then why was he hiding away? She was up before dawn, boiling the coffee grounds over an open fire, even though she had no need for such a stimulant today. She could not eat anything at all.

It took forever for the sun to come over the distant ridge, longer for her companions to get ready to depart. When she nursed Storm, she sang softly to him. "Soon, my little one, soon you shall see your father. Soon, little one, soon we shall be together."

The sun crested in the bright silver sky when they reached the approach to Endless Canyon. Norah dismounted. "I will go alone from here."

"Leave your sweet baby with me," Snow-in-Summer urged for the tenth time that day. "I have enough milk for both our sons."

"Storm will be safe with me. I know the way. I can do it." Checking her knife, strips of dried food, and canteens, she set forth. Since she was breast-feeding, she would need extra water to avoid dehydration.

Despite her slight limp, Norah had no difficulty covering the uneven terrain. She had long learned to compensate for it. Her limbs were trembling with released adrenaline when she entered the narrow defile and began her journey. It was over an hour before the way opened up before her. There, just as she remembered, was the way down to the first plateau. When she reached it, she would turn right for the ascent to the cavern. It was all mapped out in her head.

Stopping once to suckle the baby, she took a few sips of water and chewed a bit of the tough, salted meat. Here was Old Woman Rock, over there the place where she had almost fallen to her death. Higher along was the protected spot where they had often made love, and beyond that the ledge where Travis and Cut Face had plotted against her. The closer she got to the cavern the more time receded, until it seemed that only yesterday she had left this place. Living proof that this was an illusion slept peacefully in his cradleboard as she made her way up.

And then she was over the ridge, and the ladder stood propped against the limestone lip while the great maw of the cavern arched overhead. The moment she had both dreaded and longed for was at hand. If Storm Caller was not there, if there were no signs of his presence, she would have to turn back and acknowledge defeat. Grasping the ladder, Norah pulled herself up the first rung, then the next and the next until she reached the top. No voice challenged her. No form barred her entrance. She stepped inside, felt the emptiness beneath the soaring stone roof, and could have wept in disappointment. All the hopes and dreams she had nurtured so tenderly shriveled and died.

Storm Caller was not there.

She felt like dying. If she tried hard enough she could stop the beating of her heart, make her lungs go still, blot out the empty future that stretched out in her mind. She had been so sure, so very sure! The baby made a cooing sound, and Norah was startled. How could she have forgotten him, even for an instant? Perhaps Storm Caller had been here earlier. She began to search for signs. Well-hidden beneath a broken slab of rock, she found a half-full jar of water and food stores. Further exploration turned up an old hide robe. There were streaks of dried blood inside it, and a buckskin shirt. Someone had been living in the cavern. Recently.

She sat down to wait.

30

The man climbed up the rickety ladder to the cavern, slowly because of the ache in his side. The long wound that ran from shoulder to hip had festered badly; and though it was clean now, the edges finally proximating, the pain persisted. The saber had cut deeply through the muscles of the chest wall, nicking his ribs and bruising the lung beneath. Progress was so gradual he hardly noticed it from day to day, only from week to week.

He was tired when he reached the top. It was a long way up from the river, carrying the heavy jug of water and the heavier load of memories. Behind him the sky was lavender shading to mauve and glazed with golden light. He was unaware of it, just as he was unaware of so much lately. It was better not to think or feel.

Standing in the last patch of sunlight, he caught his side, damning the pain, suddenly angered at his lack of strength, the slow recovery. It was the first emotion he'd felt in weeks. And yet, he thought, what was his hurry? He had no dreams, no plans. No future. All the rivers of his mind ran backward, emptying into the sea of the past, where he had known who he was and what he was. And why.

No warning bells went off, no sense of danger threatened, yet as he moved close beneath the massive stone arch, a sixth sense alerted him to another presence. It was nothing he saw or heard, rather the impression that he was no longer alone.

His eyes adjusted to the dimness, and he saw a female outline to the left of the entrance, a short distance away. A ghost spirit of the Ancient Ones? Without thinking he reached for the turquoise talisman that used to hang around his neck, then remembered he had given it away.

She rose and came toward him, her voice soft and low. "I knew you would come here sooner or later. I knew this is where I would find you."

Not a ghost from Ancient times, but one from his own past. Or else he had gone mad. "Norah?"

It had been so long since he had spoken that his voice sounded rusty in his ears. As she drew nearer the sun touched her face, making her eyes glow a clear luminous turquoise against her tanned skin. Pieces of Sky. He looked for the talisman he had given her, here in this mystical place so many months ago. It was not there. Only a thin silver chain with an oval religious medal. Its absence should not have mattered to him so much, but it did. Perhaps she did not want any reminders of the time she had been his captive, he thought dully. And why should she? He had used her as ill as Slade had. But then why was she here? Perhaps he was in a delirium. He put a hand to his temple to steady the whirling of his thoughts.

Norah advanced softly until only a foot separated them. This was no figment of his fevered mind. He saw that she was older, with the mature ripeness of womanhood. And more beautiful than he remembered. He could not fully comprehend her presence. "What are you doing here?"

She tilted her head up and faced Storm Caller with a slight smile at the corners of her mouth. "I waited for you to come for me. You did not, and so I came to you."

Reaching up, she touched his face, letting her fingers caress the tired lines of his mouth. She could barely contain the love that welled and fountained within her. "They told me you were dead, but I never believed them."

His hand came up, against his will to cover hers. For a moment he weakened, feeling the smoothness of her skin against his cheek, the warmth of it against his palm. Then he let go and stepped away. "That is what I meant them to think so they would give up the pursuit."

"They have, but for another reason. Your name has bee

cleared and all charges against you dropped. I was afraid the
news of this had never reached you. Is that why you kept away
so long?''

His face hardened until it was cool, impersonal. "No. I never
intended to come back at all."

Norah felt a growing coldness in the pit of her stomach. Her
love for him was so great she had thought it would be enough
for the two of them, that it didn't matter if his feelings did not
mirror her own, as long as he wanted her. Now, in the face of
his indifference, it seemed that she had been terribly mistaken.
If he didn't want her, nothing she offered could change his
mind. The sense of purpose that had driven her from her home,
sustained her on the journey flew away, leaving her confidence
badly shaken. *I never intended to come back at all.*

He swung toward her. "You should not have come here."
"Why?"

It was not a question but a demand in payment for all the
anxious days, the nights spent alone, thinking of him and of
this moment, that had suddenly gone all wrong. This was not
the way it was supposed to be. She had imagined it a thousand
times: the way they would run to one another, the feeling of
his arms winding around her, the beating of his heart beneath
her cheek as they embraced. And then the outpouring of their
mutual need, the overwhelming rhapsody of the senses, the
cataclysmic union and the gentle, loving aftermath.

She inched closer to him, her fists knotted at her sides. "For
God's sake, why?" Her voice was husky with feeling. "You
owe me that, Storm Caller."

Hearing his name on her lips again was as much a shock as
seeing her had been. He had been a nameless being for a long
time, and had convinced himself he had no emotions left. That
was the only way to exist without pain. Now Norah was calling
him back to life, a reluctant Lazarus unwilling to face the pen-
alties of returning. Storm Caller looked past her shoulder with
the face of a stranger, out over the anthracite depths of the
canyon, as the sun sank behind the western buttes. His eyes
were as black as the encroaching shadows in the fading light
as he fought the sound of her voice, the pull of her nearness.

Norah waited in the oppressive silence. It wrapped around
her like dark felt, smothering her certainty. She was badly

shaken. She had gambled everything on this moment. From the first they had shared an unspoken attraction and later, even when they quarreled and fought, they had always been able to come together in the fulfillment of passion. She had counted on that factor to work for her, to smooth the way into Storm Caller's arms. She was frightened now, and wanted him to hold her and banish her fears. Instead he walked out on the ledge and leaned wearily against the wall of rock.

Norah followed at a wary distance. His scent came to her on the shifting breeze: pine, leather, man, and the subtle something that was his alone. She closed her eyes as a hundred intimate memories battered her senses, assaulting them until she felt bruised and aching.

Storm Caller peered out into the gathering dusk. What could he say to sever the cords that bounds them, one to the other? He half turned, so that his face was in profile against the starry sky. "LeBeau is dead. I told you that long ago. And now, so is Storm Caller. I am a husk, a shell that walks and talks but does not think or feel. I have no heart in me. No soul. I have no place among the living or the dead, and so I will live out my days here, in the old ways. Alone."

Norah moved closer, so that she could feel his breath ruffling the hair on the top of her head. She had to reach out to him, break through the barrier of ice that imprisoned him. She could not bear to hear the sorrow in his voice, to see the bitter set of his lips. "I would go back to that life with you now. If you will let me."

"No. It is not possible."

"Yes, it is! I am strong now, healthy and strong. I ride for hours about the ranch. Why, even when I was—" She caught herself in time. Not yet. He wasn't listening.

"The old ways are gone forever." Like Elk Dancer, who had joined her ancestors while he was gone. Like the buffalo that had provided food and shelter for his people since the beginning of time. Like the horses and mules, their wealth and transportation, their means of trade, slaughtered by Ranald Mackenzie's Cavalry in Palo Duro Canyon. He had stood there at Quanah Parker's side as they surveyed the carnage. They would fight on; but they knew their cause had received its death blow. Soon they would have to surrender or be annihilated. He eyes stung now as they had then. "That world no longer exists."

Norah rested her fingers lightly on his arm. Her retort was swift and sure. "We can build a new one. Together."

With a surge of hope she saw emotions flash briefly across his face: regret and wistfulness, a barely acknowledged longing. He had insulated himself from his feelings; if only she could break through to him! She was rendered temporarily speechless by a physical desire that had nothing to do with lust, and everything to do with love.

She wanted to hold him, to embrace him, to give herself up utterly. Her hands slid up to rest against his chest, feeling his ribs, and she was shocked at how thin he was. Muscles rippled beneath his buckskin shirt, and a tremor ran through his frame. His hands tightened on her shoulders and his chest rose and fell in a faster rhythm. Now was the time to abandon all pride, to make herself vulnerable. Remembering Abigail's words about love and pride, she found the courage she needed.

"I love you, Storm Caller. I have loved you, I think, from the first moment we met, and I will go on loving you until my last breath."

There, it was out: she could not look at his face. She was afraid to do so. Afraid of what she might not see.

He stared at her, emotions long suppressed flickering across his features. "You cannot know what you are saying! I abducted you, stole you away from your home and husband, forced you to live with me, to sleep with me. Because of me you lost the child you carried, and more than once you almost lost your life."

Norah took his hand and caught it to her lips, kissing his fingers. "You do not understand: had I known who you were when you came for me, had you asked me to go with you, I would have gone willingly." Her eyes met his. "When you sent me away, I thought I would die. I wanted to. I will not leave alone again."

He caught her face between the callused palms of his hands and held it. "There is no way to make it work, Norah, and we must both face it. I have walked in both worlds, and now I belong to neither. There is nothing left for me in either."

"No! You are wrong. More wrong than you know." She

could not tell him of the child, born of their love: the time was not ripe. Leaning her head against his chest, Norah felt his arms tighten instinctively. "I belong here with you. Here, or somewhere else, it does not matter to me! We can go back to the ranch, or we can stay in the canyon. I can make a life anywhere, as long as it is with you. If you send me away a hundred times, I will come back a hundred times!"

He shook his head in wonder. Who was this fierce little woman who could call his name and bring him back from the dead? He could no longer lie to himself: she was the woman he loved, and would continue to love until his last breath. But there was nothing for them here. Looking down at her dearly beloved face, Storm Caller found his answer. His index finger trailed along her cheek and the line of her jaw. She had already given up so much for him, yet she was willing to sacrifice more. And he had taken and taken. It was time he learned to give something back.

"I will return with you, Norah. We will begin again and make a life for ourselves. Together."

Her breath came out slowly as she searched his face. She knew how difficult it would be for Storm Caller to return and face the world that had rejected and betrayed him at every turn. "I am not asking it of you. Whatever choice you make, must be of your own free will."

"For you, with you, I can brave anything."

His lips whispered against her cheek, her temple. His mouth came down on hers, and her arms twined around his neck. He kissed her again with hungry desperation, as if he could draw some of her life and faith into himself. Norah's tears were wet against his cheeks, cleansing the old hurts away.

When the kiss ended there was no doubt in her mind, only joy. She tilted her head back and smiled wisely. "You love me."

"More than my life!"

She searched his eyes again and was contented with what she saw there. "Why did you send me away?"

"I had to! I found myself guilty of so much, where you were concerned. Guilty of almost killing the only woman I have ever loved. I could not live with that."

She wiggled closer, until her body pressed against

warmth of his, and slipped her arms around his waist. Was it possible to die of happiness?

He crushed her against him, forgetting his wound. Their mouths met, touched, opened to one another as they sought to make up for the lost months, the empty nights of their separation. His hand lifted the edge of her shirt and caught fire from the heat of her skin. "My love, my Norah."

She lost herself in his embrace, letting him pull the shirt up and off, and before she knew it they were on the ground. He worked quickly, methodically until they were both naked in the twilight glow, and she reveled in the feel of his flesh on hers. "There's something I have to tell you," she began.

"Later." He kissed her deeply, thoroughly, and she forgot what she wanted to say.

Stroking her breasts, his thumb caught in the silver chain that dangled between them. Kissing the silky skin beneath the collarbone, he felt her fingers twine in his hair, guiding him to her breast. Excitement coiled inside his loins as he caressed it with his fingertips. It was full to his cupped palm, satiny to his mouth. He sought the tip but delayed the conquest, letting his hot breath flow over its crest. His tongue ran a tingling circle around the peak and then he gathered it into his mouth, closing upon its sweetness.

His lips tugged gently, and suddenly warm liquid filled his mouth. He sat up in surprise, and Norah laughed aloud. The look on his face made her laugh again. "I wondered when you would notice!"

He saw now how much larger her breasts were, blue-veined and engorged with milk. He felt as if he'd been saber-struck again, a sharp stroke to the heart, numbing in its intensity. While he'd been gone she'd borne a child. Jealousy ate a jagged hole in his soul.

Storm, waking and staring at the strange rocks overhead, began to make soft inquisitive sounds. Storm Caller looked up and Norah laughed again. "That is my son. Would you like to see him?" Without waiting for a response, she rolled to her side and got up. She pulled the baby from the cradleboard and brought him to Storm Caller, kneeling at his side.

"Be careful, he is wet." She held the child out to Storm Caller, and he sat back on his heels.

Slowly he lifted his arms and reached out for the wriggling bundle. "I will adopt him as my own," he told her.

"I most certainly hope so!"

The boy was fine-looking, sturdy and well fleshed. His eyes were closed as he chewed upon a bit of turquoise. Storm Caller frowned. "That is my fetish he is wearing."

"It was the only thing I had to give him of his father." Placing the baby in his father's arms, she smiled at the stunned expression on his face. "That is your son you are holding! Your son and mine. His name is Storm."

Morning was breaking over the canyon, shattering the darkness, igniting the rocks into glorious colors. Storm Caller and Norah paid no heed. They had spent the night talking and making love. He knew about the ranch, about Maria and Levi, Mercy and the deed. She knew little about his recent past: it was still too fresh a wound to probe. It didn't matter.

He watched her bathe her face and felt his heart near to bursting. Quanah Parker had known the right of it: "You must go where your heart is, my friend. And it will lead you to your destiny. Search until you find it, for it is not here. Our day is gone. The sun sets on our people. If we are to survive as a nation, we must try and understand these new ways, even though they are not ours." Yes, Quanah was wise in many ways.

He pulled Norah into his arms, and she reached out to him at the same time. He kissed her lips, and she responded, her mouth trembling beneath his. She had never asked for more than to be with him, sharing his joys and sorrows. And her prayers had been answered. She filled his arms, just as the fact of her nearness filled the black void that had gaped inside Storm Caller's soul. With her dark head cradled against his breast he felt the pain ebb out, to be replaced by a strange new emotion. It took a while to put a name to it, and then he knew. Peace. For the first time he was at peace within himself.

Releasing her, he stooped down and caught up a handful of red dust, sifting some of it through his fingers; then he held the rest out toward her in his open palm. Norah inverted her own hand to him, understanding his symbolism, as Storm

Caller let the sand trickle from his hand to hers: they would make their own world, create it from the very soil of the Arizona Territory, water it with their mingled blood and sweat. A better world for their son, and for their sons and daughters yet unborn: the new breed of men and women who would inherit the West.

There was a particular magic that touched the moment, and he looked about, seeking some omen for the future. His gaze fell to Norah's face. "My beautiful woman, with eyes as blue as Pieces of Sky!"

Touching her cheek lightly, he smiled. What better talisman could a man have?

* * * * *

New York Times
Bestselling Author

LINDA

MACKENZIE'S
MOUNTAIN

HOWARD

Wolf Mackenzie is an outsider, a loner who chooses to live with his son on top of a Wyoming mountain rather than face the scorn of a town that dismisses him as a half-breed criminal. Until Mary Elizabeth Potter comes storming up his mountain. The proper, naive schoolteacher couldn't care less about the townspeople's distrust—she's just determined to give Wolf's son the education he deserves. But when Mary meets Wolf, an education of another kind begins. Now Mary and Wolf are teaching each other—and learning—about passion, forgiveness and even love.

"Howard's writing is compelling." —*Publishers Weekly*

Available mid-March 2000 wherever paperbacks are sold!

MIRA

HELEN R. MYERS

Six years ago the town of Split Creek, Texas, was rocked to its core when a young woman was brutally murdered. Her killer was never found. Now another girl has disappeared....

When Faith Ramey's abandoned car is discovered, the town feels an unwelcome sense of déjà vu. Police Chief Jared Morgan doesn't want to believe there's a connection, but Faith's sister Michaele is beginning to suspect otherwise.

LST

As secrets and scandals are exposed, old fears— and new—spawn doubt and suspicion. Is a sinister stranger lurking behind the murder and Faith's disappearance—or does someone in Split Creek have blood on their hands? Only Michaele's fierce determination—and her trust in Jared—will help her see the truth hidden in plain sight.

"Ms. Myers gives readers an incredible depth of storytelling."
—*Romantic Times*

On sale mid-March 2000 wherever paperbacks are sold!

MIRA

Visit us at www.mirabooks.com

MHRM572

If you enjoyed what you just read,
then we've got an offer you can't resist!

Take 2 bestselling love stories FREE!

Plus get a FREE surprise gift!

**It will take everything they possess to face
the truths about to come to light under
the California moon.**

CATHERINE LANIGAN

Shannon Riley is living in the shadows of a past she cannot
face. Gabe Turner is her patient, a man lying in a coma—and
the prime suspect in his business partner's murder. Just outside
the door, Officer Ben Richards stands guard, watching as the
woman he is falling in love with falls in love with his prisoner.

Then the unthinkable occurs. Gabe awakens and flees the
hospital, taking Shannon hostage in his desperate attempt to
piece together the deadly mystery threatening his life.
They are on the run from ruthless men who want them
dead—and from Ben. The three soon find themselves
trapped in a dangerous game with no clear rules—
except survival and courageous love.

CALIFORNIA MOON

MIRA

"Lanigan knows her genre well." —*Publishers Weekly*

On sale mid-February 2000 wherever paperbacks are sold!

CHRISTIANE HEGGAN

"A master at creating taut,
romantic suspense."
—*Literary Times*

ENEMY
WITHIN

When Rachel Spaulding inherits her family's Napa Valley
vineyard, it's a dream come true for the adopted daughter of
loving parents. But her bitter sister, Annie, vows to do
whatever it takes to discredit Rachel and claim the Spaulding
vineyards for herself. Including digging into Rachel's past.

What she digs up uncovers three decades of deceit. And
exposes Rachel to a killer who wants to keep the past buried.

On sale mid-February 2000 wherever paperbacks are sold!

MIRA

MCH577

USA Today Bestselling Author of
More and More

STELLA CAMERON

ALL SMILES

In this seductive tale of passion and intrigue,
Stella Cameron takes readers back to
7 Mayfair Square, an elegant town house,
during the glittering whirl of a London season.
Here, with a little help from a most unusual
matchmaker, anything is possible—even unlikely
love between a nobleman and an audacious and
determined parson's daughter....

"Stella Cameron is sensational!"
—Amanda Quick

On sale mid-February 2000 wherever paperbacks are sold!

MIRA

Visit us at www.mirabooks.com   MSC615